... of two previous novels, *Official and Doubtful*, longlisted for the Orange Prize, and *Forspoken*. *In a Sma Room*, her play about Scots poet William Soutar, toured Scotland in 2012.

Also by Ajay Close

Official and Doubtful
Forspoken

Trust

Ajay Close

TIPPERMUIR
· BOOKS LIMITED ·

First published in Great Britain in 2014 by Blackfriars,
an imprint of Little, Brown Book Group

This edition published and copyright 2014 by
Tippermuir Books Limited, Perth, Scotland
www.alternative-perth.co.uk
tippermuirbooks@blueyonder.co.uk

ISBN 978-0-9563374-6-7
A CIP catalogue record for this book is
available from the British Library.

Text styling and artwork by Bernard Chandler,
Glastonbury, England. www.graffik.co.uk
Cover design by Roben Antoniewicz
www.raphotography.co.uk

Text set in 10.7pt on 13.5pt Linotype Sabon.
Printed and bound in Great Britain by CPI Antony Rowe,
Chippenhamand Eastbourne

for Simon Duffy 1958-2012

odd, wintry flowers upon the withered stem, yet new, strange flowers such as my life has not brought forth before, new blossoms of me

DH Lawrence, 'Shadows'

Economics are the method; the object is to change the heart and soul.

Margaret Thatcher

1983

SEPTEMBER

Lexa turned to retrieve her luggage from the train and found an old man straining over her suitcase. An ageing gallant in a check sports jacket and knitted slipover, determined to prove that the age of chivalry was not dead.

She closed her fingers around the small section of handle that was not clamped in his grip. 'It's OK, thanks.'

'What've you got in here, love – bricks?'

'I can manage.'

'Can't have a young lady dragging a heavy case like this.'

She wanted to savour the moment of arrival, to linger on the platform with the smell of diesel and stewed tea and the scratchy announcements of incoming trains, so it wasn't just a question of principle.

'Really, it's fine.'

'Don't be daft.'

'I've been carrying it all day.'

'You'll do yourself an injury . . .'

'*I'm a third of your age and twice your size.*'

They glared at each other for a second before he tutted and let go of the handle.

It was dark for six o'clock. Yellow lights pierced the murk on Commercial Street, just as Atkinson Grimshaw had painted it. Old men stood on windswept corners selling newspapers. *MAGGIE SLAMS MINERS.* Lowering the taxi window, she caught the malty breath of the brewery chimneys. Leeds, her new home. She drank it in, all the lives behind the glowing windows, all the people she would get to know.

The house was a Victorian wool baron's mansion subdivided into flats. The jumble of mail on the scratched table in the hall contained three Irish names, one Russian, one Punjabi, and a note in block capitals to whoever was stealing the milk.

'You a merchant banker, then?'

'What?' The bus was idling at a red light, engine grinding.

The man beside her nodded at the letter on her lap, 'I said, are you a merchant banker?'

'Once I get started.'

She turned to look out of the window but he prodded at her arm. 'That's rhyming slang for summat else, you know.'

'So people keep telling me.'

The building wasn't hard to find. An Edwardian tower of soot-streaked white faience, the tiled lobby smelling of machine oil and floor polish. A list of companies in dull gold lettering. Solicitors, actuaries, loss adjusters, accountants. She rode the cage lift, checking her reflection in the polished brass fittings; got out at the fifth floor. The sign too was gleaming brass. *Goodison Farebrother.*

The receptionist did the usual double-take at her height. When she phoned through to the office, the person on the other end of the line made her repeat Lexa's name.

'Third on the right down the corridor.'

A long room full of light. White shirts hunched over antique desks. Pin-striped jackets draped over the backs of chairs. Piles of documents. Hewlett Packard calculators. A group in the corner were chatting, hands locked behind their heads. A man with wheat-coloured hair and old-fashioned braces made a joke which was received with barks of laughter. His open-mouthed grin showed a broken incisor. At the other end of the room a door opened, disclosing a smaller office. The man who emerged had an actor's good looks. Chestnut hair, chiselled features, a narcissistic arch to his spine. She walked up to him, right hand outstretched.

'Get Sal to make you a coffee. I'll be with you later.'

The voice of Empire, familiar from a thousand black-and-white films but never employed to address her, until now.

A secretary appeared carrying a pile of folders.

'Welcome to Grand Central Station,' she said.

As the morning passed Lexa began to make sense of the activity around her. There was a prodigious amount of paperwork undertaken in silence, interrupted periodically by the ringing of a phone. Every half-hour or so, someone would lose concentration and walk over to the windows. Seeing this, one or two others would get up and join him. In her world 'public school' was a loose insult attached to anything from an Anglo-Scots accent to a rugby shirt. She wasn't sure she'd ever met the genuine article. They *looked* better bred than the men she knew in Gemmell. Straight-backed, clear-browed, glossily confident. Most of the accents were posh Northern English, with a playing-field boom, an effortless ability to make themselves heard in the next room, if not the next county. In Gemmell, as the new girl in an office full of strangers, she would have been spoken to. Here she wasn't sure they even noticed her. Sal had distributed her pile of folders around the room and gone without making the promised coffee. Mid-morning another woman appeared and went into the boss's office; a Rossetti canvas come to life, with an eye-popping swell of bosom and a soft cloud of auburn hair.

At one o'clock she was still waiting. Several men put their heads around the door to announce where they would be lunching. Someone said he was meeting Nicola, which triggered a louche whistle. The Pre-Raphaelite emerged from the director's office and, in a little girl's voice, wheedled her colleagues into eating Chinese. They left in a gang, making jokes about sweet-and-sour poodle. Lexa tapped on the door at the end of the room.

There was a Helmut Newton print behind his desk: a woman dressed in jodhpurs, boots and lacy bra, a saddle on her back. After a couple of minutes he covered the mouthpiece and said in a tone of quiet fury,

'Can't you see I'm on the fucking phone?'

The impeccably-enunciated swearword startled her. 'I'm Lexa Strachan.'

'And?'

'And if you're Piers Kinsella you just paid me to sit on my behind doing nothing for half a day.'

He looked her up and down. Having raised the subject, she felt partly responsible when he lingered halfway. 'Have lunch on me as well.'

She went window shopping in the financial quarter.

At four o'clock he called her in.

'It's been a bitch of a day—'

A copy of *Sporting Life* lay open on his desk.

'—may I-*aah* see your letter of appointment?'

He glanced at his own signature. 'Who interviewed you?'

Her sense of foreboding increased. 'A Mister Smith . . .'

No reaction.

She racked her brains for his Christian name. He'd taken his degree at Glasgow University and had a soft spot for *the old alma mater*. However much she disapproved, it was a stroke of luck, with so many unemployed graduates around. Every Monday since finishing the accountancy course she'd sent off a dozen letters of application, casting her net ever wider as the weeks had passed. Firms she knew she didn't stand a chance with. Then Goodison Farebrother had summoned her to London. They were recruiting three trainees, one for each regional office.

'. . . *Phineus*. Phineus Smith.'

'No one else else sat in on the interview?'

'No.'

Piers Kinsella walked to the door and called out '*Gavin*—'

The man with the broken tooth turned round.

'—I'm taking Miss Strachan to the pub to-*aah* fill her in on what we expect of her.'

Her new colleagues found this funny.

She stood up, ready to go. But instead of putting on his jacket, he started reading a document from his in-tray.

'I was surprised to get the job. Pleased, of course—'

He looked up impatiently.

'—I was expecting a second interview.'

'Yes, that would have been a good idea.'

He released his jacket from the back of the chair.

*

He took her to an Edwardian drinking palace down by the river. Three men with greased quiffs and tattooed forearms were playing cards for a pile of change in the middle of their table. A pensioner leaned on the bar, a Jack Russell terrier perched on the high stool beside him.

Piers Kinsella settled himself at the table with his pint and his twenty Marlboro.

She looked at him expectantly. A taxi sounded its horn in the street outside. The card players shuffled and dealt.

'Very Otto Dix,' she said at last.

He drew on his cigarette.

'Or do I mean George Grosz? Those Weimar bar scenes where everybody looks as if they're wearing rouge and they're going to die of syphilis . . .' She smiled, then, seeing how it was received, made a mental note not to do it again. And to steer clear of art. But they couldn't sit here in silence all afternoon. 'Do you have Irish blood?'

'Do I *what*?'

There was a terrible clipped contempt to that *what*.

'Kinsella. I thought it was an Irish name.'

'I was born in Cheshire.'

'But originally—'

There was no warmth in the eyes that met hers.

'—ach well, there's no law against it.'

He didn't seem to understand this was said by way of dropping the subject.

'Against what?'

'Being English and having an Irish name.' She sipped her drink. 'They do a good Guinness here.'

'Perhaps the landlord's Irish.'

She smiled, on the off-chance that this was a joke, then remembered why smiling was a bad idea.

He stubbed out his cigarette. 'OK, here's the news. Phin's out of the picture, on leave, getting his liver dried out. If the clients ask, it's a slipped disc. Until he gets back I'm running the Northern office. We've had a reasonable nine months, given the state of the economy, but we can't afford to carry any passengers. You'll be expected to deliver the goods from day one, so you'd better be a fast learner. Do as you're told, use your brain, don't cock up, and don't listen to Gloria.'

'The woman with the hair?'

'And the big-*aah* . . . personality? No, that's Jessica. She works for Jonny Rose in Venture Capital. Gloria's in Corporate Finance. His wife calls him Keith. One of the brown suit brigade.'

'What's wrong with brown suits?'

'Nothing if you're a truss salesman. Stinks of garlic. A touch of the tarbrush, if you ask me.'

She remembered the smirks in the office when he'd announced they were going to the pub. 'Are you having me on?'

His face froze. 'I beg your pardon?'

A disconnected feeling was travelling down her arms into her fingers, a sensation like the helplessness of dreams. She had seen him smile at others. The fish-eyed stare was just for her.

'Who should I listen to, then?'

'Gavin Bawley. Knows what he's doing. Which is more than I can say for most of them.'

'The guy with the broken tooth?'

'Yep. Or Roland, if Gavin's not around.'

'Big tongue?'

For the first time Piers Kinsella looked at her with interest.

'He pokes it out the side of his mouth.' She demonstrated. 'Pushes it into his cheek when he's being funny. Tends to bump into the furniture.'

'That's him.'

'So who's the guy who sneezes when he uses the photocopier?'

'Ned Gomery. Our lawyer.'

She could tell from the way he said this they were friends.

He replaced his empty glass on the table. 'Look,' he said, with a new candour in his voice, and for a moment she allowed herself to hope, 'you won't be here long. Some of the clients like dealing with a skirt, but women don't stay the course. They can't cut it. Jess'll be the next to move on. Fucking useless. Apart from her obvious-*aah* assets.' His glance took in Lexa's A-cup breasts. 'I'll have another pint when you're ready.'

Though barely five yards from their table, the bar counter felt like sanctuary. As she arrived, the old man clamped a potato crisp between his dentures and the dog darted forward to snatch it from his mouth.

A voice behind her said, 'You should see what he does for smoky bacon.'

She turned to find one of the card school leaning on the bar. Middle-aged but still dressing like a teenager from the 1950s. Jeans turned up at the ankle, a cap-sleeved T-shirt. A dragon coiled around his bare arm.

The design was Japanese, he said. A parting gift from the man who'd trained him. Dead these past two years, but his tattoos still graced the arms of half the Scousers in the merchant navy. Lexa didn't make a habit of chatting with strange men, but after half an hour with Piers Kinsella she badly needed human contact. He dug into the back pocket of his jeans and withdrew a creased flier.

Trevor Sheldon.
Body art for the bad and beautiful.

The landlord set her drinks on the bar.

'Keep it,' the tattooist said when she tried to return the flier. 'Call in. I'll do you a free sample.'

She was carrying a fourth round of drinks back when a blast of cold air reached her from the open door. A man in a trilby hat and sodden trenchcoat made for their table.

'Thought I might find you here,' a London accent. He took off his hat.

'Well now you've found us you can fuck off,' Kinsella said.

The man offered his hand, 'Ben Wetten.'

'Lexa Strachan.'

'Not interrupting anything, am I?'

Kinsella jerked his thumb, 'I mean it. Fuck off.'

Ben glanced over his shoulder. As if on cue, the door opened.

A crowd jostled in, stamping their feet on the rubber mat, shaking the wet out of their hair, filling the pub with a boisterous hubbub of insult and laughter. In the west of Scotland she was a giant among either sex, but every one of these men was her height or taller. She saw how physical they were away from their desks, the shove and tussle and knockabout, and knew she would have to match them push for push.

The last man through the door was met with a chorus of 'Your round, Gloria'.

Chairs were dragged over from the surrounding tables. A breakaway faction set up camp around the bar. Squashed together like this, her new colleagues gave off a smell, a chutney of cold air on pink cheeks, white-collar sweat, good quality cloth, the half-digested juices of lunch and, underneath, an acrid taint of maleness. Mentally she rehearsed their names: Gavin, Roland, Ned, Ben, Simon . . .

She had the feeling she was being watched and looked up, but caught no one's eye.

'Every night. I'm telling you,' Gavin was saying, 'never sleeps alone.'

Ned flicked his head sideways, displacing his long dark fringe for a moment before it fell back into his eyes.

'But he's an ugly fucker,' Roland objected.

Gavin's broken tooth glinted in the light. 'Better goal average than Ian Rush. Top stuff too.'

'So how's he do it?'

'Infallible chat-up line. Just says the magic words.'

'Which are?'

A dozen voices chanted: 'I suppose a fuck's out of the question.'

She felt her face stiffen.

Kinsella leaned across her. 'It's not what he says, it's what he's-*aah* doing while he says it.'

A cheer rose from the bankers around the bar as a small, copper-haired woman swept in and peeled off her coat. Someone whistled.

Ned, the sneezer, noticed her interest. 'That's Rae.'

A Scottish name.

'As in Mairead,' Piers Kinsella said. 'Second generation-bogtrotter.'

'Hey Rae,' Roland called, just loudly enough to amuse the boss. 'I suppose a fuck's out of the er . . .'

Craning her neck for a better look, Lexa felt a touch on her arm. Ned again. Aquiline nose, delicate eyelashes, very white skin and very red lips. Like a fat prince in a Renaissance portrait.

'Where are you sleeping tonight?'

Out of the corner of her eye she saw a bulge appear in Roland's cheek.

She explained about the flat in Headingley, and her car failing its MOT, and having to go home next weekend to collect the rest of her belongings.

'And where's home?'

'Gemmell,' Gavin said unexpectedly.

She saw the confusion on Ned's face. 'Isn't that where . . .'

Something caused him to swallow the rest of the question. She turned round. Piers Kinsella stared back at her.

'Where the tea towels come from,' she said.

There was a frenzied barking over by the bar, followed by a sharp '*Fuck!*'

Ben had been bitten by the crisp-eating Jack Russell.

She walked into the office next morning with a hangover. Two paracetamol had taken the edge off the pain, leaving a high-pitched hum tuned to the frequency of last night's social anxiety. Corporate Finance was empty but she could hear laughter across the corridor. Pushing at the door, she found her colleagues lounging around a long table. A woman's voice was groaning. 'Oh yes, there, that's right . . . uh, just a bit . . . *ohhh yeah.*'

Ned was giving Rae a back rub, working the flesh through her dress.

Gavin sat with his feet up on the table, reading the *Financial Times*, wearing a suit of scratchy green tweed that Lexa guessed had belonged to his grandfather.

'You going tonight, Isabel?'

Rae wrinkled her nose. 'Not if I get a better offer. That French cafe crap gets on my tits—'

Her voice was smoky and slightly too loud. Lexa had studied accountancy in Sheffield, so she recognised the accent.

'—and I won't see anything. Unless Roland lets me up on his shoulders.'

Roland's tongue lolled briefly on his bottom lip.

'Get your head up there often, do you?' Gavin asked him.

'I might do.'

'Watch you don't catch anything.'

'I'm more likely to catch his dandruff.' Rae turned and saw Lexa. 'Another lamb to the slaughter,' she murmured.

She had a long flat face with a redhead's pale skin and slanting lidless eyes. Scrubbed of make-up it would have been odd, even ugly, but still sexually powerful. The only spare flesh was gathered in her lips which were shapeless, slightly rubbery.

Ben walked in. Roland and Simon started barking.

'How's the ankle?'

'Any sign of rabies yet?'

'Watch out for the next full moon.'

'Fuck off,' Ben drawled, clearly pleased to be the butt of the joke.

'Pick on something your own size next time, Benny-boy.'

'It's the small ones you have to watch, eh Isabel?'

'I don't know, Gavin. You tell me.'

'It was fucking vicious,' Ben protested, stoking their laughter. 'I could sue.'

Lexa retreated to the Cona machine by the window. Chimneys. Ventilator shafts. Buddleia growing from neglected gutters.

'Get me one while you're at it,' Rae said. 'Black, two sugars.'

Lexa placed the cup and saucer on the table. 'You're Rae, yes?'

'Last time I looked.'

'But Gavin calls you Isabel?'

'Gavin thinks he's a comedian.' She sipped her coffee. Ned had moved on to her vertebrae.

'What part of Sheffield are you from?'

The question was meant to establish a bond between them, but Rae seemed to bristle. 'Highthorpe.'

'Wino Flats?'

If she hadn't been hungover she would never have said it. Ned's hands stopped.

'That's what some people call it,' Rae said.

'*Wino Flats?*' Gavin echoed.

Rae smiled without showing her teeth. 'They charter a plane to be first with the Beaujolais Nouveau every year. Where are *you* from, Lexa?'

'Gemmell. It's near Glasgow.'

She had a dirty laugh, a witch's cackle. 'There's a coincidence.' She glanced at Gavin as if he had been keeping a good joke to himself. 'Our other graduate trainee's from your neck of the woods.'

'Gabriel Findlay.' Piers Kinsella propped an elbow on Lexa's shoulder. 'She's doing her six weeks with the City office.'

His presence put a new charge in the air.

'You're honoured,' Rae said. 'He never does that with me.'

Kinsella's gaze flickered from Rae to Ned and back. 'You have other uses.'

Rae's lips parted. She had the narrow bite of a small sharp-toothed animal. 'So you've been told,' she said.

'So I've been told.'

They had a particular tone when speaking to each other: light, and at the same time weighted with significance.

His voice lost this ambiguous timbre addressing Lexa. 'You can shadow Miss Bergin this morning. She'll show you round, since she's nothing better to do.'

Rae widened her lidless eyes. 'And you're rushed off your feet?'

'I don't keep dogs to bark myself. And you girls have your own-*aah* priorities.'

Lexa eased herself out from under his arm. 'If you mean the Tampax machine, I've found it. It's empty, by the way.'

Rae stepped into the corridor and swivelled on her high heels. Though shapely, her figure was arrestingly slender. It was hard to believe there were twenty-eight feet of intestines in the shallow spoon between her belly and buttocks.

'Goodison Farebrother. Minor merchant bank, established 1954. Annual results surprisingly healthy. Management: mediocre. On a good day. Major shareholder: Blumen's, New York. The Yanks call the shots. If it's good enough for Wall Street, it's good enough for us. So we have combination locks to preserve the Chinese wall between the corporate financier and other, *lesser*, bankers.' She kicked at the phone book in use as a doorstop. 'And don't even think about insider trading, it's a sacking offence. What else can I tell you? Divisional office opened 1960. Revolving door recruitment policy. Regular threats by head office to send in the white man. Still, you've done all right. As a trainee in Corporate Finance you can look down on everyone else in the bank. You have the best office, the only secretary who knows how to make a drinkable cup of coffee, four plexiglass tombstones to remind you of your big-time public deals, and a hundred-and-one crappy pen sets embossed with the names of your usual pissy little clients.' She nodded at a glass door etched with the words Venture Capital. 'That's Venture Capital, where they don't hand us our deals on a plate.' The next door was marked Leasing. 'That's Leasing, and that's . . .'

'Asset Management.'

'Catch on quick, don't you?'

Lexa took a risk. 'I'm not sure. It's hard to tell the insights from the paranoia.'

Rae flicked her hand to the right. 'Main meeting room, with coffee machine and fully-stocked drinks cabinet. Meeting room two. Meeting room three. I should stick with the paranoia, you won't go far wrong.'

Her profile was as inscrutably perfect as the head on a coin.

'Support staff are in here . . .'

Seven Wang word-processors sat idle on plywood desks. The secretaries were clustered around a magazine. Lexa saw permed ringlets, a gleaming blonde bob, a chic boyish crop, but within these variations the same neat-featured prettiness, and the same strained look at having been caught slacking.

'This is Alexandra Strachan.'

'Lexa,' Lexa said.

'Sal, Christine, Frankie, Linda, Cathy, Lori, Susan,' Rae recited, making no attempt to identify the owner of each name. She turned to leave. Someone tittered.

She turned back. 'I might as well take the Downey letters now, Lori. Save you a walk.'

The short-haired girl lifted her head. Above the embarrassed simper her eyes were defiant.

'Have them on my desk by ten,' Rae said.

They took the lift to the next floor.

A smell of roasting meat met them as they emerged. In the directors' dining room the table was already set for lunch, three wine glasses at every place setting.

'And this is the boardroom.'

Gilt-framed patriarchs looked down from the walls. Rae boosted herself up to sit on the long polished table, her feet dangling.

Lexa took a deep breath. 'I'm sorry about mentioning Wino Flats.'

There was a delay before Rae said 'Why would you be sorry?'

'I got the feeling I'd put my foot in it.'

'They know I grew up on a council estate. I'm not ashamed of where I come from.'

'I would have thought it would add to your cred.'

'*Cred?*' she echoed. Lexa had wanted to break through her coolness, but not like this. 'Where do you think you are, the student union? It's a merchant bank. You don't get credibility living next door to a prossie. They'll crucify you for wearing the wrong sort of shoes, having the wrong number of buttons on a suit cuff. There's a bloke in Leasing who wore a polyester tie. I mean once, two years ago. A present from his mum. They still call him "Polly".'

'But that's taking the piss out of the suburbs. It doesn't stop them being intimidated by places like Highthorpe. If they're so posh . . .'

'But they're not.'

Lexa waited.

'If they were that posh they'd be working in the City. They'll give you the crap about quality of life in the North of England, but the first sniff of a transfer and they'd be off like that.' She snapped her fingers. 'Down in London they're a joke. A bunch of Northern oiks. Oh yeah, they come from two-car homes, their daddies are solicitors and bank managers, their mummies made sure they knew which knife and fork to use, but they're second division. Minor public school. Durham and Bristol, not Oxford and Cambridge.'

She slid down from the table.

The tour was over. The chances of a sisterly alliance seemed slim.

'Thanks,' Lexa said.

Rae looked at her as if she were half-witted. 'For what?'

'Giving me a steer.'

'It's no skin off my nose.' She opened the door. 'You want a steer? Don't put too much trust in coincidence.'

'I've worked that one out for myself.'

Only eight per cent of schoolchildren in Gemmell went on to take a degree, but ninety per cent of that eight per cent went to Glasgow University. So Phin was a serial nepotist. He was also, along with the also-absent Gabriel, Lexa's best hope of a friend.

After serving behind counters and waiting on tables, Lexa found office life a revelation. All that emotion just under the surface. They affected a humorous cynicism then exploded in tantrums and rages. Did their lovers know them as intimately, she wondered? She hardly recognised herself: a banker oiling the mysterious wheels of the economy. She spent her days shadowing colleagues at meetings and checking documents for numerical errors and typing mistakes. Boring, but it was a start.

Most evenings she followed her colleagues across to Sylvester's, a gloomy basement favoured by barristers and solicitors and northern circuit judges. The low ceilings trapped a noxious cocktail of cigarette, cigar and pipe smoke. Candles in chianti bottles burned off any remaining oxygen. She was losing her taste for Guinness but it filled the stomach. By seven, lunchtime's cheese sandwich was a distant memory, with another four hours' drinking ahead before they flagged down a couple of taxis and went for a curry.

'What a waste.'

'There goes your best chance of a fuck this year.'

'*Naah*. You don't want one who turns on the waterworks.'

'You've got a point, Benny-boy.'

'Still, you don't often see a pair like that.'

'Plenty more tits in the sea.'

'Wetten! There's a lady present.'

Everyone but Lexa grinned.

Jessica's Pre-Raphaelite looks had only carried her so far. Her work was constantly disparaged for small mistakes. There was an office joke about her driving. Her babyish voice acquired an apologetic stammer which scratched at everyone's nerves. Even Lexa had been relieved to see her emerge from Kinsella's office in tears that morning, knowing the axe had fallen at last.

'You missed a trick not seeing her home. You could have-*aah* kissed it better.'

'If you'd offed her with a bit more finesse, she'd be here now, drowning her sorrows.'

'It was a mercy killing. Someone had to put her out of our misery. However-*aah* well-stacked she was. Your round, Alexandra.'

Conversation never faltered during these marathon drinking sessions, but tended to go over the same old ground, chewing the cud of office politics and replaying their meetings with clients in a range of funny voices. A nasal Brummie, a catarrhal Scouse, a Pooterish drone from the outer London suburbs, and a flat-capped 'trouble at mill' stage Yorkshire. In another hour or so, once the day's events had been thoroughly mined, they would start to tell tales on each other.

When she got back with the drinks they were debating who held the record for the swiftest dismissal.

'Susannah.'

'The one with the legs?'

'Six months.'

'Seven. Sarah was six.'

'Oh yes, *Sarah* . . .'

'Before my time.'

'Made Jess look underdeveloped.'

'What about Gina?'

'Och aye, gorgeous George*ena*.'

Lexa looked at Ned.

'Oh come on. It wasnae bad for a Sasanach.'

'Charlie, what did she manage, a fortnight?'

'Six weeks. You should know, you gave her one. In my-*aah* office, as I recall.'

'That was something she *was* good at.'

'Didn't she get the sums wrong on the Connaught sale?'

'That was Gavin. She just got the blame.'

'I-*aah* didn't hear that.'

'There was a bodybag with her name on it from day one.'

'Why?' Lexa asked.

The table fell silent.

'I mean, what did she do that was bad enough to get her sacked?'

Gavin flexed his eyebrows at Kinsella. Roland put his tongue in his cheek.

'She had a fucking awful accent,' Kinsella said.

NOVEMBER

On the Monday of her sixth week Lexa accompanied Gavin to a nine o'clock meeting and was back in the office by mid-morning. Stepping out of the lift, she saw a woman with barleywater-blonde hair striding into the men's lavatory. Lexa called out a warning, but by then the woman was backing out again, tugging at a pinstriped arm. On the other end was Roland, laughing and cursing and trying to button his flies. Ned followed them out.

Kinsella poked his head around the door of Corporate Finance. 'D'you mind? Some of us are *working*.' Noticing Ned's smirk, he switched to a gossipy undertone. 'What's going on?'

Roland checked his groin. 'She's just dragged me out of the can.'

The woman let go of his arm. 'He was having a meeting with Ned about Kingdom Alloys.'

'I was emptying my bladder.'

'For ten minutes?'

'I can piss for longer than that.'

The woman turned to Lexa. 'How can I not be impressed?' She had an Anglo-Scots accent.

Kinsella became the boss again. 'All right, Gabriel, you've made your point. Now get back to work.'

They reconvened the Kingdom Alloys meeting at Roland's desk, framed by a white rhomboid of autumn sunlight. Lexa's desk was just behind them. She moved her finger up and down the same column of figures, following every word.

It was a noisy session with plenty of laughter. Gabriel had the sort of looks that made men light-headed, but she was funny too. She spoke like a Radio 4 presenter, in punctilious sentences that she subverted with a playful inflection and strangely old-fangled slang. The posh voice, navy dress, court shoes and pearls suggested a Pony Club sweetheart marking time before marriage, but her eyes were alert to everything. Her mouth changed shape from moment to moment as thoughts and feelings moved across her face. This flux gave her a brightness, so the air around her seemed to shimmer even without sunlight. Listening, she angled her head upwards and slightly away from the person speaking, smiling at her own thoughts.

At one o'clock the office emptied. Lexa worked into the break to finish her document and stepped out for a breath of air at twenty to two. The corridor was pungent with French cigarettes. Gabriel was standing at the window. She looked too clean to have anything to do with tar and ash, too clean and blonde and expensive. The sort of woman men gave jewellery, though her fingers were ringless, with a child's short soft nails.

'Smoke?'

'No thanks.'

Gabriel turned back to the window, 'Which one is your chariot?'

In the car park were Kinsella's Audi Quattro, Gavin's soft-top TVR, Roland's Morgan, Ben's Lotus, and various souped-up Escorts and Golfs.

'Mine's a Hillman Imp. I left it at home today.'

Her eyes were pale turquoise with a darker rim the colour of ink on Victorian postcards. 'Trying to blackmail them into giving you a company car?'

'It's got wheels, an engine, four seats. It gets me from A to B.'

'Do they know they've hired a Maoist?'

This was more or less what Lexa had been wondering.

'I don't see the point of driving something developed for Brands Hatch when the speed limit's seventy miles an hour.'

Gabriel smiled, plumping the skin over her cheekbones, revealing teeth the creamy, pink-tinged colour of magnolia petals. 'How about because it's fun?'

'I wouldn't know.'

'*You've never been in a sports car?*'

She held up a forefinger – 'wait here' – and returned jangling a set of keys.

They crossed the car park to the TVR. It wasn't so unlikely that two bankers would drive similar cars. And Gavin's made him look like an overgrown child crammed into a toy. Gabriel's fitted her like a glove.

She gunned the engine.

Even at thirty miles an hour there was a thrilling sense of speed. They turned on to the ring road. It was pointless trying to speak above the roar of the engine, but the drag in their lower backs as the car accelerated, and the wind whipping their hair, and the blue of the sky, and the blurred grey of the road beneath them, struck them both with the same hilarity.

'Gabriel . . .'

The word turned cleanly on Lexa's tongue like a key opening the door to a new life. She pointed to the speedometer needle, which was flickering between ninety and a hundred. Gabriel gave her the sidelong look of a naughty child who knew she would always be forgiven. 'Fun?' she shouted.

'Fun,' Lexa mouthed back.

She eased her foot on the throttle. 'Theo drives an XJ-S. Aaron's handsome and witty and charming, but sometimes a girl just wants speed.'

Lexa presumed she was meant to ask.

'He's earning his ticket at Yorkshire Television. Ten years of bag-carrying till he proves himself worthy of actually *pointing a camera*. His big chances always come at weekends or the day before we're due to go away, and he's always so delighted. It's not very gallant of him. The sex is *bliss*, but Theo's definitely nosing ahead.' She pushed a twist of hair out of her eyes. 'Are you happy with your current swain?'

'I think the cliché is, I haven't met the right person.'

'*Ah,*' Gabriel said knowingly, 'you believe in "The One".'

'No, but I don't believe in the many, either.'

'The more the merrier, I say.'

'Then why do most relationships seem such misery?'

Gabriel's head swivelled in surprise. 'Do they? To you?'

'To anyone with eyes.' Lexa thought of her parents. Of couples she had known at university, the boys filling the air with bombast, their girlfriends smiling as if they had swallowed

poison and staring at the floor. 'Misery or boredom. I like
company, but not at any price. If you're giving up your freedom,
every second should count.'

'And by "count" you mean . . .?'

'You know, feeling you're alive.' Lexa tipped her head back
to see the tops of the buildings against the cobalt sky. 'The air
on your skin and the noise in your ears and the smell of engine
oil and leather . . .'

'*Ohh*, heightened sensation. That's just lust.'

Lexa was startled, though she seemed to mean it innocently
enough.

'No, I'm talking about the difference between living life on
the surface, and really experiencing it. Knowing you're separate
and unique and at the same time . . .' Lexa brought her fingertips
together. 'It's like a circuit. You need the connection for the
current to flow.'

These were her secret thoughts, shared with nobody until
now. Already she trusted Gabriel to understand, or to take her
seriously enough to seek clarification, so it didn't matter that she
said, 'Sounds like you're looking for an electrician.'

They were turning into the car park. Lexa recalled the way she
used to feel as a child at the shows when a ride came to an end.

Gabriel scanned the lines of cars. 'Can you remember where
it was parked?'

Lexa gave her a long look. 'Where did you get the keys?'

'His jacket was on the back of his chair.'

Gabriel slotted the TVR between one of the Golfs and Sal's
Metro, braking too late and nudging the bumper of Kinsella's
red Audi. Lexa jumped out to check for damage.

'Don't fuss. It was only a *tap*.'

'And your car is . . .?'

Gabriel nodded at a battered Land Rover Lexa had assigned
to the decorators working on the second floor. 'A bit of a tank,
but the boy racers think twice about cutting me up.' Her glance
settled on the Audi. 'If I really wanted a penile extension I'd go
to a plastic surgeon.'

Watching her reflection in the brass of the lift, Lexa wondered
how a face could be so alertly expressive and at the same time

so calm. Completely in the moment and still faintly abstracted. Half here, half there. Wherever there was.

'Are you going for a snifter tonight?'

Lexa shrugged. 'I'll probably end up in Sylvester's.'

Gabriel met her eyes in the burnished metal. 'I rather fancy trying somewhere else.'

Lexa took the glass and sniffed at the tea-coloured liquid, rearing back as the fumes singed the inside of her nostrils.

'It's bourbon,' Gabriel said.

Lexa sipped. Her tongue burned, then her lips. She wasn't sure she liked the taste, but its novelty suited the day so far.

They were in a converted factory. The corrugated-perspex ceiling was supported by girders painted with black and yellow stripes. The floor was dimpled rubber, the bar counter a slab of steel. A jazz-tinged croon seeped out of the overhead speakers. Later this space would be filled with sweating nightclubbers, but at six-fifteen the atmosphere was hushed. A youth with matted orange dreadlocks was sketching on a pad. Although no one looked towards him, Lexa detected a pleasurable self-consciousness in the drinkers at the metal tables. She had glanced over his shoulder on the way in: Belsen haircuts, dangling earrings, Doc Marten boots, the boy with the purple nail varnish and his butch friend in studded leather, the black eyes and white faces of the Goths at the bar. In the middle of this crowd sat Gabriel in her camel coat and court shoes.

'Who *are* these people?' she asked, as if coming here had been Lexa's idea.

'Students, aspiring rock stars, dealers in import records and secondhand clothes,' the bourbon was blazing a trail down to her stomach, 'anarchists, animal liberationists, fans of industrial chic . . .' She felt the need to add, 'I'm guessing.'

'So tea-break strikes at British Leyland are chic now, are they?' Gabriel cast a sceptical look at the caged wall lights, 'It'll all be gone in twenty years.'

'That's Thatcherite talk.'

She gave an extravagant shrug. 'It's inevitable. Technology advances. Mechanisation replaces the manual workforce. Multi-nationals move labour-intensive manufacturing to the Third World . . .'

Lexa was learning not to underestimate Gabriel, but she refused to believe she was right about this. Gemmell without cloth, the Clyde without ships, Motherwell without steel – 'Even Thatcher wouldn't go that far. It'd be political suicide. Industry's fundamental to everything, not just the balance of payments. Class, masculinity, Marxist theory . . . It's not going to *disappear*. A place like this exists to get young money in through the doors. Why do you think the owner chose an industrial theme?'

'The same reason they put fake oak beams in olde English tea shoppes?'

'But this isn't a pastiche of the golden past.'

'Isn't it?' Gabriel looked around her. 'Well, maybe it's the road to Thebes. The boys getting their Oedipal own back. They grow up in awe of *daddy's work*. Then they turn the factory aesthetic into fashion.' Rummaging in her handbag, she found a blue softpack of Gauloises. 'By the way, you'd better not let the Round Table hear you namedropping Marx.'

'Is that not Kinsella's?'

Gabriel looked down at the silver lighter in her hand. 'I must have picked it up in the office.' She slipped it back in her bag. 'So, how are you finding Goodison Farebrother?'

Lexa remembered Thursday's four-bottle working lunch to discuss the flotation of Ceatlin Engineering. The bread rolls Ben and Simon had lobbed across the table. The fork Roland dropped on the floor to get a glimpse up the waitress's skirt when she bent to retrieve it. Who had taken over as office lust object now Jess was gone? Rae? Gabriel? Or one of the typists? One beautiful banker she could have accepted, maybe even two, but *three*? And herself: a six-footer with a bad perm.

She let the last of the bourbon slide down her throat.

'I hate it,' she said.

Too late, it occurred to her that Gabriel might not agree. In Lexa's experience beauty made women neurotic. Jess's little-girl manner and Rae's burlesque were just different ways of coping with the strain of being looked at. But did Gabriel even notice? It was as if she were from another planet and carried around her own sustaining atmosphere. The thought of her growing up in Gemmell beggared belief.

'How do *you* find it?'

'Not as dire as I expected. Nobody's asked me which school I went to yet.'

'Which school did you go to?'

'Castlebank.'

Lexa tried to picture her in a lovat green blazer, smoking in the Peace Gardens, 'So you knew Fiona Murchieson?'

'Alas, yes.' Gabriel smiled. Her lips made Lexa think of reels of thread in a haberdasher's display. The miracle of one perfect pink among all those approximate shades.

'I had a Saturday job in Cochrane's with her brother.'

'The one whose girlfriend went to London to be a bunny girl?'

'She was a croupier,' Lexa said loyally.

'She still wore ears and a tail,' Gabriel took a luxurious lungful of French smoke, 'I went to a hooley at her flat once.'

'That place with carpet on the walls?'

'And the pirhana in the fish tank.'

'I wonder if it was the same party?'

Gabriel shook her head. 'You weren't there—'

Lexa stared at her.

'—I used to see you all the time. On the bus, in your purple flares.'

Lexa strained to recall a green blazer on the bus, or anywhere else. A fourteen-year-old Gabriel drinking coke floats in the Honeycomb, trying on clothes in the Co-Op's Fashion Korner. The two of them observing the rituals of adolescence in parallel, climbing the stairs to Mandy MacMillan's flat, swaying to Pink Floyd in a darkened room, rushing home before the town hall clock struck midnight. It made her want to laugh. The thought of them passing on the street, walking in and out of the same shops and cafes.

'I haven't been back since Cambridge,' Gabriel said the word lightly but still it clunked, 'I got a summer job with a travel firm taking tourists round the Far East. They wanted to keep me on. Not an agonisingly difficult choice: sundowners in Raffles Hotel, or Snakebite in the JCR. I popped back once a term to give my tutor some guff about glandular fever so they couldn't kick me out. A couple of friends let me borrow their essays. The funny thing is, they got 2:2s, I got a 2:1.'

Lexa was reluctantly impressed. 'You got a 2:1 in Law without going to lectures?'

'No, Arc and Anth.' She saw a translation was needed. 'Archaeology and Anthropology.'

'But I thought . . .'

'You thought I had a Law degree.' She pouted. 'I *may* have given that impression. If it really mattered, they'd've checked. And if they ever do a deal with the Polynesians, I'll be invaluable.'

The jazz tape came to an end and Lexa recognised the synthesised chords of that Human League song that seemed to be playing every time she switched on the radio. With a shriek, the girls at the bar slid off their stools and pumped their arms in a synchronised dance.

'You should have said hello. On the bus.'

Gabriel shrugged. 'I knew we'd meet sooner or later.'

'You don't seem the premonition type.'

She looked amused. '*Alter ipse amicus.*'

'Meaning what, for those of us who didn't go to Cambridge?'

One of the dancing girls yelped as her high-heeled shoe twisted beneath her.

'A friend is another self,' she said.

The shelf under the Land Rover's dashboard held a can of aerosol paint, a half-eaten apple and a tabloid newspaper.

'Why do you call them the Round Table?' Lexa asked.

'Sir Piers, Sir Roland, Sir Gawain . . .'

'Sir Ben, Sir Simon, Sir Keith?'

'Ah well, they're the serfs.'

The gearbox grumbled as she took a left turn in fourth.

'I bet Kinsella loves you driving this to client meetings.'

'Actually he does. They all assume I've got land.'

'But you haven't?'

Gabriel took her eyes off the road.

'The way you dress,' Lexa said.

'When in Rome . . .'

'And speak.'

'Oh that's an immigrant thing. My mother was German. She learned her English from Trollope and Marjorie Allingham, and then she taught me.'

'And you went to Cambridge.'

'We weren't all debutantes. Some of us were just bright.'

Lexa braced her arm against the dashboard as they stopped for a red light. Apple, paint and newspaper shot onto the floor.

'With socially ambitious parents,' Gabriel conceded.

The lights changed. The Land Rover growled and strained until Lexa released the handbrake.

'I had you down as one of Phin's Glasgow Uni mafia. I'm pretty sure Rae thinks that too.'

'The Pocket Venus?' Gabriel's magnolia-petal teeth gleamed in that irresistible smile. 'She does love a good conspiracy theory, doesn't she? What does it matter where we went? We're all in the same boat, on the same phallocentric sea.'

Lexa returned the things that had fallen off the shelf. Several loose pages had slipped out of the tabloid. Or rather, she saw now, multiple copies of the same page. A teenage girl running to fat, glistening lips parted, hands cupping her heavy naked breasts.

Gabriel glanced across. 'I do it with a razor blade,' she said. 'Never been caught. I'm very quick. I don't fling ink at the top shelf any more – they get quite shirty. And it drips down over the *New Statesman*.'

1984

JANUARY

'I need to talk to you—' Rae said.

Lexa put down her pen.

'—in the boardroom.'

The boardroom was where all Goodison Farebrother staff were taken for *a little chat*. Gavin looked over with a crooked smile. Lexa stared him down and followed Rae out of the office.

The air in here always made her want to sneeze. A compound of beeswax, dry sherry, old men, and the dust held in oriental carpets. She pulled out a chair. Rae remained on her feet, leaning against the long table. Her suit was the colour of chocolate ice cream. Her manner, too, suggested refrigeration.

'What did you do at lunchtime?'

'I had a sandwich at my desk.'

'We all went to the Wig and Pen.'

Whatever this was about, it was surely not her eating habits.

Rae shifted against the table, increasing her temporary height advantage. 'It's noticed, you know, that you don't want to eat with us. Or go for a drink in the evening.'

'It's not a drink, it's a skinful. I don't want to get paralytic night after night.'

'You don't have to drink at lunch.'

'But you all do.'

Rae's eyes narrowed. 'If I was one of two new graduates in a department as small as Corporate Finance, I'd be careful who I pissed off.'

Lexa's skin prickled. 'So who am I pissing off?'

'These things get noted.'

'Aye, you said.' Lexa heard herself slipping into Glaswegian. The English found it a threatening accent. 'Let me get this right. It's not enough to do what I'm told in working hours, I've to eat when I'm told now, and drink when I'm told. Anything else? Sleep with who I'm told?'

'I don't see that one being an issue.'

This could only be happening on Kinsella's instructions. Lexa was surprised. Management lackey wasn't Rae's style. She was a feral sex kitten, arriving at work in last night's mini-skirt and changing into the suit she kept in the ladies' loo. Yawning until someone said she looked tired, then announcing that she had been fucking all night. The whole office knew she liked to be taken from behind. Lexa found it embarrassing, but could see its advantages as a strategy. The tight clothes, the dirty talk, the stories of teenage dates tooled-up with a sharpened metal comb, all the things she did to shock while presenting herself as unshockable: they were a form of simultaneous flirtation and rebuff. 'Look at Me/Hands Off!' And it worked. For all their innuendo, the men in the office kept their distance. Only Kinsella felt free to touch without permission.

Lexa stood up, 'I've work to do.'

'You'll go when I say you can go,' Rae said in a voice left over from the days of sharpened combs, 'we need to talk about your clothes.'

'There's nothing wrong with my clothes.'

'Not if you're looking to be cast as the dyke in a James Bond movie.' Her lips twitched at her own joke. 'Have you ever asked yourself why every other woman in the building wears a skirt?'

'I can't say I've ever noticed.'

'Well, take it from me, other people notice. I'm not suggesting you develop a sense of style or anything. Half an hour in Schofield's should do it. A couple of skirts, a couple of blouses, a jacket . . .'

'So now I've to wear what I'm told?'

'It may be news to you, but women are judged on their appearance.'

Lexa laughed.

Within a month of joining Goodisons she had started to loathe her own body. In the mornings she discarded shirt after shirt until she found one which disguised her breasts. She hated her solid calves in their micromesh hose, the way her skirts bulged over the girth of her hips. And then, browsing in Oxfam, she had come across a 1940s chalk-stripe suit. A square-shouldered, almost mannish jacket and no-nonsense skirt. The following week, at the hairdresser's, she had asked for a short cut. The girl with the scissors took her at her word. Knee-length skirt, plain white shirt, no lipstick or mascara. Now she was used to it, she liked the feel of the weather on her skin, the honesty of her unadorned self striding out into the world. That morning, having laddered her last clean pair of tights, she had pulled on a pair of trousers. It hadn't seemed a big deal at the time.

Rae glanced down at her own snugly-fitting two-piece. 'You've got to be realistic. We're in business, our clients are middle-aged men. They're with us because we're a safe pair of hands, they know what they're getting. Then they see someone with a short back and sides looking like . . .'

'A dyke in a James Bond movie,' Lexa said.

Rae's face turned wary. 'You're not are you?'

'It's none of your business, but no.'

'Then what's the point of looking like one?' She moved away from the table. 'If you're going to have short hair, make sure it's a good cut. Ask Lori Cooper where she gets hers done. And wear some make-up. Try and look a bit more feminine.'

Lexa wasn't finding this funny any more. 'And then what? Lunch with Mister Let-Your-Fingers-Do-the-Walking from Arundale Paints? Client meetings over dinner at the Queen's Hotel? There's no end of advantages to being a woman at Goodison Farebrother.'

Rae's eyes slitted. 'Is that what this is about, making your little feminist protest? Grow up.'

'Like Jess, you mean?'

'You know as well as I do Jess wasn't up to it.'

'Was she any worse than Ben? Or Roland?'

Rae checked that the door was closed. 'No,' she said. 'But that's the way it is.'

Lexa looked up at the portraits on the opposite wall. Watch chains, starched collars, mutton-chop whiskers. 'You're not a feminist, then?'

Rae snorted. 'What do you think?'

'I think you're going to spontaneously combust unless you work out who you're so angry with.'

For a moment Rae was thrown. As if she had been handed a photograph of herself, taken unawares. Then she was tough again.

'Just get yourself some new clothes, OK?'

MARCH

There were two office myths about Piers Kinsella. The first was his distinctly average performance in the years he'd spent on the front line. The second: his genius as acting field marshal. While rival divisional offices wasted time and energy scuttling down to London and cutting second-string deals, Goodison Fare-brother (North) was making money. There were many worse places to start a career in banking.

'A word of advice—'

She paused, her hand raised to knock at the door. Ned had come up behind her. How could two hundred pounds move so stealthily?

'—don't tread on his tail.'

Kinsella fancied himself a country gent. Every few weeks he left the Audi at home and turned up in a Range Rover. They had all seen the game book on the back seat, alongside the Barbour and green wellies. On these country-weekend Fridays they'd find a black retriever slumped on his side in the middle of the boss's office. This was Whitby, a heaving mound of moulting hair and meaty breath, one big brown eye showing a pawky crescent of white whenever a banker stepped over or around him.

She knocked and put her head round the door. The dog's tail thumped on the carpet.

'Can I have a word?'

'Just the one.'

'Underutilisation.'

'And how could I-*aah* use you more fully?'

For Kinsella, merchant banking was a matter of virility. His favourite verb was *shaft*, at least in its active form. The competition were *poofs*, unless they caused him trouble, in which case they became *cunts*. 'Short skirt and fuck-me pumps tomorrow,' he would drawl at Rae when a difficult meeting loomed, and she would look him in the eye, and everyone present would smirk. Or else, 'I-*aah*, think we'll send Miss Findlay along to flutter her eyelashes at them.' At which point Gabriel would say that Roland too had lovely lashes, and Kinsella would reply that if the client were a fudge-packer he would be sending Gloria. He almost never spoke to Lexa like this.

She sat down. 'I want to work on my own deal start to finish. I've been here six months. It's time I got a shot at the real thing—'

His eyes returned to the folder on his desk.

'—I'm bored, and you're not getting your money's worth . . .'

He turned a page and let his pen drop in a pantomime of despair. 'You understand depreciation, don't you?'

'Of course.'

He tossed the folder into her lap. 'Well explain it to Ben. This is complete and utter bollocks—'

Ben was the previous graduate trainee, with a year's seniority over her.

'—either he hasn't got the first fucking idea what he's doing, or it's the most cack-handed window-dressing I've ever seen. The profit forecast's a joke. That machinery's never going to last twenty years. A bit of nip and tuck's one thing, but you don't take the buyer for a cunt.'

The dog whimpered, recognising his master's displeasure.

'And you want me to talk him through it?'

'But don't do it *for* him. I want to know it's his work.' He pressed a button on his telephone. 'Sal, ring Liam McVay's secretary and tell her we need to move that meeting . . . Who? Oh yeah. Well he can wait . . . I don't care what you tell him. Flash your cleavage, that should keep him happy.' He put the phone down and wrote something on his blotter.

'You still here?' he said, without looking up.

'After I've explained depreciation to Ben, do I get a deal to work on?'

'I'll think about it.'

'When?'

'I beg your pardon?' Still friendly, but letting her know how quickly things could change.

'When might you have time to think about it?'

Had he decided she *couldn't cut it*? She had no idea. He called her 'Alexandra' with a facetious smile and made drawling references to 'women's lib' and, once in a while, for no reason she could fathom, looked through her with the bored contempt he had shown on her first day. On the other hand, he had never called her a moron or flung her documents across the office or remarked on her unsuitability as sexual bait.

His gaze swept the shelf of lever-arch files on the opposite wall. 'Pass me Faxerley Colliery.'

He opened the file, glanced at the top page, closed it again, and pushed it across the desk. 'Get Lori to make three copies. It's a private pit south of Doncaster. Lockend want rid. Can't say I blame them. We're going to make it look like the bargain of the century.'

APRIL

Faxerley Colliery was an eyesore, a series of brick sheds linked by boxed chutes. A brown canal fed into a scum-choked basin. An endless line of coal trucks waited on a railway spur. Five hundred yards beyond the perimeter fence was a hay barn, a dozen Fresians grazing in the adjacent pasture. Coming from Gemmell, Lexa understood manufacturing towns, the way their squalor was tied to their beauty, but this place baffled her. A coal mine in the middle of open country. Heavy industry and animal husbandry back-to-back, like a geography textbook with two pages stuck together.

Kinsella's Audi was parked alongside a white Jaguar, ten years old but gleamingly maintained. She locked the Hillman and inspected her reflection in the driver's window. The grey linen shirt dress and matching jacket were new. She was modestly pleased with the effect: feminine enough to appease Kinsella without betraying her idea of herself. 'Oh Christ, it's Sister Clodagh,' Rae had muttered, passing her in the corridor.

The colliery offices smelled of plasterboard and stale cigars. A copy of *Woman's Realm* on the desk beside the golf-ball typewriter. Voices next door. '*Come in.*' Kinsella, Gabriel and a man squeezed into a suit two sizes too small were grouped around a low table. The colliery manager extended a puffy hand with a signet ring embedded in the third finger.

'Terry Harrison.'

The only vacant chair was beside the door. She started to draw it forward but Kinsella stopped her with a look.

Harrison sat down again. 'It's a geological lottery, this game. Some seams it comes out like shit off a shovel, some it's not worth the bother. We're two-and-a-half miles from Dudder-thorpe, NCB mine down the road. Our lot use their miners' welfare. Their top seam's under bunter sandstone, which is gassy, water-bearing and bloody hard. All we've got to worry about's magnesian limestone and Mottershaw shale. We use drill and blast method. Pillar and stall workings. The machinery they've got makes us look like something out of the Stone Age, but ton for ton we're a damn site more profitable . . .'

Kinsella listened attentively. Lexa knew that in Sylvester's tonight he would mimic Harrison's laboured breathing, his voice richly textured with phlegm.

'. . . What you've got to bear in mind is, we're all the same coalfield, but it's not the same quality coal. West Drayton gets twenty-four gigajoules a tonne out of Dudderthorpe. D'you know what they get out of us?' He turned to Gabriel. 'Go on, have a guess.'

'Twenty-nine point four.' She had done her background reading.

Harrison looked put out. 'Power stations run on cheap, low-grade coal, but they have to sweeten it with a quality product.' He counted the categories off on his swollen fingers. 'Our moisture's seven per cent. Sulphur and chlorine, less than one per cent, so they don't have to worry about fouling in the boilers. Ash fusion temperature's over fourteen hundred degrees.' He smiled at Gabriel. 'About the only thing we don't do for them's dance of the seven veils.'

Her gaze was slightly averted, a Biro balanced between her fingers above the ruled pad on her lap. Kinsella took the pen from her hand and scribbled a wavy line on the blank paper.

'Just checking,' he said.

Harrison lit a cigar. It was eleven thirty and already there were five fat butts in the ashtray. The only window was painted shut. The sun burned through the dirty glass, illuminating the blue cirrus of tobacco smoke. Lexa had a sudden intuition that he spent his life in sealed compartments. This office, the 1960s bungalow he'd call home, the glass and metal capsule of his car. His wife would be a non-smoker with a graveyard cough.

There was a tap at the door. A middle-aged woman came in with a tray of crockery and a large earthenware teapot.

They watched in silence as she lowered the tray to the table and set the cups out. In the next room the telephone shrilled. She hurried out.

Harrison resumed his hymn to the marvels of Faxerley coal. The mine was a fundamentally healthy business whose sale his bosses would live to regret. 'Flaming alphabet soup of letters after their names. They haven't got a bloody clue. No bloody balls either—'

He glanced at Gabriel. Lexa assumed he was checking her reaction to this mention of masculine potency, but when his eyes shifted to the teacups she had to bite back a smile. He was waiting for her to be mother.

'—You'll have no trouble finding a buyer. The Yanks have been sniffing round for years. The Argentinians an'all, before the Falklands . . .'

Gabriel returned his glance innocently.

Kinsella looked at Lexa. 'What are you sitting over there for?'

She moved her chair next to Gabriel's.

'Time for a cup of tea, I think,' he remarked.

Harrison turned the teapot handle to position it between the two women.

'Alexandra,' Kinsella said.

'Not for me thanks, it's a wee bit warm for tea.'

She felt a quiver at her side. 'It is, isn't it?' Gabriel agreed.

Lexa turned the teapot handle towards Kinsella. Gabriel had a sudden need to cough.

'Pour the tea, Alexandra.'

She met his eye.

'Milk and sugar?' she asked Harrison.

He stubbed out his cigar. 'No, you're right, it's too hot in here. Come on, I'll give you the tour.' He stood up. 'After you, ladies.'

Gabriel was first through the door, then Lexa. Behind them, Harrison lowered his voice.

'If they don't take dictation or make tea I hope they're bloody good at what they do.'

'I've no complaints.'

The colliery manager's laugh stirred vats of mucus deep in his chest. 'I bet you've not.'

With one hand resting on the small of Gabriel's back, Harrison showed them around. The coal preparation plant, the control room, the boilerhouse, baths and medical centre. Gabriel veered away to inspect the weighbridge, then lagged behind claiming a stone in her shoe. Each time she shook him off he regained possession.

'Mester'arrison . . .'

Orange overalls and a black donkey jacket. The first miner they had seen. The colliery manager walked him some distance away before finding out what he wanted.

Gabriel took advantage of Harrison's absence to cough. Not the discreet throat-clearing she had faked in his office, but a cacophonic hawking.

'Get a grip, Gabriel,' Kinsella said. 'You can't have developed black lung already.'

'It was the . . . cigar smoke . . .' she held her breath for a few moments and let it out in a gasp, waiting to see if the coughing would resume. 'Do you think he's keeping us away from the action for a reason?'

'I don't give a flying fuck as long as I can find some sucker to buy this dump.'

Harrison was back. 'Sorry about that, ladies and gent.'

'Is there a problem?'

'Nothing serious.' Despite their lechers' complicity in the office, Harrison had marked Kinsella as an enemy.

'So where are the surface workers?' Gabriel asked.

Up to this point Harrison had smiled at all her questions. Now he looked furtive. 'The shift's walked out—'

The bankers exchanged glances. For the past four weeks the nationalised industry had been paralysed by a strike. Kinsella's strategy for selling Faxerley was based on it being separate from, and comprehensively unlike, the National Coal Board mines. If its workforce had walked out in sympathy, they would have to come up with a new pitch. Though what were the chances of selling a coal mine which was not currently producing coal?

'—I don't know what's gone off yet. Seemingly there was a meeting in Sheffield this morning. National Union's been threatening to withdraw dispensation to work. Area said we were all right, as long as everything we produce goes to schools and hospitals.' His eyes flicked to Kinsella to check how he was taking this, then returned to their preferred resting place. 'It's bloody Scargill. He won't be happy till he's got everyone out. NCB, open-cast, private mines, the lot.'

'You let the National Union of Mineworkers tell you who you can sell your coal to?'

Harrison stared at Kinsella with undisguised loathing. 'If the alternative's a strike, I do, yes.'

'But you seem to have one on your hands anyway.'

'I don't know that yet, do I?'

'Who should we talk to, at the Union?' It was Lexa's first contribution.

'Why would you want to do that?'

She thought Kinsella was going to laugh, but the moment passed and he became once more the consummate professional. 'I think we should explain the-*aah* salient facts of their situation. Especially if they're on strike. And if by some chance they're still deigning to work, we'll want to make sure they don't spring any-*aah* surprises on us when we produce a buyer.'

Harrison looked doubtful. 'You can try, but you won't find them too co-operative. The branch president's Kevin Sproson but I wouldn't waste your time with him. Stuart Duffy's the organ grinder . . .'

His voice faltered. Gabriel was brushing at her blouse, fingers strumming briskly over each nipple.

'Toast crumbs,' she beamed at the colliery manager, 'you should have said something. I wondered what you were looking at.'

Lexa tailed Kinsella and Gabriel for a mile or so, but the Hillman was no match for the Audi's acceleration. Five minutes into the journey she was lost. She couldn't face going back to ask for directions so she kept driving, following the B roads, hoping for a lucky break. Suddenly there were houses. Semi-detached postwar redbrick. A broad urban street with a green verge lining each pavement, surrounded by open fields. Then a row of shops and a solid redbrick pub. Dudderthorpe Miners' Welfare, the sign said. The door was propped open. As her eyes adjusted from the brightness outside she realised the place was packed, eight to a table, a crowd around the bar. She turned her head, looking for a friendly face, though she knew already, she could feel it in the air: they were all men. The thickened bodies of manual labour. Broad shoulders, broad rumps, bulging forearms, beer bellies straining under their T-shirts, and everywhere the yellow sticker Coal Not Dole. She tried to catch the barman's eye but he was busy serving. She had never been in a room with so many moustaches.

When she reached the nearest table their conversation stopped. The *Guardian* had carried a piece on the strikers' paranoia. Informers and telephone taps, Special Branch trawling through Arthur Scargill's dustbins.

'Can you tell me how to get to the A1?'

A man with a face of hollows and shadows placed his cigarette in the metal ashtray. 'Through Astworth. First left. Second right on to Doncaster Road. Take last turn off roundabout . . . You know Astworth—?'

She shook her head.

'—where've you come from, love?'

'Faxerley Colliery.' She was aware of a quickening of interest around the table.

'Then you've come through Astworth.'

'Not if she came backroad, Frank.'

Lexa glanced towards the speaker, the only man wearing a collar and tie. Late twenties, prematurely grey hair, narrowed blue-green eyes.

Frank was working out an alternative route. He pulled at his earlobe, thinking. 'Right. Go to top end, turn left at T-junction, you'll see farm track. Down there you'll come to B road. Take right, second left . . .'

She held up a hand to stop him, delving in her bag for pen and paper. 'I'll need to write this down.'

Frank shrugged. 'I'll take you when I've finished my pint.'

By now she had found a scrap of paper. 'A T-junction, you said . . .'

'I said I'll take you.'

It was the surest way of getting back to Leeds. Her eyes circled the table. The man in the collar and tie was watching her.

'Can I buy anyone a drink?'

Frank did not bother to check his companions' glasses. 'You're all right, love.'

A swarthy man sitting next to him grinned. 'You can make donation to strike fund.'

She took a five pound note out of her wallet. The man drew a child's notebook from his pocket and wrote the date and the amount in a painstaking hand. Someone found a chair for her. A shout came from the bar asking what she was drinking. She wasn't thirsty, but refusing would have forced Frank to hurry his pint, maybe the only one he could afford this week. She paid for an orange juice and was handed a glass of lurid squash, a taste she had not missed since childhood. She was careful not to look towards the collar and tie, but her mind's eye furnished the details she had not consciously registered. His steel-coloured hair grew in curls which caught the light, accentuating the bloom of his skin. His mouth was a horizontal line, the flesh above and below bulging slightly, giving him an air of barely-withheld mockery.

The men around the table resumed their discussion.

'Executive's seen you jammy bastards all right, then.'

'We'll be more use donating to strike fund than standing on picket-line.'

'You'll be richer, more like. Arthur's right: one out, all out. Harder we hit 'em, sooner it'll be over.'

The Northern English Lexa was used to was an urban dialect, words formed in the nose and the back of the throat. The miners' accent started down in the belly, a mannish tongue as brawny as their flesh.

'You won't get us out without national ballot.'

'You saying you'd cross picket-line?'

'Not me, but there's some might. Two, three month down line.'

'Thatcher wants ballot, MacGregor wants ballot, media want ballot – dun't that tell you owt?'

'It tells me we're wide open and they know it.'

Turning her head as she followed the argument, she caught the burn of those blue-green eyes on the other side of the table. Flustered, she dropped her gaze and watched the men's hands, calloused and scarred, with their horny nails and nicotine-yellowed fingers. She was glad she had not bought Frank another pint. He was taking an eternity to finish this one. She gazed at the wedge of sunlight just inside the open door, awkward amid the tattoos and the dark leathery smell of beer and masculine sweat. And there was another dimension to her self-consciousness. She shifted in her seat, feeling the foolishness of being watched and knowing it and pretending it was not happening. She toyed with her disgusting drink, took a sip, put it down, ten seconds later picked it up again. Embarrassment was turning to annoyance. He was the one who ought to feel uncomfortable, staring so nakedly. At last she took a decision, setting her glass down so abruptly that some of the squash slopped onto the table. When she turned to face him he met her gaze coolly, as if he had been waiting for her to look.

'You ready, love?'

Frank had finished his pint. She followed him out to the car park.

Lexa could understand why most of her colleagues had been appointed. They had an easy way of moving through the world which silenced awkward questions. Their assurance doubled as charm or intimidation. The money they talked sounded classier than the oily, dog-eared notes in circulation. In an odd way they embodied their clients' idealism. None of this applied to Ben.

Ben was short-sighted and uncomfortable in his contact lenses. He suffered from swollen eyelids which he massaged with his fingers. On a good day he looked bleary. On a bad day, seedy. He had a smoker's sniff and chapped lips and a permanent clog of catarrh in his throat. He came from St Albans, which he couldn't help, but affected a Cockney swagger. Now that Gloria had resigned, he had inherited the role of office whipping-boy.

He knocked and went in without waiting to be asked. Lexa had half-hoped Kinsella would be out at lunch, but he was standing by the window with Gavin.

'What is it?'

Ben jerked his head towards her. 'Five minutes out of university and she's telling me how to do my job. She's still on her first deal, she hasn't even been on the fucking training scheme . . .'

Kinsella's eyes turned cold. 'Sit down.'

Gavin smiled to himself as he left the room.

Ben slapped the Wishew Refractories file down on the table. 'She's talking to me like I'm a fucking schoolboy. I've got to redo the numbers, the profit forecast's unrealistic . . . What the fuck does she know about it?'

'I can spot a bogus depreciation policy.'

'Have you been over the books? *Nah*. Have you met the MD? *Nah*. Do you even know what a fucking refractory *is*? I'm in and out of that building so often the doorman thinks I'm on the fucking payroll. I'm banging the financial director's PA—'

He had been shouting for fifteen minutes and his anger

showed no sign of abating.

'—and *she's* sitting in the middle of the fucking office telling me I don't know what I'm talking about . . .'

For the first time Kinsella looked at her. 'You didn't take him into the boardroom?'

'There was nobody around when we started. I didn't want to make it into a big deal . . .'

Ben's lips pulled back, exposing the nicotine seams between his teeth. 'So it's no big deal when she rips the shit out of me in front of everybody? She's never worked anywhere else, she's only here because—' he caught sight of Kinsella's expression and aborted whatever he was about to say next '—I've spent three months on this deal. *Nobody* knows that company better, and it's complicated. If the miners block supplies to the strip mills, the blast furnaces go cold. When they're cold they crack. If they get replaced, that's a lot of refractories, yeah. But what if Maggie says "time to cut our losses, we can buy steel cheaper than we can make it, we're pulling the plug"? They'd go tits-up overnight. We *need* to make it look sweet. She doesn't have a clue about any of this, but I've got to do as I'm told . . .'

'You said that?' Kinsella asked her.

'I said I was acting on your authority.'

Ben was blinking almost continuously now. 'You've always said we run our own deals. If we cock-up, OK, we take the consequences, but we use our own judgement. I don't need the graduate trainee telling me I've missed a trick . . .'

The words poured out of him, the same points made over and over again. Kinsella seemed mesmerised, his eyes moving from Ben's face to the file on the table and back.

'Look, Ben,' she made her voice calmly reasonable, 'this has got blown up out of proportion. It's just a mistake. I know you're good at your job . . .'

Kinsella cut her off. 'OK Ben, you can get back to work now. I want a word with Alexandra.'

For a moment Ben seemed inclined to stay and argue, but he settled for banging the door on his way out. Kinsella flicked through the file. Lexa waited for him to look up with a conspiratorial grin.

'You made a real pig's arse of that, didn't you?' He closed the file in disgust. 'You're going to have to sharpen up the way you deal with people. If I hear of anything like this with the clients you're off the Faxerley deal, I'm telling you now. What the fuck were you doing telling him he had to do as he was told?'

'It wasn't the way he made it sound.'

'Are you saying you didn't say it?'

'You told me to sort it out.'

'I asked you to have a word. I didn't say you could put him up against the wall and have him shot.'

'He wouldn't listen.'

'You should have found a way of saying it he would listen to. Why do you have to make everything into a battle?' There was a knock at the door. '*Come in*. And when you told him he was good at his job, it was embarrassing. He's been here two years, he knows he can do the job . . .'

'Can he? That's not what you told me. Before he walked in here and appealed to the universal brotherhood . . .'

The door opened. The combined staff of Corporate Finance, Asset Management, Leasing and Venture Capital filed into Kinsella's office, ties loosened, faces boozily flushed, reeking of smoked cigarettes and restaurant garlic. Everyone except Rae and Gabriel. Lexa was the only woman in the room.

Though it was clearly a prearranged meeting, for a moment Kinsella seemed surprised. Then he caught their mood. His posture relaxed. He stood up, motioning her towards the door, 'We'll talk about this later.'

But the way out was blocked by her colleagues, still shuffling into the room. She had to stand and wait.

Kinsella smiled for the benefit of the audience. 'And try to look a bit more cheerful, Alexandra. We're not a firm of undertakers.'

His fingers found the flesh under her ribs and tickled her.

For a moment she stood frozen in disbelief, then she snatched his hands away and grabbed at his midriff in savage parody of his touch. 'That's enough overfamiliarity, thanks.'

Nineteen pairs of eyes watched her, bright with cruelty.

Kinsella made a pantomime noise, '*Ooooo*, I am *sorry*.'

Someone murmured 'Must be the wrong time of the month.'

'And when's the right time of the month for touching up female staff?'

Her smirking colleagues caught each other's glances.

Closing the door behind her, she heard the explosion of laughter.

Gabriel unlocked the door at the top of the staircase, releasing a smell of Penhaligon's Gardenia laced with Gauloises.

'Next time, I'll choose,' she said.

The *Guardian* women's page had praised the film's frisson-free treatment of sexual coercion and rejection of ideologically-compromised genre norms. Lexa had had to see it, if only to find out what they meant. And now she knew. Shaky camerawork, downbeat locations, every shot composed to minimise visual appeal.

'And the script!' Gabriel said. 'Why couldn't anyone manage to string more than three words together?'

Lexa stooped to lift the post from the mat. 'That's how people talk.'

'I don't.'

'Your mother was a German philosophy graduate and you went to Cambridge.'

The rape scene hadn't bothered Gabriel. It was the heroine's *pornographic violence* that offended her. Those *revolting* shots of the victim out on the firing range, putting bullet holes in man-shaped targets. The *self-righteous sadism* of the revenge scene. Lexa listened, trying not to smile. Gabriel had the knack of squeezing enjoyment out of anything. Even her repugnance was half a game, an excuse for exclamation marks and gesticulation.

'. . . cut your hair, throw away your skirts, get yourself a phallic symbol and teach them the meaning of fear. In other words, let's all act just like men.'

Lexa followed her into the kitchen, where Blake's 'Wise and Foolish Virgins' and Klimt's 'Salome' were pinned to the cornflower-coloured walls. 'You're not averse to a spot of direct action.'

'That's tearing page three out of the *Sun*. It doesn't involve live ammunition.' She picked up the corkscrew. 'I don't mind women wearing dungarees and neglecting the tweezers. What I *do* mind is being told I'm a quisling because I own a lipstick.'

Lexa found the wine glasses. 'Do you never get tired of being the charming sex?'

'No.'

'Having to smile instead of saying what you mean?'

'What's wrong with smiling?'

'Nothing, if you feel like smiling. But I don't want to have to do it all the time because if I don't I'll be seen as a bitch.'

'I take it Kinsella's still giving you the big freeze.'

Lexa was about to reply that she wasn't talking about Kinsella. Only of course she was.

'You think I should have put up with it? Stood there like an idiot while he had a good grapple?'

Gabriel tilted her head to consider this. 'If you were going to get physical, you could at least have drawn blood.'

'It's not funny,' Lexa said. But they were smiling.

Together they could talk about anything. How they never saw a pregnant woman on television. What men found so arousing about stiletto heels. Why every blonde actress cast in a cop show got her face slapped or her blouse ripped, or both. To Gabriel there was no such thing as a self-evident truth. She would start with a simple question, to which Lexa would supply the obvious answer. Then she would unpick its logic with another question, and another, until the obvious answers ran out and Lexa, sweating lightly, was using all her ingenuity to defend what she *just knew*. In this way, for the first time, she was gaining an overview of her own opinions and prejudices, a sense of who she was. And a sense of Gabriel too. So principled in some ways, so unscrupulous in others. Her barleywater hair. Her rapt smile. Her eyes, swimming-pool pale in sunlight, Prussian blue in cloud.

The wine tasted strangely delicious, as if it held some precious metal in solution.

'You like?'

'It's incredible.' Lexa turned the bottle. The label meant nothing to her.

'Same grape as St-Émilion.' Gabriel pronounced the name in an effortless French accent. 'Grown on the same slope, but the wrong side of the road. Twenty yards west it'd cost forty quid a bottle and taste exactly the same.'

'How do you know this stuff?'

'I used to work for a wine importer.'

'Before or after the tour operator?'

'Before, but after Pinewood.'

'The *film studio*?'

Lexa loved Gabriel's laugh, a triumphant pealing shout. 'That's just the way Aaron said it.'

'And you told them what?' It was one of their jokes, the way Gabriel bent the truth to get what she wanted.

'Oh I don't know.' But she did. 'Something about working in Australian television.'

'Did they not check your references?'

'I had three weeks' grace while they blamed the post for not getting a reply. And after that, they couldn't manage without me.'

Lexa took another sip of the wine, holding it in her mouth for a moment so she would always remember the taste. 'Have you ever been knocked back?'

'Oh *yes*.'

'When?'

Gabriel thought for a few moments. 'D'you know, I can't remember.' She topped up Lexa's glass. 'Someone has to do the interesting jobs. It might as well be me.'

'Even if there are people better qualified?'

'They're only better qualified because they've been given a chance.'

Lexa opened her mouth, then shut it again.

'What?' Gabriel said.

'How is it you think the world's your oyster?'

Gabriel's Prussian blue eyes lightened in wonder. 'How is it you don't?'

Gabriel's bathroom had the predictable trappings – deep-pile towels, bubble bath, expensive soaps – but also a feature Lexa had not expected. Several labourer's rubber gloves had been fixed to the wall above the bath. Some were limp and passive, others seemed to be reaching towards her. Impossible to look at them without thinking of building-site cat calls, obscenities shouted from passing vans, the wolf-whistles that were surely satiric (or meant for someone else).

Down the corridor the telephone rang.

'I never knew you were so artistic,' she said, walking into the sitting room. Then she saw Gabriel's expression. The telephone receiver rested on its cradle, but there was a tension in the air, as if it had only just been replaced.

'Who was that?'

Gabriel's voice was flat. 'They didn't say.'

'Wrong number?'

'I doubt it.' She tipped the remains of her glass of wine back into the bottle. 'It's been going on for about a week. Every night. Sometimes there are noises in the background, as if he's in a bar.' Anticipating Lexa's question, she added, 'It's not a heavy breather.'

'You could always let it ring.'

'What if it's Ma phoning to tell me Pa's in hospital? Or the police, to say you've had an accident?'

Lexa's heart squeezed. 'You could have your calls intercepted by the operator—'

The double note of a train horn carried through the open window.

'—could it be Theo?'

She shook her head. 'He's besotted with a primary teacher now.'

'Aaron, then. He sounds the type to get aggressive.'

'Are silent phone calls aggressive?' Gabriel pulled at a loose thread in the arm of the settee. 'I feel *watched*, which is creepy but not actively threatening. After it happens the first time, you're waiting for it to happen again, and that makes you feel *complicit*. That's what the silence is saying: "you know what it's about, really. By pretending you don't you're just making it worse for yourself . . ." and I suppose "worse" presumes it's already bad, so maybe it is aggressive. But it's not Aaron. He's on a six-month attachment in New Zealand.'

'Which leaves . . .?'

She shrugged. 'No peeved ex-lovers, no jealous rivals, no deadly enemies . . .'

'It's somebody in the office, then.'

Gabriel stopped playing with the thread. 'Who?'

All at once Lexa felt tired. She wanted to go home to bed, and walk in to Goodisons in the morning to find Gabriel her usual irrepressible self. 'Well it's not Ben. You'd hear him sniffing. Gavin couldn't pick up the phone without speaking . . .'

'And Ned only has eyes for you.' Gabriel jumped up and crossed to the door. 'Leave your wine, you can finish it when we get back.'

'From where?'

She picked up the car keys. 'You're right. No more smiling.'

When they arrived at the cinema the doors were locked. Gabriel retrieved the aerosol can she kept under the dashboard. All the lifts Lexa had accepted in the Land Rover, all the times she had seen this can of paint, and still she was shocked.

'Do you do this often?'

'Never done it before, officer, I don't know *what* came over me.'

Lexa had to laugh. Gabriel jumped every queue, shot most red lights, reversed the wrong way down one-way streets, lit up in the no-smoking seats. Once, at a sherry and *bonne-bouches* do in the boardroom, Lexa had seen her wipe her fingers on a curtain. She flouted every rule of civilised behaviour, but she did it with such *panache*.

Beside the doors was a poster showing the actress in a figure-hugging dress she had not worn in the film, looking down the sights of a gun. Even without the benefit of airbrushing, Gabriel was more beautiful.

'Any ideas?'

Lexa cast a nervous glance along the empty street. 'Women are Angry?'

'Not hugely original.'

'I never even wrote my name on a desk at school.'

'You were a goody gumdrops.' Gabriel shook the can.

The aerosol hissed and paused, hissed and paused. Across the poster she had written MORE PRICKS THAN KICKS.

'What do you think?'

'I think the police'll be looking for a university-educated vandal.'

'Catch.' Gabriel threw the can.

'No!' But Lexa caught it. 'You're the one with strong feelings. I was just bored.'

'So write that.'

'Why?'

'Because I'd like to meet the naughty Lexa.'

A police car crossed the junction fifty yards away.

Lexa sprayed a cross topped by a circle. She had never quite felt entitled to this symbol. As if there were such a thing as an accredited feminist. Another cross, another circle. It was unexpectedly gratifying. The weight of the can in her hand. The pungent hiss of the paint. Such a slight pressure on the nozzle to do something so irreversible.

'Welcome to the criminal classes,' Gabriel said.

Two or three days a week now Lexa drove to Faxerley Colliery. If she took the direct route and there were no road blocks to stop the flying pickets she could do the journey in half an hour, but she preferred to set off earlier and follow the B roads. Every trip revealed some fresh curiosity. A Norman chapel surrounded by farmland. A seventeenth-century dovecote. A shop window mannequin, bald and startle-eyed, pressed into service as a scarecrow. That morning she passed a ploughed field and, next to it, what she had been brought up to call a 'bing' but the locals called a 'slag heap'. Four women were crouched on the slope, heads down, blackened fingers rooting through the spoil.

Jean, Harrison's secretary, removed her glasses as Lexa walked in, embarrassed to be caught wearing them, though they had etched permanent grooves either side of her nose. 'He's got somebody with him.' Jean never referred to Harrison by name. She made a worried face and mouthed 'N-U-M'.

Lexa knocked and went in.

'Just in time.' Harrison treated her with a lack of ceremony which bordered on disrespect but was preferable to the attention he paid Gabriel. 'Have you met Mester Duffy?'

A man in his late twenties was sitting in front of the desk. She noted the indigo shirt worn with a pale cream tie, the close-cropped grey curls, the narrowed eyes burning out of his squarish face . . . And then she knew him.

'Stuart,' he said pleasantly.

The eyes were more green than blue, and alive with something she had to look away from. Not amusement, though she was reminded of a private joke: the straight face and the second meaning.

'You got back all right then?'

'Thanks to Frank.'

Harrison was looking at her suspiciously. She started

to explain but he talked over her. 'Mester Duffy thinks I'm keeping him in the dark, holding things back from his members. Maybe you can put him right.' He turned to the Union delegate. 'Miss Strachan here works for Goodison Farebrother, the merchant bank.'

Stuart Duffy nodded as if enlightened, though she had the feeling he already knew exactly who she was.

'Any interested parties yet?' he asked her.

'None so interested they'd want me to breach confidentiality by naming them.'

'But you'll be wanting our co-operation?' His accent was like Harrison's, but his voice was deeper.

'She wants to know if your lot are going to start playing silly buggers, aye.'

Stuart Duffy took out a pocket diary and a stainless steel fountain pen. The nib scratched across the paper. He tore out the page, folded it in half and tucked it in his shirt pocket. 'I can't say anything until I've put it to the men, but I know they'll want some answers before they commit themselves. For instance, is Mester Harrison included in the fixed assets?'

'That's my business,' Harrison said.

'And ours. We'd like a manager who can deliver on his promises.'

'And I'd like a workforce who can see further than their next pay packet.'

'The money's a side issue.'

'Do you think I was born yesterday?'

It was a circular argument. After five minutes she had grasped all the salient points. The Union objected to the production levels used to calculate incentive payments. The manager said they were wanting bonuses for turning up to work. From where she was sitting, the boss and the workers' champion did not seem so far apart. They spoke the same dialect, faced each other with the same combative pose. They didn't even have to discuss their agreement to ignore her.

'. . . it's a different game now, I can't incur any extra costs.'

'All we're asking's to be paid for the work we do.'

'We were down two thousand tonnes last month.'

'Be even lower if we go back to "work to rule".'

'Don't threaten me, lad.' Harrison stabbed the desktop with a finger. 'I told you, it's a new game. You can't cut my throat without cutting your own. *I* don't know if they're going to want redundancies, but if you want to make it more likely, fastest way to do it's working to rule. Tell you what, join your pals out on strike. Ask her how that's going to impress a buyer?'

Stuart Duffy turned towards her. 'Would it make any difference to Beronex?'

Kinsella and Gabriel had met the chief executive of Beronex UK a week ago. No one else was meant to know.

'You're asking the wrong person. My colleagues are handling the buyer side.'

She could see Beronex was news to Harrison, but he wasn't prepared to admit his ignorance in front of the Union official and she wasn't prepared to wait around to enlighten him. Let him phone Kinsella. See how far that got him.

When she excused herself, Stuart Duffy got up to open the door for her. He stood five feet six inches in his shoes, which – she looked down to check – had a generous heel. She stared at him and his green-blue eyes contracted with a look she hadn't seen before. At least, not aimed at her. He was closing the door behind her when she felt the touch at her waist, two fingers tucked into the band of her skirt. She almost turned, but she was afraid of meeting that look again. Or afraid it would be gone.

In the empty office next door she retrieved the slip of paper. It was the page she had watched him write and tear out of his diary.

The car park beside the miners' welfare was full. She left the Hillman across the road, behind a minibus with 'Camden Car Hire' painted on the side. The sky was a less punishing blue than earlier in the day but the heat remained, stored in the pavements, aggravating the smell from the dustbins.

She stepped over the threshold into a wall of talk and laughter. Moustaches and tattoos. Lipstick and blusher. The women all sitting together in a clash of turquoise, coral, fuscia, jade. Some were singing along to the jukebox, word-perfect. The men sat at separate tables or stood at the bar. An acne-crusted youth fiddled with the microphone stands on the makeshift stage. A homemade banner hung from the ceiling: *Victory to the Miners*.

There was no sign of him. She stood frozen for an instant in the grey linen dress she had already worn half to death, a novitiate among the gaudy milkmaids. Thank God for the jukebox. She studied the list. Bill Hailey, Eddie Cochran, Jerry Lee Lewis, Del Shannon, Johnny Kidd and the Pirates, songs recorded before she was born. Age did not seem a great divider here. Old and young, male and female were united by an overriding similarity. Padded jaw, putty-lump nose, solid slabs of cheek. Only the women in the corner broke the mould. More delicate than the local girls, they had city haircuts and wore 1940s dresses in prettily-faded shades of forget-me-not and lavender. *Camden Car Hire*. Lexa felt a hot sluice of antipathy, though she too was a tourist. She turned away and there he was, watching from a table near the dartboard, an empty chair beside him.

His short-sleeved shirt looked silver where it caught the light, echoing his hair.

'What are you drinking?' he asked.

Eight men looked up at her expectantly.

'I'll get my own.'

'She'll serve me quicker.'

The miners grinned.

'I'll have a Guinness, then.'

She sat down, smiling at everyone and no one.

The man next to her nodded, 'All right?'

There was something familiar about his Mungo Jerry hairstyle. 'Do you work at Faxerley?'

'Us lot do.' His gesture took in several tables. 'Not Pecker, he's Dudderthorpe, but we don't hold it against him.'

Pecker had cement-blond hair and a blue line around the gum of his capped front tooth. 'It's a man's pit, George.' Disconcertingly he winked at her. 'Some of us've got what it takes, and some of us haven't.'

George leaned towards her. 'Most of us started at Dudderthorpe, but we've moved on to better things.'

'Softer, you mean,' Pecker said.

George laughed. 'I work in lamp room, on pit top. I did face-training. Waste of time, that were. Five minutes down there and I'd be dropping off. It were atmosphere. Cun't keep me eyes open.' He had a boxer's boneless nose and a ragged amateur tattoo spelling O-W-L-S across the knuckles of his left hand, but his mildness reminded Lexa of the ease she felt with women. 'Dayshift, backshift, made no odds.'

'You should have tried sleeping in your own bed once in a while.' Stuart was back with her Guinness. When he sat down the table became crowded. 'George, Pat, Mick, Dave, Pecker, Tommo, Dean.'

'I'm Lexa,' she said, since he had not.

'They know. You're famous.'

A microphone whistled and all heads turned towards the stage where an old man with arms big as pistons was calling for quiet.

'I'm glad to see so many faces here tonight, even ugly ones—'

A heckler shouted something Lexa didn't catch.

'—reason you're all here is to have a bloody good time. Any miserable sods'll answer to me. But before kick-off I want to say summat. I don't need to tell any of you how important this strike is. Thatcher knows what she's doing. It's war, and if she wins, God help us all . . .'

Lexa became aware of a glancing touch. Stuart had moved closer, his bare forearm beside hers. The old man on stage was talking about Arthur Scargill, how the government had tried to dismiss his warnings as scaremongering, but again and again he had been proved right. Stuart's skin was warm against her own. She held her breath. It had to be deliberate. She could feel her fine hairs bristling as they met the denser growth along his muscled arm. He had hardly looked at her since she sat down, which deepened their conspiracy, listening to the speech poker-faced while an electric seam crackled between them.

'. . . Bucket's going round, so if you've too many pound notes in your pockets, here's chance to get shut of 'em. And now, you've heard enough from me, so here they are, allt' way from Pontefract—' his voice rose to a bellow '—Beale Street Brew.'

Five men in jeans and flannel shirts stepped onto the tiny stage and struck up a hybrid of rock and country-and-western. The bass notes fuzzed in the battered speakers. Between vocals the lead singer played a wailing harmonica, stamping out the beat with a metal-toed cowboy boot. The crowd could not get enough of this music, feet tapping, heads nodding, hands beating out the rhythm on their thighs. Each song ended to a roar of appreciation. For the last number of the set the band stepped down from the stage. The singer took up an acoustic guitar and, with a crack in his voice, delivered a ballad, the lament of a plain, hard-working man who could not give his lady the pretty things she found in the city, but who offered her the truest heart. Lexa studied the faces in the audience. Everything about them was foreign. Their luxuriant sideburns, the girth of their arms, the granular texture of their skin. Even the smell of them, inhaled briefly and then lost amid the beer and cigarette smoke. Some instinct made her turn her head. Stuart was watching her. Colouring, she looked towards the stage. At the end of the song the room erupted. The table-thumping lasted a full five minutes, by which time the singer was at the bar, halfway through his pint. The jukebox started up again and the women drifted on to the dance floor. Mick stood up to buy a round of drinks.

Still shy of Stuart, Lexa turned to George. 'This is a benefit night for the strikers, but everyone here's a miner, or a miner's wife or girlfriend, and Faxerley's already paying a strike levy?'

'Aye,' George said.

'So where's the money supposed to come from?'

'You,' said Tommo, or Dean, she wasn't sure which.

Everyone laughed.

Pecker lit a cigarette, 'You'll be loaded. Merchant banker. Pied-a-terre in Leeds.' He mispronounced the French, possibly for comic effect.

'Waterbed upstairs.'

'Black satin sheets.'

'Mink bedspread.'

'Mirror ont' ceiling.'

The conversation had become a free-for-all.

'Champagne breakfast Sunday morning.'

'Caviar on toast.'

They all grinned at this.

'Jensen Interceptor.'

'XJ6, I reckon.'

'Don't be daft, it'll be a Porsche 944.'

'You want to know what I drive?'

'Aye,' they chorused.

'A Hillman Imp—'

They burst out laughing, as they were meant to.

'—eight-fifty CC, runs on three-star.'

'Metallic blue? Parked across road?' Pecker said. 'Your silencer's going. Lads'll do it if you give 'em a fiver.'

George looked wistful, 'I did my courting in a Hillman Imp.'

She smiled at the old-fashioned verb. No one else found it funny.

Mick returned with the drinks and tossed a cellophane-wrapped panatella across the table. From the careless way Stuart pocketed it she saw that they were more than drinking friends. An unlikely alliance: the Union man small and dapper and quick-witted; Mick burly and beetle-browed, not a sparkling conversationalist, but treated with quiet deference by the men around the table.

A girl in a tomato-red dress approached Mick from behind, placing her hands over his eyes. He got up to dance.

'Lucky bastard,' Pecker said. 'Sixteen-year-old and insatiable.'

Lexa looked down at her Guinness.

'What's *she* doing here?'

The man pointing at her was lean and sallow-skinned, not a typical product of the local gene pool.

'This is Lexa. She's my guest.'

'I know *who* she is. She's one of them bankers trying to sell Faxerley to asset strippers. What I *don't* know is what you think you're doing with her.'

Stuart's manner suggested he had limited reserves of patience. 'She's looking for a buyer who'll take it on as a going concern.'

'She's paid to make profit for bosses on back of our sweat, or on back of our idleness if there's more money in it. Fat lot of good scabbing through national strike'll do us then.'

Lexa did not like the turn the conversation was taking.

Stuart waved his hand as if batting away a fly. 'Piss off, Tony, I'm trying to enjoy myself.'

Tony raised his voice to be heard by the other tables of Faxerley miners. 'Mester Duffy'll do all right when we get our P45s. He'll get Area job, driving round in Union car, claiming overtime for sitting in pub all night—'

It wasn't only the Faxerley men who were listening. Heads were turning on the other side of the room. Tony's eyes glinted. Lexa had seen that look in children, before a calculated act of transgression.

'—I hope you count it.'

Stuart stood up, his chair scraping the floor. He was several inches shorter, but there was a compacted power in his arms. 'You what?'

'Your pieces of silver. Make sure you get all thirty.'

George and Pecker pushed their chairs back from the table. Mick made no move but she sensed his readiness.

'You've had too much to drink, Tony.' Stuart spoke quietly, reinforcing Lexa's suspicion that he was about to do something violent. 'If you still feel like this int' morning, come and see me and we'll discuss it.'

'We can discuss it now, outside.'

Abruptly George and Pecker were on their feet. 'Come on, Tony,' George said, pulling him away, 'let's get you back to your table.'

Tony tried to shake him off. 'You going to get your big pals to rough me up?'

'I wouldn't miss chance of doing it myself, if it came to it.' Stuart sat down and picked up his pint. 'But it won't.'

The stand-off was over. Muttering to himself, Tony returned to his seat. Stuart's colour was high but he seemed calm. She wondered whether George and Pecker were protective because he was short, or loyal because he was a big enough man to make his height irrelevant.

'Thanks,' she said.

He pulled a dismissive face. 'Happens every week. Some idiot gets pissed and thinks it's high noon.'

Mick glanced across. 'All right?'

'Aye.' Stuart's narrowed gaze was focused on the bar. He drained his pint, 'there's somebody I need to have a word with.'

She stood up to let him pass. He was careful not to touch her but she felt the pull of his body at the top of her thighs, in the upper slope of her breasts. She knew he felt it too. For all their differences, there was a symmetry between them.

George touched her elbow. 'Is it going to be all right?'

'Faxerley?'

He nodded.

'I can't promise anything, but I'll do my best.'

'Good lass.'

Stuart had stopped at a table in the corner, where the Camden Miners Support Group had been joined by several locals. A red-haired woman offered him a chair. Her friends headed for the dance floor. The Northern girls in their tight dresses and precarious stilettos jigged on the spot, while the Londoners moved with the freedom of flat shoes and flowing skirts. An elfin blonde pirouetted with outstretched arms until a miner pulled her into a clinch. They danced body-to-body, his hands clamped on her buttocks.

George caught Lexa's eye. 'He'll be back in a minute.'

She gave him an icy look. 'I've only met him twice.'

'I just thought . . .'

'I know what you thought.'

He grinned. 'As long as you're having a good time.'

And she was, she realised. Part of the fun was anthropological, but she liked them too. They did not know the first thing about her, yet they included her so readily. After eight months at Goodison Farebrother she still felt like an outsider. Then there was the pleasure of seeing their intimacy with Stuart and knowing that, tonight at least, hers was the privileged connection. Even as he had laughed with Mick or leaned across the table to catch what Pecker was saying, the electrical disturbance had continued between them. She could feel when he was watching her. Like now. Slowly she turned. He was standing at the bar, waiting to be served. Their eyes connected and a flame rose from her midriff to lick the contour of her breasts.

She turned to George, 'How long have you known him?'

'Must be seven year. He were faceworker then. Well, he din't shift much coal. Always in meetings with branch committee. Then he went full-time on Union. Branch secretary. It were only last year he got delegate's job. They don't like 'em too clever.'

'And is he? Too clever?'

'Clever enough. Harrison's a slippery bastard, ran rings round last delegate. Stuart's a good negotiator. Keeps his head.'

'He nearly lost it just now.'

'What – with Tony?'

'I thought he was going to hit him.'

'*Give over.*'

The only man in the room wearing glasses stopped at their table.

'Are you dancing?'

She looked at George.

'Go on,' he said.

The light in the car park was broken. House martins criss-crossed the thick dusk, diving and swooping after insects. She walked until she lost the pungency of the dustbins and could breathe in the night. The air was foreign, warm with the dusty scent of places where it never rained.

'All right?'

She turned. Stuart was behind her, by the wooden rail separating the car park from the football field.

'Yeah.' She fanned her face. 'Just hot.'

He was smoking the panatella Mick had given him. The end glowed, a red eye in the dark. For a small man he took up a lot of space: his feet planted unnecessarily wide, that big head, the beginnings of a barrel chest.

She perched on the fence. 'Too much dancing.'

'Who with?'

'Glen.'

'And you've still got both arms in their sockets? You're doing well.'

It was her turn to speak but she couldn't think what to say.

'Where're you from?'

'Scotland.'

He grinned. '*Where* in Scotland?'

'A place called Gemmell. You won't have heard of it.'

'I know Gemmell. My grandad was a miner in Fife. Digging up parrot coal.'

The term meant nothing to her.

'Top grade anthracite. Clicks when you burn it, like a parrot. It's the density. That hard, they used to carve it into furniture. There's a parrot coal gravestone somewhere.'

She laughed, taken with the idea. She liked incongruity, things which did not fit into easy categories. Like a man fluent in masculine pub talk who shared her taste for eccentric detail. A man built along the same lines as his companions, with the same muscular shoulders, the same strength in his broad hands, and yet unmistakeably different.

'George was saying you worked underground.'

'Six years, aye. Left school on the Friday, started my face-training Monday morning.'

'You must have been glad to get the Union job.'

She saw him jib at this, then decide not to take offence.

'Glad some ways. It's hard work, primitive. Taking pick to thirty-inch seam. No toilets down there.' He had slipped into the miners' brawny dialect. 'That hot, you take clothes off sometimes, work with nowt on. You watch each other allt' time. You have to. You never see roof coming down on your own head.'

'You sound as if you miss it.'

'Aye. But you don't know it at time, do you? I weren't going to spend fifty year knocking myself out, pissing it away int' pub, coming out at sixty-five with a brass Davy lamp and half a lung. You want to get on. So I moved onto Union side – you get same production bonus as face-workers, but it's hell of a lot safer. We had three fatals last year. It's delegate's job to tell wife. By Christmas I felt like angel o' death.' He cleared his throat and spat. 'On face, they think Union officials are living life o' Reilly. But it's not as easy as it looks. You're paid to take blame, carry can for what majority want. Dun't matter what your personal feelings are.'

'You'd like Faxerley to come out on strike?'

'Nobody *likes* being on strike.'

She didn't mind the rebuke, since she did not believe him.

A thought struck her. 'So you're not a graduate—'

She had never seen anyone smile showing only their lower teeth.

'—I don't see what's funny.'

'You don't need a degree to string an intelligent sentence together.'

'That's not what I meant.'

He drew on the cigar. 'I did a week at Oxford once. Ruskin College. NUM send so many every year. It din't teach me owt I din't already know.'

'About the class struggle?'

'Summat like that.' He was watching her again. It felt less collusive now they were alone. 'Are you going to be my inside woman on this sale?'

'Is that why you asked me here tonight?"

'Of course. Is that not why you came?'

She was being teased.

'I'm sorry, I've got my own battles to fight.'

'More important than jobs and communities?'

'Men's jobs,' she said.

'And women's.'

'Part-time, in the canteen.'

'They matter to them.'

'I'm sure. I just don't think they matter to you—'

He gave her the look he had given Tony.

'—I'm not saying you're any different from anyone else. It's just the way things are.' She nodded towards the miners' welfare, 'Separate tables, separate interests. It's the same in banking. But you can't live like that and pretend everyone's on the same side. If you can put together a no-strike deal, that'd be good for us and good for you. But I'm not going to climb into your pocket any more than you're going to climb into mine.'

'Hard nut, aren't you?'

'I just like things clear.'

'And you think I don't?'

She hesitated. It was a long time since she'd shared her thoughts with a man. There was a power in it, opening herself up, forcing him to know her, but it didn't come easily.

'Those London women in there, teachers or social workers or whatever they are, driving two hundred and fifty miles to show their solidarity and bag off with a bit of rough: what were you really thinking when you were talking to them?'

'That I'd rather be talking to you—'

She held her breath.

'—OK, they're on a jolly. Piss-up on charabanc, bit of dancing, get a click. At least they're not Tories. And they've come to see for themselves. Whether we win or lose, that's worth summat. I'd like to get 'em all up here. MPs, media, university lecturers, company directors. Drag 'em through these godforsaken villages and show 'em how we live.'

'Does that go for bankers too?'

'If cap fits . . .'

'It doesn't.'

'That's all right then.' He turned her arm to see the watch on her wrist. 'Twenty past ten. They'll be calling last orders.'

The evening was over. She felt a terrible disappointment.

'Did you really think I was going to be your . . . informer?'

She glimpsed his bottom teeth again. 'Anyone would think you din't trust us.'

'Anyone would be right.'

He ground the panatella under his shoe. 'We'll have to see what we can do about that.'

Panic fizzed in her chest as his face closed on hers. Then she caught his scent. Dark, earthy, disgusting and delicious, the musky tang of cigar on his breath.

The delicacy of the kiss took her by surprise. A dry sip. He pulled back and she assumed it was over, but he moved towards her again, their lips brushing against each other, pushing and retreating. Again he pulled away, and their eyes locked. Other than their lips, no part of their bodies had touched, but she felt him fix her with that look as surely as if his hands had grasped her shoulders. There was no question and no answer, just an exchange of facts. The way he looked at her, and the way she looked back.

Corporate Finance was half-empty. Gavin, Roland and Simon were out at meetings. Rae came in from Venture Capital to pour herself a coffee. There was a click as Kinsella's door opened.

'Have you done it?'

Surreptitiously, Lexa, Ben and Gabriel looked up.

Rae waited a second too long before replying, 'Done what?'

Kinsella turned his back to the office, but his words were crisply audible. 'What we discussed yesterday.'

'If you mean Adrian Lennard, I'm seeing him this afternoon.'

'Not Lennard. What we talked about in Sylvester's.'

Lexa recognised the resistant look on Rae's face, but had never seen it turned against Kinsella.

'No.'

'That must be why I've just seen her in the back office.'

'Must be.' Rae reached over and picked up Gavin's copy of *The Spectator.*

From behind they made an odd couple. Kinsella in his shirt-sleeves like a six-foot schoolboy. Rae chic and groomed and womanly, though no bigger than a child.

'So when are you going to do it?'

She shrugged.

'What's that supposed to mean?'

'I don't think it's such a good idea.'

'I don't give a toss what you think.'

She turned a page of the magazine. 'OK.'

Kinsella bent towards her, 'I thought we had an understanding,' he hissed.

Ben slid his eyes towards Lexa. Ever since the showdown in Kinsella's office he had been trying to make her smile. Having won, he wanted no hard feelings.

'I'm not going to sack her.'

Kinsella moved closer. Even at a whisper, his consonants

could slice concrete. 'You were the one who said it, she's fucking useless. Everything she does has to be done again.'

'Yeah she's a crap typist, but that's not why you want rid of her, is it?'

They were talking about Lori Cooper, the secretary who couldn't spell 'sincerely'. Nineteen last month, with a thirty-five-year-old's orange mask of make-up, a short skirt and a selection of skinny-rib sweaters that showed off her bust.

'Do you remember the conversation we had? About you-*aah* taking on more responsibility with a view to an assistant directorship?'

Rae closed the magazine. 'I am taking responsibility. I'm trying to make sure I'm not sitting in an industrial tribunal in three months' time, explaining that she was canned because Gavin got bored sticking his dick in her.'

Kinsella was frequently crude, but if crudeness were used against him he reacted with disapproval. 'Her work isn't up to standard.'

'And hasn't been for two years. But it's only since she caught him flashing those Polaroids around that the situation's got critical.'

'You've become very high-minded since ten o'clock last night.'

Lexa could see his point. Nothing at Goodisons happened for the right reason. Usually Rae relished her cynic's understanding of the way the place worked.

'I was a bit slow working out the implications,' she said.

'What implications?'

In a voice that parodied seduction, she murmured, 'Who're you going to get to sack me when the time comes?'

'Is that a proposition?'

'No,' She dropped the magazine on Gavin's desk, taking advantage of the movement to dart a sly glance at Lexa, 'it's a knock-back.'

'That ought to get me a mention in the *Guinness Book of Records*.'

'Yeah,' For the first time Rae's toughness rang hollow, 'It probably will.'

The narcissistic schoolboy had vanished. In his place stood a

figure of absolute authority. Father, headmaster, hanging judge.
'I don't want to see her here tomorrow.'

'She hasn't even had a verbal warning.'

It was Rae's first tactical error, but a decisive one.

'Then you'd better warn her, hadn't you?'

Gabriel rummaged through her bag, tossing out several crumpled tissues, a tube of superglue, a contraceptive diaphragm flecked with lint, and a fish knife with *Reynolds Hotel* in copperplate on its silverware handle. At last she found the matches.

'So,' she said, exhaling, 'the Pocket Venus has a conscience.'

Lexa took one of the tissues and collected the cigarette ends on the stone windowsill, handing the twist of paper to Gabriel, who stowed it in her bag. The eighth floor was untenanted, but there was no point in advertising their presence.

'And they're not sleeping together.'

Gabriel bowed. 'So you were right.'

'Which means you're not as safe as you thought.'

'His right-hand man is the more pressing threat, I fear.'

Gavin. Lexa wasn't surprised. 'He's asked you out?'

'I don't think *wining and dining* is on the agenda.'

'You can handle him.'

Gabriel gave a theatrical shudder, 'Not even with rubber gloves.'

'He wouldn't be so bad if he sorted out that tooth.'

'And left his camera at home.'

'And cut out the aftershave.'

'Oh he has to wear that. It's the only way to cover up the wee on his heirloom tweeds.'

They met in this corridor two or three times a day for as long as it took Gabriel to finish a Gauloise at the open window. The other bankers smoked at their desks, but she preferred to take her poison in unpolluted air. And it was a break from Corporate Finance. Lexa had grown to depend on these stolen minutes to get through the working day. The marble-look floor, the old-gold iron radiators, the panelled and frosted-glass doors were identical to those on the floors below, but when their laughter rang in the empty rooms it felt like a different world.

Gabriel gestured with her cigarette, 'Weren't you meeting the working-class hero on Friday night?'

Lexa began to smile.

Gabriel cocked her head.

'He kissed me.'

'And was it very Lawrentian?'

'Not particularly.'

'Slobbery?'

'No.'

Gabriel lowered her voice, 'Probing?'

'*No.*' Lexa moved around to stand on her other side.

'What are you doing?'

'The wind's changed, I don't want to stink of Gauloises.'

'Do I stink of Gauloises?'

'You smell of pavement cafes in the sixteenth *arrondissement.*'

'I'll take that as a yes.' She directed a plume of smoke through the window. 'So you kissed him back?'

'After I'd got over the surprise.'

Gabriel gave her a sidelong look. 'You had *no idea* when he tucked that note in your skirt?'

'He's five foot five.'

'So what? Oh, you mean he can't reach. Did he stand on a box?'

'I *mean* when you're my height you don't expect to be kissed.'

'I don't see why not.'

Lexa loved her for that. Though it begged an uncomfortable question. If six-footers were fair game, why had so few men tried with her?

'Looking up at a woman makes a man feel inadequate, never mind kissing one who towers above him. It's embarrassing – I know it shouldn't be, but it is. Unless I find myself a basketball player I'll always be a joke.'

'Then he's a joke too. Unless he goes round kissing midgets.' As usual Gabriel had struck at the heart of the matter. 'So what's he like? Besides five foot four?'

'He's five foot *five.*'

'*I beg your pardon.*'

Lexa caught sight of the town hall clock. 'We're meeting the lawyers in ten minutes.'

'Handsome? Witty? Napoleonic?'

She knew Gabriel would persist until she received an answer.

'Intelligent, not the centre of attention but somehow in charge.' She found herself smiling again. 'Manly.'

'I thought that was an insult.'

'I said manly, not macho.'

'And the difference is . . .?'

The scrape of his chair as he'd stood up to Tony. Catching her wrist to see her watch.

'He can do macho, but it's optional. The rest of the time he's normal.'

Gabriel raised her eyebrows.

Lexa shrugged. 'Like me.'

'*Aha.*'

Lexa nodded towards the town hall clock. 'And we've got to get the paperwork copied.'

'So was it a serious pass or an impulse snog?'

'*Gabe*,' Lexa thrust her watch under Gabriel's nose. 'We were late last time.'

Gabriel stubbed out her cigarette. 'Have you got a coin?'

'Of course.' It was a given of these meetings, like Gabriel forgetting to bring one. 'Heads or tails?'

'Tails.'

When Lexa lifted her hand they laughed. They tossed to decide who went down first, to introduce a properly random element into the pattern, but since Lexa always had the coin and Gabriel the luck, the outcome was always the same.

'Oh by the way,' Gabriel pulled a small package wrapped in pink tissue paper out of her bag, 'happy birthday.'

'You promised you wouldn't!'

'And you believed me?'

Inside the pink paper was a pair of pants. Lace-trimmed cream silk.

'I thought they might come in useful,' Gabriel said, 'when you play Lady Chatterley.'

The phone rang, insinuating into her dream and, finally, waking her.

'There's something you should see.'

'Stuart?' She knew who it was, but she could not remember giving him her number.

'Meet me at the Jolly Sausage at five—'

She peered through the window at the darkness outside.

'—big transport caff on the A1 just past Doncaster. I'll see you in the car park. You've got an hour.'

The Jolly Sausage was a one-storey building with *CAFE* emulsioned in block capitals across its pitched roof. Four container lorries were silhouetted against the eastern sky. He flashed his headlights and, when she had parked alongside, got into the Hillman's passenger seat.

'Head south—'

She looked at him.

'—I'm guessing your numberplate's not on the police computer.'

'I start work at nine.'

'You'll be there by ten.'

'Ten's too late.'

'Take the day off.'

'I can't.'

'Take a sickie then.'

She didn't want to hear herself making another prim objection.

They drove in silence. She switched the radio on but it was tuned to a station which hadn't yet started broadcasting. Her stomach felt scoured, as if she were breaking some basic rule of health by being up at this hour.

He reached across and cancelled the indicator as they neared the Dudderthorpe turn-off. 'No point picketing Dudderthorpe, it's solid.' He pointed to the car in front, a Datsun sitting low on its wheels under the weight of four passengers, 'Follow them.'

'We're going to Mosby?'

'Very good. Let's hope the police haven't worked it out.'

Mosby was ten times the size of Dudderthorpe but built to the same plan. The semi-detached houses, the broad pavements, the palette of red brick, green verge and black road, muted in the grey dawn. The main street was lined bumper-to-bumper with cars. She squeezed the Hillman into a gap by the shops. Men streamed along both pavements, three and four abreast. As Lexa and Stuart joined the flow the group in front broke into a jog. They heard the crowd before they saw it: several hundred pickets standing in front of the colliery gates, spilling onto the grass at either side. They huddled together, chatting, smoking, coughing up the first phlegm of the day, shivering in T-shirts in anticipation of another sweltering morning. Mick was there, the map of dark hair on his chest showing through his singlet. Pecker came up and put his arm round her. She shrugged him off. There was a showground smell of churned turf.

Stuart went to talk to a trio of miners she recognised from the benefit night. She walked over to the pit gates. The crowd was denser here: young men, a few pink-and-white with puppy-fat, the rest hardened by the job. Judging by the voices most were from Yorkshire, though one group spoke with the twang of places south of London. Kent, she saw from their badges. The sun rose, painting the pickets' faces with warming light. The grass took on a buttery shine. There were no other women here, yet she felt at ease, free to stare, and eavesdrop, and smile at jokes that had not been cracked for her benefit. Today everybody knew their enemy. All subsidiary hostilities – men against women, North against South, worker against bourgeois – were forgotten in the elemental struggle between picket and scab.

Stuart came to find her, bearing the plastic cup from a Thermos flask half-filled with tea, 'Get that down you.'

She swallowed it and grimaced. 'Ugh, sugar.'

'Some people are never satisfied.' He retrieved the cup, shook out the last drops and, with a shout of 'Frank', tossed it over the heads of the crowd. A hand reached up and caught it.

'Aye aye,' he said, 'here they come.'

A convoy of police vans drove up the main street. White transits with orange stripes, dark uniforms packed shoulder-to-shoulder inside. The pickets struck up a chant of '*The miners. United. Will never be defeated*'. The police emptied out of the vans and herded the crowd on to the grass, then lined up in front of the two blocks of pickets. Lexa and Stuart found themselves on the east verge, hemmed in on all sides. She nudged his arm and nodded at the far side of the main road.

'Shouldn't we . . .'

Before she could finish her sentence, the crowd contracted in a surge towards the pit gates. Stuart was jammed into her left side, another man pressing on her from the right. She could feel someone behind straining to keep his weight off her. Turning her head, she saw that it was Mick. A red and green striped jersey was in front, the shoulders flaked with dandruff.

'Any minute now,' Stuart warned.

She felt the solidity of his body against hers.

'What do we do?'

He grinned at the question. 'We push.'

The vans roared through, one after another, their rear windows painted out so the strike-breakers could not be seen. Lexa felt the press of the crowd forcing her forward. Beside her Stuart was grunting with effort. The strikers were singing the football chorus '*here we go, here we go, here we go*'. The air was savoury with masculine odours, belch and fart and unwashed body hair. The pressure at her back was immense. The only way to avoid being crushed against the red and green stripes was to join in the push, but her hands were trapped at her sides. The crowd was a heaving, unpredictable thing prone to sudden bucklings and sideways shifts. After one of these she caught a glimpse of the police line on the other side of the access road, arms linked, returning the shoving of the strikers. Hilarity was welling up inside her, a joke so rich she could not open her mouth wide enough to let the laughter out. She squeezed her upper body around in a quarter-turn, put her shoulder to the man in front, and started to push. The vans were still coming, turning in to the access road too quickly and gathering speed as they passed. With each van the crowd pushed harder, and the police pushed harder back. And then the last one was through and the pressure relented. The police retreated to the main road. Stuart stepped to one side, breaking the contact between them.

'What now?' she asked, panting.

He looked at her strangely. She could feel tears of laughter in her eyes.

'Now you buy me breakfast,' he said.

There were twenty lorries in the Jolly Sausage car park. After the holiday mood on the picket-line its customers seemed a dour bunch, queuing in silence for their fry-ups, sitting one to a table, doggedly smoking.

'It's that feeling of power combined with total impotence.' She unloaded her tray and stowed it under the table. 'Everyone's waiting for the big moment. All that expectation. *Something's going to happen.* And then it does and it's a big fat nothing. I don't know how they can do it day after day, the same anticipation and the same let-down. You'd think there'd be more real violence.'

Stuart looked up from his plate. 'Have you never been on a picket-line?'

'I've been on marches. Abortion. Take back the night.'

He exhaled, as if daunted by how much there was to explain.

'You don't need anything to happen. The *crowd* is what happens . . . You know about the Black Act, don't you?'

She didn't.

'Seventeen twenty-three. Made blacking your face a capital offence. The Rebekah Riots—?'

She shook her head.

'—protest against tollbooths. Some folk dressed up as women. It happened in the bread riots an'all. The ruling class were changing the status quo in their own favour. It was the people's way of saying "do that and anything's fair game". Cross one line, you might as well cross 'em all, turn world upside down. That lad in the cardboard copper's helmet, he's making the same point. He doesn't need to knock anybody's teeth out.'

'But it happens.'

'It happens, but it's not us that starts it.'

'It's always the police's fault?'

The mocking bulge of flesh around his mouth became more pronounced.

'You still think British bobbies are best int' world, don't you—?'

Gradually she was learning to interpret the fluctuations in his accent. Relaxing with the miners, he spoke the broad dialect he had learned at his mother's knee. But addressing them in his official capacity, or talking to Harrison, or her, he used standard English, unless he became angry or otherwise impassioned, when his definite and indefinite articles would start to slip.

'—they could've arrested you, you know. I've seen 'em lift folk for less.' He grinned. 'If I achieve nothing else in my life, I'll have turned a member of ruling class into a picket-line hooligan.'

'I told you, that cap doesn't fit.'

'Aye, you did.'

'If you really want to know, my dad sells secondhand cars. His dad was a village postman.'

'Working on his own?'

'Uh-huh.'

He shook his head. 'Country postmaster – dun't count.'

'*His* father was an illiterate agricultural worker.'

'Aye, peasant stock. Last link with feudalism. Centuries of deference in the genes.'

'And whose loins do you think the proletariat sprang from?' She realised they were flirting, 'I suppose you're descended from an unbroken line of class warriors?'

'Five generations of miners on my mother's side. My grandad moved from Fife in the twenties. There were a few came down then. I remember Jim Thwaite standing for local council on a "get the Jocks out of Dudderthorpe" ticket. My father's side's Irish, fairground family originally, but my dad were a miner.'

'So you're the transitional one?'

He squinted at her.

'Desk job. Virtually white collar. Your kids'll be middle class.'

All at once he looked guarded. So he was married.

'How many've you got?' The question chimed too politely in

the air between them, but she had to say something.

'One, and he won't be middle class.' He glanced at his watch. 'I'd best be off.'

She had a sudden physical memory of him pulling back from the kiss. 'You're going to work?'

'I've got a job to do.'

'Me too.'

That grin again. 'It can't be that important if you can take a morning off to go gallivanting round the countryside.' He pushed himself up from the table. 'You can tell them you've been working on a no-strike deal with the Union representative.'

'Is that a real option?'

He took a last swig of tea and replaced the mug on the table. 'Everything's up for negotiation.'

It was early Monday morning in meeting room three. Twenty bankers sat drinking coffee and chatting about the weekend. The half-hour before work was the only social time Lexa spent with them nowadays.

Gavin was complaining about a traffic jam which had delayed his journey in to the office.

'. . . like a bloody Roman battalion on the move. Transits, Land Rovers, horse boxes. It went on for fucking miles. How much is that little lot costing us—?'

Ned offered her a slice of his buttered toast. She shook her head.

'—all they have to do is pass emergency powers. Anyone within a mile of Coal Board property who's not on their way to work gets arrested and held until the end of the strike. They'll have to pull in a few hundred on day one, but by day three there'll be no problem.'

Lexa kept her eyes on her newspaper.

'It won't last much longer,' Roland said, 'Scargill's had it. Every day there's more of them back at work.'

'And in the meantime we're letting a few hundred yobs bring the motorways to a standstill.' Gavin's glance fell on Lexa. 'Have I said something funny?'

She carried on reading the *Guardian*. Gavin rarely spoke to her. She was neither predator nor sexual prey. For him, there were no other categories.

'Please,' he said, 'share the joke with us.'

'I was just wondering when you said *a few hundred yobs* whether you meant the pickets or the police?'

Gavin looked around the room, priming his audience. 'I do believe we've got a Scargillite in the camp.'

Ben and Simon laughed.

Gabriel would have turned the moment with a joke. Lexa

couldn't. Or wouldn't. She didn't want to leave. Goodisons was the quickest route to her future as an ethical banker. But being different from her colleagues was crucial to her sense of self-worth.

She folded the newspaper. 'Why do you think the government hasn't gone for your solution? There's a lot of us support the strike.'

'A lot of vegetarians in Hebden Bridge,' Roland said.

'Dudderthorpe NUM collected a thousand pounds on Albion Street on Saturday.'

A mistake. She knew as soon as she'd said it.

Ben blinked. 'How do you know?'

Ned paused from licking the butter off his fingers, 'She was with them.'

Kinsella looked up, 'I beg your pardon?'

Gavin tongued his broken incisor, 'Like a bit of rough, do you?'

A smirk circled the table.

Rae appeared in the doorway. 'Phone for you, Kinsella. It's your broker—'

Lexa had never seen him move so quickly.

'—Lexa, you're wanted as well.'

In the corridor Kinsella kicked the *Yellow Pages* out of the way and closed the door of his office.

Rae smiled to herself, 'I think someone's just made himself a bit of pocket money.'

'So who wants me?'

Rae nodded at the door opposite.

The ladies' lavatories were reached through an old-fashioned powder room with pink wallpaper and a Formica shelf at dressing-table height. Gabriel was sitting in one of the Lloyd Loom chairs.

One glance told Lexa something was wrong. 'Are you ill?'

'Do I look ill?'

'You've looked better.'

'Cheers. Lovely to see you too.'

Lexa had been putting in long hours at Faxerley. They hadn't spoken for several days.

'Who's in this morning?' Gabriel asked.

'Full house. Gavin's noticed there's a strike on. He makes

Thatcher sound like a bleeding-heart liberal—'

Gabriel did not smile.

'—do you want to go up for a cigarette?'

She shook her head. On her arm was a patch of dry-textured skin like a fading burn. She tugged her sleeve down when she saw Lexa looking. 'Can you get some papers out of my desk—'

An odd request.

'—I'll be working at Faxerley today, but I need a file.'

The door opened. Lori Cooper crossed the pink carpet and disappeared into the washroom.

'What's happened?' Lexa asked.

Gabriel's breath was warm on her ear. 'Not while she's in there.'

They waited.

'What's she *doing*?' Lexa hissed.

Another couple of minutes passed.

Lexa lost patience. 'This is ridiculous.'

Gabriel flashed her a warning look.

Lexa sighed, dropping her voice. 'You might as well get it over with. I had mine yesterday.'

'Had your what?' Gabriel mouthed. They started to giggle.

'My bollocking. "In case you haven't noticed, we're-*aah* trying to put a deal together. There's a little thing called a deadline . . ."'

From the washroom came the sound of flushing. Lexa and Gabriel sprang apart, which made their giggling worse. The connecting door swung open.

When Lori had gone, Gabriel asked if there was any news on the reorganisation.

Every hour brought some fresh rumour. Phin was coming back; London was sending up a new divisional head; Kinsella had been offered the job in exchange for cutting the payroll; his friend at Hill Samuel would be moving across as soon as someone was sacked to make room. In Sylvester's they talked of little else, which was another reason not to drink there.

'You could always ask Kinsella,' Lexa said, 'he might even tell *you*.'

Gabriel stopped scratching her arm. 'Kinsella's not speaking to me. Unless you count Friday, when he told me to take the coffee cups into the pantry.'

'And you said . . .?' Lexa was looking forward to this.

'I didn't say anything.'

It was hard to believe they had been laughing a few moments before.

'What's happened, Gabriel—?'

There were violet shadows under her eyes.

'—are you still getting those nuisance calls?'

A weary look crossed Gabriel's face. 'Are you going to fetch that file or not?'

'Not unless you tell me what's going on.'

Gabriel examined herself in the mirror above the shelf, widening her eyes and sucking in her cheeks, turning her head to left and right. 'Am I really so unsightly?'

'Look at me,' Lexa said.

Gabriel threw a glance over her shoulder.

'No, I mean stand up, turn round.'

She did as she was asked. She had the beginnings of a tan, which made her hair seem lighter.

'You're fine,' Lexa said, 'you just don't look like you.'

'And how do I look when I'm looking like me?'

'Calm. Relaxed. Not embattled.'

Gabriel looked away.

'It's Kinsella, isn't it?' Lexa said.

She nodded.

His eyes on her in meetings as he issued instructions to somebody else. Standing watching while she used the photocopier. Leaning over her from behind to drop a file on her desk. Nothing really, but something.

'What did you do—?'

Gabriel's eyes blazed.

'—I'm not saying it's your *fault*. It's just, ringing you at all hours and not speaking: it's so childish, so humiliating for him.'

'That'll be something else I'm paying for.'

'But he didn't just start doing it for no reason?'

'Clearly not.'

Lexa sat on the dressing-table shelf.

If Gabriel's face was uncharacteristically opaque, her voice was as clear as ever.

'The first meeting with Beronex was an absolute fiasco. I was convinced they were going to tell us to take a running jump. He didn't want to tell London he'd blown it, so he rang the Norwegians. We were lucky. The big banana was in Birmingham, he could see us the next day. We had sixteen hours to put together a knockout presentation—'

Lexa remembered that day. More than four weeks ago. Gabriel had had countless opportunities to tell her before now.

'—we got it finished by ten. Sal stayed behind to type it up. Panic over. So he said he'd buy me dinner. I suggested Chinese, I couldn't see him trying anything over a paper tablecloth and a cup of tea. But we ended up at this place with dimmed lighting and a wine list, where they took about three-and-a-half weeks to bring the food. I tried to steer the conversation on to neutral ground, but he wanted to talk about some sexpot he'd slept with in Hong Kong and how eastern women are *different*, and this girl he knew at university who had three nipples, and getting the glad-eye from the prostitutes in Chapeltown . . . I've never been so pleased to get to the end of a meal. And then he drove me home and parked outside the flat and—' she kept her voice light '—there was an *embarrassing interlude* when he made it clear he was going to maul me and I made it clear I didn't want him to . . .' She took a breath. 'I got out of the car. He drove off. And twenty minutes later the phone rang.'

'So you knew all along.'

She tilted her head. 'I suppose I didn't think you'd have much sympathy. You told me to be careful often enough, and you were right.'

Lexa knew there would be more to the story. There weren't enough minutes in the day for Kinsella to make nuisance calls to all the women who'd knocked him back. Something had salted the wound of Gabriel's rejection. Perhaps he'd lost face with Gavin and Ned, or maybe everyone knew, maybe it was an office joke.

She stood up. 'Keep a log. Write it all down. We'll take it to London.'

Gabriel stopped pretending she was telling an amusing anecdote. 'He's running the Northern office for them.'

'That doesn't give him the right to sleep with you.'

'I've been here eleven months. He's supervising my first deal.'

Lexa had never seen her defeated before. Normally she was like a river, running over or around whatever stood in her way. 'He's supervising me too. We haven't spoken more than twenty words since the day I told him not to tickle me. I get by.'

'And you know why that is?' Gabriel's voice was sharp. 'Because anything that requires detailed instruction is done by *me*.'

They turned as the door from the corridor opened. Lori Cooper stood on the threshold, so poker-faced that she could only be hiding a smirk.

'Mister Kinsella told me to tell you—' she paused, making sure she got the message right, '—if you're not too busy slapping on the warpaint, could you get your lardy-arses into Corporate Finance now.'

The miners' welfare was deserted. The woman behind the bar smiled. While Lexa was pleased to be recognised, there was a knowingness in the smile she didn't like. She was wary of honey-blondes with sugar-frosted nails and lips and a tangle of gold at neck and wrist. They were too blatant in their soliciting of desire, too exposed. Generally a second look revealed the dark roots, leathery tan, fleshy mole and discoloured tooth. But not this time. This one was sweet-faced, soft-skinned, full-breasted: a bona fide blonde.

'They're upstairs.'

The meeting room covered the entire upper floor of the building. Eight hundred striking miners, and Lexa, standing room only. She felt a nervousness that had never afflicted her on the picket-line, a reminder of how the situation had changed. Yesterday morning she had arrived at Faxerley to find six members of Dudderthorpe NUM huddled around an oil drum filled with smoking plywood. They'd stepped aside when she explained who she was, but she still hated the idea of crossing a picket-line. Harrison was in a foul temper. The early shift had turned up at the gates and gone home again. Word spread quickly, and the afternoon and night shifts failed to appear. Faxerley Colliery had been picketed out. They knew they were cutting their own throats, as far as the sale went, but there was no mistaking the relief in this room. Gone was the edginess of recent weeks. Now everyone was in the same boat. Those who'd wanted to strike all along. Those who saw it as an empty gesture. Those who only cared about feathering their own nests. And the Dudderthorpe men, all-forgiving in the exultation of their victory against the bosses.

The old man who had acted as master of ceremonies at the benefit night tapped the microphone. The room fell silent. He told them whom they had to thank for the latest batch of food parcels and read out the list of Union members up in court. Stuart was standing by the stage. Behind his mask of attention, she could tell his thoughts were elsewhere. She read him easily, up to a point. Beyond this point was the dazzle of wishful thinking, the euphoria that filled her every time they met. Nodding across the colliery yard, a quick coffee in the canteen, the odd evening she drove home via the welfare. And on the picket-line, when they pushed side by side and she saw the set of his jaw, the assertion of self in the teeth of the other, and a voice inside her murmured *we're the same.* As if hooked by this thought, his eyes flicked towards her. She had the impression that he smiled to himself as she looked away.

It was time for the speakers. He stepped up to the platform, his face lit by a grin which he quickly subdued. Since the clapping wasn't really for him.

'I want to talk to you about law and order—'

Sly smirks appeared on the faces of the miners nearest Lexa.

'—anyone here think bussing seven thousand coppers up North is an efficient use of police resources?' He paused theatrically. 'No? I bet the good people of Surrey don't think it's such a spiffing idea, either. Burglars are having a field day down there, while the constabulary are up here cashing in on overtime and expenses. And for what? What crime are they preventing?'

'Shutting pits is the crime,' someone shouted from the floor.

He jabbed a finger towards the crowd. 'Morally, you're dead right. But police can only deal with what parliament says is a crime. Criminal damage, for instance. You can't just go round snapping wing mirrors off cars, bashing eight bells out of bodywork with a ruddy great stick. They come down hard on that sort of thing. Same goes for assault. Giving somebody a black eye, dislocating their shoulder. Serious offences. They'll put you away for that.' Lexa's neighbours were smiling, even the slowest could see where this was leading. 'So when are they going to arrest coppers who got stuck into Wayne Stone's head with a truncheon and broke Darren Saville's nose arresting him for shouting "scab"? They say there's the odd bad apple in every barrel, but it's funny how even good apples are wearing coats with no number on so you can't make a complaint . . .'

It was like seeing him properly for the first time. Blazing with anger. Completely assured of his ability to sway the crowd.

'. . . They tell us we're all equal under the law, but if government dun't like law, they can change it. Ring bell, get sheep off their backsides and walk 'em through right door. It's that easy for 'em, and they're still breaking rules. Pulling miners off picket-line and not telling families where they are. Pushing 'em through courts with "the usual" bail conditions. And guess what they are? Stay away from picket-lines. Bail's meant to be tailored to individual case. They're stapling pre-printed form to your file before you've seen bloody beak. Secondary picketing in't even a criminal offence. It's a civil matter, for civil courts. All this garbage Thatcher talks about law and order: it's one rule for them and another for us.' His voice rose. '"Miners are on strike? Get DHSS to knock fifteen quid off wives' benefits for strike pay. We know full well they're not getting strike pay, but that's not our problem. There's pensioners collecting for support groups? Charge 'em under Vagrancy Act. If bastards try to picket, we'll block roads. They're still getting through? Charge 'em with riotous assembly, then we can send 'em down for life".' He was shouting now, his face red, teeth bared. '*Life imprisonment*. For trying to defend right to work.'

Lexa knew she shouldn't be here. It was only a matter of time before some trouble-maker told Harrison. But how could she walk away from this?

Stuart took a breath. 'You know real tragedy of this strike? We're all ont' same side. Scabs don't have to watch riot boys waving their pay packets at 'em, but at end o't'day do you think Thatcher feels less contempt for them than she does for us? You think their jobs'll be any more secure? Will they 'ellaslike. In any class divide you get brown-nosers, ones who toe line. They see some bloke getting his head kicked in by uniform and they say "it's his own fault". Dun't matter whether he's black, Irish Catholic, or just an ordinary working-class joe. He must have been asking for it. These things happen for a reason. If you keep your nose clean you've nowt to worry about. They're so bloody brain-dead they an't realised there dun't have to be a reason. Asking for a roof over your head and food ont' table and a fair day's pay for an honest day's work – that's reason enough. Dun't matter whether we roll over and lick their jackboots, they'll stamp on us just same. As long as we keep letting 'em. And you know why? You know real *reason*?' The hairs rose on Lexa's arms. 'Because they hate us. You can come up with all sorts of fancy words for it, profit motive, economic considerations, but what it boils down to is hate. "Enemy within" she calls us, and she's dead right, and you'd better be ready, because at end o't'day it's them or us.'

The crowd started to applaud, stamping on the floor, faces flushed with the heat Lexa felt in her own cheeks. Black, Catholic, Worker, Woman: *we're the same.* A youth in a Spandau Ballet T-shirt pushed his way through the hall towards the stage. Stuart hesitated before relinquishing the microphone. The boy's panting was loud through the amplifier.

'They've arrested Jim Whittlestone. His wife Rita just died of cancer on Tuesday. They've lifted his lad Gary an' all.'

Eight hundred miners bellowed, '*NO!*'

'They've got them down cells at Manton Road.'

The crowd surged towards the doors.

He found her on the pavement outside the police station, looking down on the men in the car park.

'What's happening?' he asked.

'The police have locked themselves in.'

He turned his head, scanning the street. The only person visible beyond the crowd was an old woman watering her roses with a hosepipe. Lexa saw his face darken.

'What?'

'Ammunition.' He nodded. 'Over there—'

She saw a pile of bricks beside a part-dismantled garden wall.

'—any minute now somebody's going to start chucking 'em.' He grabbed her arm. 'Come on.'

She glanced down at his hand. 'Afraid you'll get done for inciting a riot?'

'You can't afford to stick around either.'

'I'll take my chances.'

His mouth tightened with frustration.

It was another broiling early summer day. The heat had melted the tarmac, making it tacky underfoot. The men in the car park started to sing 'You'll Never Walk Alone', their voices surprisingly musical, unlike the rough chants on the picket-line. The old woman left her garden and shouted across the road.

'What do you think you're doing?'

The crowd on the pavement swivelled towards her. Some of the smiles were fond, others derisive.

'I thought Dudderthorpe was solid,' Lexa said.

'It is. That's Lily. If she were American she'd be against apple pie.'

'You should be ashamed of yourselves.' She had a powerful voice for such a small frame. 'That's a police station, you know.'

'It's never!' somebody shouted, to laughter.

'You should be down that pit doing day's work, not causing trouble ont' street.'

There was less laughter this time.

'I see you, Stuart Duffy. You should know better. You always think you do, anyroad.'

Stuart swore under his breath. The strikers were grinning, looking towards him.

'You need wages, you've got responsibilities.'

In the car park two miners began to hammer on the reinforced glass of the double doors. Upstairs a casement window opened and a uniformed figure appeared, retreating when a stone smacked off the brickwork beside him.

Stuart grimaced. 'The cavalry'll be here in a couple of minutes—'

Lexa kept her eyes on the crowd.

'—do you want to end up with a record?'

'I'm just watching.'

'Weren't you listening in there? They can send you down for life. Even if they just do you for breach o' peace, what sort of future do you think you've got in merchant banking, taking every Wednesday off to do your community service?'

He was right. There was no reason to resist him. Other than the desire to pay him back for resisting her. She resented the power he had wielded on the platform, his words touching the quick of her as they had touched everyone in the hall. She wanted to do the same to him, turn his world upside down. Failing that, the least he could do was acknowledge the woman she was becoming through his agency.

'You were the one who took me on to the picket-line.'

'Aye, that were picketing. This is a siege. Of a police station.'

The crowd was singing 'Arthur Scargill walks on water'. A voice inside the building spoke through the muddied amplification of a loudhailer.

'*This is a police warning. Disperse now or you will be arrested.*'

'We want Jim and Gary,' a miner shouted. It became a chant, taken up by the others. They were banging on the doors in time to the words. Someone altered the format to call-and-response:

'What do we want?'

'Jim and Gary!'

'When do we want them?'

'Now!'

The loudhailer repeated the order to disperse. A half-brick smashed one of the downstairs windows. A cheer went up.

Stuart's voice sharpened. 'Are you *trying* to get us arrested?'

The banging was getting louder. Three men were taking it in turns to kick at the seam between the double doors, the chant inciting them, adding to the pressure on the straining lock.

'I want to see what's going to happen,' she said.

'I can tell you now. Wayne Stone and Darren Saville have been telling world and his wife how pigs gave 'em a beating. Then John Worsley's bloody pride-and-joy Triumph Herald got done over. On Friday they went to picket Gundy and some jokers reckoned they'd put scabs' windows in. Half of Dudderthorpe got shit kicked out of 'em, other half are kicking themselves for missing it. Yesterday Faxerley comes out. Now they've lifted Jim and Gary. Police know Rita's just died, so *they're* trying to crank it up an' all. When both sides are spoiling for a fight they usually get one.' He threw an anxious glance towards the car park. 'Listen to me, this is not a picket-line. This is a mob.'

The roar from the crowd did not quite drown the sound of splintering wood as the doors gave way. The men at the front stormed the building. Stuart's head swung round in the direction of the main road. Lexa heard them too.

'Lexa, *come on—*'

The sirens were getting louder.

'—you've nowt to prove to me.' His voice was a growl, 'I knew first time I saw you.'

The police vans turned off the main road towards them. The crowd on the pavement started to run.

'Where's your car?' she asked.

'This way.' He caught her hand, pulling her across the road in the path of a police transit. For one disjointed moment she saw the white metal closing on her, the blue light flashing weakly in the scouring sun, and then they were on the opposite pavement, still running, their shoes catching on the sticky tarmac as they swerved into Lily's garden.

'Short cut,' he barked at the astonished old woman, dragging Lexa down the path beside the house, across the back lawn and flowerbeds and over the bottom wall into the garden of a house in the next street. She landed on a set of rusted bedsprings, twisting her ankle, crying out as the flaking metal pierced her skin.

He grabbed her hand again but she shook him off, fighting for the breath to tell him she was going no further.

'*Lexa,*' he hissed in such an odd voice that she glanced over her shoulder. In Lily's garden were two uniformed men, their heads protected by round helmets, their batons drawn.

She leapt the next wall, soared clean over, while Stuart had to use his arms to vault it. Her body was a machine, covering the ground effortlessly as she did in dreams, bounding from one garden to the next, terrified and perversely exhilarated. The strip of twinned gardens was half a mile long. Close-cropped lawns yellowing with lack of rain. Prim concrete paths. Marigolds, peonies, red hot pokers. A model windmill, a garish painted gnome. Her long legs scissored past them all, the taste of blood raw in her throat. She looked around to see Stuart a couple of yards behind her, pounding over the grass, his face scarlet. Just two walls separated them from the police.

'Where?' she gasped.

He jerked his thumb, incapable of speech. She sprinted

towards the house, thinking he meant her to make for the road beyond, but when they were in the narrow side passage she felt her shirt yanked backwards. He dropped a key, retrieved it, inserted it in the lock. She could see the faster of the two policemen scaling the last wall. Her heart was bursting in her chest. Stuart jiggled the key in the door, cursing between heaving breaths. The policeman was halfway across the lawn, his partner close behind. Stuart put his shoulder to the door. The lock gave and they were in. He shot the bolt. There was a cupboard under the stairs in the hall. He pushed her inside as the policeman's baton hammered on the door.

They crouched in the dark, panting, breathing in the smell of whitewash. Neither of them spoke. She sensed ordered clutter, stacked seedboxes, screws in jars. A shelf jutted painfully into her shoulder. The banging gave way to silence and then, just as she was about to suggest venturing out, started up again. Long after her breathing had steadied, he was still taking rasping breaths. She could feel the heat coming off his skin and taste the chalky-vinegary tang of his sweat. He shifted his weight beside her but took care that they did not touch.

'Are you sure I can't help?' she said.

He tipped another tablespoonful of oil into the salad dressing. 'There's nothing to do.'

No mess on the work surfaces, no dishes in the sink. The vinyl floor was spotless. Not that she would have offered to clean it. Her gaze travelled over the countertop wine rack, the glass spaghetti jar, the HP Sauce apron hanging from the back of the door. She envied the way men could take pleasure in cooking. She could not scramble an egg without feeling the shackles of domestic slavery.

'Go and sit down,' he nodded towards the front room, 'tell me if you see owt.'

She wandered around, taking in the dust-free surfaces, the showroom condition of the three-piece suite. Only the books connected with the man she knew. Well-thumbed copies of Gramsci and Marx. Crispin Aubrey's *Who's Watching You?* A cloth-bound edition of *The Ragged Trousered Philanthropists*.

Too restless to sit still, she climbed the stairs.

The window looked out over the gardens. She counted the walls she had jumped, the lawns she had crossed. The rusty bedsprings in the sole untended garden called to mind her injured ankle. Sitting down on the bed, she rolled up her trouser leg to examine the raised welt. The navy blue sheets gave off a smell of washing powder and sleep-drenched skin. The slippers under the bed looked child-size when she placed her own foot alongside one.

'Grub's up.'

He was standing in the doorway.

'I was looking for the bathroom.'

He let this pass without comment. 'That were Mick ont' phone. They've put cordon round village. They're arresting anyone who leaves their own house.'

He had made a cold buffet. Bread, salad, pickled beetroot. She wondered at the wisdom of putting out corned beef *and* pork pie, given that he was now on strike. She would have refused the wine, but he'd already opened the bottle.

Had they shared this meal in the evening she might have suspected his motives, but it was three o'clock on a summer afternoon. She could hear a blackbird on the telegraph pole outside, and children, just out of school, being hurried along the street.

'Do you think the police'll be back?'

He shook his head. 'They weren't local. They dun't know I live here.'

'They must have seen us.'

'They had sun in their eyes. If they'd seen us they'd've battered door down.'

She wanted to relive the chase with him and find out if he had felt the same exhilaration, flying over those walls. 'We're lucky they were so slow coming after us.'

'Lily held 'em up.'

'The old lady? I thought she was going to turn the hose on you.'

'When it comes to crunch, blood's thicker than water. She's still my mother-in-law—'

Lexa put down her glass.

'—Irena's mother died when she were four. Lily brought her up. She's a rum duckie but she did a good job. Well, you've seen for yourself.'

'I don't think I . . .'

'Behind bar at welfare.'

'Blonde hair?'

'That's right.'

'She's beautiful,' Lexa said flatly.

'Oh aye, she's beautiful.'

She looked at her watch. 'I should see if the police'll let me through.'

He started to laugh and she had to pretend she didn't know why.

'We had nowt in common. Just growing up here. She wanted out, had a look round, reckoned I were her best bet.'

Lexa heard the past tense but phrased her question in the present just in case, 'So you're a trophy husband?'

'Aye, we were well-matched. Neither of us wanted t'other when we got down to it. At least she had honesty to do summat about it.'

'Maybe you weren't that unhappy with the situation.'

'Some ways I weren't. Lads at welfare kept telling me what a lucky bastard I were. They reckoned we were at it every hour God sent. If they were in my shoes . . . Most nights it were peck on cheek and cup of cocoa. And not always peck on cheek.' Lexa looked down at her plate. 'My choice as much as hers. It takes two not to tango. She moved in with Nacods delegate, took Ryan with her. I kept this place. We're civil now, but that's about it. Daft thing is, I were never that keen on blondes.'

'Not even blondes with perfect figures?'

It was meant to sound playful but it came out sour.

He leaned back in his chair. 'And I thought you were different.'

'Oh I'm different all right,' she said.

He sighed and she had the shaming sense that, for him, this was old ground. 'Every woman I know's on a diet, even my mother. Fifty-seven. You'd think she'd earned right to eat what she liked by now. Forty year o' starving herself, bleaching her hair, trying to turn into summat she's not. Waste of time. Men want all sorts – just like women. Some want blondes with Miss World figures, aye, but for every one like that there's another one who can take 'em or leave 'em. But a woman with long legs and mouth that kinks up at corner . . .'

Who else could he be describing? And yet. She knew what people saw. Remarkable height and an unremarkable face. A useful woman to have on your side in a tug-of-war or an ethical debate, but not a sexual provocation.

'What did you know the first time you saw me?'

He cleared his throat with a scraping grunt. 'You what?'

'When we were outside the police station, you said I didn't need to prove anything, you knew the first time you saw me.'

'Oh aye.' He drained his glass. 'You walked into welfare and I thought, she's scared of nowt, that one.'

She wondered if he were playing her as he had played the crowd earlier. 'You don't strike me as the timid type yourself.'

The afternoon sun flooded through the window, catching the glass salad bowl, filling his narrowed eyes with light. She felt the weight of something about to happen.

'I'm scared o' you,' he said.

Trying to recall it, later, was like developing an over-exposed film. Most of the pictures bleached to whiteness. Just the odd surviving fragment. The quickening of his will as she leaned across the table. The glimpse of lower teeth as his mouth opened to hers. A flutter of panic, climbing the stairs. The sense of a line crossed, her life divided, before and after. Slipping his shirt buttons to find the black fur on his chest. The smell of him all around her, the wine and that chalk-and-vinegar tang. The feeling of being poured towards him until the momentum became unstoppable. And the voice inside her.

We're the same.

First there was the drinks waiter who pulled up a chair to talk Rae through the wine list. Then the food waiter moved in to point out the specialities of the house. Then the pasta arrived, followed by the chatty boy with the black pepper and his smiling friend with the parmesan. And now one of the chefs had come through because he used to go out with Ciara and he'd heard she was married, and how were Brigid and Josephine and poor little Theresa . . .?

'How many Bergins are there?' Lexa asked when the chef had retreated to the kitchen.

'Seven girls. All redheads. We were the school Catholics, one in each year. An under-fourteens swimming champion, a shoplifter, a tart, a teacher's pet, an asthmatic, a retard and a psychopath.'

'And which were you?'

'Can't you guess? I was the accident. Well, we were all accidents really. They couldn't afford to feed themselves, never mind seven kids. If we'd all brought something in for harvest festival there'd've been nothing in the house to eat. One year I took a tin that'd lost its label and the teacher made me take it home again, the bitch. I used to bin the letters about parents' evening. I couldn't face them turning up in the van.' She shot Lexa a defensive look. 'We didn't all have dads who drove Jaguars.'

Lexa had told her about the endless succession of Austin Allegros, Ford Cortinas, Morris Marinas – and yes, once, a Jag, but a Jag with trade plates. Here today and gone tomorrow. Like the idea of emigrating to Canada, and buying the hotel on Skye, and all the other grand schemes her father dreamed up and forgot, all the other reasons her mother had to be so relentlessly disappointed. No tins in the Strachan house. Every meal was home-cooked and tasted of unhappiness. Well *boo-hoo*, as

Gabriel would say.

'One Christmas the drivers all got hampers. Tinned ham and a bottle of sweet sherry and a little tartan tablecloth. Mum cut it up and made me a pinafore. First new clothes I ever had.' She menaced Lexa with a breadstick. 'I don't want this going any further . . .'

'Any further than what?' Lexa told Gabriel everything, as Rae knew full well.

'Bonus time's coming up. I don't want them thinking they can pay me half as much as everybody else because I used to get free school dinners.'

'They know about the gang fights.'

'That's different. You get all sorts in gangs. Ian Leigh's mum was the school nurse.'

'That must impress Kinsella.'

Rae's lidless eyes turned to glass.

They had been out to lunch every Tuesday for the past three weeks and still there was a tension between them. Lexa suspected it was a quality Rae's relationships never lost. Men seemed to find the spikiness erotic, but the secretaries didn't like her. Their eyes acquired the careful look Lexa remembered around the dangerous girl at school, the hard-faced girl with the loud dragging voice. Lexa too had given her a wide berth, returning many monosyllabic replies before it had dawned on her that, in a take-it-or-leave-it way, she was being offered the hand of friendship. Even now it seemed unlikely. Rae had no time for women who couldn't work sex to their own advantage. She smiled at attractive strangers in bars, and looked traffic wardens in the eye, and could stop the cars on Westgate just by stepping off the kerb. At the first of these lunches Lexa had asked why Gavin called her Isabel. 'You know: the knock-knock joke.' But Lexa had not known, so Rae had had to explain: *'Knock-knock. Who's there? Isabel. Isabel who? Isabel necessary on a bicycle?'*

They were talking, between interruptions, about the office.

'Does Lori Cooper know you saved her job?'

Rae's nose wrinkled. 'I haven't saved anything. I didn't sack her, that's all. Kinsella hasn't forgotten.'

'He must know she'd win at a tribunal.'

'The maximum pay-out's fourpence ha'penny. He doesn't give a shit.'

'Presumably Phin'd have something to say about it.'

Rae's furtive glance said she had privileged information to impart. 'Phin's not coming back. They're giving him his pension and seventy grand so he can drink himself to death in his garden shed. Kinsella's the big boss now, or he will be as soon as London makes it official—' Lexa caught a glimpse of sharp teeth between her painted lips, '—So Jonny Rose's days are numbered.'

'Which is good news for you.'

The waiter was back with the sweet menu. Rae ordered zabaglione and he leaned in close to tell her she spoke beautiful Italian. She rolled her eyes at his departing back, plainly delighted.

'I've got some ground to make up if I'm going to be in with a chance. This Lori Cooper thing is a pain in the arse. He's going to want his pound of flesh.'

'And you're going to give it to him?'

Rae gave her another glassy look.

The dessert arrived. She dipped a finger in the creamy gloop and sucked. 'Better than sex.'

The waiter told her she'd been sleeping with the wrong men. She pushed a spoonful at Lexa. She was always doing this sort of thing, offering you second bite of her sandwich, taking a swig of your coffee as she passed your desk. Maybe it was normal if you had six sisters.

Lexa shook her head at the zabaglione and was paid back with, 'I hear your colliery deal's on the skids.'

'Says who?' But Lexa knew the answer. It had been topic of the night in Sylvester's. 'Kinsella's been nagging us to get a move on, that's all.'

'Yeah, well, I wouldn't work too closely with the Angel, if I were you. Make sure everything's down on the time allocation sheets. That way you get your fair share of the credit, and if it goes pear-shaped you don't get more than your share of the shit.'

Lexa sighed. 'Put another record on, will you?'

'I'm trying to give you some good advice.'

'And I don't want to hear it.'

Rae licked her spoon clean. 'It's your funeral.'

They walked back to the office. It had not rained for a month and the pavements had started to smell. The shops in this part of town sold cheap luxuries for the bedsit population up the hill. Secondhand books and records, hookahs and incense. One shopfront was painted like the Confederate flag, its window filled with photographs of tattooed bodies. As they stopped to look, a heavy thump and a volley of swear words echoed down the covered passage at the side of the shop.

A stringy figure in a cap-sleeved T-shirt and drainpipe jeans emerged. The dragon around his bicep brought back Lexa's first day at Goodisons. That awful evening in the pub.

'Aye aye,' he said, 'Haven't seen you at the Trafalgar for a while.'

He was limping. It was only polite to ask.

'Locked myself out. I was trying to get in through the upstairs window. Not the brightest idea I've had this week . . .'

Lexa didn't have to follow him down the passage. They could have wished him luck and walked on. But it was a chance to step out of the middle-class box Rae had put her in.

Behind the shop was a concrete yard. The bottom window was boarded and barred, the upstairs sash slightly open.

'I'm Rae, in case you're wondering.'

Turning, Lexa saw her chin tilted up at him, her cheeks flushed from the wine at lunch.

'Trevor.' He flashed a chipped smile, holding out his hand, palm-up. She yielded hers to be kissed.

Lexa hoisted herself onto the coal bunker built against the back wall of the house, but the window was still too high. She looked down into the yard.

'You are joking,' Rae said. 'Do you know what this suit cost?'

'Take it off, then.'

Trevor laughed.

She unbuttoned her jacket.

Where Lexa had jutting hip bones and angular shoulder blades, Rae's body seemed to have been poured into a mould. She was smooth all over, her skin a luminous white made creamy by a faint, even covering of freckles. Lexa felt slightly sick, as she had felt in the restaurant, watching her eat the zabaglione. The shape of her breasts was clearly visible through her bra. A couple of orange pubic hairs escaped the legs of her lacy pants.

Lexa hauled her up on to the bunker and locked hands to make a stirrup. Rae shook her head.

'Kneel down.'

A flash of painted toenails, and she was standing on Lexa's shoulders.

'*Ooof.*'

'This was your idea, remember?'

Slowly Lexa pulled herself upright. One leg began to tremble.

'Hold still,' Rae barked.

Ten seconds later she was standing in the open doorway, easier in her near-nakedness than Lexa was fully clothed.

Trevor stepped forward with her suit, 'You two should be in the circus.'

Rae zipped her skirt and smoothed the fabric over her hips. 'Actually we are,' she said.

The fluorescent light flared and died and flared again.

'Sweet Jesus,' Rae muttered.

The walls were covered floor to ceiling. Fading Polaroids of tattooed body parts, posters, jokey signs, pages torn from girlie magazines. A dried snakeskin had been drawing-pinned around a pair of gold-fringed knickers. Signed photographs of minor movie stars were framed above the black vinyl couch. Adam Faith, Farrah Fawcett-Majors, a face from *Coronation Street*. A table beside the cracked sink held an assortment of plastic bottles filled with coloured inks. The device itself had a worryingly improvised look. Brass screws and wires and wingnuts, red insulating tape, a rod attached with rubber bands. Trevor picked it up.

'So that's the gun?' Lexa said.

'That's the *machine*. You connect it—' he picked up a flex ending in a crocodile clip, '—like this, and you're ready to go.' There was a high-pitched buzzing and a blue spark. 'I could show you, if you like. On the house?'

'Thanks, but no thanks.'

Rae's eyes glittered. 'What did you have in mind?'

'Whatever you want.'

Lexa looked from the tattooist to Rae. How did she do it? One smoky-voiced question and the game was on. Or had they been playing ever since he kissed her hand?

Rae scanned the pictures pinned to the walls.

'Daisy?' he suggested, 'Rose? Butterfly? A little heart?'

Rae touched a page ripped from a magazine. A bare-chested man, his jeans fastened by a death's head belt buckle, his tattooed hand on the point of removing a pair of mirror shades. 'This,' she said.

His face fell. Lexa smiled to herself.

'If that's what you want. Most ladies go for the ankle, or the wrist, or the arm.'

'On the arse.' Rae tapped her left buttock. 'But keep it small.'

Was she bluffing? Lexa was no longer sure. 'Do you really want a scorpion on your bum?'

'Yeah, I do.'

'When you're forty?'

'Why not?'

'When you're *sixty*?'

'By the time I'm sixty it's going to be halfway to my knees anyway—'

Trevor unhooked an ink-stained white coat from the back of the door.

'—all right then, if it makes you feel better,' Rae took off her jacket, 'on my shoulder blade.'

Two wooden chairs faced each other in the middle of the grimy linoleum. She straddled one and unhooked her bra.

'Why don't you think it over? Come back next week.'

Rae twisted around to catch Trevor's eye. 'D'you get the feeling she thinks I'm making a mistake?'

He opened a jar of Vaseline and smeared some on her skin.

'I think you should sleep on it,' Lexa said. Rae put so much effort into trying to pass. Her clothes, her car, her riding lessons. She even voted Tory. 'Once you do it, that's it, you know. You'll always be the kid who had free school meals.'

Rae's face hardened, 'And you think that bothers me?'

'I think it'll limit your freedom—'

Trevor fished in the pocket of his white coat and, sitting back in his chair, lit a cigarette.

'—I'm not saying you *shouldn't* . . .'

'Yeah you are.' Rae's upper lip lifted, showing her narrow V-shaped bite. 'What you mean by "freedom" is other people letting me in. Keeping my nose clean, watching my table manners, on the off-chance that some chinless twat'll ask me to the right dinner parties, maybe even walk me up the aisle . . . It's *my body* and I do what I like with it. Which doesn't include fucking Kinsella, as it happens. You should listen to yourself sometime, Lexa. Getting up on your high horse because you have to wear a skirt. Looking down your nose at me, thinking I'm going to prostitute myself for a job. You're the one who's been bought and sold. You don't even own your own skin. What's so terrible about a woman with a tattoo? Why're you so desperate to stop me? 'Cos it's *common*? Yeah, that's part of it. Snobbery. But it's more than that. I'm going to *limit my freedom*. God forbid I put anybody off. Because it's not just a bit of ink, is it? When I take off the clothes I wear to work, it'll still be there, and you know what it'll be saying? *This is my body and I decide, not you.*' She looked at Trevor. 'What are you waiting for?'

He started up the machine. Rae flinched as the needles touched her back.

'It'll sting to start with.' The cigarette waggled in his mouth as he spoke. His right hand traced the outline, his left hand using a dirty towel to wipe the surplus ink from her skin. Raising his voice over the buzzing, he told Lexa, 'It feels like being drawn on with a hot pen.'

'It feels like some bastard's carving his initials on me with a piece of broken glass.'

Trevor grinned around his cigarette. 'I had you down as one of the tough ones.'

'Make a mistake with that thing and you'll find out how tough I am.'

He worked intently, one eye squinting against the smoke. When he removed the cigarette from his mouth to flick ash onto the lino, Rae took a puff.

'Is that blood?' Lexa said.

'That's right: I'm sticking needles into her skin.' He touched Rae on the arm. 'It'll bleed for an hour after, like any scratch. You'll have a scab for a week. Bit of Savlon if you like, but no picking, and no lying on your back.'

'I prefer it on top anyway.' She took another drag of his cigarette. Even with her eyes closed against the pain she looked invulnerable.

'You what?' she asked, though no one had spoken.

'Nothing,' Lexa said.

Rae opened her eyes.

Lexa shrugged. 'Me and You. Tall and small, plain and pretty.'

'Good girl and slut?'

'If you like.'

Rae's rubbery lips bunched in amusement, 'What *do* we see in each other?'

Lexa knew. Despite her scarlet toes and her lacy pants and her string of turbulent romances, Rae was a closet feminist. And all Lexa wanted was to learn to be a vamp.

JUNE

In his normal voice Stuart said, 'What were you shushing me for? You were noisy one.'

Lexa laughed, a bit of her wanting to cry as always, and they pulled apart.

She knelt up and looked over the wall. Green wheatfields startled with poppies. The brilliance of a high summer sky. The only building visible was the little Norman chapel in whose grounds they had spent the past hour. Stuart was lying down, his penis still swollen on the damp hair that thinned to a strip along his belly before fanning out over his chest. His hair, his green-blue eyes, the bullish way his neck rose out of his shoulders. Each carried its own erotic charge. She reached out to touch, then changed her mind and pressed her hands into the turf, feeling it give, cool under her fingers despite the day's heat. There were no headstones but it had to have been a burial ground. The earth was so springy. *All flesh is grass.*

'What are you doing, trying to contact other side?'

'I'm touching time,' she said. 'A thousand years under my fingers.'

'Eight hundred.'

'You always have to be right, don't you?'

'I don't have to be, I am.'

Sometimes they were slow and tender together, their lips as tentative as the first time they had kissed, sensation spreading its intricate patterns across her skin while her throat held an ache like unshed tears. Sometimes sex was a sort of contest, more like wrestling, rolling over and over, neither one yielding, until they reached a quivering stasis. Then her breathing came quick and ragged, like in the films.

It was the affection that surprised her most. The more than sensual way his lips sought hers, as if she were running water to a man dying of thirst, or a crying child he was trying to console, or a gift so unexpected she made him want to laugh. It wasn't just that the sex was better than the sex she'd had before: it felt like *making love*. There. She'd said it now, if only to herself. Like jumping out of a plane. Not shutting her senses down in terror but relishing the cold and the windrush and the adrenaline in her chest, trusting the air to buoy her up, astonished by how different the world looked from here. She had learned the bleak lesson of her parents' marriage early: men's and women's interests were irreconcilable. But somehow Stuart bridged the gulf. He *saw* her, that was it. To be seen and, having been seen, to be loved: the possibility had never occurred to her.

'This is part o' Barlby estate—'

It always amused her, how quickly he returned to making general conversation.

'—my uncle worked in stables. Had one o' tied cottages.'

'Peasant stock,' she murmured, but he didn't catch the reference.

'By time I knew him he were eighty-odd. We'd call in and he'd be sitting there, watching rats run up curtain. My mother were always ringing estate office. He could rot for all they cared. They were quick enough to take advantage when he were on payroll. They'd have him and gamekeeper and head lad in on Boxing Night to entertain Lords and Ladies. Then they decided they din't want riff-raff dirtying furniture so they buried that tradition, came round with bottle of Harvey's Bristol Cream on New Year's Day. They'd let him make a cup of tea, take one sip and piss off to patronise next poor bastard. They still own Levinwell. Pub, shop, cricket pitch, houses. It's like feudalism never died out.'

'Centuries of forelock-tugging in the genes.'

This time he rose to the bait. 'Not in my genes. He were only my uncle by marriage.' He pulled her towards him, 'I know whose side I'm on, unlike some I could mention.'

She folded onto the grass, 'Someone has to fight the system from the inside.'

He unfastened a couple of her shirt buttons, 'I heard Beronex were having second thoughts.'

He said it idly, but she wasn't fooled. She found it sexy, him running two agendas, the power she had to determine which was uppermost in his mind.

She took hold of him. He liked to be twisted gently.

He shut his eyes. 'I thought deal'd be done by now.'

'Things are progressing.'

His hand moved down her body. She sighed noisily, making him smile.

'Progressing how?' he asked.

'Satisfactorily.'

He increased the pressure of his finger. 'How?'

She squeezed him in response and heard his breath catch. Then he was on top of her. She started to protest, it was too quick, not the way they did things, but as his face loomed above hers, enquiring if she wanted him out, her body sucked him in deeper.

He moved slowly, letting her take his weight. It was still strange to her that he could be both the doll-size snappy dresser and this landmass of flesh and muscle. The shoulders her hands could barely span, the continent of his back, the savanna of his chest. She felt his lips vibrate against her neck, a groan, or a word . . . was it *love*?

A dog barked. She opened her eyes. A shaggy-faced mongrel was staring down at her, its front paws propped on the churchyard wall.

'Stuart.'

He rolled off her.

In the distance a man's voice called 'Tess.'

Stuart flattened himself against the wall. Lexa buttoned her shirt and pulled on her trousers. The dog met her at the gate, tail wagging. A middle-aged man was walking up the road, his windcheater jacket zipped to the neck despite the sweaty glow on his face.

'Tess!' he called again. Lexa moved towards him, the dog frisking at her side.

She met him a few feet from the car, coming to a sudden halt, blocking his path. She knew it looked odd. The mongrel was sniffing at her thighs, obviously interested in the scents higher up.

'*Tess*.'

The dog ignored him.

'Afternoon,' Lexa smiled, pushing away the persistent snout.

'Afternoon.' He was one of those slow, grudging speakers. 'Taking a break from Mester Harrison. Or is it Mester Duffy today?'

She reminded herself that these words did not necessarily bear an offensive construction. 'I've seen you around Faxerley, haven't I?'

'Not recently.' Seeing no alternative, he added, 'I'm the pipe-fitter.'

'Lexa Strachan.' She put out her hand.

'Brian Netley.' He kept his in his pocket. His eyes were small behind those wire-rimmed glasses.

'I'm just admiring your Norman chapel. Such a weird thing to find in the middle of nowhere.'

'Ah well, this is somewhere to us.'

She found this funny. He did not return her smile.

His gaze shifted. She turned to see Stuart, fully clothed, strolling towards them. The dog stopped snuffling at her legs and went to investigate.

'Afternoon Brian,' he said in a casual voice she knew was put on to amuse her.

Brian nodded at him, 'I thought that were your car.'

Lexa checked that all her buttons were fastened. By mid-afternoon everyone on the colliery payroll would have heard about this.

The pipe-fitter lowered his voice. 'I need to talk to you.'

'You're talking to me now,' Stuart said.

The man's glance flicked towards Lexa. 'Officially I mean. I've been down to Nottingham. I've to collect some samples, get them in for analysis.'

All at once the axis changed. The men were united, she was on the outside. Stuart became businesslike. 'I'll come round later. Will you be in at six?'

'They say they've heard of a case in Czechoslovakia . . .'

'Six o'clock,' Stuart repeated.

Lexa saw a look pass between them, an agreement that there were words which could not presently be said. Brian Netley turned away. The dog gave a whimpering bark.

Stuart watched them disappear round the bend in the road. 'Fuck,' he breathed.

She started to laugh. 'So nobody ever comes here?'

'All right, all right, you win that one.'

'I don't think Mr Netley likes me very much.'

'You're t'least of his problems.'

'Really?'

'Never mind.' He unlocked the car.

'We're virtually living together,' she said. 'I've heard you talking in your sleep. I know what the bathroom smells like when you've been in there first thing in the morning. If you really want, I can do an impression of the sound you make when you come—'

He was grinning in embarrassment.

'—so what's the big secret?'

He started the engine. 'There's things you don't tell me about your job.'

'You don't want me to tell you. It'd spoil the fun of tricking them out of me.'

'It's not interesting.'

'I know. I just want you to break his confidence.'

'Why?'

'Because we sleep together.'

He gave her a sidelong look. 'He thinks pit's given him cancer.'

They stopped at a *Give Way* sign, waiting for a horsebox to pass the junction. The hedgerows to either side were dense with nettles and cow parsley and flowering brambles.

'Have you told Harrison?'

Stuart sighed as if it were her question, not his disclosure, which had soured the atmosphere.

'Between you and me he's not all there. He's got bee in his bonnet about electricity pylons. His hobby's UFOs. He gets obsessed and starts keeping files. Reckons Faxerley's got a higher mortality rate than it should've.'

'Is he right?'

He grimaced. 'There's a few've died in their late fifties, early sixties. It's not unusual round here. They like their beer and fags and fried food. There's diseases you're prone to, working underground, everyone knows that. But not what he's talking about.'

'And what is he talking about?'

'God knows. He reckons there's something in Mottershaw shale gives you cancer. It's got into air down there and everyone's breathing it in. Next thing he'll be blaming CIA.'

'So it's rubbish, is it—?'

He looked the other way, checking for traffic before pulling out.

'—he's making a fuss about nothing?'

'He's found a couple of old timers. Reckons they've got same thing he's got.'

They overtook the horsebox. The road stretched straight and empty ahead of them.

'Any mention of legal action?' The random way this had come to light made Lexa anxious. How much more was there she didn't know? 'If there's litigation in the works it has a bearing on the deal.'

'Could it stop sale?'

'I wouldn't have thought so, but it qualifies as material disclosure. The buyer has to be told. Have you got names and addresses for these two guys?'

'They don't live local.'

'It doesn't matter if they live in Timbuktu. Is Netley talking about money—?'

He was staring through the windscreen.

'—Stuart.'

'I told you, he's a conspiracy nut. He's more interested in proving things're wrong than getting 'em put right.'

'Will he go to the press?'

'Nah.'

'How can you be so sure?'

'He dun't trust them either.'

He switched the radio on. The dry spell was set to continue. The water board was considering a hosepipe ban.

'Has anyone said anything to Harrison?'

'I've no idea. Believe it or not I've one or two other things on my plate.'

'Wouldn't you rather know if it's dangerous?'

'Course I would—'

He braked and turned off the road on to the uneven ground in front of a five-barred gate. They sat there with the engine running. A tractor chugged past them, the farmhand staring.

'—I tell you what I don't want. If sale falls through because of an unproven safety scare and it comes out vendor's agent were acting on information from Union delegate, that's me finished. There's not much call for branch officials who put their members out o' work.'

'Gabriel'll be the one who raises it, not me. She's been told to look at the pension fund anyway. There's all sorts of ways it could come out.'

He studied her with narrowed eyes. 'Come here.'

They kissed. The aftershave he applied every morning had almost worn off. His skin smelled of fresh air and sweat and a fishy residue of arousal. He sucked her earlobe, grinding it gently between his incisors.

'Just make sure nobody knows it came from me.'

Lexa sat outside Kinsella's office, trying to look unconcerned. If he had wanted to talk about the deal, he could have stopped off at her desk, or picked up the phone, but he'd got Sal to ring her. And now he was keeping her waiting.

The intercom light came on. Sal stopped typing and lifted the receiver.

'He's free now.'

Kinsella was sitting at his desk, reading a file. 'Open the window,' he said.

She crossed the room and lifted the sash. An oyster-tinted sky, the air thick as felt between her fingers. A rivulet of sweat trickled between her breasts.

'Sit down.'

He had caught the sun at the weekend, which made his eyes unusually piercing when he looked up. 'Have you seen this?'

He tossed the folder across his desk. Several pages slithered to the floor. Ever since the tickling he had kept her at arm's length, making sure she understood this as a loss of favour.

She gathered the scattered sheets of paper, which were limp from the humidity. *Wishew Refractories*. Ben's deal.

'I told you to sort it out, but it went to the client as it was, so now we all look like cunts.'

'I am a cunt,' she said.

'I might as well take out an ad in the *Yorkshire Post*: Goodison Farebrother would like it to be known that they're a bunch of fucking amateurs. I ask you to do *one thing* for me . . .'

Kinsella threw two kinds of tantrum, sarcastic and hysteric. The sarcasm wasn't pleasant, but preferable to his saliva-flecked arias of rage.

'You told me I couldn't handle it.'

'*Don't* tell me what I did or didn't say. You know the rules. You cock it up: you sort it out.' Through the open window came a rumble of thunder. He paused, distracted. 'And why've you got a fucking Mediterranean tan? I'm not paying you to spend your days at Faxerley sunbathing.'

'We're in the middle of a heat wave. I get outside at lunchtime.'

'So I hear.'

Her heart stopped.

Was that a smile hovering at the corners of his mouth? And if it was, was that good or bad?

'Is there anything you want to tell me, Alexandra? Anything you think I ought to know?' He turned to a pile of correspondence, scribbling across the letters and dropping them in his out-tray. 'No? Gavin tells me you've-*aah* been on television. Several seconds apparently. He says you're wasting your talents, you should be playing prop forward, you'd be a natural in the scrum.'

The cameras. As one face among thousands, she hadn't given them a thought.

His cut-glass accent sharpened. 'Has it ever-*aah* crossed your mind that our clients might not be happy about you supporting the workshy fuckers who've walked out on strike? Since we're selling the fucking colliery—?'

What could she say? The risk was insane. But it was the only thing that made the job bearable.

'—What am I supposed to tell them? "This is Alexandra Strachan. You might recognise her face from the six o'clock news, but don't worry, she's got a management perspective"? You think they'll swallow that, do you? Hmm? Lucky for you we're in the middle of a deal, and I haven't got time to get anyone else up to speed, otherwise you'd be out. Now fuck off before I change my mind.'

Lexa stood up.

Rae burst through the door. 'Are you trying to take the piss—?'

Lexa sat down again.

'—all the hours I put in training Peter Lawrence, the work I did on the Symons deal, the Mercer result, all those client dinners with Dick Harkness. "Can you do me a favour Rae?" Oh sure. I don't mind giving up my weekends, working late. Even though I'm the only one with a fucking social life round here . . .'

'I'm busy,' Kinsella said. 'If you want to see me, make an appointment with Sal.'

'Why would I want to see you? So you can feed me another load of bullshit?'

He got up and shut the door. Lexa watched his reflection in the glass over the Helmut Newton print on the wall.

'You were the one who stopped co-operating, as I recall.' He was standing so close that Rae had to choose between stepping backwards and craning her neck to see his face.

'You're crowding me,' she said.

'It never used to worry you.'

'I didn't say it *worried* me, I just don't like it.'

'But you used to.' Since Stuart, Lexa understood physical pull. She knew that Rae was feeling it now, and that Kinsella was aware of this fact. 'Why don't you calm down and we'll-*aah* talk about it later.'

'What's there to talk about?' She looked up at him. 'I get a performance-related bonus of two thousand pounds. Fucking Ben gets three. Gavin gets fifteen. *Fifteen thousand quid*, seven-and-a-half times as much as me. I'd love to see the figures that stand that up.'

'It's not about comparisons.'

'What else is it about?'

He fingered her necklace. 'I like this—'

She twitched her head away. A few strands of hair stuck to the sweat on her cheek.

'—The last twelve months we've been doing the groundwork. It's the next twelve that are going to be interesting. That's when we find out who's worth the money. You've got to play the long game.'

Lexa could feel Rae's indecision.

'What long game?' she said at last.

'There's going to be big changes round here.' His voice dropped to a murmur. 'Do you trust me?'

'What do you think?'

'Do you *trust* me?' he repeated.

'Not on the evidence of what's happened, no.'

He said it a third time, slowly. 'Do you trust me?'

Their reflections gave nothing away. After a long time Rae said, 'I suppose I've got no choice.'

'That's better.' Kinsella had reverted to his habitual tone with her. Light, intimate, pregnant with meaning. 'The way I see it there'll be two senior vacancies, one in Venture Capital and one in Corporate Finance – I'll have enough to do without running a department day-to-day. But there's-*aah* a problem with the natural candidate for Corporate Finance and a member of the current support staff. I've been thinking we could do with someone to deal with this kind of thing formally. The new director of Venture Capital could have a personnel role, with an extra five grand to make it worth her while. It's the sort of thing a woman might be better at—'

Lexa smiled. Any minute now Rae was going to tell him where he could stick his personnel role.

'—there's going to be a lot of expansion in the North over the next few years, a lot of opportunities for a bank like us, but I have to know the people I'm relying on are fully behind me. It's all about trust: you trust me, I trust you.' In the glass over the print Lexa saw him brush a strand of hair out of Rae's eyes. 'You understand?'

There was another long pause.

'I'm getting the general idea,' Rae said.

'Good girl,' he breathed.

The eighth floor smelled just the same. Dusty radiators and a stale reminder of Gauloises Disque Bleu. For the second time in an hour Lexa opened a window and felt the clamminess outside. The sky had an artificial brilliance, as if the electricity in the atmosphere had been harnessed in fluorescent tubes. She didn't hear the footsteps on the stairs. Gabriel was suddenly beside her, looking even thinner than the last time she had seen her. Her cheeks had developed a horsey contour, her neck was a stalk.

'You made it!' Lexa said, and heard the grating note of false cheer in her voice.

They had not gone for a drink or to see a movie in three weeks. Instead of meeting up here a couple of times a day, it had become once every two days, then every three or four.

Increasingly, Gabriel couldn't face climbing the stairs. A hangover. Pains in her legs. An energy-sapping bug. *Bored with me*, Lexa thought. But she knew it was more than that.

Gabriel dropped her bag, which was weighted with something bulky and rectangular. Then she had to stoop to find her cigarettes and matches.

'Aren't you hot?' Lexa asked.

She was wearing a navy flannel shirt and brown tweed skirt, the two items in her wardrobe which went least pleasingly together.

Lexa tried again. 'Were you at Faxerley yesterday?'

'Some of the time.' Her voice was sluggish.

'And it's going OK?'

'Uh-huh.'

'If things are slipping I could help.'

'They're OK.'

'Have you checked out the cancer angle?'

'Uh-huh.'

'And?'

Gabriel raised a hand and rubbed at her eyelid. Lexa took the cigarette from her fingers before it singed her hair.

'Nothing.'

'No litigation in the works?'

'No.'

'And the widows' pensions?'

'What you'd expect.'

'So Kinsella's happy?'

Gabriel hunkered down and began to search through her bag.

Lexa held out the cigarette. 'You've already got one lit.'

Gabriel put it to her lips. There was a clap of thunder almost directly overhead, but she did not look up.

'Gabriel?'

'Mmm?'

'Have you spoken to Kinsella about it—?'

It was like trying to reach her through a cloud.

'—we need to talk about what's happening to you, Gabe.'

'Do you mind if we don't?'

'You have to get on top of it.'

'I've seen the doctor.'

'What for?'

'Pills.'

'It's this place that's sick, not you.'

Gabriel managed a thin smile. 'He wouldn't give me pills for them.'

'So you're going to dose yourself with tranquillisers?'

'Anti-depressants.'

'Chemicals to blot out reality instead of getting to grips with it.'

'What do you know?'

Lexa's stomach shrank, but hostility was good. She had done some reading. Depression was repressed anger. Release the anger and you began to shift the despair.

'So tell me.'

Gabriel stared out of the window. 'I'm too tired.'

'We're supposed to be friends, Gabe. I need to know how you're feeling.'

'I *feel* tired.'

'So you've got some pills to help you sleepwalk through it. Is that what you want?'

'I don't want anything . . .'

Her voice tailed off. More shocking than the weight loss or the listlessness was the absence of expression in her face.

'Are you sleeping at night?'

She half-shrugged. 'I suppose so. I dream. It's like watching myself on close-circuit television. This person I don't recognise.'

'But *I* recognise you.'

Gabriel turned from the window. 'Bully for you.'

Lexa told herself this was the real meaning of love: swallowing the hurt and keeping yourself open. 'You're not the only one who feels alienated. If we weren't alienated by this place there'd *really* be something wrong with us. We've just got to hang on. It'll change. In a few months' time we'll look back and think "thank God that's over".'

'A few months?'

'A year at the most.'

'A *day's* like a . . .'

It was important not to rush to fill her silences. These days she could pause for fifteen seconds in the middle of a thought. Lexa waited. The humidity was getting worse. Her hands were so swollen the skin felt tight.

'. . . do you know what time is?' Gabriel said in her new, unnervingly affectless voice. 'It's wanting things. Wanting to eat, drink, piss, shit—' She never used these words, it was almost a surprise to Lexa that she knew them. '—go to bed, get up . . . things you wouldn't even call wanting until you don't want anything. Wanting's what moves the clock.'

'But you want to get back to normal, don't you—?'

Gabriel looked at her.

'—You got so much out of life.'

'Did I?'

'You know you did. Every moment. Oh Gabe, I don't know whether I should be saying this or not. It was like you had this . . . *lightbulb* inside you—'

Gabriel turned to the window again. The cigarette burned forgotten between her fingers.

'—you were interested in everything. From the moment you woke up you'd be taking it all in. It's not as if I'm talking about the distant past. This was three or four weeks ago. You've got a temporary depression. Today's Tuesday, we last saw each other on Thursday. I know it doesn't feel like it, but time is passing. This will pass.' Lexa heard the inadequacy of her words, and cringed inside, and yet she meant them. 'Move in with me. You can have the spare room, we'll take it in turns to cook. I'll keep the clock moving, I'll do the wanting for both of us.'

'That's how I got into this in the first place.'

Lexa's face contracted. 'Because of me?'

'Not everything comes back to you.'

The thunder was so close Lexa felt it in her diaphragm. A deep clang like struck metal. The next moment the air was noisy with rain. Relief swept through her. Gabriel crouched on the floor and began to wrestle with her bag. Another deafening thunderclap dragged Lexa's gaze back to the sky. It was like no rain she had ever seen. Wrathful, relentless, determined to drown the world. Gabriel gave a final tug at the bag and pulled out her desk diary.

'You want to know what's happening in my life?'

Lexa felt a shiver of apprehension as she turned the pages.

Monday May 24: 8.40 tits. 9.15 arse. 9.57 tits. 10.41 tits. 10.53 legs. 11.25 tits. 11.26 legs. 11.30 tits, arse. 11.59 arse. 12.37 arse. 12.49 tits. 12.52 arse. 12.56 tits

She looked down at Gabriel, still hunched on the floor.

'It was your idea. "Keep a log, we'll take it to London".'

'Kinsella,' Lexa said.

'Every time he looks at me. And what he's looking at.'

Lexa's eyes flicked to the facing page. It was the same. She turned to the following week, and the one after that. The same painstaking record. Page after page covered with the same four words.

tits arse legs tits arse legs arse tits arse arse tits cunt tits legs tits arse arse tits arse legs tits arse legs arse tits arse tits arse tits arse legs arse tits legs arse tits tits legs tits arse arse tits legs arse legs arse tits arse tits legs arse tits arse

They picked her up in a Ford Cortina with a blown silencer. She got in the back with Stuart. A sunburned miner introduced to her as 'Cappo' sat in the front. She didn't catch the driver's name. He took them off the A1, cutting between B roads on farm lanes, bumping over tractor ruts of dried mud. Usually these trips to the picket-line were high-spirited jaunts, but today she sensed bad temper like a fifth passenger in the car.

'Hello,' she murmured to Stuart.

His smile turned into a yawn.

'Late night?'

'Early morning.'

She put her hand on his leg and he patted it twice, which made her feel about as sexy as an old Labrador.

'I've taken the day off—' she said.

He glanced warningly towards the front seats.

'—they can't hear—'

His narrowed eyes followed something outside the window.

'—will you have time, after?'

'I don't know.' He looked grim. 'It's not going to be normal turn up, see 'em in, piss off again. There's two convoys, morning and afternoon. After that, your guess is as good as mine. I don't even know what we're going for, except to rub steelworkers' scabbing noses in it.'

'Isn't that enough?'

'Not for Arthur. Word's gone out: *this is the big one.* They're coming down from Scotland. Bloody Wales. We can't stop lorries. We know that. We've tried. So what are we doing? It's enough to make you believe in infiltration.'

'Don't look at me, I'm *your* double agent,' she said, to make him smile.

He rubbed a hand over his face. 'I don't like it.'

In the front seat Cappo lit a cigarette. Stuart wound down his window, 'I saw you in Leeds yesterday.'

'Why didn't you. . .?'

'I did. You din't hear me. You were across road with a redhead.'

'Rae. We went out to lunch.'

'Pal of yours, is she?'

'A colleague—'

Lexa had drunk a glass and a half of wine and asked if there was a role for Lori Cooper in Kinsella's long game? Later she had used the word 'collaborator', and Rae had retorted that she had better collaborate too, if she wanted to keep her job once Faxerley was sold.

'—she's a venture capitalist.'

'You what?' He was tickled by this. 'That's what it says in her passport, capitalist?'

'She invests in new start-ups. High risk, high return. Sorts the entrepreneurs from the out-and-out chancers.'

His smile showed a glimpse of lower teeth. 'Classy.'

At that moment she hated him, a principled rejection contaminated by a thought she had previously suppressed. Both he and Rae were short, both could hold their own with senior management but remained indelibly working class. Had she spotted him yesterday she would have had to introduce them. Both had a way of talking to strangers as if they were old friends. Lexa would have felt pushed out. As she was feeling now.

'She's not a pal, then?'

'Rae doesn't really have women pals.'

His grin turned wolfish. 'Does she intimidate you?'

She knew exactly what he meant. 'No, why should she? I don't want to fuck her.'

That wiped the smile off his face. He looked furious but said nothing, being in the wrong, which she knew from experience would only prolong his sulk. Cappo glanced into the back of the car, smirking.

They passed the rest of the journey in silence, staring out of opposite windows. At night when they were alone together he desired her, she knew. But when was sex just a meeting of two people? The bed was crowded with ghosts. Old lovers, prospects, movie stars, archetypes, every one with their ranking in the sexual league. And now Rae would be between the sheets too. *Does she intimidate you?* It wasn't just that he'd let slip he saw her as second class. He thought she saw herself like that.

'Where are you going, boys?'

A Sheffield accent. Lexa could see a silver-buttoned tranche of blue-black serge from thigh to breast pocket.

'That's our business,' the driver said.

The arm pointed off the road, across a stretch of open ground covered in yellow scrub. 'If you're picketing, your best bet's up there.'

Lexa had heard about policemen who played it by the book, refusing to take sides, but she didn't believe they existed.

Evidently the driver felt similarly. 'We'll stick to t'road.'

'There's nowhere to leave your car.'

'We'll risk it.'

'Don't say I didn't warn you.' He banged the flat of his hand on the car roof to send them on their way. Cappo and the driver were still laughing when they turned off the roundabout.

'Fookinell,' Cappo breathed.

As far as the eye could see the road was lined with blue and white horseboxes, coaches, caravans, Land Rovers, transit vans, and on every vehicle was blazoned the word *Police*. Gavin had been right: it was like the Romans. Formidable organisation. Military might.

Cappo pursed his lips. 'Couple of thousand?'

'Four or five,' Stuart said.

As predicted, there was nowhere to park. They drove back onto the dual carriageway and through the suburbs, a detour that put them on the other side of the coking plant. They left the Cortina on the last street of houses before the farmland began. An old man scowled at them through a bay window. The crops were worthless now. The crowd overflowed the road, spilling into the fields. Thousands of young men, many bare-chested and ruddy under the already-burning sun. It was like the exodus from a football ground on Saturday afternoon, only they were going nowhere.

Lexa and Stuart walked a couple of paces behind Cappo and the driver.

'I think they're going to sack me,' she said.

He raised his head. 'You're talking to me now, are you?'

'Looks like it, doesn't it?'

She waited for him to say something more, since she had made the first move, but he was staring into the distance.

'I knew as a woman I was living on borrowed time, but still . . .' Still what? Still she had managed to forget. Told herself she was different. It made no sense that she had been hired in the first place, why shouldn't she continue to buck the trend? 'I get something wrong, a slip of the tongue, it doesn't matter how small, somebody'll pick me up on it. I make a suggestion, it gets shot down. My name comes up and they give each other this look . . .' She wasn't sure he was listening. '*Stuart.*'

'*What?*'

'I just told you something important. To me anyway.'

'What do you want me to say?'

'Well you could say "I'm sorry, that must be tough" or "they'd be mad to let you go" or even "are you sure you're not imagining it?" which would piss me off, but at least it'd be some sort of response.'

'Will it affect sale?'

'No, don't worry, I'm not that important.'

He shrugged. 'Just make most of money while it's coming in, then. No point worrying while it happens. Without trade union backing there's nothing you can do. You don't like working there anyway. You're always moaning about it.'

'Moaning' she particularly disliked: a feminine verb, second cousin to 'nagging'. Nothing to do with the airing of justified grievance that was a union rep's stock-in-trade.

'Are you this sympathetic when your members' jobs are threatened?'

'God's sake Lexa, it's seven o'clock int' morning. I'm sorry they might sack you. I'm sorry I said your pal were nice-looking. I've got two hundred men with families who stand to lose everything if your deal falls through, and I'm getting by on four hours' sleep a night for a strike there in't a cat in hell's chance of winning. So I've got other things on my mind.'

'Right,' she said.

Several hundred police with perspex shields and visored helmets were blocking the road in front of the coking plant. The strikers in their jeans and T-shirts a few yards away looked like actors in the wrong movie.

'Where are you going *now*?'

She had heard men take this exasperated tone with their wives.

'I'm leaving you free to concentrate on other things.' She lengthened her stride so he would have to jog if he came after her, 'Don't worry about meeting up later, I'll make my own way home.'

'Suit yourself,' he said.

Some of the pickets were sunbathing, stretched out in the field. Others stood in clusters, chatting, laughing, playing kickabout with a ball. Just before nine the languor went out of the crowd. The miner beside Lexa cocked his head. She felt it before she heard it: a vibration in her bones. The strikers fell silent. Squinting into the distance, she counted thirty-five tipper trucks approaching through the heat shimmer on the metalled road. The pickets' faces wore a sacramental gravity, ten thousand people standing tensed and still. The convoy was moving fast, hurtling towards them, the steel grilles around each cab making the drivers eerily invisible. Lexa started to shake with the clamour of metal, the grinding engines, the heat and the glare and the pressure in her chest. Then the push began and she surrendered to the press of sweating, straining bodies. For five minutes nothing mattered more than gaining the next few inches of ground. Until the last truck in the convoy disappeared inside the plant and, with that sudden dissipation of energy she could never quite get used to, nothing mattered less. The crowd relaxed, drifting into the fields for the half-hour wait until the lorries were loaded. Rows of mounted police stood in formation halfway up the hill.

The noise of engines gunning into life brought the crowd back together for another push. Lexa was squashed again, but the tension was gone. No one seriously thought the convoy could be stopped, so there was a moment of confusion when the police line broke. The wall of shields opened and through the gap charged the horses. She felt her features sag into a replica of the stunned expressions all around her. The pickets at the back turned and ran, but where she was standing the crowd was packed too tightly to permit retreat. A wave of fear passed through the men in front of her and then, abruptly, the charge stopped. The horses turned and trotted back behind police lines. A couple of missiles flew towards the uniforms – a half brick, a lemonade bottle – but it was astonishing how quickly equanimity returned. As if the previous fifteen minutes had never happened.

She was on the road when she heard the drumming. She saw heads turning, seeking the source. A man's voice said 'What the fuck . . .?' It was the police using their truncheons to beat a tattoo on their shields. They were chanting too, not words but war cries. As she watched, the line of shields parted and the horses cantered through. The crowd made a sound she remembered hearing on the big dipper when she was a child. The world turned more slowly. She had time to take in the gleaming chestnut flank, the plate-size perspex blinkers fixed to the bridle, the lift of its hooves, the power in its breast, before she ran. Everywhere men were scattering in panic, scrambling over walls and fences, criss-crossing the cornfield, fleeing alongside her. If she could just find a stretch of open ground she knew she could outrun them all, but there were too many people in her way, and those hooves too close behind. A few yards to her right the horses had overtaken her, the riders swinging long staves, striking at anyone within reach, men staggering and dropping as they were hit. Behind the horsemen came the infantry, in black boiler suits and cannonball helmets, with truncheons and round gladiatorial shields. An officer with a megaphone was shouting orders, pointing out which pickets to arrest, barking 'bodies not heads' while his men hit out indiscriminately and their quarry ran blundering into the backs of those running before them.

And then Lexa could run no further. She threw herself to the ground face-down and waited for the trampling hooves, but the horse whose breath she had felt hot on her neck must have changed course in pursuit of someone else. Effortfully she got to her feet, hands on her thighs, lungs heaving, as the miners fled past her. She knew she was putting herself in danger, that by standing still she presented too easy a target, but her legs refused to move and an unsuspected corruption in her whispered that she would be safe, they would not hurt a woman. In the chaos around her she could see handcuffed miners being led to the waiting vans, miners fighting with policemen, miners with blood streaming down their faces. Ambulancemen were loading people into a Land Rover, mopping up the casualties even as the boiler-suited gladiators were making more. A picket cowered on the ground, naked from the waist up, the bruises flowering on his bony back as the truncheon descended again and again.

'Stop!' she shouted, but the word was swallowed by the din.

A few steps nearer and she could hear the laboured breathing of the policeman as he worked, and the animal sounds of the man he was beating.

'Press,' she yelled. It was all she could think of, and miraculously there was a picket at her side raising a pocket camera to his eye. She did not see the blow that caught her head. The pain surpassed anything she had felt before. The camera was smashed from the picket's hands. His arms took the next blow, rising to protect his skull. Then the policemen were gone. Lexa bent over the miner on the ground and stood up again, afraid she was going to pass out. At the same time she felt immensely calm. There was something she had to do, if she could only remember what it was. She made herself breathe. In and out. *Stuart*: that was it. She had to find him. But first she was going to sit down.

'Oh no you don't.' There were hands under her armpits hauling her to her feet. 'Come on. Walk. One foot in front o't'other.'

He smelled of sweat and something sharper that might have been excrement, but he was helping her so she breathed in his scent, took it down deep inside her.

'Not far now. See that ambulance over there? Dun't look much like ambulance, does it? That's 'cos it's army vehicle with respray. Hard cases in overalls are army too. Nato helmets. They come out of Newark every morning but it's "only a billet". They must think we're fucking soft.'

She realised he was talking to keep her conscious, but she was not sleepy, just very calm. Aware of everything, but at a distance. She felt the ground moving under her feet as they walked. She heard the shouts and groans and curses. She saw men stooping and straightening with stones in their hands, and others sitting on the ground in shock, or lying curled into themselves as their fellow pickets charged over and around them. Further off, the police were still lashing out. It all seemed so unreal.

'I'm all right,' she said to the ambulancemen. Up the hill she could see hundreds of miners walking along the road towards Sheffield. 'But there's a man on the ground back there, no shirt, you'll see the bruises.'

'She took crack ont' nut,' the hand was still clamped around her arm, 'if you ask me she's got concussion.'

For the first time she looked at him. He was an inch or so shorter than her, dark and wiry, with a moustache.

'What about your camera?' she said.

'Eff all use now.' He patted his trouser pocket. 'But I've got film.'

'I'm fine,' she repeated, disengaging her arm.

He stared into her eyes and seemed satisfied. 'Come on then.'

'Where?'

'To find lads.'

There were five of them, faceworkers at Carbeck Colliery. Her rescuer's name was Gaz. His brother had a can of beer. It was warm, but it wetted the inside of her mouth.

They followed a narrow lane down to a scrapyard. Pickets were clambering over the metal carcasses, scavenging for anything light enough to be hurled through the air but dense enough to do damage. Gaz found an Austin A40 minus its wheels and windscreen. 'One, two . . .' The 'three' came out in a straining grunt as they lifted it off the ground. A couple of hundred yards from the coking plant two rusting cars had been laid bumper-to-bumper across the road. They placed the Austin on the end and stepped back, panting. Lexa smiled, feeling her arms float upwards of their own accord. Fifty yards away a second barricade was being built out of rocks and scrap metal.

The crowd engaged in this task displayed the same slabs of sun-reddened flesh, wore the same jeans and T-shirts dotted with badges and stickers, but they were no longer the men who had fled from the police horses. Their faces were hard, a new purpose in their movements. Others were collecting stones, bottles, lumps of metal, to use as ammunition. The police watched inscrutably from behind their perspex visors.

Lexa jumped at the sound of diesel engines.

'Second convoy,' Gaz said.

There were no direct hits at first. The stones fell short, cracking on the road or bouncing harmlessly off the raised shields. The next wave of missiles was better aimed. There were cheers as a rider was felled from his horse. The police started to advance. Lexa laughed, which had always been the way she showed fear. A miner jogged along the line of scrap cars shaking a petrol can, his hairy belly wobbling as he ran. A balding picket caught up with him, pulling at his arm. Gaz dragged the older man away and they argued, shouting, neither listening to the other. Gaz's voice was louder and in the end his opponent was silenced.

'We had agreement, nob'dy said it but we all knew: no stones, no horses. So we didn't throw stones. We kept our side of bargain. And what do they do? Fucking cavalry charge. I saw that lass—' he pointed at Lexa '—smacked over the head for nowt. We could've been sat in that field making daisy chains, it would've been same difference. They were under orders from the off. So don't talk to me about playing by rules. They've beaten us like dogs today, and now we're going to bite back.'

Lexa did not see who threw the milk bottle but she watched the burning rag in its neck soar through the brilliant air, heard the musical smash on the Austin's roof a split-second before the whoosh of flame, and her blood thrilled. Behind the second barricade the picket with the petrol can was filling a row of bottles. Another miner had torn up his shirt and was dunking the rags in petrol. He looked at her doubtfully.

'Light and throw. No fucking about.'

The first two matches went out but the third lit the petrol-soused fabric. Her skin quivered. Day after day she toed the line. Kept her head down and her mouth shut. She was so sick of being careful. Gaz looked towards her, gesturing urgently. She smiled back. Windmilling her arms like a bowler, she let go. Sunlight caught the neck of the bottle against the breathless blue.

They were calling last orders as she stepped inside the door. The public bar was packed with strikers. She worked her way to the end of the counter to wait her turn. And then she saw him, in the snug with Mick. His face was dirty, his shirt pocket torn, but he seemed unscathed. The landlord called 'Time' and an unseen hand pushed the snug door closed. She reached for the handle. A thickset man stepped in front of her.

'Not now, love.'

'But a friend of mine's . . .'

'Not now,' he snapped.

The saloon bar was deserted. No striker was going to pay a penny a pint more for red velour seats and fringed lampshades. By leaning over the counter she could see into the snug. Ten pickets were crammed around a table laden with pints. She recognised a face from the television news, one of the NUM Area officials. Stuart was at a smaller table by the bar, his back to her. She was about to call to him when she heard her name spoken.

Stuart picked up his glass, 'She'll've been up road by ten.'

'You reckon?'

'Not her fight, is it?'

Her eyes stung at the injustice. Now they would have to have a row, when what she wanted was a slow, shared bath soaping each other's aching flesh before they fell into bed, the sheets smooth and cool, sunlight picking out the weave in the curtain pulled across the open window.

Mick grinned, 'You going to kiss and make up?'

Not being able to see Stuart's face, she could only guess at his response.

Mick's eyebrows flexed suggestively, 'Grateful sort, is she?'

'Fuck off.' But his voice was smiling.

Mick's grin widened, 'Bit different from Irena.' His eyes lifted and connected with Lexa's, showing no surprise.

Stuart leaned back in his chair.

'All cats are grey int' dark,' he said.

JULY

The bouncer ticked Lexa's name off his clipboard and stepped aside. Lori Cooper was leaning against the inner door. The walls leaked a muffled throb of bass.

'You're going to love it in there.'

'Am I?' Lexa took off her raincoat and saw Lori's eyes widen.

The typist peered into the mirror of her powder compact, scratching at a mascara smudge with a silvered fingernail. 'Still, it's all a matter of taste, isn't it?'

'What is?'

'Sex.'

'When it's not prostitution,' Lexa said.

On the other side of the door the music assaulted her. The club was a smoky semi-darkness, pitch black at one end where the lights had been turned off to concentrate the revellers in a more intimate space. It wasn't that they were drunk, or not only that. Every movement was exaggerated by their determination to have a good time. Their voices were raised to carry above the music. Their laughter was louder, readier, to Lexa's ears more forced. Their faces, painted by the dance floor's flashing lights, loomed out of the shadows, familiar and grotesque.

Goodisons' summer parties had previously been held in the walled garden of a stately home, with Pimms and Chinese lanterns and puddles of sick behind the delphiniums. This year Kinsella had broken with tradition, conning the solicitors on the second floor and the receivers on the third into splitting the bill and beefing-up the quota of beddable secretaries. The Skool Club. Lexa had heard of the place but never been inside. The walls were covered in blackboard paint and chalked with cutelymisspelled graffiti. A tall woman in a mortar board and gown strode between refectory-style tables swishing a cane, the black cloth parting to reveal fishnet stockings and an overflowing basque. Passing the Leasing boys, she took a playful swipe at Mark Burgess. Jonty Cordwainer bent over, presenting the seat of his trousers, tongue clamped lewdly between his teeth.

Sal lurched towards Lexa in a white sheath so tight it showed the outline of her underwear, 'You came in fancy dress!'

The suit was Tommy Nutter. Another Oxfam find. On Annie Lennox, the magazines Sal read would have called it *androgynous chic.*

Sal put down the glasses she was carrying, 'Have you seen Piers?'

His PA was the only person who called Kinsella by his first name.

'Sorry, no.'

'Must be seeing to the surprise.' She tapped the side of her nose.

Lexa said she was going to get a drink.

An apprehensive look crossed Sal's face, 'He rang again, your friend. Just after lunch.'

Her heart leapt in spite of herself. 'But you told him I was out?'

'He asked if you'd left a message. I said no, and he said it sounded like that was the message . . .'

'And you said it was.'

'He asked me straight out.'

'OK.'

'There's only so many times you can tell someone the person's in a meeting . . .'

'I said it's OK.'

It wasn't, but she would have to live with it. There was no way of explaining to him how hurt she was without compounding her humiliation. *You see, I actually thought you found me attractive. I didn't realise I was just marginally better than masturbation.*

She turned to watch the dance floor. The ultraviolet light picked out white shirts teamed with striped ties and ultra-short pleated skirts. Gavin was dancing with one of these professional schoolgirls. Roland jerked arrhythmically in the orbit of another.

Ben was all over the place, dancing with everyone and no one, shuffling backwards in a moon walk, spinning on one foot and blundering into a secretary as he recovered. One of the lawyers snapped at him and he lifted his hands appeasingly.

'What's happened to those drinks, Sal . . . *Fucking Norah.*' Kinsella's lips curled into an oddly effeminate simper. 'Remind me to give you the name of my tailor.' He took her by the elbow, steering her away from Sal. The first time he had touched her in months. 'I want a word with you.'

She moved her arm free of his grip. 'Can't it wait till Monday?'

'No it fucking can't.' He screwed up his face as if she were behaving oddly, 'You need a drink.'

Though stone-cold sober, she stumbled as she followed him across the floor, uncoordinated with loathing. She had felt like this ever since reading Gabriel's diary. She wanted to strike him, spit in his face, humiliate him in public, but Gabriel had made her promise she would not. It was unbearable, and daily she had borne it, as she had put up with everything else, until she was poisoned with self-doubt. But say she had made her feelings clear: he would only have laughed. And in the face of his laughter, whatever she said or did would have been ridiculous.

She took one sip of the sugary punch and returned her glass to the tray. Kinsella nodded across the club, 'Gabriel finds it very quaffable.'

She was standing by the dance floor. As they watched, she drained her glass. The lights flashed from blue to green and Lexa saw the skeletal prominence of her collarbone, the whittled contour of her arms.

'Where d'you think you're going?' he said.

'She shouldn't be drinking.'

'Since when did you join the Band of Hope?' His fingers closed around her elbow again. 'We haven't had our little talk. While you were at Companies House today I was finalising the reorganisation.'

So her time was up.

'Do you have to do it here?'

'Somebody else'll tell you if I don't—'

Lexa reclaimed her glass from the gymslipped waitress. The punch wasn't so bad if you swigged it straight down.

'—it's official now, I'm in charge. Jonny Rose'll be leaving. It's about time Venture Capital had a shake-up. Nick's in charge of Leasing for now, see how he does, and I'm giving Andrew one last chance to turn round Asset Management. I'll still be running Corporate Finance but there'll be fewer of us. Everyone's going to have to pull their weight. No room for dead wood—'

She steeled herself.

'—you'll have to work for it, but there'll be a bit more in your bank account every month.'

The shock of reprieve welled up inside her, threatening to spill over into tears. 'Is that the surprise?'

'What? No, that's something else.' He glanced over at the bar where Gavin was laughing with a couple of legal secretaries. 'Come on, let's get a proper drink.'

She crossed the club at his side. She still had a job. He hated her clothes and her politics, but her work was too good to let her go.

'A Bloody Mary and a . . .' he turned to Lexa, 'Virgin?'

The barmaid tittered.

Lexa understood then that nothing had really changed. 'Champagne,' she said, to see what would happen.

'Why not? A bottle. And three glasses. Forget the Bloody Mary.' Propping his elbow on her shoulder, he spoke into her ear. 'I've been meaning to thank you for your work on Faxerley Colliery. It was looking dicey for a while, selling in the middle of a strike. London's very pleased with both of us.'

'And Gabriel,' she said.

Gavin was staring at her suit. 'You got a dildo strapped on under there? Only I'd like some warning if I'm going to be meeting you in the Gents.'

Kinsella guffawed.

The barmaid poured the champagne.

'To the director of Venture Capital.'

Gavin dipped his head in acknowledgement.

Lexa blinked as wetness sprayed across her face. Kinsella's shirt was soaked red. Rioja dripped from Gavin's chin. Rae was standing in front of them in a T-shirt and a pair of leather jeans.

'You know what I can't understand—?'

A couple on the edge of the dance floor turned at the sound of her voice.

'—the way you kept saying "do you trust me"? Why would anybody do that when they were going to break every promise they'd ever made? I bet you had a right laugh. Silly cow thinks she's going to get promotion.' She was slipping into dialect, which only happened when she drank. 'But I'll tell you something. You might think I'm a mug for trusting you, but I'm not half as stupid as you are, putting this clown in charge . . .'

A circle of spectators was forming around the bar. The accountants at one of the long tables stood up to get a better view. Kinsella plucked his sopping shirt between thumb and finger, holding it off his chest. He had decided to be amused.

'Can I get you a drink, Rae? Your-*aah* glass seems to be empty.'

Lexa saw that she had rehearsed this scene and, by deviating from the script, Kinsella had thrown her, but she recovered. 'Let's look at the *long game*. Isn't that your thing? You promote your drinking buddy who doesn't have a clue about venture capital. London are making so much money right now, they don't give a toss. But what happens when things get tight? When the market crashes and they start counting the pennies and find the old pals' act up North isn't doing the business, in fact it's been going down the pan from day one? You can sack him, but you're still going to be in a sewerful of shit.'

'This is getting very fecal,' Kinsella murmured, 'do you think she's been taking it up the arse?'

Rae bared her narrow teeth. '*You promised me.* You knew I had other offers. You wanted to keep me, but you didn't want to pay me what I'm worth, so you lied to me.'

'As I remember, the promise cut two ways.'

'So you weren't always going to promote him? Come off it. He doesn't believe it, and neither do I. You're a liar. And the thing about liars is, word gets round. You're a joke. Piers "my word is my bond" Kinsella, with your morning calls to your broker, a grand on this, two grand on that, you woke up with a good feeling about it. *Of course* you've got a good feeling about it: your client's taking over the fucking company the day after tomorrow . . .'

Kinsella moved casually, interposing himself between her and the spectators. 'Shut up, you little tart,' he hissed, 'you don't know what you're talking about.'

'But I do know. You've got a big mouth. You want to lower your voice when you're on the phone.'

'And who are you? Some cunt with a briefcase who lets the clients fuck her all ways up so she can come back to the office with a result.' He remembered the audience, and his venom gave way to a stagey regret, 'You should have offed her when you had the chance.'

Rae gave a breathy laugh. 'What difference does it make to you whether Lori Cooper works here or not?'

'No difference at all,' he said, 'I just wanted you to do it.'

She placed her empty glass on the bar. 'And I didn't want to.'

He waited until she was almost out of earshot. 'Oh-*aah* Rae—'

Her pace slowed but she didn't look back.

He winked at Lexa, '—love the leather.'

Sal had hooked up with the back-office boy who went rally driving at weekends. Ben and one of the schoolgirls were doing a synchronised bump and grind. Lori Cooper danced alone, shifting her weight from leg to leg with a rapid pelvic flick, unaware of the solicitors' clerks behind her, pointing at her buttocks as they sang along with the chorus. 'That's en-ter-tain-ment.'

Lexa clambered on to a table whose chairs had all been stolen, to see the far side of the club. Gabriel had vanished.

'You won, then.'

Ned was looking up at her.

'What?'

'The job. Congratulations.' He flicked the fringe out of his eyes. 'Is the air fresher up there?'

'I'll get down, if you move out of the way.'

'Put your hands on my shoulders.'

'I'll be fine if you move back.'

'Put your hands on my shoulders.'

In the end, it was easier to comply. He lifted her down, staggering under her unexpected weight. In the blurred moment before her feet touched the floor she had the impression he was going to kiss her.

'Thanks.' She stepped back.

'You're on your way now. Team manager in a couple of years, a director in five. You'll be ordering me around before you know it.'

'It's just a rise.'

'And a fall.'

He had the shiny look people gained when things went wrong for others.

'I don't know what you're talking about.'

'Have a guess.'

Goodisons had taught her to expect the worst. 'Not Gabriel?'

'Got it in one.'

She tried, and failed, to think of other ways Gabriel might have fallen. 'Sacked?'

'Surplus to requirements. You got her job.'

'I've got my own job.'

He pulled his high court judge face. 'That's not *strictly* true—'

A waitress moved towards them with a tray of empty glasses. Lexa flattened herself against the blackboard paint to let her past but Ned closed the gap, placing his hands on the wall either side of her head. The waitress went the other way.

'—It's the law of the jungle. Survival of the fittest.' He mimed a lion's snarl in her face. 'The best woman won.'

'I'm not the best woman. And it's got nothing to do with merit. This is down to Kinsella. I'm just the accidental beneficiary.' Behind her distress, she was aware that Ned was standing too close. 'He's been harassing her because she won't sleep with him . . .'

Ned grinned. 'What, old Kinsella?'

'I didn't *win* anything. She's my friend.'

'She'll get another job. She's a looker.'

'Yeah, and that's why they've sacked her.'

He was swaying slightly, his arms not quite braced against the wall.

'I like you, sexy Lexy. But I'm not sure you like me.'

'You're the only one of them I can stomach.'

He giggled. 'That wasn't quite the answer I was hoping for.' He took one hand off the wall and loosened her tie, then unfastened the top button of her shirt, his index finger pressing against the base of her throat. 'That's better, isn't it?'

'You're pissed—'

She ducked her head to get out from under his arm but he moved with her, leaning forward to pin her against the wall.

'—I've got to find Gabriel.'

'As your lawyer I wouldn't recommend it.'

'You're not my lawyer and I need to talk to her.'

'Tell me you like me first.'

'Get off me, Ned, I mean it.'

'Just say it.'

She pushed him off. He yielded a little, then let his whole weight slump against her.

'Come on,' he coaxed. 'It's not much to ask. Three little words. I . . . like . . .'

She hit him, as hard as she could, just under his ribs. The awkward angle diluted the blow but it took him by surprise and he buckled. She twisted under his arm and away. A narrow corridor had opened up along the edge of the dance floor. She shouldered her way through, scanning the faces under the flashing lights, checking the long tables, the bar, the ladies' lavatory.

Rae appeared and handed her a glass.

'I thought you'd gone,' Lexa said.

'If they want me out they can throw me out.'

The expensively-womanly clothes Rae wore at work gave her the tapered elegance of a fashion sketch. In T-shirt and leather jeans, without heels, she was simply undergrown, like the women smoking at bus stops on council estates with a buggy and two toddlers in tow. For the first time Lexa understood just how far she had travelled to become the classy Rae Bergin.

'I don't know about you, but at my school the teachers didn't wear gowns and silly hats. Or carry canes. We got detention, which wasn't that big an influence on our sexuality—'

Lexa's gaze swept the room.

'—if you're looking for Gabriel, she was over there a few

minutes ago, but I shouldn't think she wants to see you.'

Lexa met her eye. 'You know, then.'

'Everyone knows.'

'But do they know why?'

'Do you?'

'They cut one of the jobs. Gabriel won't sleep with Kinsella so she's out.'

Rae laughed nastily. 'There's only – ever – been – one – job. I tried to tell you but you wouldn't listen.'

It made so much sense that Lexa wondered if she had not always known, deep down. 'I'm listening now.'

The DJ put Duran Duran on the turntable, causing most of the men to leave the dance floor.

'Phin was carted off to the booze clinic three days after he did the interviews. His secretary couldn't stand Kinsella so she went sick too. Everyone thought they'd be back in a month. Sal says the files were unbelievable. She had to go through Sheila's shorthand notebook to find out what the hell was going on. "The stunner from Gemmell". So pissed he couldn't remember her name. Sal finds the applications file. Lexa Strachan, from Gemmell. Only Sheila'd already exchanged letters with the Angel Gabriel and opened another file. You should have seen his face the morning she turned up. They could have written to you, bunged you a couple of hundred quid for the misunderstanding, but you know Kinsella: if it's his cock-up he doesn't want to know. Then you were here and it was too late. Alistair Lowe'd just walked out, you'd done accountancy. By the time we knew Phin wasn't coming back, you'd turned out quite useful. But there was no way they were ever going to keep two female graduate trainees . . .'

Lexa's mind was racing, re-assessing everything that had happened over the past ten months.

'. . . funny how things work out. You and Lori Cooper staying. Me and the Angel out the door.' She smiled at Lexa's reaction. 'I think a glass of house red in the kisser counts as a resignation, don't you?'

There was a stir of excitement over by the long tables. Waitresses hastily clearing glasses.

'Ey up,' Rae said, 'looks like it's surprise time.'

Duran Duran faded out and was replaced by a distinctive metronomic beat. A spotlight came on. Kinsella had found a clean shirt from somewhere. He climbed on to one of the long tables, a microphone in his hand. The secretaries stepped on to the benches either side of him and began to dance, shaking their hair and backstroking with their arms in a parody of sixties go-go dancers. He strutted along the table, timing a series of pelvic thrusts to the beat.

It was a rhythm and blues number given the art college treatment. Synthesised cash registers, the melody beaten out on a tin can. But the original female vocals had been erased. Instead, Kinsella half-spoke, half-chanted the lyrics in his crisply patrician voice, the secretaries joining in the call-and-response of the chorus. The upturned faces on the floor soon got the hang of this. When he said 'I want money,' the whole club yelled back *'That's what I want'*.

Lori Cooper climbed on to the makeshift stage. He swaggered towards her and they moved body to body. She unbuttoned his shirt. Sal joined the dance, sandwiching him between them. Julie, the new typist, unlaced his shoes. He stepped out of them, switching the microphone from hand to hand, allowing Sal to remove his shirt. Meanwhile Lori had slipped the top button of his trousers.

He had the body of an overgrown boy, hairless and lacking in muscular definition. Flaunting his head like Mick Jagger, he thrust out his concave chest. Lori lowered herself down his body and tugged the trousers over his stockinged feet. Sal performed a parallel movement behind him, easing down the waistband of his boxer shorts. Rae's eyebrows lifted. He was wearing a gold jockstrap which cupped his genitalia and disappeared into a thong between his buttocks.

Across the table, Ben grinned at Roland. Ned caught Gavin's eye with a conspiratorial look that said *one of us just got away with it*. As if the world were not run by naughty boys.

'I need some fresh air,' Rae said.

The cloakroom was shut, Lexa's mac locked inside. Looking

around for a member of staff, she spotted Gabriel with Kinsella, who was now fully dressed, at the empty end of the club. The darkness made it difficult to read their faces. Then the dance floor lights changed. His hand was fastened around her wrist. She wrenched free and he snatched her bag, emptying it over a table.

Lexa broke into a run.

The sudden alteration in Gabriel's expression reminded her of couples caught rowing in public. That smiling instinct to conceal.

'Lexa.' She gave the name the celebratory boost Lexa remembered from their meetings on the eighth floor, only now it sounded like a stranger's good manners. 'Are you having fun?'

'What's Kinsella doing with your handbag?'

'None of your business,' he said. He unfolded a sheet of paper and tossed it aside. 'And it's Mister Kinsella to you.'

Gabriel was watching him raking through her possessions. 'Congrats on the job by the way, you must be thrilled.'

'I was, until I heard you were out.'

'Oh well,' she said, '*c'est la guerre.*'

She was so thin Lexa could count the ribs above her décolletage. Her throat was flushed, a sign that she had drunk too much. Unless it was the alcohol interacting with the pills. Kinsella started to cram the clutter back into her handbag, cursing as a lipstick rolled off the table, though he made no effort to retrieve it. Lexa was used to seeing him well-oiled, but not like this, so stotious that he had to lean against the furniture. She didn't understand what Gabriel was doing within fifty yards of him.

He pushed the bag across the table, 'Time to go.'

'Bye,' Gabriel sang.

'Both of us,' he said.

Lexa stepped between them. 'You don't have to go anywhere.'

'I don't have to go anywhere,' Gabriel echoed.

Lexa wasn't sure who was being mocked. Over by the bar a cheer went up. Asset Management were standing on the long table, bellowing about not doing it when you want to come, turning an arch gay anthem into a rugby song. She touched Gabriel's wrist. 'What do you say we get a drink at the bar?'

Unsteady as he was, Kinsella could still muster a residual authority. 'You're in danger of making a very stupid career move, Alexandra, so why don't you mind your own business?' He moved towards Gabriel. 'Come on.'

'Come on where?' she inquired, but her mouth betrayed her with a crooked grin.

He grabbed her arm. 'Don't fuck me about—'

Lexa tried to break his grip. He knocked her hand away.

'—I know you took it and I want it back.'

'Want what back?' Lexa asked.

'Want what back?' Gabriel parroted, then yelped as her arm was twisted behind her.

Lexa had never been physically frightened of Kinsella. He had never been violent. But nor had he done a striptease on a tabletop before.

'*Let go of her.*'

'I tell you what, I'll fight you for her.' He laughed in anticipation of his own punchline. 'Or aren't you-*aah* man enough?'

Gabriel tried to pull away. He forced her arm higher up her back.

'You're hurting me.'

He brought his face close to hers. 'Do you want me to let go—?'

She cried out in pain.

'—do you?'

'Yes.' There were tears in her eyes.

'Then hand it over.'

'*I haven't got it,*' she screamed.

'Got *what*?' Lexa was near to screaming herself.

'His bank statement.'

'No one else has been in my bedroom in the last ten days.'

At the other end of the club a slow handclap started up.

Kinsella smiled at the look on Lexa's face. 'Your friend here fucked me then picked my pockets.'

'*Please,*' Gabriel whimpered.

'Is it at your flat?' Lexa asked.

She nodded.

'Let her go. She'll bring it in to work on Monday.'

Kinsella's teeth reflected yellow light from the dance floor,

'Wrong answer.'

Gabriel's face twisted in agony, '*Lexa.*'

'All right,' Lexa said, 'we'll get it now.'

Gabriel staggered as Kinsella released her.

Ben, Simon and Mark Burgess had taken over the long table and were stamping their way through 'I Can't Get No Satisfaction'.

Rae intercepted Kinsella at the door. It was clear from her face that she had seen everything.

'Is this a private party or can anyone come along?'

The streets were quiet, no taxis to hail. An old man asked them for a light, two teenage girls stepped into the gutter to avoid them. They met no one else. The sound of Gabriel's voice made Lexa jump, 'I need the loo.' The bars they had passed had long since closed and she would not hear of peeing down an alley. It was Rae who got them moving again, leading them across the road and round the corner. They stopped outside a row of darkened shops and Lexa recognised the tattoo parlour.

Second time around it was easy. Onto the coal bunker, pulling Rae up after her. *Hoop-la!* Their party trick.

Gabriel was sitting on the edge of the bath. The white enamel glimmered in the sodium light through the window.

'Are you OK?' Lexa asked.

She came closer and heard the breath catch in Gabriel's throat as if she were weeping, yet when she lifted her head her eyes were dry.

'I'm sorry,' she said.

Lexa shrugged.

There was movement beneath them. Gabriel looked towards the stairs in panic, 'Lock the door.'

Lexa shot the puny bolt and perched alongside her. Cartons of Vaseline jars stacked in a corner, a first aid kit, a plumber's wrench. The tiled walls rotated. She was drunk.

Gabriel stared at the floor. 'Every morning it was the first thought in my head: when I get to the office he'll be there. I'd walk out of the lift and I couldn't breathe. This tightness . . .' She pressed a hand to her sternum, as if talking about the symptoms was bringing them back. 'Into the loos, try to take some deep breaths. Every morning. I'd think I was having a heart attack. Lori Cooper was going to find me on the floor and dash through to Corporate Finance to spread the news . . . I hadn't even *seen* him yet. I'd sit in there for twenty minutes, half an hour – all the secretaries knew – until I heard your voice. If I was still in there at quarter past nine, I'd know you'd gone to Faxerley—'

Lexa heard the unspoken accusation.

'—he'd look straight at me when I walked in. It didn't matter who was there. I'd sit down, try to concentrate on what I was supposed to be doing, but my skin would be *crawling*. I couldn't work, I couldn't even *think*. Every word I spoke, he'd be listening. I'd be talking on the phone and he'd be reacting to what I was saying . . .'

'But he spends most of the day in his office.'

Gabriel's smile said that even Lexa had turned against her. 'The door's always open. He's always *popping through*. And once in a while he'd walk in and not look. That really used to get to me. But he was always aware of me. Believe me, I know—'

Into Lexa's head, against her will, came the incredulous face Kinsella would have pulled.

'—you know that radar you have for someone when you're completely infatuated? It's like that. He has the crush, I have the symptoms.'

'It's not a *crush*, it's harassment.'

Gabriel looked up, 'Can't it be both?'

'He's not a schoolboy scribbling your name on his jotter. He was trying to pressurise you into having sex with him. And he succeeded.'

She shook her head. 'It's not that straightforward.'

'No?'

Gabriel looked at the floor again. At last she said, 'You know how when someone's attracted to you, even if you're not interested, you're aware of their awareness of you?'

'Mmm.' It sounded logical.

'They need you, or they need their fantasy of you, and they know you're *not* their fantasy, so they sort of hate you too, or those bits of you that aren't what they want . . . I mean anyone, not just him—'

It had been a long time since Lexa had heard her talk like this.

'—and if you're a woman you've had the conditioning, so

even though you're not attracted to him, and you're picking up the mixed messages, you're still flattered. Somebody wants me, I'm desirable. And then you start to wonder. What is it they desire? What do they see? Is it all fantasy or is some of it real? Maybe they see something you don't see yourself. They're obsessed with you. You're obsessed with their obsession. It's not as if he was operating in a vacuum. I did my bit.'

Lexa couldn't listen to much more of this. 'You know what's wrong with you, Gabriel? You think because you're intelligent you must be the exception to the rule. Everyone else, but not you. It's *sexual harassment*. The victim ends up feeling responsible, asking for it because she wore the wrong clothes, or looked at him the wrong way. She turns the anger she should be feeling towards him against herself. You *know* all this. It's how men get away with it. Do you really think mooning over yourself in the mirror compares with making anonymous phone calls and intimidating you in the office? I'm telling you, you looked *hunted*. You still do.'

A tremor crossed Gabriel's face. Lexa willed her to break down and weep, whatever it took to purge the strain of the past few weeks, but she pulled herself together.

'I just wanted it to *stop*. All the staring and controlling, all the . . .' she made a gift of the word '. . . harassment. You want it to stop, but you *dread* it stopping. Because then he won't want you, and that matters more than anything you feel inside. That's all you are: the thing he wants. And you think, how can I use it while I've still got it? Do you understand?'

There was a beseeching note in her voice, as if Lexa, not Kinsella, were the source of her pain.

'Do you understand?' she repeated.

'I suppose so, but I still don't know why you had to sleep with him.'

Gabriel gave a brief, bitter laugh. 'In other words you don't understand at all.'

'What I don't understand is how you're turning a textbook case of sexual harassment into some sort of tribute to your charms.'

'*I'm trying to explain how it happened.*'

Lexa flinched. Gabriel had never shouted at her before.

She tipped her head back, exposing her throat, that long neck so starved it looked snappable. 'I thought I could control him with sex. I thought if I gave him what he wanted . . . Half an hour, maybe twenty minutes. How bad could it be?'

'And how bad was it?'

She shook her head. 'I'm sorry.'

'There's nothing to apologise . . .'

'*There is.*' She took a breath. 'There is—'

The pink-lipped, plump-cheeked prettiness was gone, along with the bright chase of thoughts, that moment-by-moment engagement with the world, but she was still Gabriel, and Lexa had forgiven her everything for all time.

'—I knew there was only one job. I knew they'd hired you by mistake and Kinsella was letting it slide because it was easier than telling London it was his fault. I knew it couldn't go on for ever. I knew when he put us both on the Faxerley deal that we were in competition. And I knew you didn't know.'

Lexa nodded, relieved that she did not have to feel quite so guilty about getting the job at Gabriel's expense. 'If I'd had half a brain I could have worked it out for myself.'

'I'm surprised the Pocket Venus didn't tell you.'

'She tried, but I wouldn't hear it.'

Gabriel bit her lip. 'I'm sorry.'

'It's all right.'

'*No*, no it's *not*.' Her voice rose as if Lexa were goading her. 'I knew we were competing and I knew you'd win. You don't mind thinking the way they think, going over and over the pointless details. He wasn't even that interested to begin with, but I worked on him. It was supposed to be low-level, just enough to make him feel it might be worth his while keeping me around. He didn't like you anyway, I could see you rubbing his fur the wrong way and I thought I might as well make the most of the situation.'

'So you didn't tell me because you thought it wouldn't make any . . .'

Gabriel cut across her, 'Because you're my best friend and I was trying to cheat you out of a job that was rightfully yours.

Though technically mine. Because when I saw you getting something wrong, on the *extremely rare* occasions I've seen you get *anything* wrong, I thought *hooray!* He could see what was happening. It was a joke between us at first. Then when things turned nasty he used it against me, telling everyone what a *tremendous* job you were doing, how *infinitely superior* you were to me in every way. I knew the reorganisation was coming up, so I played my last card . . .'

A fist hammered on wood. '*Open the fucking door—*' Gabriel screamed.

'*—I need a leak.*'

Lexa slipped the toytown bolt. In the instant before his face appeared she had a vision of her hand picking up the plumber's wrench and striking him. The impact of cast iron on flesh, the crunch of bone and tooth. He pushed past her. Gabriel leapt to her feet. He had his flies open before they were out of the room.

Rae was sitting in the tattooist's chair, leafing through a dog-eared copy of *Playboy*. Catching sight of Gabriel's expression, her eyes flicked enquiringly at Lexa. They heard the cistern flush and Kinsella came downstairs, missing his footing at the bottom, steadying himself with a drunken assurance that no one had noticed. He prowled the room, inspecting the photographs of women in leather bikinis, a slack-jawed grin on his face.

'So this is where you hang out.'

Had he forgotten about the bank statement? Lexa caught Rae's eye and nodded towards the door, but Rae returned to the magazine.

He switched on the electric kettle. 'Now what would you three be doing in a place like this?' He looked at Gabriel, who looked away. 'I know she hasn't got one, unless she's had it done since last week.' Rae's eyes widened at this news. 'My money's on Rae, but it could be-*aah* . . . Are tattoos part of the cross-dressing thing? Or does it get the shop steward's motor running? *Fuck*, he'd need something.'

Without lifting her head Rae said, 'Shut up, Kinsella.'

'Make me—'

She darted a glance at Lexa.

'—or have you both had it done . . .?'

In a single fluid movement Rae stood up, turned her back and peeled her T-shirt over her head. She wasn't wearing a bra.

Lexa was reminded of a dog picking up a scent.

'So that's what they're wearing on the council estates this year.'

Rae pulled the T-shirt down again, but it was too late, she had moved the evening on to a different level. They all felt it.

Kinsella slumped onto the vinyl couch, kicking Lexa's jacket to the floor. On the draining board, the electric kettle started to grumble.

'Shame about the-*aah* job,' he said. 'It was London's idea—'

Rae was back in the tattooist's chair, flipping through the magazine too rapidly to be looking at the pages.

'—they've pulled in some deals that have to be serviced up here and they want someone they can trust, with the right background. You can't expect them to put a girl from the slums in charge.'

Rae lifted her eyes to Lexa. 'The trouble with Kinsella is he thinks there are only two sorts of people. The ones with tattoos and criminal records, and the ones who leave the bottom button of their waistcoat undone. He hasn't worked out that anyone can have a tattoo. People get pissed, spur of the moment. And there's plenty of crooks don't have a mark on them. Like the sort of bloke who makes himself a few thou' every year insider dealing.'

The bubbling kettle switched itself off. Kinsella yawned, 'If there's no milk I'll have two sugars.'

Gabriel was nearest the draining board, leaning against the wall, arms folded.

Rae dropped the magazine, 'Course, insider trading's legal in this country. It's bent, obviously, but it's not against the law, not like shoplifting or fiddling the meter, the sort of thing the criminals on council estates get put away for. The trouble with working for the Americans is, they've got no sense of proportion. They'll sack him anyway.'

Lexa bent down to retrieve her jacket from under the couch. The floor canted like a ship's deck, and then Kinsella was on top of her, forcing her head down, tugging the shirt out of her trousers. Her stomach heaved at the stink of cigarettes, the hot touch of his clumsy fingers pulling the cloth up over her back.

As abruptly as he had overpowered her, he let her go and fell back on the couch. 'Just checking. I thought you might have a matching one, you two being such good friends. Don't worry, I-*aah* don't want to see the rest—'

She straightened up.

'—make me a coffee, Gabriel, there's a good girl.'

Gabriel had stepped away from the wall. Her now-redundant intention was still readable on her face.

Rae swivelled in her chair. 'So Gabriel, what's all this about a bank statement?'

'I found it on his bedside table—'

To Lexa's knowledge this was the first conversation Gabriel and Rae had ever had.

'—I was bored, listening to him snoring.'

He leered at Lexa. 'I'd-*aah* had a bit of a workout.'

As if he hadn't spoken, Rae said 'I don't suppose it shows any credits from a broker. Like Grilse Dearing or . . .'

Gabriel moved towards the kettle. 'Rutherford Cornwallis. Four thousand pounds.'

Rae nodded. 'That *is* interesting.'

He stretched out, swinging his feet up onto the arm of the couch. 'She's not what you'd call-*aah* active in the sack. Makes you sweat for it, if you know what I mean—'

Gabriel pulled back the curtain under the sink and found a jar of Maxwell House and a bag of sugar. The spoon clinked rhythmically as she stirred.

'—I've seen it before with her type. They go on and on about equality, but what they really want is a bit of force—'

Gabriel carried the steaming mug across the room and held it above his groin.

'—Rae here likes it doggy-style. Apparently. I'm not speaking from personal-*aah* . . . It's all those years hanging around the streets, watching the strays going at it. But you're the-*aah* shocker. We all thought you liked cunt. Well, Ned kept hoping. Then we find out you've spread 'em for a proletarian dwarf . . .'

His arm lashed out and knocked the mug from Gabriel's hand. The coffee flew in an arc across the room, the china smashing on the floor. Lexa wasn't sure which of them moved first, only that she was pinning his legs, knotting her tie around his ankles, and Rae was on his chest, struggling with his arms, as Gabriel pulled the belt from his trousers to bind his wrists. He fought them, thrashing under their weight, one hand escaping to clout Rae so hard that Lexa was afraid he'd broken her jaw. He had a drunk's blundering strength, but they had three times the adrenaline.

Tenderly Rae patted the side of her face. 'Now what were we talking about? Oh yeah . . .'

She got up and crossed the room. Gabriel took her place on his chest. Dimly, Lexa was aware of a sober world in which Kinsella would not have been tied up. But this was better. Let him see how it felt.

She was startled to hear the whine of the tattooing machine.

'I think we should do an experiment,' Rae said, 'in the interests of science. Does having a tattoo make you any more of a shithead? I'd say not, but I'm ready to be proved wrong.' She brought the machine up to his face so he could see the needles. 'What do you reckon, ladies? On the bicep? Oh no, that's right, he hasn't got one.'

'That's enough.' He sounded surprisingly normal under the circumstances.

Rae frowned. 'It'll have to be a word. I was rubbish at art.'

'Crook?' Gabriel suggested.

'Why not?'

With a tearing groan Kinsella launched himself upwards, dislodging Gabriel and cutting off the machine. Lexa moved fast, slamming her weight down into his solar plexus. Winded, he gasped.

Gabriel fiddled with the crocodile clips until the noise started up again.

'OK,' Rae said. 'Crook it is. On the right hand. So the clients see it every time he shakes on a deal.'

'*Fuck off.*' His voice was hoarse.

Gabriel double-checked the belt around his wrists, making

sure it would hold.

Rae tested the needles against the vinyl skin of the couch, 'Or we could write arsehole on his arse.'

Gabriel sniggered, revealing an unexpected current of affinity between them.

When she unzipped his trousers his resistance became frenzied. He bucked and swore. The buzzing machine fell to the lino. But Lexa knew how to control him now.

He retched.

'You going to be a good boy and turn over?' Rae said.

Experimentally, Lexa got up.

He lay there with his flies open, taking wheezing breaths.

Rae put one hand on his ribcage, the other hand on his hip, and pushed, but he was heavy and the couch too narrow. She couldn't turn him. 'Looks like it's going to have to be crook.'

He didn't believe they would do it, even now. Lexa could tell. But if it was all a bluff, who was going to say stop?

'What about *prick*, on his prick?' Gabriel suggested.

'*You frigid bitch.*'

'Manners,' Rae said.

'You know her problem, don't you?' He was looking at Lexa. 'What this is really about. She came round to my place, all tarted up . . .'

'She knows,' Gabriel said loudly.

'. . . "I've got a proposition for you"—'

It was startling how accurately he caught her intonation.

'—"I do something for you, you do something for me".'

'*I've told her*,' Gabriel said.

Rae reached for the bottle of ink.

'"I'll fuck you any way you want",' his lips made the faint smack of a kiss, '"if you sack Lexa".'

Gabriel struck his face.

It must have hurt, but he laughed.

Lexa felt a tearing as if her heart were being dragged out through her chest.

Rae poured a capful of ink. 'We're going with crook, yeah?'

'No.' Lexa pushed down the waistband of his boxer shorts, exposing the strip of pale skin just above his pubic hair. '*Rapist.*'

2006

FEBRUARY

At parties, when Lexa was asked what she did for a living, she always said 'I work in Cambusdyke'. It was easier than watching them struggle for an intelligent question about conflict resolution. And they were so titillated by vicarious contact with Scotland's most notorious housing scheme, it would have been cruel to deny them. Eyes agleam, they would ask what it was *really like*, and she'd describe a typical day, neglecting to mention that this day came round just once a week and was, strictly speaking, an afternoon. It seemed to her everyone had a stake in the Cambusdyke mythology: politicians; suburban ghouls; the red-top press; the residents, of course; and the army of carers and support workers and facilitators paid to improve its deprivation-index rating.

On her first visit she'd had to drive on to the pavement to avoid a three-piece suite on fire in the middle of the road. Cambusdyke was known for recreational arson and the stoning of the firemen who arrived to extinguish these blazes. Millions had been spent on the brand-new school, health centre, community complex (library, theatre, recording studio, cafe and gym) and twelve state-of-the-art, vandal-proof bus shelters, none of which had survived. Streets had been renamed to shed their stigma and, when the local taxi firms still refused to pick up fares from them, demolished. Artists-in-residence had supervised the creation of several community murals (immediately defaced). A dreadlocked muso had led drumming workshops and known a brief, unhappy fame as the one black face on the scheme. Resting actors in clown costumes toured the high school giving out free fruit and multicoloured condoms. And still Cambusdyke led Scotland in heart disease, hepatitis B, registered heroin use, benefit fraud, teenage pregnancy, illiteracy, innumeracy, unemployment, mental illness, and a type of facial scarring known as the 'Cambusdyke smile'.

Lexa had other clients. The revolting reference librarians and their book-hating, jargon-spouting managers. The Parks Department gardeners who refused to replace their bedding plants with wildflowers (or, as they saw them, 'weeds'). The blue-rinsed volunteers who couldn't understand why the 'coloured gentlemen' in the hospital canteen were making such a fuss. Plus all the boards and committees and steering groups wanting quick-fix resolutions. In almost every case, she made a small but observable difference. On Thursdays she adjusted her definition of success. Getting past the methodone-nodders slumped around the chemist's doorway. Persuading the hash-smokers not to light up. Finishing a session without the police being called (not that they came, or never in time to break up the fight). Returning to the car park to discover that she would not be taking the Micra in for another respray in the morning, assuming she wasn't car-jacked on her way home. She wasn't disliked. A figure of sly amusement, sometimes, but it wasn't like being thrown to the lions. She was friendly with most, and fond of some, as they seemed fond of her. When she'd started in Cambusdyke the key phrase had been 'social inclusion', now it was 'community capacity building', but the principle was the same: salvation by self-esteem. And the community's self-esteem had been bolstered by Lexa and others like her. But what the social policy-makers could not afford to see, and the community saw only too clearly, was that becoming less dysfunctional could only erode community pride. God forbid they should lose their regular slot on the television news.

'Tell him, Miss.'

They all called her 'Miss' in the sessions, as if she were a schoolteacher. With the mingled deference and disrespect implied.

'Lexa,' she corrected for the thousandth time, and then, to a grey-faced largely-toothless man who was all of thirty-five, 'let Gemma have the talking-stick, Billy.'

'Naw. I'm talking the noo, amn't I?'

'Ye urny.'

'Aye I am.'

'All right,' Lexa interposed, 'Billy can finish and then we'll hear from Gemma.'

Silence.

'Billy?'

'I canny mind what I was gonny say, can I?'

'Gie us the fucking stick, then.'

Lexa's policy was to treat swearing as working-class vernacular unless used with aggressive intent. But in Cambusdyke aggression, too, was intrinsic to local speech.

The problem – the *presenting* problem – was territorial gangs. Children couldn't get to school. The Glennie Young Team couldn't cross Meadow Street without getting a *doin'* from the Cambie Mental Posse. The CMP took similar risks west of Hamilton Road. Gang membership was automatic, a birthright of both sexes, but had hitherto lapsed past the age of twenty. Now there were men as old as twenty-seven turning up in A&E, and not just for the stitching of their Cambusdyke smiles. Every few weeks the injury was a bullet wound. When Lexa convened her weekly session there was real fear in the room. Fear, excitement, vainglorious exaggeration, and the lust to avenge their own with spectacular violence to others. And no one present was an actual gang member. They would attend in the indefinitely-postponed Phase Two. Investment in the conflict was a feature of all resolution work. It wasn't meant to be easy: that's why she was paid. But still sometimes she asked herself why she had chosen a career in this particular line of difficulty?

'Are youse the prayer meeting?'

Even Lexa twitched a smile. He stood in the doorway, surveying the twenty-odd people in the room, and letting himself be surveyed. White trainers, Adidas tracksuit bottoms, a sliver of Rangers' blue revealed by the half-open zip of his waterproof jacket, his skunk-dyed hair long on top, with a hip-hop pattern shaved into the back. It was the standard look for local males between the ages of two and fifty.

'We're the neighbourhood council,' she said, gesturing to the ever-empty seat beside her, 'join us, if you like'.

This was his cue to turn and go, cutting short the interruption, but instead he advanced into the room to grasp, turn and straddle the profferred chair.

'I'm Lexa.'

'Bammer.'

'Bammer,' she echoed coolly.

No one laughed. She wondered if they didn't dare.

Gemma was handed the talking-stick, and returned to the perennial rumour that a paedophile was haunting the children's play area. Chelsi interrupted to complain about Gemma's Barbie-pink Clio with the Powerflow exhaust and LED down-lights. This prompted Corinna to raise Chelsi and Kyle's noisy sex sessions, and Kyle to accuse Corinna's Staffordshire bull terrier of shiteing all over the pavements night after night. At which point Lexa reminded them that they were here to address the issue of no-go areas.

Bammer turned, fastening her with his blinkless blue stare. 'Can I say something?'

She nodded. Kyle handed him the stick without being asked.

'When the CMP stop selling on our turf they can walk where they like.'

Wee Kenny McQ slipped out at the back to tell God knew who, and Lexa understood that if they hadn't turned up by the end of this session they'd be there mob-handed at the next. And even as her stomach knotted in anxiety she felt a sort of relief, because the great unspoken was out in the open and the real work could now begin.

'Got a light?'

Bammer was standing in front of the Micra.

'I don't smoke,' she said.

He shrugged and, pulling a book of matches from his pocket, lit his joint. 'Gonny gie us a lift?'

'I'm not insured to carry clients.'

'I'll no sue you, then.'

She moved past him, towards the car. He put out a hand to block her and, when she looked him in the eye, pointed at the large turd she had almost stepped on. 'Corinna's dug,' he said. So then she had to smile.

He was going into Glasgow. It was on her way. And there was just a chance he would tell her something helpful. In the close confines of the Micra he was even younger than she'd thought. No scars as yet, and no shaving line that she could detect. He said he had a lot of customers like her. Businessmen and women. She told him he was wasting his time but either he didn't believe her or he was desperate to impress. West End folk. Faces he saw on telly sometimes. They could rely on him for the quality gear. She let him talk, trying to calculate the number of links in the chain between him and the people she needed to attend her Thursday afternoon sessions.

Her mobile rang. Before she could stop him, he lifted it from the dashboard.

'She's busy the now. She'll call you in five.'

'Who was it?' she asked.

'Some guy Stuart,' he said.

The hotel dated from the mid-1990s. Mirrored glass, electric revolving doors, muzak battling with running water and the bass notes of manly conversation. Lexa was reminded of an airport departure lounge: a sealed capsule indifferent to day or night. The same headachy charge in the air, the same subliminal hum of air conditioning and lights. And that sense of being about to leave solid ground. Looking around, she spotted the indoor fountain, saw the muzak was a pianist at a shiny black baby grand. She should have bought new clothes, a thought she had dismissed a dozen times over the past twenty-four hours. Too late now to do anything but dismiss it again. Why not new shoes, too? With heels of course (no woman here was wearing flats), in which case she'd have needed sheer tights, and a leg wax, and a manicure so she didn't snag the micromesh, and a face pack before the full make-up she wouldn't have known how to apply, and maybe a Botox jag on her frown lines and a chicken-fillet bra. And who would he have met after all this preparation? What chance would she have had of being herself?

She spent several weeks a year working away from home so she was used to hotels. She had some paperwork in her bag. Not that she was so very early, but she had a hunch he'd be late. She didn't want to sit here watching the lifts and have to pounce on him the minute he arrived. Let him recognise her. If there was anything left to recognise.

'Lexa?'

She turned.

His beautiful, abundant, steel-coloured hair was gone; in its place a colourless stubble cut to a quarter-centimetre all over, the pink of his scalp showing through. His face too was pink: the close-shaven jaw, the weathered flush of forehead and cheek. He was lucky with that strong square head, not all men carried the loss of their best feature so successfully. He was wearing moleskin trousers and Gore-Tex boots. On his wrist, amid the thickly-curling hairs, was a chunky black rubber watch. One more prop and he could have stepped off a mountain.

He stood up and she was briefly disconcerted by his lack of height. She sat down quickly before he could kiss her. Or show no intention of doing so.

'Long time,' he said.

She felt her lips set in a sceptical line.

There was a pause while each waited for the other to broach the reason for this meeting. He seemed equally relieved when the moment was postponed. First – he tried to catch the eye of a waitress, who veered off to the other side of the lounge – first, the exchange of news. He had left the NUM five years ago for a career post with a bigger union, and was now touring the regions to canvas support for the deputy general secretary's job.

'A wee tip. Don't tell your Scottish voters they're a region.'

He fixed her with his narrowed gaze. 'Are you going to be setting tartan traps for me all night?'

'I don't know, are we going to be together all night?'

She realised what she'd said.

He pulled his old lower-tooth grin.

She had planned to take him out to eat, had pictured herself in a booth at Gillies, explaining clapshot and crappit heids and cranachan, but he'd booked a table in the hotel restaurant. He hoped she liked fusion cooking. He dabbled in the kitchen. Made a mean stir-fry, if he said it himself. Finding the time, that was the problem. She'd be the same, now she'd left equal opps for conflict resolution. So that was her news scooped. She had Googled him too, of course, but she'd had the grace to feign ignorance.

He thought she'd be living in New York by now. 'Bankrupting the Third World from your office on Wall Street.'

'You never really knew me, did you?'

For a moment he was taken aback. He looked away, his eyes following another retreating waitress. 'I thought I did,' he muttered, 'but maybe not.'

The pianist was playing the Arctic Monkeys in the style of Mantovani. She used the pretext of scanning the room to avert her burning face. 'Have they got something against our table?'

'Search me.' He stood up. 'White wine, wasn't it?'

She watched him make his way to the bar. He had lost that lightness on his feet, his old animal grace. He looked like a football manager: stocky, still powerful, but never again to run with the crowd's roar behind him. She recalled the man he had been so vividly, she could not believe he was gone. It was as if she could look past the paunchy impostor crossing the floor and find him leaning on the bar, still twenty-eight with a full head of hair, still pretending to be the fixer he had since become.

'You never used to drink spirits,' she said when he came back.

'It's water.'

She put down her wine, 'I didn't realise I was drinking alone.'

'Does it bother you?'

'Yes,' she lifted the glass again, 'but I'll get over it.'

'I'm not an alcoholic, if that's what you're thinking. It wasn't helping with the weight. I went on a diet for a month, gave it up, couldn't believe how much better I felt . . .' He tailed off, seeing her smile.

'Do you belong to a gym, Stuart?'

'Yeah.'

'And you've given up red meat and panatellas, and you use a light moisturiser on your skin?'

His green-blue eyes flashed. 'What are you saying?'

She had been trying to tease him, but even she could hear it hadn't come out like that. 'Just trying to position you. Metrosexual. Health-conscious. Hillwalker. Brownite? Blairite?'

'Nobody's a Blairite now.'

'But you used to be.'

'And you weren't?' His look swept her head-to-foot. 'In equal opps?'

All at once she felt tired, foreseeing an evening filled with these abrasions. The pianist had switched to The Beatles. 'The Long and Winding Road.' They let its schmaltz wash over them.

'You used to be a six-pints-a-night man.'

'That were when I were with you, on best behaviour,' he said in dialect, and something inside her almost broke.

'Are you still living there?' she said at last.

'Nah. It's bandit country now. They shut Dudderthorpe pit in ninety-two. That were start of it. Lads who got jobs moved out, nobody wanted to move in. Faxerley shut Christmas 2000. Council shipped in problem families. Kids got into houses they couldn't let. You can buy smack on Thomas Street now. I go back every two week, see lads at welfare, but I wouldn't want to live there.'

Vandalism, drug addiction, spiralling decline . . . What could be more familiar? And yet a part of her was shocked. She had thought it would never change. Like that twenty-eight year old with his stainless-steel hair.

He was living in Leeds now. The Union headquarters was behind Park Square. He had a flat just along from Leeds Bridge, in one of the new blocks they'd built to look like warehouse conversions.

'I saw a kingfisher last week. There's a bar downstairs. Couple o' decent restaurants five minutes up the road. Live music if I fancy it. Dawn chorus o' pile-drivers every morning. It's still the North but it's not a museum.' He sipped his water. 'You went back to Gemmell?'

'I've got a flat in a street of millworkers' tenements. The mill's a business centre now.'

He was waiting for her to say more, supply a few cues he could pick up over the course of the evening. It was uncivil not to oblige. She owed him nothing, but she had agreed to meet him.

'It's a nice community. A lot of single mothers in their thirties and forties, the odd Polish family. We run our own ceilidhs, hold a freecycle shop on Saturday mornings in the credit union—'

He choked.

'—you find that funny?'

He pointed at his throat. 'The water. Went down wrong way.' His eyes dropped to the table, embarrassed for her.

She groped for a remark to move things on, but her mind was blank. They were working too quickly through their quota of possible conversations. Another five minutes and there'd be nothing left to talk about. Nothing except the real reason they were sitting here.

*

They were led to a table with a view over the Clyde. The waiter unfolded Lexa's napkin with a matador flourish and spread it across her lap. She looked around at their fellow diners. A couple of custom-tailored cowboys (haulage contractors? landfill millionaires?), but mostly middle-managers in Hugo Boss treating their secretaries or girlfriends on expenses. There was a good deal of cleavage on show in various shades of toffee and buttermilk and tanning-shop orange, all of it expensively wrapped.

Stuart seemed at home here, sitting in his throne-size Empire chair poring over the menu. One glance had been enough for her to make up her mind. The restaurant was heated for the comfort of its semi-naked customers and she was starting to sweat in her merino wool. She stared longingly at the flags staking out the hotel courtyard as they snapped against the oxtail sky. She could have been out there walking along the river, the wind sharp across the water, jouncing the reflected lights.

Turning away from the window, she found him watching her. 'You're just the same.'

She raised an eyebrow. 'Did no one ever tell you the art of paying a compliment is to make it half-believable?'

'You've still got your long legs. Or am I not allowed to say that?'

'It's a free country. So I'm told.'

She noticed a huddle of waitresses, all slim and pretty and under twenty-five, looking towards their table. Evidently they were being discussed. Not with smirks or suppressed laughter, but with the conspiratorial body language of social drama.

Stuart leaned back in his chair, 'Have I changed much?'

She studied the tangle of grizzled hair in the open neck of his shirt. He had learned the power of understatement in dress: luxury in neutral shades, textures which begged to be touched. His eyebrows too were turning grey, but his lashes, like his hairy arms, were still coal black.

'Unrecogniseably,' she said.

'You'd walk past me in the street?'

'I don't just mean physically.'

'What then?'

It occurred to her that he, too, wanted a reunion with his twenty-eight-year-old self.

'You wouldn't have asked me that before, in case you didn't like the answer.'

'So I'm more confident?'

'Or more used to people telling you what you want to hear.'

He laughed. 'You could be right.'

She had a sudden memory of him sitting up in bed, bare-chested, wearing this same self-satisfied look. Her first real love affair. That way her body would click into his orbit.

Their eyes met. For a long moment neither spoke.

'Are you married, Lexa?'

Somehow the use of her name made the question less personal. She waggled the fingers of her left hand, 'No ring.'

'Boyfriend?'

'Not at the moment.' She felt her eyes become shifty. The truth was *not for three years*. 'And you?'

'Do I have a boyfriend?'

'Are you married?'

'No. Well, yeah, separated. You know how it is—'

Not really, she thought.

'—least there's no kids this time round. Ryan's in America now, postgraduate research at MIT. Polymer hydrogels as drug delivery vehicles, whatever that is when it's at home.' He picked up the wine list. 'How do you feel about Chablis?'

'Not keen enough to drink a bottle on my own.'

'I'll help you out with a glass or two.'

'I thought you were off it.'

'It's not every day I meet up with an old friend.'

'Is that what I am?'

He met her look. 'I don't know. You tell me.'

The waiter stepped forward to take their order.

The elaborate rituals of pricey restaurants. After the wine, which Stuart insisted she taste, the *amuse bouches* turned up. Then there was the food to be chosen, the advice about what was especially good that night. The starters. The solicitous enquiry: was everything all right? She nodded, but actually it was pretty average.

Stuart took a sip of Chablis and pouted appreciatively. 'How come you left Goodisons?'

'I'm not sure I remember now.'

He looked at her over the rim of his glass, 'They didn't catch you doing something you shouldn't've?'

'Like what?'

Another pout, 'Sleeping with the other side?'

'You think it was because of you?'

'It crossed my mind, mulling it over in the lonely nights.'

'They didn't sack me, I resigned, and it had nothing to do with you.'

He cut into his langoustine. 'I'm glad to hear it.'

The lonely nights. She was swept by a wave of irritation. It wasn't just that he was flirting with her, he was flirting with the facts, inventing this hokey ending when they both knew fine what had happened. Forcing her to play along because she didn't want to look like the kind of woman who would brood over a twenty-year-old slight.

'What was it, then?' he persisted.

She drank. The wine was just right. Faintly mineral, cold and clean. 'I was a fish out of water. I used to do that. Go for jobs where I'd have nothing in common with anyone around me. I should never have worked there in the first place.'

'Aye well, if we could take every decision with twenty-twenty hindsight . . .'

A different sort of silence fell between them.

'You mean Faxerley?' She felt stronger for being the one to say it.

'It weren't me who took decisions at Faxerley.'

'Is it a . . .' She realised where this sentence was going and had to start again. 'Are they in a lot of pain?'

'What do you think?'

She put down her fork. The food had turned to ashes in her mouth.

Ten dead. Another thirty-five in the queue. Men she had known. As soon as Bammer got out of the car, she had returned Stuart's call, her heart thudding at the ringing tone. The sound of his voice snatched the breath from her throat. Her fluster was shaming now. The tumours were caused by asbestos, that was the sick joke. All that coal dust they'd breathed in, only to contract an asbestos-related cancer. They were sueing for compensation, but – guess what? – liability was disputed. A chain of torts stretched from the mine's last owners, Inverspall, to Beronex, to Lockend, now in the hands of the receivers, to Lockend's insurers, who had also gone bust. And finally, to Lockend's agents in the sale, long since swallowed by a continental bank.

He finished his langoustines, leaving the garnish. 'And they've not asked you for an affidavit?'

'I told you, no.' But her expression gave her away.

'Let's have it,' he said.

By chance she knew someone in the firm of solicitors instructed by Inverspall. An old lover. Not that they'd parted on friendly terms. He'd told her a little, but put the phone down on her when she rang back.

'The share price has been shaky for a while. It makes more sense for them to stall for a court hearing than have a pay-out put a hole in this year's results.'

'You're saying they're not going to settle?'

'It doesn't look like it.'

His face contorted. 'We need that money now. Once you get diagnosis you're looking at life expectancy of eighteen month. If you're lucky. We haven't got time to fuck about for t'sake of Inverspall's annual results—'

There was nothing she could say.

'—you know what happens to 'em? Their lungs seize up. They put 'em on pure oxygen but it dun't make any difference. They can't get a breath. You wouldn't know Mick now. Fifty-four and he's like an old man—'

So Mick was one of the claimants. She was sorry, though she found she still bore him a grudge.

'—remember deep voice he had? You can hardly hear him now. They won't take him into hospital. They say he's better off at home. He'll be dead this time next year, if he lasts that long. Money's no good to him then.'

She took a gulp of wine. 'I don't know what you think I can *do*.'

He leaned across the table, 'I want the lot. Who they're talking to, what they're thinking, QC they'll be using.' He pointed a finger at her. 'And don't tell me you don't know. If lawyer won't tell you, there's your old pals from Goodisons. You can find out.'

The diners at the next table were looking at them.

She dropped her voice. 'You don't understand. I can't have contact with them.'

'Course you can.' Belatedly something in her tone got through to him, 'What don't I understand?'

She shook her head, 'I just can't.'

'And that's it, is it?'

Last night, after they'd spoken on the phone, she'd spent hours on the net, then gone to bed and dreamed of wasting bodies, fluid-choked lungs, corpses dissected on the pathologist's slab. There were hundreds of Dieters and Gustavos and Bobby Joes out there, all with the same determination to beat this thing, the same trust in some miracle-working maverick on the other side of the world. And the widow's postscript, added a year or two later. The medical sites were worse. Brachytherapy, pleurectomy, thoracentesis, extrapleural pneumonectomy. So much ingenious intervention but, in the end, the same futility. They were dying. And yes, that was it.

'I left Goodison Farebrother *twenty-two years ago*. I didn't even deal with the buyer. That was Gabriel's job. I can't drag Inverspall into court. If they want to stall it . . .'

He shook his head, talking over her. 'No. You're wrong. They'll settle. They've no choice. Every month they put it off it'll end up costing 'em more. There's men *dying*, counting days, lying awake nights worrying what's going to happen to wife and kids when they're gone. Money won't give 'em their health back, but it'll make hell of a difference to time they've got left.'

'And I really hope you get them some, but I can't help.'

Finally he heard her. It was more than disappointment, he looked stunned. She was furious with him for pinning his hopes on her, and sorrier than she could bear.

A waitress approached the table. Avoiding their eyes, she collected the dirty plates. Lifting Stuart's langoustine shells, her awkwardness intensified. No sooner had she left than a colleague arrived with the next course. Polish or Czech, a dancer's shapely legs under her long starched apron. She saw Stuart looking and let go of his plate a fraction too early so that a drop of creamy sauce splashed his shirt.

'Excuse,' she said curtly, turning away.

Once she was out of earshot, Lexa asked, 'Have you eaten here before?'

'I just got in this morning.'

'And you've not been harassing the chambermaids?'

'You what?'

'I'm joking, Stuart.' Though she wasn't, necessarily. 'The staff don't seem to like you.'

'I'm not that struck on them. You don't expect to interrupt 'em shagging in the ensuite in a five-star hotel.'

'You didn't?'

'It's not sort o' thing you make a mistake about.'

'And you complained?'

'You're dead right I did.'

'And they've been disciplined?'

'They won't do it again.'

She waited in vain for the irony to dawn on him.

'Whatever happened to the class struggle?' she said.

'Same as happened to feminism. It stopped being easy excuse for folk who've only theirselves to blame.'

He raised his hand to call their waiter, making a little squiggle in the air to signify the bill. Neither of them had touched the food in front of them. She remembered sitting on the other side of the negotiating table from him, how she would have given anything to get his mouth to relent from this grim line. Only now she had nothing to give.

The bill was a long time coming.

'If I were sort to take bat and ball home,' he said, 'I reckon it's me who should have face on.'

'What d'you mean?'

He exhaled in disgust. 'Think about it.'

'Just tell me, Stuart.'

He looked at her as if they had been skirting this subject all evening. 'A goodbye would have been nice. I were bit slow on uptake in them days. I din't catch on you'd be finished with me when pit were sold.'

She stared at him in amazement. Mick had never told him. He had no idea why she had dropped him. She reminded herself that he had said it just the same. "All cats are grey int' dark". But in his eyes *he* was the injured party. She didn't like him thinking ill of her all these years, but it drew some of the sting of her own humiliation. And what was the point of reopening old wounds? They would never see each other again.

'It was a bad time,' she said, 'Gabriel had a sort of breakdown.'

'Gabriel?' He frowned, 'When were this?'

'That summer. The boss pressured her into having sex with him, then sacked her. If it happened now it'd cost them a couple of million.'

But he wasn't really interested in what had happened to Gabriel. She watched him sign the dinner to his room. She had told herself she held no expectations of this evening, but all day her pulse had been racing. She had changed her clothes three times, smiling into the mirror, trying to see herself with unaccustomed eyes. And now it was over. When the taxi pulled up to the hotel forecourt, he didn't even shake her hand.

2009

JULY

The vehicle in front was a forty-year-old camper van. A screeching fan belt, more rust than paint. Two security guards stepped out of their bomb-proof glass to watch it pass, fingers on the triggers of their rubber radios. Only bankers took this road. The black tarmac pavements were patchless, gum-free, sleek as wall-to-wall carpet and empty as far as the eye could see. Fifteen thousand people worked here, and it looked like the aftermath of a neutron bomb. That dated her. Who remembered neutron bombs these days? Who remembered WMD, and that was just six years ago? Things changed so fast, if you didn't delete your old files you might run out of capacity.

It was less than twenty years since this patch of monochrome Edinburgh had been razed and rebuilt as a slice of Technicolor America. Lexa had often walked through the old quarter but had no clear memory of it now. It seemed to her that the super-size chunks of tinted glass and yellow stone with their vast, blank plazas had redrawn the map, squatting across the web of former streets. Most Edinburgh buildings were narrow and high, like plants straining for the northern light. These corporate headquarters suggested the ozoneless skies of Houston or Phoenix. Even on a sunny day they looked wrong, the fatty deposits of a boom that already felt like ancient history.

Rae turned the radio off. 'Well?'

'Well what?'

'Just checking you've not lost the power of speech.'

'You don't want to hear it,' Lexa said reasonably.

'You got that right.'

They turned down the ramp into the car park.

'I just think you're making a mistake.'

Rae's features reflected the wearying predictability of her taking such a view, 'Bloody profitable mistake.'

'If it doesn't blow up in your face.'

Rae slotted the Porsche into a parking bay. 'I have salaries to pay.'

Her turnover was down fifteen per cent, and this was just the beginning. In a couple of years she'd remember this as Easy Street. Lexa too. When they looked down the list at schools, social work, refuse collection and touchy-feely luxuries like conflict resolution, which did she think they were going to choose?

'And you really want to be the front-woman for public enemy number one?'

Rae grinned, 'That's RBS.'

'You're still supping with the devil.'

'Give us a break, it's not like I'm fronting-up land mines. Or even cigarettes.'

She killed the engine, and made her case.

'All right, banks aren't very popular just now. You think they're going to go away? Alison Babbington's a decent woman who walked into a wasps' nest. She could do with a bit of support. They're all waiting for Caledonian to go belly-up so they can say "they should never have had a woman CEO". She's a walking XX chromosome. But Fred and Andy, they're *individuals*. And while we're on the subject of double standards—'

Lexa raised her hands.

'—and *supping with the devil . . .*'

'OK, OK.'

They looked at each other.

'Say it, then.'

Lexa sighed, 'Gabriel sold her soul a long time ago.'

It was one of those magnesium-bright summer mornings. Emerging, dazzled, from the underworld of the car park, Lexa saw the vista she was expecting, an empty expanse of grey marble crossed only by the flagpoles' slanting shadows. Then the sun dipped behind a cloud. There were several hundred people in the plaza. Women in the office-worker spectrum of navy, grey and black. Men in suits. Lipsticked smilers in straw boaters ribboned with Caledonian's pink-and purple tartan. Reporters, television camera crews. And the focus of their interest, a battalion of suburban capitalists in white T-shirts blazoned with the slogan *I was robbed by Ali Baba*.

Rae took out her phone. 'I thought you had a meeting to go to?'

'Not till half eleven.' Lexa lifted a hand in greeting, recognising the banking union equality officer. She had been planning to find a cafe and read the paper before walking over to the City Chambers, but she might as well stand in the sun and watch the show. After all these years, she still got a buzz from an angry crowd.

Caledonian Bank's share price had fallen sharply overnight, forcing the CEO to release the profit warning she had hoped to hold back till the next annual results. Rae had been online since five, trying to give the figures a bit of *bounce*. It could have been worse, no one was talking about a taxpayer bail-out. But the people who'd invested their savings twenty or thirty or forty years ago were not looking on the bright side. No good telling them that a couple of lean years after decades of steady dividends wasn't such a bad average. They felt every bit as aggrieved as the subscribers to the rights issue that had been Alison Babbington's first big decision as CEO. Lexa remembered the triumphal interview on the *Guardian* women's page, and the cartoon in the *Independent* depicting her as Midas turning old ladies' shopping trolleys to gold. Just five years ago. And now they drew her as the blindfold figurehead on a sinking ship. The balance sheet was better than at HBOS or RBS, but the sense of betrayal was worse. Cally had always been the couthie bank: more prudent, less nakedly greedy, more *Scottish*. It was like finding your granny had been out on the razz in fur coat and nae knickers. The headlines had been negative enough for Alison Babbington to bypass the bank's own Corporate Relations department in favour of a crisis-management gun for hire: Rae Bergin, of Left Brain Communications.

While Rae flirted with the camera crews, Lexa mingled with

the shares protesters. A heterodox crowd. The T-shirts were worn over every kind of flesh from toned-and-tanned to liverspotted. No one looked within hailing-distance of the breadline, but there was wide variation in what Lexa, if no one else, still called 'class'. That woman crossing the plaza, for instance. Her slogan printed on a singlet cut flatteringly low, a flouncy skirt showing too much leg, an advert-perfect curtain of blonde hair reaching halfway down her back. She looked like a supermarket celebrity, one of the Coleens and Abbeys and Cheryls whose glamorous heartache sold cheap magazines to the checkout queue, but with a peculiarly intent expression on her face.

She turned away, raising one hand. There was a synchronised kerfuffling in the crowd, and when she turned back it was Alison Babbington's face Lexa saw above the skimpy vest and perky little skirt. The plump shine of Alison Babbington's skin, that seed-pearl smile and distinctive second chin. Lexa's gaze swept the plaza, finding the expected transformation, an army of clones. And even as she was thinking it was a hoary old cliché, the risen hairs on her neck proved the stunt had hit home.

By the time she reached Rae's side the woman had removed her mask and was being interviewed on camera.

'Who?' she breathed in Rae's ear.

Rae twitched her away and, when they were safe from the microphones, muttered, 'Christie Dodds. Spokeswoman for the Shareholders Action Group.' She paused to listen to a point the woman was making, before adding, 'ShAG.'

'How postmodern.'

Rae bestowed an eloquently expressionless glance.

This close, Lexa could see that there was more to Christie Dodds than hair extensions and high heels. The reporter was nodding eagerly at everything she said. Not that she needed encouragement. She had the Glaswegian's rapid, discordant eloquence. The CEO and board were liars as well as thieves. They had lied about the state of the balance sheet at the time of the rights issue, and thousands of shareholders had seen their dividends disappear.

'. . . hard-working people who've thought, aye, OK, I'll go

without the now, while I'm earning. I won't take that three weeks in Gran Canaria the neighbours are having, I'll give the new suite a by, the new car, whatever, so I can save for my old age, so I won't be a burden on the taxpayer. So we've looked around and thought "what's safer than a bank?" And where's it got us? That's what we're asking Ali Baba and her fourteen thieves. If she's not too busy counting her three million pound bonus. What's happened to our money . . . ?'

Rae's mobile rang. She took the call in her *public relations* voice. From the end of the conversation Lexa could hear, she gathered that the priority was knocking Christie Dodds off the lead in the hourly bulletins. There wasn't much hope of trumping the pictures, unless Sir Mungo was willing to do a striptease on the boardroom table, but they could set the agenda on Radio Scotland and *The World at One* . . . Whoever was on the other end of the line seemed to have larger expectations. Rae listened, rolling her eyes, then hung up.

'Lex . . .?'

'No,' she said as a joke, not knowing what she was refusing, which was Rae's cue to look exasperated (maybe jokingly, maybe not).

Instead, she did the hamster-cheeked grimace that was as close as she ever came to entreaty, 'Just say hello.'

Alison Babbington wanted to meet her. Her name had cropped up during discussion of the *internal presentational challenges*. The bonus boys had caused the problem, but it was the drones who would pay. Three thousand call centre and back office redundancies were planned. Another three hundred posts in Invoicing, Accounts, and Payroll would be transferred to outside agencies. Negotiations with the Union had ended in deadlock and threats of disruption.

'She just wants a bit of advice.'

'What, like "get yourself a conflict resolution consultant – but it's not going to be me"?'

'Five minutes, tops. A handshake, a bit of eye contact, and out. As a favour to me.'

'Why?'

Rae looked around, making doubly sure no one could hear.

'She's *hired* me, but she doesn't *like* me. She meets you: she sees me as the kind of woman who's got friends like you. It'll help.'

'And what if she doesn't like me?'

'She will.'

It had happened once or twice before. Female clients taking against Rae's sluttish face, her tight little bed-gymnast's body. But she'd never asked Lexa to step in. It would certainly impress the warring freemasons next Monday. It might even be instructive: a few minutes one-to-one with a business legend who fetishised the personal touch. How had she made KostLess a market leader and taken Aubreys department stores out of twenty-four-piece tea sets into Barbour and Cath Kidston? By treating customers as *people*. Lexa was curious to see whether the persona that was so effective on screen survived a meeting in the flesh. And it'd be something to tell Gabriel when they next met.

'Ten thirty in her office,' Rae said, already turning to the next task on her list.

A helicopter arrived to film the plaza from above, though there was nothing to see. Just the television crews chatting among themselves, the protesters mooching around, the union activists in their M&S suits, the boater brigade looking bored until they were approached and their smiles snapped into place. Lexa spotted a couple of policemen in tight black T-shirts standing near Christie Dodds, and another two over by the bank doors, but that seemed to be it. No sign of the paramilitary battalions who'd kettled the G20 protesters in London. For all the resentment about bankers and their bonuses, there was no serious risk of disorder. No one had liked the panicky queues outside Northern Rock and the nation's cash dispensers coming *this close* to running out of money, but Rae was right, what was the alternative?

She was roused from these thoughts by a tap on her arm. The woman nodded at the far side of the plaza. A yellow tipper truck was moving across the marble, the grind of its engine just audible above the racket of the helicopter. The ground seemed to sink under the weight of its tractor-sized wheels. It was closing on a brushed-steel sculpture to the left of the flagpoles. The bright air bulged with anticipation. Every face but one wore the same look of suspense. The exception was Christie Dodds, standing behind the cameras with a smile that said *film this*.

It had to be slurry. Unless it was baked beans, a thousand-gallon insult to the banking executive some newspapers still called the 'baked bean queen'. The truck halted with a squawk of hydraulic brakes. The back began to rise and tilt. There was a sound like pebbles shifting on a beach. It occurred to Lexa that what was going to be dumped was nothing wittier than shingle. Then she saw the flashing discs, the greens and blues and pinks and yellows. Sweeties? No: *buttons*. She laughed. The same laugh she saw on the faces of the union activists, the shareholders, the reporters and photographers, the uniformed security guards and the women in tartan boaters. Thousands upon thousands of buttons were gushing from the back of the lorry. Here they were, in what even the Chancellor was calling the worst recession since the 1930s, and all of them – the couples who'd lost their nest eggs, the suits who would lose their jobs, the fund managers who'd gambled away the pensions of millions of workers – all of them stood laughing at the gaudy, glinting colours in the sunlit air.

'I'm Alison.'

The unnerving thing was, she looked less like herself than those masks had out in the plaza. The face, so familiar from newspaper and screen, was younger in person, a mixed-message of bloom and blowse. Too much flesh, but luxuriously too much, pouring across brow and cheek and chin like double cream. Her body was unambiguously middle-aged. Wider than in the photographs. Clad in a costly, concealing drape of black, with a necklace of linked gold whorls like something Boudicca might have worn. The hand she offered was warm and white and plump-backed.

'Ooh, you're cold,' she said in the husky half-whisper she had used to such reassuring effect in the supermarket commercials. Though it sounded less democratic when you'd had to get past five tiers of personal assistants to hear it. She brought her other hand across to sandwich Lexa's fingers between soft flesh, 'It must be chilly out there.'

'It's . . . hotting up.'

Alison Babbington laughed, releasing Lexa's hand. 'That fucking woman.'

Whooman. Her accent occupied the exotic end of the Highlander spectrum. She almost sounded German.

'Have I shocked you?' she asked.

'It's not exactly your public image.'

'Oh,' another laugh, 'that.'

On television, Alison Babbington tended to be shown in stereotypically feminine activity. Rearranging window displays in her retailing days, or, since moving to Cally, presiding over the boardroom table like a mother of strapping sons. Caricaturists picked on that touch of the pouter pigeon in her second chin and bolster breast. It took Lexa a matter of seconds to tune in to what they missed. An irony so pervasive it didn't show in her face, or showed only as a provocative blankness. She refused to cram her soft bulk into tailored suits, preferring artfully-unstructured jackets in beautiful fabrics and sweeping skirts that ended just above her tidy ankles. Rae called these outfits burkas, and was proceeding on the assumption that Alison Babbington had chosen the sexless route to power. Now that she was in her presence, Lexa doubted this.

They were standing at one of the floor-to-ceiling windows, hidden from anyone looking in by the tinted glass. The room was big enough to hold an oval table that seated twelve, and four low-slung chrome-and-leather chairs positioned in a cosy huddle, but the CEO seemed happy to have Lexa tower over her.

'Security think I should have a permanent bodyguard.'

'Really?'

'Yes, that was my reaction,' Alison Babbington said drily. 'I suppose you never know . . .'

'It doesn't feel violent out there.'

'Are you an expert on violence?'

'I went to a few protests. Twenty-odd years ago.'

'Another young radical who grew up?'

Lexa looked at her.

'It's just a conversation,' Alison Babbington said. She touched the gold whorls at her neck. 'So are you? An ex-radical?'

'Conflict resolution *is* radical. But anyone who does it well has to be seen to be neutral.'

The chief executive officer flashed her a deadpan glance. 'And you think you can get the unions to buy it?'

Lexa laughed. 'Not me. But I can give you a couple of names. People the unions will trust.'

'We pay very competitively.'

'If pay was a priority I'd be in another line of work.'

'We're a happier environment than Goodison Farebrother.'

Lexa stopped smiling.

Alison Babbington let the subject drop. 'So how *does* it feel, out there? To a neutral radical.'

Lexa shrugged. 'There's a lot of anger. What I'm not hearing is any definite sense of what they want—'

The CEO looked interested.

'—it might be worth trying for a face-to-face. If you haven't already. Channel the anger into some specific aspirations . . .'

Alison Babbington was shaking her head. 'She doesn't want to *resolve* anything. She's an activist shareholder. She doesn't care about the long-term interests of the bank. Or the staff. She's not even interested in the dividend. She's just looking for the biggest hike in the share price so she can get out again at a profit. And she doesn't care who she sells to.'

'Looks like it's a contract killing then,' Lexa said.

'Now you're putting ideas in my head.'

The first few bars of a Suzanne Vega song Lexa had always loved sounded from the desk behind them. The CEO retrieved her Blackberry. 'I see,' she said at last, 'yes please.'

A tartan-ribboned boater appeared from the outer office.

'Duty calls,' Alison Babbington said. 'Good to meet you.'

The handshake was more perfunctory this time.

On impulse, Lexa asked, 'Am I anywhere near Gabriel Findlay's office?'

Whatever it was that crossed Alison Babbington's face, it was gone as soon as it came, but the room temperature dropped by several degrees.

'Terrie,' she said to the woman in the boater, 'would you take Ms Strachan along?'

Had Lexa been told that one of them would still be in banking two decades after leaving Goodisons, she would have guessed Rae. Failing that, as a result of some unimaginable exigency, herself. Never in a million years would she have fingered Gabriel. It was Rae who'd brought them North that summer, after one of her ex-lovers put in a word with a two-bit investment bank in Glasgow. It was an excuse for a holiday. Cycling round Arran, dragging themselves up Goat Fell, a nostalgic trip back to Gemmell. Within a week Rae had taken the job and was looking for somewhere to live, but there was nothing between bedsits and business lets. She didn't want a room in a scuzzy student flat, and if the three of them clubbed together they could rent a house with a garden. And after everything that had happened, did Lexa and Gabriel really want to live in Leeds? They spent three days criss-crossing the city from one unsuitable let to another, until Gabriel produced a small ad torn from the Gemmell evening paper. They couldn't believe how cheap it was (though that made more sense once they saw the décor), and the train took twenty minutes into Glasgow, which was quicker than the bus from Hyndland, and on the thirty-first of July they signed a six-month lease on Mackenzie Square.

It rained around the clock that August. The garden was a jungle. They spent their days in the old conservatory, the rain drilling on the glass roof as they squinted in the watery light, breathing the scent of pummelled earth through the open windows. The two of them alone until Rae got back at six. Closing her eyes, Lexa could still feel the narcotic relaxation of those weeks. The radio playing, next door's children squabbling, banana bread cooling on a wire tray. When *PM* came on at five they'd strip to T-shirts and knickers and slap white emulsion on the walls just so Rae wouldn't ask 'what do you *do* all day?' It couldn't last forever, but it had felt as if it might. By mid-

September Lexa was volunteering at a Citizens Advice Bureau. By December, this had become a salaried post. Meanwhile Gabriel kept them entertained with a string of short-lived careers. Market researcher, colour consultant, mystery shopper. Finally, declaring that if she was going to do a joke job she might as well earn serious money, she talked herself into four weeks' work experience at Caledonian Bank. It was the only way around the reference problem. Gavin had written Rae's while Kinsella was on holiday, but that sort of luck didn't strike twice. And in a way Gabriel's internship wasn't so dishonest. They were all starting again, turning the clock back, wiping the slate clean, as if Leeds had never happened.

Lexa was washing up after dinner when the phone rang.

'Everything A-OK?'

'Fine. Except you're late.'

'Rae hasn't phoned?'

'No. So when can can I expect you?'

'I'm here. In the Smiddy.' An old man's bar round the corner, not a place either of them frequented. 'Talk about God's waiting room,' she added in her carrying voice, 'be a chum and bring your yellow mac.'

She was sitting in a corner, reading the *Daily Record*.

'Happy birthday,' Lexa said.

Gabriel put on the yolk-yellow coat. One of the old men stopped them on their way out. She'd left her Burberry on the seat.

Outside, under the unthreatening sky, Lexa asked, 'So why do you need two macs?'

'That's a very good point.'

She rolled the Burberry into a sausage and forced it into a litter bin.

'It's ruined.'

'Ruined how?'

Her eyes flicked left and right along the empty street. 'Look, Lex, I need you to promise me something.'

'You don't want to talk about the coat.'

They grinned.

'Half an hour's peace. I've had a hellish day.'

They cut through the town centre, crossed the homicidal sequence of traffic lights over the ring road intersection, and followed the river. The last time Lexa had walked this path the air had been sticky with the garlic reek of ransoms. Now the island parting the current was crowded with giant hogweed, their cauliflower blooms aglimmer in the just-failing light. Upstream, the river widened into a dam fed by a tumult of stepped rock and white water that some unsentimental Victorian industrialist had blighted with an enormous mill. Over time the mill, too, had been blighted, and in its decay had become picturesque, and that prettiness had been spotted and sold to a developer, and now it held what the sign in the window of the show flat described as 'forty desirable urban living spaces'.

'Rae says they've knocked ten thousand off the price and they're still not selling.'

Gabriel held a finger to her lips and pointed.

A heron was standing on the bank, half-hidden in the tangle of Himalayan balsam, fishing in the once-poisoned water. As they watched, he seemed to draw the twilight into his voluminous wings. The long white neck retracted and, flapping, he took to the air.

'I never thought I'd see that here,' Lexa said.

Gabriel followed the bird's flight across the river, 'He's here every night.'

Lexa glanced at her.

She shrugged, 'It's somewhere I can think. And nobody can find me.'

'Is this about Martin?'

Gabriel raised her eyebrows in mute reproach.

Lexa mimed zipping her lips.

They walked upstream to the falls with its dimly phosphorescent froth, the water roiling and churning in the pool beneath. The river had flooded so often this past year that the local paper was running headlines about climate change. A tidemark of twigs, branches, scuffed plastic bottles and aluminium cans lined both sloping banks. The concrete path above was strewn with more substantial debris, accretions of matted weed and polystyrene packaging, a tree trunk stripped of its bark and smoothed by the water.

Gabriel picked her way across this obstacle course and jumped down to a slab of rock which, though wet and slippery-looking, was not actually submerged. She stretched, locking her hips, extending her arms out and back. The yellow coat like a cinematographer's trick in the monochrome palette of the long summer gloaming.

She looked up at the bank. 'What are you waiting for?'

Lexa jumped down to join her, uttering an involuntary *oof*.

'The old knees complaining, are they?'

'Anything you can do . . .'

Despite the jokes, neither regretted getting older. They could look back over the wreckage of failed relationships and still say they had been lucky with their lives. Lucky with each other, and lucky to have come back to Gemmell when they had. Ten years younger, and they'd have been stuck in a field, off their faces on ecstasy, flailing to a pile-driver beat. In 1984 music had been political. Music, stand-up, theatre, all those peace festivals and pride marches and multicultural fairs. If there was a Tory voter in the west of Scotland under the age of thirty, Lexa never met them. Even Rae tagged along to those street concerts for Nelson Mandela.

The late-eighties were their carefree years. Out every night at a salsa class, or the screening of a German expressionist silent classic, or some comedy club open mic. They joined an acapella choir though they both sang flat, ducking behind big Rona to escape the choir leader's gimlet eye. Mostly Rae had had something better to do. Taking trips from Duck Bay on somebody's boat. Driving up to Loch Fyne for oysters and champagne with whoever she was sleeping with that night. Conveniently for Lexa, Gabriel's lovers had been the once-a-week kind. She went for winners. An astrophysicist, an investigative journalist, a Scottish front bench spokesman. Lexa could understand the aphrodisiac of success, but not Gabriel's indignation when they proved to be so driven that the job always came first. Was it to do with her father, the workaholic town clerk? After each disaster she claimed to know herself a little better. Then she went and did it again. It was a relief when she settled down with Martin, who was only a king of the dunghill.

It was noisy on this rock, so near the roaring water. Lexa had to raise her voice to say, 'I met your boss today.'

'Was that before or after you barged into my meeting?'

'And you gave me the bum's rush. Before.' Lexa buttoned her jacket against the spray from the falls. 'I tell you who she reminded me of: Lucy, when she's off her medication.'

'Psychotically depressed?'

'When she's manic. Telling you exactly what she's thinking, whether she knows you or not. Creating this instant bond between you. I suppose she does it to everyone.'

The heron, which had settled on the opposite bank of the river, took off again.

Gabriel's face was pearly in the half-light, and wet with spray. 'I hope Martin's fed the kids.'

When the property market started to go crazy Lexa and Rae had done the sensible thing and bought their own homes. Gabriel sat tight until the landlord died and she was offered Mackenzie Square at a knockdown price. A Regency villa of blackened sandstone, with its original shutters, skirting boards, fireplaces, door handles and escutcheons, and a certain amount of original woodworm: all for what Lexa had spent on a two-bedroom flat. The weekend she moved out, Martin moved in – 'Just till the builders finish the dry rot work at my place.' She hadn't been fooled for a second. The only surprise was that it took him so long to get Gabriel pregnant.

She was thirty-six when Amy was born. Martin had just been head-hunted to run a domestic abusers' rehabilitation programme in Inverness. He'd complained about missing *these precious early weeks* but looked mightily relieved to be packing his bag come Sunday. Mondays to Thursdays, Lexa slept on his side of the bed, or paced the floor with the crying baby. Rae called her a mug ("It's not like she can't afford a nanny"), not seeing the generosity in Gabriel's taking, the love she made possible between her daughter and her childless friend.

After eighteen months the Inverness project ran out of funding and Martin found a social work job back in Gemmell. A year later Gabriel had Joe. Lexa found it hard not being needed, but Niall had moved in by then, so there were other dramas to distract her. The underpaid school dinner ladies and hospital cleaners whose cases she took on, the ever-deepening disappointment of New Labour, Niall's parents' divorce. New names were inked into the calendar on her kitchen wall. Liz and Stefan, Neve and David. There were three or four years when Rae saw more of Gabriel, what with lunching in big-ticket restaurants on expenses and Christmas shopping in New York. But when Martin moved out and Niall got his unmissable opportunity in Australia, Lexa and Gabriel slotted back into each other's lives. Daily emails and phone calls. Midweek movies. The Friday night wind-down at Mackenzie Square: Gabriel overcooking the pasta, Lexa bringing the wine, Rae with provolone from the Italian deli in Glasgow.

They scrambled back up to the concrete path and headed for Martin's to pick up the children. Lexa had been looking forward to a long gossipy dissection of Alison Babbington's character, and was feeling cheated. She tried again.

'Rae asked me to have a word with her about the unions. Turned out to be a job interview.'

Gabriel lifted her eyes to Lexa's face. 'You jest.'

'She must have thought I'd be so flattered, I'd cave in. Teasing me like we were old friends—'

Gabriel's hands closed either side of her nose, as if in prayer, before brushing the river spray off her cheeks.

'—how come we've never talked about her?'

Gabriel stopped dead on the path. 'Because I work *hideously* long hours in an *extremely* high-pressure job, with an hour's commute back to this dump, and I don't want to waste what little free time I have left on conversations like this.'

Lexa took a long breath. 'You really have had a bad day.'

She closed her eyes. 'Horror ubique,' she said.

They walked on. Towards the town centre, the river path was planted with the same industrial foliage that was used to line the ring road central reservation. Synthetic-looking shrubs, spikily indifferent to the seasons. Mixed in with these were self-seeded weeds and saplings and a carpet of ivy that gave off a faint rank scent of growth.

Gabriel's mobile rang. She snatched it out of her pocket and, without looking to see who was calling, turned it off.

'Don't mind me.'

Her face was suddenly intent. 'Lex . . .'

'What?'

But she turned away. A black rectangle was silhouetted against the sky as it flew from her hand to fall, with a splash, in the river.

'Is it broken?'

'It is now.'

Lexa had to laugh. 'That's about seven hundred quid's worth of kit you've trashed tonight. Still, I suppose it's only two-and-a-half hours of your labour.'

Gabriel looked surprised.

'Have you never worked it out?' Mental arithmetic wasn't her strongest suit. 'It takes you three weeks to make what I earn all year.'

'*Really?*'

'Yup.'

For the past seven years she had been working in Structured Finance. At first she'd assessed portfolios of American loans put together by an investment bank in the City. Caledonian was buying them like they were going out of style. As was everyone else. The London boys were making a packet, and it wasn't rocket science, so one day Gabriel walked into the CEO's office and said, raising her index finger, *ahem, why don't I do that?* And Caledonian had bought a little bank in Boston to source the loans for her to repackage. They'd tossed her another ten thousand, nowhere near what she was worth to them, so she'd planted a rumour. A certain bank in Broadgate was being very attentive . . . And *hey presto!* They put an extra nought on her package and made her a managing director. Banking was rife with title inflation, an American vanity that had caught on over here. She could ask a vice-president to do her photocopying, if she smiled nicely. Three-quarters of what they gave her was bonus, and most of that was stock. Nevertheless, on paper she was paid half a million pounds a year.

They had reached the section of the path lined with laurels and rhododendrons. Teenagers used the caves inside these bushes to have sex and smoke bud and drink cider they bribed the jakeys to buy them from Sanjay's Seven-Eleven. Lexa heard the pounding footfall of a jogger approaching them from behind. Gemmell wasn't a muggers' town, even at dusk. She moved to the side of the path without looking, but Gabriel wheeled in alarm. The runner nodded at them as he passed. It was Elliott, Joe's basketball coach.

From the far side of the rhododendrons the town hall clock struck the half-hour, its illuminated face like a yellow moon stuck to the sandstone tower. Around it, shreds of mauve cloud were layered over a dimming blue that was still, just, daylight. They rounded a bend and the sycamore on Weavers' Green came into view, silhouetted against the sky. Invisible in its leafage, hundreds of starlings were emitting their sci-fi bleeps and whistles.

'You could afford to move to Edinburgh,' Lexa said.

Gabriel batted an insect out of her face. 'I suppose I could.'

'So why don't you? If this place is such a *dump*.'

In a single thrilling impulse the starlings took flight.

Gabriel looked up into the shrieking sky. 'Because you're here,' she said.

Turning the corner into Swiss Street, where the tenements had been cut down to a row of single-storey shops, Lexa noticed a brightness reflected in the cloud cover. Like the glow from the floodlit football ground in winter, but on the north side of town, towards Mackenzie Square.

Martin answered the door before they had a chance to ring the bell.

'I've been calling you,' he said.

'I've lost my phone.'

'A warning would have been nice.'

'They haven't been here?'

'Not yet. It won't be long.' He nodded at Lexa. 'When did you find out?'

She looked at Gabriel.

'We were going to watch the news,' Gabriel said.

Martin released a humorous breath, 'In you come.'

Amy and Joe were sitting in front of the X-box. On the table were the plates of spaghetti that neither had touched. The air was charged to a pitch of excitement that could only end in tears. Or vomit. Joe started babbling about Christine Bleakley and Rio Ferdinand, both of whom he seemed to think Gabriel would soon know. Amy seemed to think her mother was going to jail.

Martin tipped his head at Lexa to indicate that she should follow him into the living room.

He closed the door behind him.

Even at forty-eight he was a man of unignorable physicality, a leaner into others' space, hands curved off his hips in a gunslinger's readiness. Lexa had known him almost half her life, eaten at the same table, swigged from the same bottle, heard him making love in the middle of the night, but if she ever found herself alone with him she'd take the first excuse to leave.

'Have you heard from Rae?' he asked.

'Not since this morning.'

'Funny, that.' He rubbed his jaw, which needed a shave. His T-shirt was spattered with spaghetti sauce. She could smell the garlic and olive oil on his skin.

'What's happened?'

He turned on Sky News.

A media stake-out in some tree-lined suburb, the liveried estate cars and four by fours and vans double-parked. Fluffy microphones and long lenses. The blue dusk pierced by very bright white lights. Lexa knew every rusted railing and pavement crack in Mackenzie Square. On screen, it looked like a different street.

They had shot some footage of Gabriel leaving the bank in her Burberry mac, ignoring the cameras, the simple business of putting one foot in front of the other almost too much for her. Watching her reverse the Jag out of its parking space, Lexa's heart was in her mouth. As if grazing a colleague's Mercedes could matter now.

Alison Babbington was interviewed in her office. Behind her, just in shot, was the spot by the window where Lexa had stood with her that morning. The protesters' masks and buttons were allotted seven seconds at the end of the report.

As an exercise in crisis management, it couldn't be faulted. The story had been turned. The bank was as much a victim as its shareholders, the villain a rogue trader in Structured Finance working off-piste with Cally's money. The shareholders were right to be concerned about the quality of information they'd received before the rights issue, but the bank's management too had been misled. The trader in question had been suspended. Steps were being taken to remove her registration. The Financial Services Authority, with whom the bank had extremely friendly relations, was helping them get to the bottom of this.

Gabriel came in.

'It's a stitch-up,' she said.

And so began the fugitive days.

Amy and Joe stayed on at their father's while Gabriel moved in with Lexa. The all-expenses-paid mob camped in Mackenzie Square soon found out, but Lexa's neighbours rallied round and refused to let strangers inside the building. After a week the invasion had shrunk to an unshaven photographer and two chain-smoking reporters. Gabriel suggested taking them mugs of tea, in the manner of adulterous members of parliament, but Lexa said it would only lead to a picture in the next day's papers, which would bring the television cameras back. ITN had trawled through the archives and found some film of her as a young analyst commenting on Scotland's whisky sector but, after that, with no new footage, the story had dropped off the bulletins. The newspapers were more ingenious. A seven-figure salary was plucked out of the air, with a breakdown of how she spent it. Anonymous sources were quoted on her taste for champagne cocktails and ordering off-menu. They found a hairdresser who never named his celebrity clients; a designer clothes shop that was understood to open up after hours for her; the health spa she supposedly used, with its steroid-built personal trainer. One of the tabloids ran the by-now famous photograph of her unlocking the Jaguar alongside full-length colour pictures of Christie Dodds and Alison Babbington. Underneath, some hack had compiled a dossier of each woman's 'vital statistics'. Age, weight and height. Marital status. Signature drink, shoe and handbag. The restaurants and dress labels they favoured. The cars they drove. The men they dated. ('Peter Andre types' in Gabriel's case, which gave them both a good laugh.) One morning Lexa opened the *Herald* to find a picture of herself, taken on the street, with a caption describing her as 'friend and community worker'.

'You look like Vanessa Redgrave.'

'She's seventy-odd.'

'In her *heyday*.'

To her relief, it didn't happen again. The story was the blonde banker with the lottery-winner's bonus, not an Oxfam-clad Amazon climbing into a Nissan Micra.

For a week Gabriel didn't set foot outside the flat, and took Lexa's advice on not answering the phone. Rae rang daily, but Gabriel wouldn't speak to her.

'At least listen to what she has to say.'

'I *know* what she has to say. She had *no idea* what the CEO was up to. Even though she's running the media strategy. She wanted to resign in protest, but decided she'd be more help to me *on the inside*.'

'She misses you.'

'Not as much as she'd miss six thousand pounds a week.'

So it was just the two of them. When Lexa got in from work, she'd make the pea and broad bean risotto Gabriel liked, or cook *pasta puttanesca* with extra olives, so that every mouthful tasted of luck. But there was only so much food Gabriel could eat, only so many bottles of merlot they could split, so many Jane Campion DVDs they could sit through, so many Joni Mitchell songs they could source on YouTube and sing along to. Only so many hours of Lexa's solicitude Gabriel could stand.

'*The Scotsman* says you were selling mortgage debt for slums in the American rustbelt.'

'They don't know what they're talking about.'

'All right then, why don't you tell me?'

'Because there's *nothing to tell*.'

After ten days she was climbing the walls. Lexa bought her a hoodie and some trackie bottoms in the Red Cross shop and she went to meet Amy and Joe in the park. It was fun, feeding her hair into a baseball cap, coaching her in the Cambusdyke slouch. As far as fooling the media went, the expedition was a success, but later Martin rang to say he wouldn't co-operate a second time. The kids found it too upsetting. They missed their mother, but the way she'd kept scanning the bushes freaked them out. She was often distracted with them, they'd learned to live with that, so long as she was physically present. But not seeing her for days on end, and the dogs' abuse they had taken at school, to go through all that for an hour with Paranoid Pam, and the swings too wet and the café closed . . . It was no one's idea of a good time. Lexa offered to have the children stay with her, but could only agree when Martin pointed out that four people going stir crazy in a two-bedroom flat wasn't going to work. They needed a holiday. If Gabriel was going to take them far enough away to permit some form of normal life, then he was prepared to help.

The whole island was on holiday that week. The stone-flagged streets behind the harbour were clogged with people. Women showing their bra straps under shoe-string vests pushed babies dressed in Celtic strips and miniature Nike trainers. Raw-chinned faces under gel-mussed hair scanned the talent with stares so frank that Gabriel had to look away. Though her own mother wouldn't have known her in those sunglasses. There was a carousel for the wee ones, and a shooting gallery for the teens, and drinking competitions, and a burger van with its delinquent smell of caramelised onions, and a pub band over from Ullapool and, upstaging all of these, on the breakwater across the harbour, a fifty-metre bungee jump.

That morning, as usual, they drove to the sandy side of the island for a few hours' windbathing on a North Atlantic beach. By three, the rain had set in. At the north end of the harbour stood a metal hangar with a red-and-yellow sign. *Pleasureland.* Inside was a purgatory of garish plastic and flashing lights and a thousand-and-one attention-getting noises all blaring at the same time. The amusements themselves hadn't changed much since Lexa's childhood. What was new was the nicheing of every machine, the frenetic ingenuity put in to catching the customer's eye. Aliens, pirates, zombies, vampires, Tutankhamun's Egypt, Al Capone's Chicago, Seventies Disco, invasion Iraq, the one-gag universe of television sketch shows, and, endlessly repeated, the cops'n'robbers dystopia of downtown America.

Gabriel smiled at her dismay. 'Auntie Lexa was hoping for a what-the-butler-saw.'

The children were given twenty-pound notes and sent to the change booth.

'I feel like I'm trapped in the tabloid subconscious,' Lexa murmured.

'It's the most fun the kids have had all day.'

'It's pornographic—'

Gabriel's smile broadened.

'—worse than pornographic. At least sex is a primal instinct.'

'And gambling's not?'

'Not for me. Or you.'

Gabriel flexed her eyebrows. 'That'll be why I was on half-a-mill.'

'You were paid to *minimise* the risk.'

'Was I?'

'You said.'

'I lied.'

Lexa stared at her.

Gabriel laughed for so long that the woman in the change booth looked over. 'You should see the look on your face.'

'Very funny.'

This redoubled Gabriel's mirth. She dipped at the knees with the force of it, helpless in its whoops and whinnies. Amy looked up from the tuppenny nudger and crossed the orange carpet to stand by her mother's side.

'Ah God,' Gabriel said weakly, wiping her eyes.

After dinner, they left Amy and Joe in front of the television at the bed and breakfast. The curtains didn't meet in the middle and the quarry-tile floors were waxed with a dim sheen that smelled of sick, but it was in Lexa's price-range, and their land-lady was happy to keep one ear open for squabbling. The bar down the street was a fisherman's cottage. They claimed the vacant table without a view of the wall-mounted wide-screen, and tried to decide between Gewürztraminer and Spanish rosé, the only wines sold by the glass. Gabriel had changed into a top which showed off the pink of her windburn and the tender cross-hatched skin above her breasts. A young man, big, as they bred them on the island, flashed her a second glance. Another giant, with a tribal shoulder tattoo showing under his camouflage vest, rose to greet him. They locked hands like Roman centurions, arm-wrestling in mid-air, and for the first time in years Lexa thought of the miners.

'How's your rosé?'

'Corked, I think.'

Gabriel glanced over at the frowning Lithuanian behind the bar. 'Good luck with explaining that.'

A small silence opened up.

They had come three-hundred-and-fifty miles only to find reminders of what they were fleeing around every corner. Newspapers left on cafe tables. Old men grumbling in the chip shop. The ice-cream seller's bad jokes. It seemed to Lexa that she and Gabriel were the only two people in Scotland not talking about it.

Gabriel lifted her glass of Gewürztraminer, sipped, grimaced, and set it back on the table. 'You should have tried the electric shock box.'

'Fun, was it?'

'It wasn't like being tasered.'

At the neglected end of Pleasureland, where the orange nylon carpet gave way to a trodden earth floor, they had found a machine the size of a small wardrobe, decorated with a picture of Frankenstein's monster. A retro-styled monochrome screen showed a zig-zagging graphic. When a pound coin was inserted and the handles were grasped, it produced a rising whine and an electric current that increased in strength, or perhaps only seemed to, as the graphic leapt and fuzzed. A digital counter displayed a rapidly-escalating sequence of numbers. It had been impossible to prise Amy and Joe away from this game.

'Capitalism,' Lexa said, 'the system that sells you your own pain.'

'Isn't it more of a socialist thing? You've got a room full of machines dealing in gain . . .'

'The *illusion* of gain,' Lexa corrected.

'The possibility of gain,' she conceded, 'and one machine selling the certainty of pain. And my children would rather have the pain.'

Lexa sniffed at, and again rejected, her vinegary wine. 'At least they know where they are.'

'Don't tell me you're not a *teeny* bit pleased that the whole financial house of cards has collapsed.'

'I'm not.'

'Not even a smidgeon,' she held finger and thumb a millimetre apart, 'when you see how everyone hates us?'

'I don't think of you as one of them. You're my good Nazi.'

'Sweet of you to say so, but I loved every minute. I wouldn't have missed it for the world. It's like . . .' her head tilted '. . . riding a comet's tail. This blazing ball of attractional force streaking across the sky. Who can resist? Governments, churches, charities, the absolute bright-as-a-button best people: they all get sucked in.'

'It's not comets that do that,' Lexa said, 'it's black holes.'

There was nothing quite so blithe as Gabriel's shrug. 'It's the zeitgeist.'

'Your *zeitgeist* has left us with a world financial crisis.'

'Which will pass,' another shrug, 'as crises do.'

'And what'll be left?'

'More than we'd have, had the banks not been given their head.'

'If we'd kept a bigger manufacturing base . . .'

'But we didn't. We don't have Australia's mineral resources or Asia's cheap labour or Germany's work ethic.' She held up her index finger. 'What we *can* do – some of us – is money. *We get it.*'

Lexa siezed her chance, 'Is there any possibility you'll be cleared by the FSA?'

'None whatsoever.' For a moment Gabriel's face belonged to someone Lexa didn't know. 'Unless they've put a complete idiot in charge.'

'So. . .?'

Gabriel glanced towards the pool table where the young giants were setting up a break. 'I've done mystery shopping before. I can do it again.'

'You're not going to fight it?'

'I'll fight to keep my pension. We won't have much of a future living off Martin's child support.'

'But you've got savings?' Even Gabriel couldn't get through all that money.

'Cally defers bonuses for three years, cash and stock. Not that the stock options are worth much now.'

'You must have *something* put away?'

'You know me. Spend spend spend.' She reached for her handbag. 'I vote we switch to gin.'

There was a continuous traffic of drinkers past their table, heading out to the street to smoke their cigarettes in sociable clusters. Gabriel joined them while Lexa queued to buy the drinks. The island was far enough north for the backpackers to sit and read on the harbour wall at midnight. Lexa loved these long, gentle evenings when the wind dropped and the sky was hued in mother of pearl. The door of the bar was propped open. She could see a slice of creamy sunlight on the wall of the butcher's across the way. A cat yawned on the warm pavement. One of the pool players gave Gabriel a light. Lexa watched her chatting to them. They smirked at their trainers, shifty and flattered.

'Gordon or Tankray?' the Lithuanian barman asked.

Gabriel was back in her seat by the time she got the drinks to their table.

Lexa sat down. 'Just tell me one thing . . .'

'Mmm?' Then she understood. 'Gin first.' She took a grateful sip. 'All right.'

'What did you do?'

Gabriel took a longer sip. 'The risk managers lost their nerve. If they'd left everything alone we'd have been fine.'

Lexa had read every newspaper report online, and the more she read the clearer it became that no one really understood why the bankers had suddenly lost their touch. But one fact had been repeated so often it was beyond doubt.

'You were dealing in *sub-prime mortgages.*'

Gabriel's chin lifted. 'Define "sub-prime mortgage".'

'You're the banker, you tell me.'

What the media called a sub-prime mortgage, Gabriel called a leg-up for poor black families in East St Louis who couldn't get a foot on the property ladder. And for others on the very bottom rung, paying crippling rates of interest on their credit cards and car loans. When those debts were consolidated into a second mortgage, the interest rate dropped by half.

'It's a way of taking people on the *outside* and bringing them *inside*, if that sounds familiar.'

Lexa decided to leave the argument about banking as an instrument of social inclusion for another day. 'You must have known those loans were never going to be paid off.'

Gabriel gave her other trademark shrug, that slow-motion wriggle of playful equivocation. 'You've never been to East St Louis. Nor have I. We can't say who's going to default. There's a *risk*, a bigger risk than with mortgages in Manhattan, so they pay a rate of interest reflecting that. And the investors buying packages of that debt receive a higher rate of return. They're all consenting adults . . .' She looked up, smiling. The tattooed youth loomed above them.

'I'm going to the bar.'

The possibility that this long-postponed conversation might be scuppered by a priapic twenty-four-year-old was more than Lexa could bear. 'We're fine,' she said.

'But thank you,' Gabriel added with a twinkle.

He moved off, grinning.

'What is it you *get*—?' It had been nagging at Lexa ever since she'd said it.

Gabriel quizzed her eyebrows.

'—"*Money. We get it*".'

'*Oh*. You know.'

'No, I don't.'

That rapt look, half-present, half-abstracted. Lexa had seen it a million times and it had never lost its charm. 'The thing about money these days is it's an idea. A hundred ideas. And then one day . . .' she opened her hand, looked into her palm and up at Lexa '. . . there it is: number one-hundred-and-one. *What if . . .*? When we were at Goodisons there was no such thing as a mortgage bond market. If we'd strung those words together, they'd have laughed. And then someone had the idea: why not sell parcels of mortgage debt? You're a bank. You've got squillions of these things on your books. You know they're going to pay out over twenty-five years, but you don't want to wait. You sell them on, you get your money now, do something else with it. Next, they're selling parcels of health club subscriptions, credit card debt, car loans. *A multi-billion-dollar market* that hadn't existed six months before.' A left-handed flick: 'Nothing.' Her right hand snatched at the air: 'Something.'

Lexa had never seen her make either gesture before. 'And these things you sold, these . . .'

'Asset-backed securities. Collateralised debt obligations. CDOs. It doesn't matter what you call them. The mortgage bonds that didn't sell because they were rated as too risky, until someone had the idea of slicing them and mixing them up to spread the risk.'

'Debt coleslaw,' Lexa said.

Gabriel leaned forward, her face shining. 'One minute it's unsellable. The next, the market can't get enough of it. There weren't enough people in America wanting to buy homes to meet the demand. So what did they do?' Her blue eyes were alight with a sort of joy. 'Someone came up with the idea of a synthetic financial product, modelled on a real CDO. A shadow. It would perform exactly the same way, only instead of the *actual* loans – or slices of those loans – which would *actually* pay out, it had a swap. Basically, an insurance policy. Investors in the shadow gambled on the loans in the real CDO being repaid. Investors in the *swap* reckoned there was likely to be a certain percentage of default. The two bets cancelled each other out, so there was no need for any of it to show up on the bank's books.' She picked up her glass. 'And that's what I did.'

'But I don't see . . .'

'What's in it for the bank? Two per cent off the top, risk free.'

Lexa thought about it for a while, until she more or less understood.

'Nothing on the balance sheet?'

'Nothing on the balance sheet.'

'And, with this synthetic whatsit . . .' Lexa found herself grasping thin air as Gabriel had done a moment before. '. . . there was actually nothing there?'

'Fiendish, isn't it?'

Lexa shook her head. 'It's insane.' She turned it over in her mind. 'Just an idea . . .?'

'And it was making us *millions*.'

At school Lexa had loved maths, the sweet finality of it, solving quadratic equations, getting ninety-eight per cent in the exam. Her mistake was assuming that working with money would offer the same certainty, the same *justice*. Gabriel had never been good with figures. Even now Lexa double-checked anything she added up. Just the other day, doing her homework, Amy had had to explain to her mother that nothing squared was still nothing.

'A wee bit less ingenuity,' Lexa said, 'and someone might have noticed that those sub-prime mortgage-holders couldn't meet the payments.'

'Ah but they *could*.' Gabriel lifted that didactic forefinger. 'For the first two years, while the interest rate was pegged.'

'And then?'

'And then the value of their homes had risen so they could remortgage.'

'*What?*'

'It kept things ticking over.'

'Till the property market crashed and they went bust.'

The tattooed pool player was back, offering an opened packet of crisps. Lexa didn't recognise the brand but construed the off-colour packaging at a glance. When Gabriel took one the boy smirked at his friend, who was watching from the pool table.

She took another. 'Spicy beaver. My favourite.'

The boy returned to his game of pool.

'Being a banker isn't *hugely* different from being a painter, or a poet, or a composer, or an inventor . . .' She saw Lexa's expression. 'I mean it.' And she did. As she said it, she lit up all over again. 'Blu Ray technology, a cure for cancer, a new derivatives market: it's the *same impulse*. People want more. More art, more life, more money, more things . . .'

'More credit they can't pay for.'

'It's human nature.'

'It's a global disaster.' Lexa took the plunge. 'How much?'

Gabriel's brightness flickered. 'How much what?'

'How much did the bank lose on these things you packaged, these . . . CDOs?'

There had been speculation in the press but, on Rae's advice, Alison Babbington was refusing to pre-empt the investigation.

'I told you,' Gabriel said, 'the risk managers lost their nerve

They've got models. The market panicked. The swings in price from day to day were greater than the models allowed, so they said no: we had to get rid of them. The market didn't know what any CDO was worth, so they made the most adverse assumptions on all of them.'

'But *how much?*'

Gabriel met her eye. 'Half a billion.'

'*Dollars?*'

'Pounds.'

The figure hung in the air like a cartoon graphic, something that could not possibly exist in three dimensions. It occurred to Lexa that Amy had a stronger grasp of the situation than any of them. Her mother might indeed go to jail.

Gabriel stood up and walked out, leaving her handbag and cigarettes under the table. On the pavement, visible through the open door, she turned her back on the bar. It was obvious from her posture that she was on the phone.

'Everything OK?' Lexa asked, when she sat down again.

Over at the pool table the tattooed boy potted the black.

'Tickety-boo,' she said.

The last night of the holiday there was a fancy dress parade through the town. A procession of thickset farmhands, lipsticked and lewd in their wives' satin nightwear, pouting and hitching up their balloon breasts. It was the custom for children to be given ten- and twenty-pence pieces to throw at the tractor-drawn floats. Joe laughed as loudly as the local boys when this shower of silver popped a balloon. Amy copied Lexa's stony look. The pageant was over by ten. The guisers removed their makeshift prosthetics, returned their wives' undergarments slightly stretched, and the town retreated indoors to line its stomachs before the midnight bonfire. It was time to get the kids to bed. They had an early start in the morning. Amy wheedled the twelve-year-old's privilege of an extra half-hour and Lexa offered to take Joe back. She was gone twenty minutes. Thirty at most. Just long enough to wonder later if staying would have made a difference.

She left mother and daughter strolling along the breakwater, stalking the pedestrian gulls. It didn't take much to make Amy happy. The fact of being out so late in the not-yet-failing light, the moored boats creaking in the harbour, the oily rainbows looping the surface of the water, the prettily-painted lettering on each prow. Persephone, Clarinda Mae, Queen of the South. Such highfalutin names to sweeten the stink of fish. Gabriel was the old style of mother, *laissez-faire*, only distantly watchful. But then, Amy was the old style of child.

Lexa got Joe showered and toothbrushed and tucked up in bed. He fell asleep mid-sentence, asking for a story. Daylight sliced through the gap in the curtains. She decided to go out again.

A few islanders still loitered around the bungee jump, knowing it would be another twelve months before they saw anything half as spectacular. Four Englishmen in baseball caps and matching sweatshirts took it in turns to fit the harness, tightening the straps around the chest and shoulders, the customers standing shy under their hands. Amy told her all this, after. About the fearless girl with the strawberry mark across one eye, and the youth so drunk he could hardly stand. She didn't notice her mother leaving her side, but there she was at the foot of the crane, easing off the gold band she wore on her index finger, along with her earrings and a tube of lipsalve from her pocket. She slipped them into her handbag. Then, carelessly, she dropped the bag on the ground.

Halfway to the top her face disappeared. A trick of the light, or perhaps her escort told her to step back. This was the moment Lexa arrived and asked Amy where she was. They both looked up. The sky had clouded to a dingy brown, a brackish wind blowing off the sea and rocking the crane as it pulled the cage upwards. When it reached the top there was just enough delay to suggest the jump might be aborted. And then she fell. Down almost to the water, and up again, three-quarters of the distance fallen, before the second plunge and the never-to-be-forgotten sight of her, head slumped, limbs dangling, like some grisly find from the dredged harbour, jerking lifelessly on the end of the rubber rope.

Lexa studied the rents in the vinyl seating, the dust balls by the skirtingboard, the scuff marks on the gloss-painted walls. There were two cracked panes in the astragal window. She read posters about swine flu and the lifeboatmen's ceilidh. She noted the peculiar forsakenness of a cottage hospital after hours, the faint playing of Radio Scotland somewhere down the strip-lit corridor. She drummed her fingers, bit a ragged nail, found herself listening to the low buzz of the storage heaters. Gradually she came to understand what it meant to watch through the night: to know the doubleness of time, its passing and its eternal present, to feel the weight of each minute without the distraction of thoughts. A muddy darkness pressed on the window. She watched it turn through indigo and cobalt blue to a translucence that was greenish and lemony and no colour at all, until a pallid sky striated with thin cloud painted a square of watery light on the wall beside her. A van stopped outside. The whistling driver unloaded his crate of milk.

Gemmell Royal Infirmary had a hum. Which was good. A hum meant centre-of-excellence, state-of-the-art, scanners, resuscitators, technology that crooned and bleeped. The hospital on the island had had an echo, and a smell of carbolic, and floral curtains washed too many times that closed with a rattle of metal hooks and runners. Walking in through the Infirmary's automatic doors, Lexa thought: she's safe now.

The stroke ward was stark and gloomy at the same time. White walls, white sheets, white sky on the other side of the windows. Old ladies in bed, some fast asleep, some propped-up and watchful. At the far end was a private room. The occupant lay on a mound of pillows. Her mouth was open, her chin collapsing into folds of neck, her face a ruined soufflé.

'Gabriel.'

Lexa felt quite calm, but her cheeks were scalding.

She came closer and saw the transparent hose snaking from under the bedclothes to the satchel of orange liquid. A thinner tube ran from a drip suspended above the bedside cupboard.

'*Gabriel.*'

Her eyelids fluttered but she did not wake. Lexa pulled up a chair and sat holding the hand pierced by the canula. A smell, faint but distinctive, teased at her nostrils.

Occasionally Gabriel's forehead puckered with the ghost of a frown, or her cracked lips showed the nuance of a smile, only to fall slack again. Once, her swollen eyelids half-opened sightlessly. Lexa was reminded of the summer Amy had been born, those long days watching the dreamlife of the sleeping baby. She finally identified the smell, the tarnished-metal taint of old lady.

She had handled every stage of the crisis with the same efficiency. Insisting that the air ambulance be despatched from Aberdeen. Booking herself and the kids on a later flight to Glasgow. Seeing Gabriel on to the helicopter, keeping out from under the paramedics' feet but letting them know that if anything went wrong they would regret it. No one could have done more. It was the thinking she found difficult. Out of nowhere she would grasp the enormity of what had happened, and then it was gone. Her mind refused it.

'Am I intruding?'

She looked up. Alison Babbington was standing at the end of the bed.

'Not on me,' Lexa said, 'I can't speak for Gabriel.'

She came closer. A detached part of Lexa's brain noted how lightly she moved, as if she had wheels, not legs, under that long skirt.

'You're quick off the mark.'

Alison Babbington ignored this barely-coded hostility. 'She's sleeping?'

'Unconscious. I suppose Rae tipped you off?'

There was a steeling, and then a softening, in Alison Babbington's face. 'It's not a PR stunt,' she said. It seemed to that detached portion of Lexa's brain that her accent was even more Germanic. 'If the media find out, it won't be from me.'

She fetched a chair from the ward and placed it on the other side of the bed. 'Rae says you've been friends for a long time—'

Lexa said nothing. She didn't know what this was – a forty-eight-hour blackout, the start of a long convalesence, *please God not a deathbed* – but she knew she couldn't afford to be distracted from it.

'—I didn't know. That day we met.'

'The day you hung her out to dry,' Lexa said.

Alison Babbington breathed in, and out again. 'Should I leave?'

Lexa looked at her.

'What if I just sit here for a while,' Alison Babbington said. 'I won't speak.'

Lexa went back to watching Gabriel.

AUGUST

'Don't worry about your shoes.'

But Lexa stepped out of her wet sandals and left them on the mat, just to feel the Indian runner under her feet. Woven claret and port and venous blood. A whiff of cedar as she passed the Moorish cabinet with its antique doodads. The PA nodding hello and goodbye as she left with that enormous diary. The big black tom cat hoisting his tail to cross the Turkmenistan rug. Every detail was filed in her memory and kept for the day when she would recount this evening to Gabriel. A walnut table beside the sofa displayed five silver-framed photographs of her hostess, variously aged but wearing the same look of pouter-pigeon complacency. Glad-handing Angela Merkel. Raising her glass to a young Alex Salmond. Sharing a joke with Prince Charles. Red-nosed on a ski slope arm-in-arm with a smiling woman. And in a more recent snap, holding a baby.

Alison Babbington had appeared at the hospital on three successive Friday nights, drawing up a chair, turning off her BlackBerry, and chatting in a voice so discreetly hushed that Lexa had had to lean towards her to catch what she was saying. It was a trick of power, she supposed, to induce this straining, hyper-attentiveness. When the bell rang to signal the end of visiting, they had walked to the car park – Lexa to the Micra, the CEO to her chauffeured BMW – and gone their separate ways. The last thing she had expected was an invitation to dinner. But here she was, nursing a glass of Sancerre, watching her hostess peel and chop at the granite counter in her enormous kitchen.

The excuse was giving her a square meal, since she had no chance to shop or cook. Lexa couldn't see how the head of a bank was any less time-pressed, but let it go. Nothing mattered but Gabriel. She visited her every night. Or, today, at lunchtime. This was her life now: putting in a distracted day at work, dashing home to make herself an omelette and run Gabriel's nightclothes through the wash, then spending the evening at the hospital.

'When I opened the door just now, you looked shocked.'

'It is a sort of shock, seeing a public figure in a domestic setting.' Lexa looked around her. 'Even one as palatial as this.'

Alison Babbington caught her eye. 'You mean ostentatious.'

Lexa wondered if she was supposed to deny it. 'Modestly ostentatious,' she said.

When the salad was prepared and Lexa had tasted and approved the sauce, Alison Babbington turned off the heat and took her on a tour of the house. A curious thing to do with anyone other than a close friend or newly-hired domestic, Lexa thought, as she was ushered up the corkscrew stair to another two floors of presidential proportions. The laundry room smelling of tumble-dried clothes was bigger than her sitting room in Gemmell, so she wasn't expecting this cosy little chamber papered in yellow.

The child had kicked away the covers and lay on her side, her pyjama top ridden up to expose a sweet sausage of midriff. She seemed caught in a dream of running, open-mouthed, fine hair streaming in a breathless wind, one plump pink heel lifted, the other foot bearing down.

'And this is Natasha, my perimenopausal miracle—'

Lexa took five years off her previous estimate of Alison Babbington's age.

'—who's very good at pretending to be asleep.'

She leaned down to scoop the suddenly-grinning child into the air and swung her across so that Lexa had to take the warm weight of her. Natasha seemed happy enough, wrapping her legs around Lexa's waist, fitting her silky head into the crook of neck and shoulder.

'She likes you.'

Downstairs again, her hostess lit the candles on the chimney piece, their flames doubling in the over-mantel mirror. 'Her father's found other fish to fry,' she said with a smile that ran against the grain of her voice. 'A younger fish. Not very original of him. But that's what you get for liking alpha males. They should write it into the wedding vows. To have and to hold, till the twenty-eight-year-old comes along.' Her voice changed register. 'Or am I just unlucky, with unlucky friends?'

Lexa stroked the purring tom cat on her lap. 'I've had my share of bad luck, but not that kind. So far.'

Alison Babbington's reflection vanished as she stooped to hide the spent match amid the artistically-arranged logs in the fireplace. 'And what sort of luck has Gabriel had?'

Three weeks since her stroke, but to Lexa – endlessly, obsessively, reviewing all that had happened since – it felt like three years.

Martin said it would give the kids nightmares, seeing their mother like that: inert, as good as dead. Really it was his own nightmares he feared. As long as the children didn't visit, he had to stay at home to look after them. It had taken Lexa four days to wear him down. He left Amy with her for a couple of hours while he took Joe to the dentist. It was a way of allowing it to happen but leaving himself some shouting room should his misgivings prove justified.

Amy listened calmly enough when Lexa gave her the pep talk about being brave and not getting upset, but when they walked into the private room, the colour drained from her cheeks. Gabriel's head was bent to one side. The skin sagged on her face, draping around her eyes in glistening purple folds. Her eyelashes were crusted, the corners of her mouth caked with white. Nudged forward by Lexa, Amy sat by the bedside, her eyes darting towards the mound of bedclothes and away, plainly horrified, and fascinated, by the drip. Surreptitiously she pinched the back of her own hand but the flesh would not yield to her fingers.

Lexa urged her to talk to her mother, suspended somewhere between sleep and coma. For all they knew she could hear every word. Reluctantly, Amy described life at Martin's, what he cooked for tea, the fillings he put in their sandwiches when they walked up Ben Lomond, the red shoes he'd bought her, the television shows he allowed her to watch when Joe was in bed.

Gradually this forced chatter became more natural. Lifting her eyes from the bedspread, she noticed that her mother's nightdress was exposing an immodest amount of sun-mottled flesh. Reaching across to pull the covers higher, her sleeve brushed Gabriel's hand. To her vivid alarm, the fingers moved. One crusted eye opened and looked straight at Lexa.

She had been unconscious for five days.

'Habt ihr das Gewehr?'

This was not Gabriel's voice. Her eyes moved restlessly under half-closed lids. Amy's face flashed panic.

Then she said it in English, 'Do you have the gun?'

Lexa tried to smile but her mouth was frozen. 'How are you feeling, Gabe?'

'My head hurts.' She sounded querulous, like an old woman.

'What about the rest of you?'

Gabriel looked down at her body under the hospital sheet. She seemed puzzled by the hand with the drip. It was impossible to say whether she recognised either of them.

'Mumma . . .'

Gabriel's eyes closed, her forehead creasing into a frown.

Amy looked helplessly at Lexa.

Without opening her eyes, Gabriel murmured 'Harry'll do it.'

They knew no one called Harry.

Natasha had a nanny who'd gone home by the time Lexa arrived. Hard to know what to do for the best; she had a filthy Niddrie accent, but Tashie loved her. Alison Babbington glanced at Lexa. 'Have I offended the neutral radical?' Her BlackBerry played that snatch of Suzanne Vega. She excused herself, leaving her guest with the Sancerre. Lexa stood up to examine the paintings, a Jenny Saville nude and one of Alison Watt's exquisitely rumpled bedsheets. Someone – not necessarily the householder – had an eye for contemporary Scottish art. But she couldn't see an interior designer taking the trouble to source all these paperbacks. Virago's bitten apple. The iron logo of the Women's Press. Virginia Woolf. Angela Carter. Beatrix Campbell. Melanie Klein. A well-thumbed copy of *Our Bodies Ourselves*. Lexa and Gabriel owned most of these titles, the same editions. *Sweet Freedom*.

Eve Was Framed. My Secret Garden. The Hite Report ('144 women in this study said they preferred sex with women'). She associated these books with cheerfully-decrepit tenements, their sandstone crumbling like brown sugar, the woodchipped walls brightened with theatre posters and sprawling cheese plants and cheap Indian bedspreads thrown over sagging sofas. Planks of unvarnished pine propped on salvaged bricks. It was disorientating to glance away from these same cracked spines and out of Alison Babbington's window. Street after street of neo-classical restraint. Pilasters, fluted columns, filigree ironwork, a grid of soot-blackened ashlar descending to the firth of Forth. When this quarter was built there had been no cars or planes, no medical treatment worth mentioning, no birth control except widowhood, no cyberspace. Yet these terraced town houses would still be home to the Edinburgh establishment when Cally's corporate Xanadu was dust.

Alison Babbington came back.

'Ah, good old Shere,' she said, seeing the volume in Lexa's hand, 'I always meant to write and thank her for saving my sex life from DH Lawrence.'

Although no longer in a coma, Gabriel slept at least twenty hours a day. No knowing when she would wake, or what she would say in the few minutes before sleep reclaimed her. The websites warned that recovery from stroke was a long haul. Patients showed an early improvement as the swelling in the brain went down, but serious repair was the work of months or years. Lexa understood this. What she could not comprehend were the dramatic fluctuations. There were days when Gabriel's gaze was wounded but lucid, like herself hungover or after a sleepless night, and other days when she talked of hidden cameras and fighting dogs fed on human blood. Then there were the days in between, when sanity's coat blew open to show a snazzy lining of delusion.

One evening she complained that the doctors kept asking her questions. What day was it, what month was it, where was she, who was the prime minister? Reciting this list, a change came over her. She beckoned Amy closer, her eyes pleading. Lexa could not remember when she'd last seen such naked feeling. She wanted Amy to stay and prompt her with the answers. Amy protested that the doctors would hear her. A look of immense cunning crossed Gabriel's face. Without moving from the pillows, she seemed to stretch towards her daughter. '*Whisper.*' And then, as suddenly as it had descended, her agitation was gone. Her gaze strayed to the get-well cards on top of the bedside cupboard. Her hand moved towards her head, causing the drip to tug at her skin.

'Who am I?' she asked in her old woman's voice.

'You're my mum.'

'Am I?'

By this time Amy had learned not to answer every question. 'You've had an accident but you're getting better.'

It was her eyes Lexa found most disturbing. Their new way of rolling and swivelling, that strange provisional hovering.

'They said they'd bring the gun.'

This again. Lexa had no idea whether she meant an actual gun or whether the word was a dysphasic substitution. Attempts to resolve the issue had only led to further confusion.

She sat on the bed. 'Who said—?'

Amy shot her a grateful look.

'—do you mean the doctors? The ones who were asking you questions?'

The hovering gaze clouded. 'What questions?'

Lexa had the sensation of falling into a trap. '"What day is it, what month is it, where are you?"'

Gabriel's eyes widened in alarm, exposing the whites above and below each iris. Like ping-pong balls, Lexa thought.

'It's all right, Gabriel. You don't have to answer.'

'My head hurts.'

For the next twenty minutes Lexa sat, holding a damp flannel to Gabriel's forehead, as she had done the night Amy was born, after the epidural.

When she awoke, Gabriel said 'What day is it?'

'Monday,' Amy told her.

'What month is it?'

'August.'

'Where am I?'

'*In hospital,* Mumma.'

Gabriel smiled like someone harbouring a great secret. 'I know who the prime minister is.'

Lexa smiled back. 'Who?'

'McSporran,' she said.

'You never call me by my name, Lexa.' Alison Babbington kicked off her shoes and tucked her feet up under her on the sofa. 'Why is that?'

'Do I not?' Lexa said.

'Call me Alison.'

'What, now?'

Alison Babbington showed her seed-pearl teeth. 'Within the next hour will do.'

In the course of their *sotto voce* chats on the stroke ward, while Gabriel slept the sleep of the dead, Lexa had learned a great deal about Alison Babbington. The sandalwood soap she used for its subliminal masculine authority ('I draw the line at aftershave'). The flat in Kensington, the castle near Inverness, the farmhouse in Brittany she saw once a year, if that. The formidably-capable private secretary who ran her four homes and her social diary and was locked in a turf war with Brenda, her PA at the bank. The personal shopper who weeded-out any colour that would not have been worn by a man. The cleaner. The nanny. The night nanny in case she had a *bank thing* to go to – but since she was at her desk by six each morning, she kept those to a minimum. Home by seven was her rule, and if she heard about staff in the office after eight she made sure they were asked why they couldn't use their time more effectively . . .

And of course it was flattering, being taken into her confidence. Alison Babbington wasn't short of potential friends. Her senior executives. The lords and ladies, knights and dames, corporate chairmen and university vice-chancellors she met at gatherings of the great and good. Her fellow gallery trustees and theatre board members. Yet who had she chosen to cook for? A conflict resolution consultant lucky to make £30,000 a year. Where Lexa saw only the gulf between them, Alison found affinities. Had they not read the same books, loved the same movies, hummed along to and then sickened of the same drippy singer-songwriters? Both had trained as accountants, and worked in banking. More by luck than judgement Alison had timed her career just right, starting in retail, making the switch to finance when she was senior enough to stand up for herself. By the time she was running KostLess, with an MBA from INSEAD under her belt, she'd thought she had nothing to learn. She'd never admit it outwith these four walls, but coming to Cally had been good for her, curing her of her obsession with detail. She'd had to toughen up, gain a strategic overview and make decisions fast, acquiring the macho skills she'd once shunned as a matter of principle. That sort of superstition seemed silly now. 'By our age, women' – *wheemen* – 'are the powerful sex. That's why the boys are so keen on twenty-eight-year-olds. I can think of any number of strong women. You, Rae, any of my senior staff. Where are the men?'

'Heading up your competitors,' Lexa said.

The rain had cleared away the clouds. The open window held fifteen rectangles of near-colourless dusk. Meltwater and lavender. A moth flew towards the candles. The black tom cat lifted his head.

Alison tucked a hand inside her shirt and deftly rearranged a strap. 'But you and I are worth ten of them. Why aren't you at the top table, Lexa? What is it that puts women off? I didn't want it either, when I was younger. I think we're nostalgic for male power. It's eroticised for us. It works against us in every way, but it's a hard thing to give up . . .'

Lexa was thinking about that breathy, supple voice. So much more expressive than her face.

'. . . Or is it just cowardice? We know what it's like to live under the whip and how much we hate the men with the whip hand. We'd rather work for a man we don't respect than be hated like that.'

'I work for myself,' Lexa said.

'I suppose that's one answer.' She smiled, lifting the bottle. 'Another half-glass?'

*

Just when Lexa was thinking Gabriel was over the worst, the doctors had announced she needed surgery. Trauma sustained during the bungee jump had ruptured an artery. The bleeding had stopped, but there was a complication: a build-up of cerebrospinal fluid. A shunt would be inserted to divert it into the peritoneal cavity. Afterwards, the surgeon reported that when he'd tapped through her skull, fluid had spurted across the operating theatre. Without prompt action to ease the pressure, his patient would certainly have died. Lexa broke into a sweat of relief at this news. Then she saw the reservation in the anaesthetist's smile.

Gabriel was back in her room the following day. Lexa and Amy found her sleeping. The nurses had shaved off half her hair, making her look like a dandelion clock part-blown. Ten centimetres above what had been her hairline was a surgical dressing. A tube, roughly the width of a drinking straw, ran from this dressing, under the skin, past her ear and down the side of her neck. The procedure had been explained to Lexa, but still the sight shocked her. The mystery of Gabriel had been violated. Her body was a machine with a botched repair. One day her flesh would rot in the earth and this plastic pipe would be all that was left of her.

Amy said nothing when she saw what the doctors had done to her mother. She sat on the edge of the hospital bed and held the fingers that never moved. Lexa placed a comforting hand over the warm crown of the child's head. Amy pretended not to notice that she was crying.

'It's hard for you,' Alison said.

Lexa drained her glass. 'Hard or not, it has to be done.'

'Yes.' The word was drawn out, sibilant. 'But you have to take care of yourself too.'

'I thought you were doing that.' She watched Alison's face. The pouter-pigeon complacency remained unruffled, 'It's good of you, coming to the hospital, but what she needs is to be let off the hook.'

Alison shook her head, smiling, 'The FSA are running the investigation.'

'You could retire her on health grounds.'

'We have to restore investor confidence.'

'She has *brain damage*.'

'Then she won't care.'

Lexa stared.

Softly, Alison Babbington quoted, '"Hard or not, it has to be done".'

Lexa got to her feet. No point prolonging the evening.

Alison Babbington looked up from her nest on the sofa. 'Now you're punishing me,' she said. 'I *can't do it*. Even for you. Look, Lexa, I don't want to see her suffer for what she did. But none of us can escape the consequences, and . . . if it didn't sound callous, I'd say she's getting off lightly.'

'You're right. It does sound callous.'

A trundling noise came through the open window. Lexa turned her head to look. Just a car on the cobbles, the road's greasy surface catching the evening light with a seal-coloured shine.

'I wouldn't have thought she was your type,' Alison Babbington said lightly.

'You don't really know her.'

A cool smile crossed Alison Babbington's face. 'Tell me.'

'She doesn't have a *type*. Even when she's infuriating, there's no one like her. She's . . . magical, really.'

A faint *huf* of amused breath. 'The thing about magicians is their audience does most of the work.'

'What I don't understand,' Lexa said abruptly, 'is why you keep coming to the hospital.'

Alison Babbington brushed a cat hair off her skirt. 'Not this week.'

'Unless it's to ease a guilty conscience—'

The CEO's eyebrows lifted fractionally.

'—once maybe, if Rae thought it'd look good. But week after week . . .'

'Not this week,' she repeated.

'Because she's conscious now. You don't want to find her awake. You might have to *talk* to her.'

'Because I realised it wasn't Gabriel I was coming to see.'

The cat stretched, pushing its claws into the arm of the sofa.

Lexa said, 'Did you know what she was doing in Structured Finance?'

The effect on her hostess was shocking. She had been trying to puncture that ironic poise, not to strip it away altogether.

'You're not being very logical, Lexa. If I knew, then I'm implicated. I couldn't afford' – *afforrt* – 'to have anything to do with her, or with her friends. Let alone sit at her hospital bedside. Why would I not do exactly what you want, get rid of her, using her illness to keep the FSA away? Hmm—?'

The whispering quality was gone from her voice, its teasing fricatives now sharp as broken glass.

'—and why would she not point the finger at me, get the media off her back and on to mine? Why would she make *no effort* to put up *any sort of defence?*' She paused. 'Maybe because she did something else.'

'What?' Lexa asked, worried now. 'What did she do?'

Alison Babbington pushed the cat off the sofa. 'That's what we and the FSA are trying to unravel.'

In the right mood, Rae would concede an irony to her making a living out of public relations. But she was just as likely to snap that the ingratiating stereotype was lazy liberal-arts bollocks: PRs were professionals these days. To Lexa, they looked like a dozen young women with shiny hair, good legs, nice manners and no reason to go home at five. Rae did not deny they'd been hired for their looks, but there was nothing the boss demanded of them that she did not do herself. She too flirted with the clients, in her wasp-waist suit and her red-soled shoes. She could tolerate the sexism of the Scottish business male, as long as he was paying her a thousand pounds a day.

She had managed a decade in Scottish banking. The same old battles to be fought, but they hadn't felt like *her* battles. She couldn't be bothered with the taxonomy of the Edinburgh private school system, and she hated being lumped with the west coast wide boys who still dressed like Gordon Gekko. For Rae, success was always tied to her rivals' capacity to trigger her street-fighter's instincts. It was her bad luck that the bank she'd joined in Glasgow had been staffed almost entirely by democratically-inclined Scots. Without her grudge against the English upper middle classes she was nothing. So she got out. If every Scottish PR had been a Jackie or Tricia in magic pants and hot-stuff lipstick, she would never have progressed beyond launching helium balloons and lunching local radio DJs. But she had enough self-knowledge to seek out the Sophies and Amandas who'd gone to ceilidh classes in South Ken and migrated North to nab some Barbour-clad James or Archie. The sort of women who moved with a coltish sway and trip, and tossed their long manes, driving the hair back from their foreheads with thumb and second finger. She had bought them jugs of mojito just to listen to their tortured vowels, to watch them flinch when she said 'serviette'. And ambition had been born out of her loathing.

Her strategy was to identify the client's core value and sell it straight, building a brand profile around integrity. And if Lexa recognised this as just another kind of spin, she could see that it played well with the self-made MDs and corporate chief execs. Along with the smiling geishas, and the spearmint-leaf tea they served in meetings, and Rae's throwaway line about its calming effect on excessive testosterone. She'd always believed in presentation, in the have-your-cake-and-eat-it bluff of maverick-cum-company woman, and never mind who she was inside.

Yuki – according to the Perspex sign on the reception desk – greeted Lexa like an old friend, though she was ninety per cent sure they'd never met. Now that one of the team was Japanese, she was going to have to stop thinking of them as geishas.

'I'll just see if Mrs Bergin is free.'

'Mrs' was a professional title. There had been two false alarms, each involving a fiancé who had lived at a distance necessitating air travel. The last wedding cancellation, nine days before the scheduled event, had been an expensive business for almost all concerned. But not for Lexa and Gabriel, who still had the outfits they'd bought for the previous fiasco and had made a pact to purchase their gifts the day before the ceremony. Since then, Rae had taken to wearing a ring and rebranded herself as a 'cougar', a detail that did the business no harm. Not that she was such a fool as to sleep with the clients. These days her lovers weren't just a decade or more younger but, as often as not, Asian and of a different faith. If Lexa felt complicated about these mutually-exploitative couplings, it was nothing to Rae's horror at her lengthening streak of celibacy. How could she stand it? *Because once you get to my age – if you look your age – you don't get asked.* Which was Rae's cue to explode, Why don't *you* fucking ask?

The door to her office opened.

'Come through, Lex.'

She was standing in front of the wall-sized window, her hair like glinting copper wire, those gym-toned arms shining silver through their screen of ghostly freckles. Her grey skirt was long and full, the tastefully-mismatched jacket on her coat stand loosely cut.

'Fashion seems to be having an Alison Babbington moment.'

'It doesn't suit me?'

Lexa looked at her.

'Oh Christ, I can't stand it when you lie.'

'I haven't said anything.'

'I could see you working up to it.' She checked her watch. 'Make it quick. I've got a meeting in ten.'

This was one of the reasons Lexa preferred not to see Rae at the office. Every conversation was conducted against the clock. She billed her clients in fifteen-minute chunks. Lexa sold herself by the morning or afternoon, but not always both in the same day.

'You need to get Alison Babbington to call off the dogs on Gabriel.'

Rae sat down at her meeting table, a fourteen-seater chunk of yellow glass and steel. 'And can she end child poverty while she's at it?'

Lexa took the seat opposite. 'The situation's changed.'

'Not for Caledonian Bank it hasn't.'

'She'll look like a bully.'

Rae's chin lifted. 'Tell you what, *you* ask her.'

'I have.'

'Course you have. And if she won't do it for you, she ain't gonna do it for me.'

So Rae knew about her dinner in Edinburgh.

'What about the PR case? "Compassionate bank boss decides not to persecute brain-damaged employee".'

'Whose medical confidentiality has been respected so far.'

'Cheers Rae. I'm sure Gabe would say the same.'

There was a short, charged pause.

Rae sketched a triangle on her spiral-bound pad. 'I've done everything I can.'

'I know,' Lexa said. She felt the same. Out of her depth. 'But we can't let her walk out of hospital into the arms of the FSA.'

Rae drew another, intersecting triangle. 'The news agenda's moving on. If she can get through the next three weeks we'll be into party conference season. She's bought herself some time . . .'

'By having a stroke?'

For the first time since Lexa's arrival Rae looked shamefaced. 'I'm just saying there's ways of playing it. She can say nothing, keep her head down. There's an election next year. Who knows what's going to happen six months down the line . . .?'

'Is that Gabriel's friend speaking, or Caledonian's PR?'

Rae's lips parted, showing her sharp-toothed bite. 'I've been down at that hospital *every afternoon*. She's my pal too. She didn't just get put in a box when she wasn't with you.' She tore out the page, scrunched it into a ball. 'You really think I don't want her to walk away from this? Course I do. I just can't say it in public. It's my *job*. She understood.'

Lexa didn't blame Rae for what had happened. Her credibility had been on the line. She'd heard her in the plaza, assuring Alison Babbington that she could deal with Christie Dodds. She was paid a hundred-and-twenty pounds an hour: she had to pull a rabbit out of the hat. Or a scapegoat. A safely anonymous sacrifice, she must have thought. Until the CEO suggested a candidate.

'Alison Babbington says she did something worse than the stuff in the press.'

Rae drew a fresh triangle on her pad. 'Yeah?'

'"Yeah?"'

Rae seemed startled by the attack she put into the word. 'Shit, Lexa. It's news to me. I just meant . . . yeah: she's Gabriel.'

Lexa had spoken to a solicitor. He was willing, and came highly recommended, but he needed to know what the FSA was likely to throw at him. Gabriel was no help. She couldn't even remember the password on her laptop, and none of the obvious candidates (including 'password') had worked.

'You could put out some feelers at Cally.'

Rae rolled her eyes. 'No, I couldn't, because no one's going to tell me.'

'And you don't want Alison Babbington finding out you're Gabriel's friend.'

'Fuck off, Lexa.'

They listened to the rumble of the traffic nine floors below.

Rae sighed. 'All right, you win. It won't work, but I'll have a go.' Her glance flicked up from the table-top, 'You've checked her mobile?'

'Yup.'

The island police had finally forwarded her handbag.

'And there's nothing?'

'Nup.'

But Rae knew her better than that. 'Oh, right. Let's not invade her privacy. I'll just read it in the *FT* in three months' time.'

Lexa shifted in her seat. 'If it's anything to do with the bank, you'll be the first to know.'

His PA said to come on Monday at four. No, Lexa couldn't speak to him, but she had passed on the message and he knew what it was about. And now it was Monday and Lexa was sitting between the disabled ramp and the crèche area, trying not to look at the wall covered in clip-art posters. All those competing stand-out colours and blocky fonts. Ethical trading, people before profit, challenging discrimination, stopping the BNP . . . She agreed with every lofty ideal. Which was why they depressed the hell out of her.

She was a *Guardian*-reading baby boomer who'd moved from squishy centre to hard left just by standing still. Not a fashionable position. She told herself she wasn't a real dinosaur, not like the fifty-year-olds in leather biker jackets still flogging agitprop tabloids outside Boots on Saturday mornings. At least she knew she was a spectator on the banks of the great river that had once swept her along. Since the Strike, or the end of the Cold War or, at any rate, *since her youth*, politics had moved outwards to religious and ethnic strife and inwards to the nursery, becoming at once too vast and too small to fully engage her. Her childlessness disenfranchised her. She couldn't seem to get worked up over campaigns for school crossings and *20's plenty* zones and combating *stranger danger*. It wasn't that she doubted the epidemic of abuse. She had enough friends who, late at night over one too many drinks, had blurted *actually it happened to me* . . . But for Lexa, the cult of the victim-child was the acceptable face of an insidious myopia. Why wrestle with inequality when you could privilege the innocent instead? Children had become a politics. Not just the sexually and physically and emotionally at risk, but all children. Which was the same old song but to a newly-righteous tune: *me and mine come first*. Me and mine's right to jump the queue for hospital treatment, and breathe clean air, and eat a locally-sourced organic diet, and have a wee greet over the polar bears, and be driven to school in a four-wheel-drive tank and taught alongside other lucky wee boys and girls who might save their stamps and bottle tops to help the barefoot children in Africa but would never kick a ball with the ferals on the other side of town. And this was more than OK: it was aspiration, the new civic virtue, a reason to mortgage yourself to thirty per cent over the hilt and max out the credit cards. Until the global economy had gone bust.

And of course Lexa cared about Amy and Joe and paedophile rings and cyber bullying and food additives and air quality and the melting ice cap. But what no one in power – or with any hope of power – was prepared to say was that they couldn't have it all. And yes, she took the odd forty-quid flight (the train was so expensive) and drank gallons of milk from those evil farting cows (she didn't want osteoporosis in ten years' time) . . . At which point Gabriel – the old Gabriel, before her stroke – would have tilted her head and wondered why those left stranded when the socialist tide went out were so keen on self-imposed guilt. Forever beating themselves up about throwing away the *Big Issue* unread or grinding the Third World under the wheels of their cheap-pineapple-and-king-prawn-laden supermarket trolleys. And Lexa would have answered that she saw nothing wrong with a wee bit of guilt. The haves feeling guilty about the have-nots had worked well enough as a redistributive principle, before guilt was redistributed to those too lazy or feckless to become filthy rich and famous. Before self-interest became the only respectable position. Before she'd caught herself saying, in a certain sort of company, that she earned her living keeping the burglar-class out of middle-class homes.

She had hung on for longer than most, refusing to read that John O'Farrell book her ex-lefty friends kept pressing on her, buying the *Observer* for Nick Cohen (until he went rogue over Saddam Hussein), even getting a brief heady sip of *history-is-on-our-side* during the campaign for Scottish devolution. Before reverting to righteous futility with the protest against war in Iraq. But politics as reflex, that all-encompassing binary system, us or them, for or against, everyone she cared about on the same side . . . all that was gone, replaced by politics as shopping, as issue-based pick'n'mix. She could stand in the climate change checkout queue with a basket of genetically-modified foods, behind advocates of nuclear power and the eco-gadget route to unconstrained domestic growth. Right and wrong – even right and left – were debatable positions these days, because the big picture was economic, and no one really understood it. Not the ex-Marxists or the Muslims or the Greens or the high rollers in the City, or even Gordon Brown. How could she live in such a world and not become a little jaded?

Anyway, she didn't have to read the posters on the wall. There were other distractions. Four cubicles had been created out of office dividers and a seated queue of women waited to receive aromatherapy, reiki, shiatsu massage and reflexology. A stress-busting therapies taster day, according to the receptionist who, when four o'clock became half-past, was sure no one would mind Lexa having a go. Then it was five. And then five-thirty. The receptionist was sorry, he must have been held up. By now Lexa could have used a little stress-busting, but the therapists had gone, and the receptionist was buttoning her jacket and warning that the janitor locked the building at six. Lexa said she'd give it another few minutes. It wasn't as if she had anywhere else to go.

At five to six she slung her bag over her shoulder. Down the pink art deco staircase, the colour of some German cold-cut left on the platter at the end of the party. Was it Woolworths that had had stairs like this, with this same curved chrome banister rail . . .?

'Are you lost, love?'

He was coming up the flight below, emerging out of the shadowed stairwell, looking straight at her.

'It's me,' she said.

His shock was unfakeable.

She wasn't the only appointment he'd missed lately. His diary was all over the place. His PA was having a few problems at home. He was cutting her as much slack as he could but, God's sake, when they'd come from the other end of the country . . .

He was really sorry, but he had to be somewhere twenty minutes ago. He'd only come back to pick up some papers.

She said 'Gabriel's had a stroke. I found your message on her phone.'

He nodded, twice. 'Can you stay till tomorrow—?'

She watched him realise the question was open to misunderstanding.

'—in a hotel? On me. I'll pick you up first thing.'

The room they were sitting in was just big enough to contain the white leather suite and widescreen television. Heat blazed from the radiators. Despite the air freshener tucked behind the potted begonia on the windowsill, a smell of sickness hung over the house. There was the sound of a lavatory flushing and, somewhere closer, the clatter of crockery being set on a tray. 'He'll be with you in a minute,' the woman called out. Caroline. Hair the colour of bitter chocolate, so thick it could have been a wig. Lexa had been shocked, keeking under the lush fringe to find that monkey face, as if she were the one doing her husband's dying. He took a long time making his way down the hall. They could hear his laboured breathing, and Caroline murmuring encouragements at his side. Lexa tried to prepare herself but was nowhere near ready for the apparition in the doorway: skeletal, blue-faced, suffocating as he stood. It was hard to believe there was a grown man's body within the cinched folds of that brown velour dressing gown. He had the feet of a Pieta, alabaster-white and slightly less than life-size, without corns or bunions, the tendons clearly visible. She had never paid him much attention back then. He was just Stuart's friend, a beefy man with a moustache. Now he had lost both muscle and hair, there was nothing for her to recognise. She refused to consult her one clear memory, the day of the rout at the coking plant. Meeting his eyes as he'd glanced up to find her eavesdropping from the other bar.

'You remember Lexa,' Stuart said.

'A,' Mick gasped. His eyes were black jelly glistening in a face small as a child's, though no child ever had that toneless skin. Clinging to his wife for support, he extended his free hand. Lexa moved towards him, clumsy with health. His palm was cold and papery. She hoped his bones wouldn't snap in her grip.

'How're you doing?' she asked.

'Not too . . . bad . . . today.'

She was afraid to let go in case she was helping to hold him up.

Caroline nodded towards the armchair with a look that acknowledged, and resented, Lexa's discomfort. A wife could not afford the luxury of squeamishness. Her job was the efficient management of her husband's dependence while continuing to seem the submissive little woman he had married.

It was several minutes before Mick was settled in his chair. Cushions were brought out from behind the sofa to wedge him upright. The top button of his pyjama jacket was unfastened. Slippers were found for his feet. His dressing gown was tugged from the hem until it sat smoothly beneath him. There was a further interval while he recovered from the exertion of sitting down. Caroline left the room and returned with the tea tray. Two types of chocolate biscuits wrapped in coloured foil. Mick's tea, milky and already cooled, was in a turquoise plastic picnic mug. There were three cups and saucers but he dismissed her with a feeble, impatient flick of his hand.

Stuart began to talk football. Their team was having a run of bad luck. Bernie had to be wishing he'd signed Cocker when he'd had the chance, though they'd done better than they'd any right to in that friendly against Wednesday. Lexa gathered that the art of these visits was to simulate ordinary conversation, ignoring the fact that one of the parties was too wasted even to nod. There were no questions and no pauses to allow their host to volunteer his opinion. Mick appeared to listen, though she could not believe he was thinking of anything but the ceaseless struggle for breath. For her part, she was torn between boredom and savage embarrassment. Normally she would have looked at Stuart, since he was speaking, and normality was the illusion they were striving for, but it was Mick she was visiting and, each time she turned to face him, she felt dismay rearranging her features. Her sense of smell was unusually acute that morning. She still had the scent of Stuart's nubuck jacket in her nostrils, though Caroline had taken it at the door. A mouth-furring tang rose from the teacups, meeting the synthetic citrus of a chocolate biscuit whose orange foil was partly unwrapped. The air freshener was coconut-flavoured. Her tongue baulked at the plaster taste of sterilised milk. But all of these were preferable to the underlying smell.

Her gaze wandered the room and, out of habit, she put together a description for Gabriel's benefit. A feminine space. The grandchildren in gold-coloured frames, a couple of Julia Roberts movies on DVD, an *ER* box set, the latest *Hello!* magazine, but no evidence of a shared life. Maybe that explained why Caroline seemed both vindicated and bitter now that her dying husband had need of her.

Stuart handed Mick the picnic mug. Lexa watched the liquid travel down his throat.

'You'll see . . . changes . . . round here.'

For one awful moment she couldn't understand what he was saying. Stuart came to the rescue.

'I din't take her along William Street, din't want to scare her off when she'd just got here.'

Mick's mouth widened fractionally in what she took to be a smile. All his expressions were vestigial, expending energy he could ill afford. 'I saw her . . . on picket-line . . .'

'And she weren't scared then,' Stuart finished for him. Mick let this stand, though she wondered if he had been trying to say something less complimentary.

'You're too . . . late . . .'

'Too late for what?'

Stuart frowned in surprise at her tone. Mick tensed with the effort of further speech and began to struggle. His head strained, pushing against some constriction in his throat. His mouth opened and closed as if to rid itself of a vile taste. The gasping breaths were punctuated by a faint glottal clicking. Stuart took the mug of cold tea from his hand. His manner suggested this was a regular occurrence, best ignored.

'Too late to see pit again, that's for sure,' he said when Mick's fit had subsided. 'They capped Dudderthorpe six week after it shut. Left half machinery down there, leaking acids, oils, all sorts. Faxerley took 'em eight week. They got compulsory purchase order on scrap metal merchants so they could join up two sites. European money to grass land over. It's a country park now. Six square mile. All they left were Faxerley baths block.

Converted it into industrial units. Panel-beater and lad who prints wedding invitations. Six jobs where there used to be nine hundred.'

'The price of solidarity,' she said. Then she saw Stuart's face.

'There were twenty-four still out at end. Thirty-seven at Dudderthorpe. Allt' rest scabbed.' He met her eye. 'It's all right you looking like that. You weren't on strike, up to your neck in debt, patching kids' shoes with cardboard. There were another eight month of it after you left.'

Mick saw her discomfort and, though his face showed nothing, she felt his satisfaction. His mocking glance over the bar counter that day had taken a quasi-sexual pleasure in her humiliation.

'It weren't all . . . bad . . . We had . . . film stars.'

She looked at Stuart and he named an English actress famous for taking her bra off for foreign directors in the 1970s. An Equity activist, a wearer of badges and signer of letters to the newspapers.

'I wrote to her, asked her up to see for herself what it were really like. She came on picket line, got pissed-up with lads . . .'

Lexa knew he had slept with her, and she was jealous. Even after all these years. Not jealous of the sex, that would have been ridiculous, but of standing shoulder-to-shoulder with him on the picket-line and, later, surrounded by the baritone chorus of drunken voices in the miners' welfare.

Mick inclined his head confidentially. 'She took shine . . . to Stuart.'

'Didn't we all?'

He sank back against the chair, having hit his target.

'Mick's still got monk on because she wun't go down cellar with him. He wanted to switch lights off, show her how dark it were down pit. She din't fancy it for some reason.'

Mick laughed. A painful, wheezy staccato. Then his shoulders and chest began to heave and Lexa heard that ominous clicking in his throat. The coughing started as a repetitive scrape, escalating into spasms, then convulsions which ripped through him, each seeming to promise a violent release until overtaken by the next. Standing, Stuart reached for the beaker of cold tea, then thought better of it. Mick's hands clawed the air. The breath was rattling in his throat, his blue face turning puce. Stuart put out his hands, palm-up, and Mick clutched them, bracing himself against the racking coughs, letting the attack work its way through him until it had slowed to a rhythmic flinching and, finally, they came to rest, the healthy man and the sick, heads bowed together, hands clasped. Stuart looked huge beside him, though Mick had been a good six inches taller and probably three stones heavier. Lexa could picture him now. Dependable on the picket-line, humorously taciturn in his cups. Never far from Stuart, tossing him a cigar across the table, ready to spring to his aid at the threat of a bar-room brawl.

Mick pulled away first. His eyes, before they closed, were bloodshot. Stuart sat down and drained his teacup. She understood that they would be leaving soon.

Mick opened his eyes and nodded towards Lexa. 'What's she . . . doing here?'

A good question. She was a stranger in his home. There would be many he knew better whom he refused to see in this condition.

'She's helping with campaign.'

She hoped her surprise didn't show.

Mick's red-rimmed eyes were studying her. One hand was pressed against his sternum, the other rested on the arm of his chair. Curving his fingers, he beckoned. She took the three steps needed to cross the room. The smell was overpowering. He beckoned again. Reluctantly she knelt to put her face on a level with his. His hand grasped her fingers. In the dark jelly of his eyes she saw no trace of dislike or contempt or sexualised spite, no memory of that long-distant act of malice. Just the loneliness of a dying man.

Stuart drove her around Dudderthorpe village. Boarded-up houses. Smoke-blackened steel shutters. An ice-blue Rover abandoned on the football pitch. The police station they had besieged, its windows now darkened with heavy-duty metal mesh. From the elevated seats of his silver four-by-four it was possible to see over the exploding privet into once neatly-tended gardens run to seed.

'There's sandwich factory at Levinwell. They took canteen staff and some o' face-workers. Painting and decorating. Hot foam car wash. Security jobs. Time-served tradesmen taking Alsatian for a walk round building sites . . .' He brought his speed down, noticing a police car parked in a lay-by up ahead. 'One or two did all right. Tommo went to college, ended up with a degree. He's an inspector with Health and Safety now. Frank's a magistrate. Started off in Worksop, had to move down to Mansfield. Knew every family up in court.'

He nodded at the policemen as he drove past.

Lexa turned her head, feigning interest in the squad car, but really watching Stuart at the wheel. If anything, he looked younger than the man she'd met in Glasgow three years ago, his arms tanned and taut above their gauntlets of black fur, his T-shirt cut to forgive what needed forgiveness but still snug enough to be butch. He seemed to have more hair, though it must have been that what little remained was more visible against his tan. He'd spent the drive from Leeds taking a conference call with his phone on loudspeaker, a duty he had to discharge to be free for the rest of the morning. Then at Mick's, the drama of Mick had left no time for awkwardness. But now it was just the two of them.

'So what's this campaign I'm supposed to be helping with?'

'Justice for Faxerley—'

She gave him a wary look.

'—Nowt to do with your old pals. Deadline's passed. We cun't get it to court in time. Government's our last hope.'

'You think they'll compensate men from a private pit?'

'No,' he said, 'but lads could do with a fight. Strengthens immune system.'

All the miners had had this streak of black humour. The trick was to know when they were letting you in on the joke, and when they were turning it against you.

The last time she'd driven along this stretch of road it had cut through open country, now it was lined with identical pink-bricked houses. Most had a PVC conservatory tacked on the back, doubling the amount of floor space downstairs. A village-sized estate of detached homes, each less than two metres from its next-door neighbours.

'I can see how you wouldn't want to live here,' she said.

'Why's that then?'

She recalled this tone from the days when she first knew him, when she'd had to vet every innocuous remark in case it was misconstrued.

'It's lost its romance,' she said.

His lips set in their old mocking line.

Another mile and they'd left the houses behind. He pulled in to the side of the road and turned off the engine. She looked around. Streetlights burned uselessly above grey tarmac. Ragged grassland on either side. Her heartbeat quickened.

'Where are we?'

'Have a guess.'

Birkdale Country Park. She saw the sign and understood.

'Come on,' he said. 'Fresh air'll do you good.'

The grass was a lifeless yellow-brown, though the summer hadn't been particularly dry. She remarked on this.

'They din't put enough topsoil down. It's just slag underneath.'

'Where are the birches?'

He looked confused, until she pointed to the sign.

'Ah. They din't take. Still, they looked good on Dobbie's turf when John Prescott cut ribbon.'

She didn't like the idea of all that toil and danger smoothed over, remade as a public amenity. Yet the thought that money had been spent, some debt to those men supposedly paid off, and it was now a waste ground . . . that seemed worse. It wasn't only the place she had romanticised. So much of the man she had loved had been context. The pits, the village, his class politics. Now he stood stripped of all that, did she even know him, let alone like him? Other than physically. Her blood still warmed at his proximity, that much had not changed. The coarsening of middle age suited him. She guessed he attracted more female interest these days, though he had lost the touching blend of slightness and muscle, swagger and reserve, that had first penetrated her defences.

He took her to see the canal basin with its towpath of chipped herringbone brick and the holiday barges roped to rusting green-

and-gold bollards. They trudged up the slope to the cast-iron plaques embedded in the ground over Faxerley's two shafts, then walked around the single-storey block that had once held the pithead baths. She tried to fill in the rest of the site – the coal preparation plant, the medical centre, the offices – but the pictures in her head bore no relation to the geography around her. They climbed higher, up what she was increasingly certain was an artificial gradient, across the bridge over the railway cutting, to a paddock where two horses and a white-nosed donkey left off tugging at the grass and plodded towards them. The piebald horse leaned over the barbed-wire fence to nuzzle her hand.

It was one of those seasonless English days she associated with this place. A soiled white sky. Flat calm. A day to be whiled away over a sausage sandwich in the pit canteen, or a tomato juice in the miners' welfare, her gums stinging from too much Worcester sauce. Back then most bars had shut at two o'clock, to reopen at six. It had been her first experience of the illicit world of afternoon drinking. Desultory talk in lowered tones, beer froth licked from an upper lip, the phosphorus hit from a struck match. Someone's salt-and-pepper dog settling with a groan under the table. At this distance it was hard to recapture the appeal, that faint thrum of excitement under the boredom.

'A bungee jump, at her age,' he said. 'What did she think she were doing?'

Lexa picked at a twist of horsehair snagged on the barbed wire. 'I didn't even know you knew her.'

'Harrison introduced us.'

She had to search her memory. Harrison: the colliery manager. Strange how some details faded while others were fresh as yesterday.

'When was this?'

'Before Faxerley sale went through.'

'While I still knew you?'

She saw a sardonic glint in his green-blue eyes.

'Before you packed me, yeah.'

She felt warm suddenly, though the day was cool.

'And you've kept in touch for twenty-five years?'

'Three year. I looked her up after you wun't help. It's thanks to her Mick's still alive—'

Lexa's face fell apart.

'—drugs she got him. From America.'

There had been forty of them worth spending the money on, their cancers still at the stage where a difference could be made. It wouldn't work forever, and it wasn't much of a life, but better than no life at all. The drug was not yet approved, but the pharmaceutical company had been willing to include them in its international trials. For a price. *A fuck of a lot*, he said. So then it made more sense that Gabriel had no savings.

'Is that why you phoned her—?'

He squinted as if she'd asked a trick question.

'—about the drugs?'

'Ah, no.' He grunted to clear his throat, a sound as familiar to her once as her own breathing. 'I'm a trustee on a pension fund. I thought she could give us some investment advice.'

'I hope you haven't bought any of her CDOs.'

She said it as a joke, but he looked startled.

'No,' he said, 'we steered clear o' them.'

The donkey came up to the fence. Instead of clapping the shaggy neck as she would have, Stuart made a claw of his fingers and gave it a good scratch.

'How long till she's up and about?'

The innocence of the question made her want to weep, the news she had to impart like a poison inside her. And then she told him and had the strangest sense that he was relieved.

'That's FSA off her back, anyroad—'

She shook her head.

'—if she's not all there they shun't be questioning her.'

'You don't have to tell *me*.' She took a breath flavoured with horsehide and grass. 'They won't see her till she's out of hospital. They're looking at everything, it'll take them months. The CEO's saying it's a one-woman problem, but they can't just take her word for it.'

Down the slope, a young couple were playing with their bichon frise. Stuart turned to watch the dog scurrying after the ball.

'*Jesus*,' he muttered, as if the news were still sinking in. 'She din't deserve that.'

With the baths block behind them, the view was almost completely rural. The horses. A Dutch barn. Crows flapping between the oaks on the Levinwell road. The patchwork panorama of ripening corn, striped hay meadow and green potato fields. Lexa heard Gabriel's voice in her head, as clearly as if she were standing behind her. *You can't go back*. And of course she knew that. That wasn't why she was here. But how could she not remember? The games they'd played, the sparks they'd struck from their conflicting interests, the balance of power ever-shifting, the struggle both fierce and somehow collusive, like the way they'd made love. His left hand was resting on the fence post. His eyes followed her glance. Reddening, she returned her attention to the view, looking south to where Dudderthorpe pit had once stood, searching for the headgears until she remembered that the girders would have been sold for scrap. Then west, past the village with its concentric crescents of red brick, the mini-mart, the miners' welfare, to the parkland of the Barlby estate. A small building caught her eye. Curved at one end, the other end squared-off, an ancient gravity in its grey stone. The Norman chapel. And now another detail floated to the surface of her memory. The dog-walker who'd caught them in the churchyard that day, who was hostile, and furtive, and had been to Nottingham for tests.

'We knew,' she breathed.

Stuart stood very still.

'That miner, the day we made love at the chapel—' or should she have said *shagged*? '—he had something wrong with his lungs . . .'

'Brian Netley,' he said.

The name slotted neatly into her memory, as if it had been there all along. Just as likely she had never known it. That was the way memory worked, like a computer file corrupted each time it was called up. It was impossible to retrieve what she had felt at the time: if she had had some premonition of disaster. Maybe she had just taken him for a heavy smoker. But no: it was coming back to her. There had been others with the same symptoms. She would not have ignored them, surely? The more she thought about it, the more dislocated she felt. It was *Gabriel* who had come to the rescue; *Gabriel* who had seen that it was drugs they needed, not the righteous satisfaction of their day in court. While she, Lexa, had done nothing. This was not the person she thought she was. A dab hand at telling them what they wanted to hear in a funding proposal, yes, or a tender for a public contract, but not a woman to ignore the early warnings of a disease that would decimate a workforce . . .

'We *knew*.'

'We *knew nothing*.' He lowered his voice, though there was no chance of being heard by the dog walkers. 'There were that much dust about you cun't tell what it were. Waterpipe range were always leaking. Safety officer told me it were matrix o' cement and fibreglass. Pipe-fitters'd chop lump out, put seals on ends, fit another piece. Week after they'd be doing same somewhere else. Dust is dust – fibreglass, asbestos: it din't look any different.' He passed a hand over his scalp. 'Some o' old timers'd been doing job forty year, they weren't going to listen to me. I tried to get 'em to wear masks. They thought I were taking piss—'

She knew she should say something. It was cruelty to stand here accusing him with her silence.

'—Christ, Lexa, d'you know how much asbestos there is in Britain? Dudderthorpe Infants, clinic where we had us injections, Shepswell baths . . .' His skin had turned grey beneath his tan. 'Life's full of risks and people take 'em. Near enough everyone at that pit were a smoker. They knew it'd likely kill 'em. Their grandads were miners, most of 'em. They could see 'em sat in chair all day, coughing up muck. Working underground's more dangerous than sitting behind a desk. They weren't daft, they knew that.'

'They didn't know they were taking thirty years off the end of their lives.'

He looked down at the barbed wire. 'No,' he said.

She studied his lowered head, its downy fuzz, that shallow spoon-sized dip at the top of his neck, and an ache of pity spread through her. She wanted to tell him that no one could blame him: he'd called it as he'd seen it at the time. And it was true. But it meant nothing now she'd seen Mick.

'What *am* I doing here, Stuart?'

There was a moment's delay before he looked up. 'What d'you mean?'

'You've taken the morning off work.'

'You've taken whole day.'

'I told you, I thought you might know what she's been up to.'

And, of course, she'd had another motive.

He sighed. 'They're all on benefits. If DWP find out, they'll prosecute. Stress'd kill 'em, never mind cancer.'

'But if the money went on medical treatment . . .'

His eyes met hers.

'I see.' She recalled the smartness of Caroline's leather suite, the shiny Golf parked outside the house. What was Gabriel doing buying them cars and furniture? What was she doing helping them at all? But that was a double-edged sword of a question, too easily turned against herself.

'They must be safe enough by now. If anybody was going to shop them to the fraud hotline, they'd have done it at the time.'

But he wasn't looking for reassurance.

'I need her laptop,' he said. 'It had a yellow case.'

'Do you know the password?'

'No.'

'Forget it.'

'It'll take FSA two minutes to crack it.'

'And what they find might help her keep her pension.'

'And it might not an' all. Forty men. And their families. It's a fucking smoking gun.'

'I said no.'

His mouth tightened. 'So you're just going to hand it over to 'em?'

'Not necessarily.'

They stood there, listening to the crows. The horses had given up on them and were cropping the grass a few metres away. A breeze had blown up out of nowhere, bringing the smell of rain.

'Are you worried the press'll get hold of the story?' she said. 'Is that it?'

'Oh aye. Hold the front page.' He made a breathy sound,

notionally amused but a long way from laughter. 'We've got these lasses in Union office. Clerical. They can't get enough of 1980s. Tony Hadley. ABC. Boy George lookalike nights in town. I can just see 'em opening *Daily Mail* at coffee break. *They did what: dug coal out o't'ground? Bloody 'ell, bit primitive, weren't it?*—'

Down the hill, the dog walkers were calling their bichon frise.

'—fifty-odd blokes with cancer from summat they did in olden days. You've more chance getting mistreated dog into papers now. Unless some lottery-funded wanker's turning it into performance art.'

She thought about the irrelevance of the past. The Gabriel who'd been introduced to Stuart all those years ago, her shimmering skin, her razor-sharp brain. And Lexa's own vanished self, flirting with him in the vanished canteen. Those hot summer nights, with just a sheet to cover them. Waking to the smell of him. The daily drama of the strike. The thrill of knowing that, if not actually *making* history, she was *living* it, her heart beating to its pulse. Alive. Alive.

Maggie. That was the name the dog's owners were calling.

Stuart said, 'It dun't do me any good, seeing Mick.'

She laid her fingers on his ringless left hand where it rested on the fence post. He accepted the touch, and they stayed like this awhile before he turned towards her. She felt a tightness in her throat, her belly, in the air between them. He took her by the shoulders and chafed her bare arms.

'Sodding August. You look frozzen.'

They began the walk back to his car.

SEPTEMBER

Lexa locked the Micra, buttoning her coat as she walked. The wind was blowing from the north, driving the year's first fall of leaves across the hospital car park. Nine weeks since Gabriel's stroke. She felt a moment's hopelessness, which was all she ever allowed herself. There would be other autumns when this one was over, other seven o'clock dusks with boys shouting on the practice pitch and wood smoke in the air, and boxes of fireworks in the newsagents, and Gabriel back home in Mackenzie Square.

Meanwhile she was keeping a diary of the patient's recovery, noting improvements in diction and manual dexterity. She could dress herself now, and brush her own hair. Daily her sentences grew more sophisticated, her train of thought less prone to jump the rails. Her skin still had the bloodless tint of poultry in the butcher's window but, even asleep, she looked more alive.

'Have you come to see me?'

She was shambling along the corridor towards Lexa in a crumpled Gieves and Hawkes shirt and Matalan jogging bottoms. That dragging left foot made her progress painfully slow, but Lexa didn't mind. As she didn't mind coaxing her into eating her dinner, and reading out the same crossword clue five times over, and turning a blind eye when she cheated at Snakes and Ladders. What good was love if it couldn't be put to the test?

She was making for the lavatories at the other end of the corridor.

'Come in with me.'

The cubicle was designed to accommodate a wheelchair, so there was plenty of room. Gabriel slumped on to the horseshoe of moulded plastic that turned the lavatory bowl into a giant potty. Lexa tried to work the joggers down between her thighs and the seat but had to give up and haul her back to her feet. It wasn't easy. She looked like skin and bone but lifted like dead weight. Seated again, she swung her right foot and her slipper fell off.

For several seconds nothing happened but, once the flow started, it seemed it would never stop. Gabriel smiled her new smile. Passive. Vacantly expectant.

'Gabriel, do you remember . . .?'

Outside, someone rattled the door handle. Lexa jumped, but whoever it was went away. Rae disapproved of these interrogations, afraid that the wrong question could raise Gabriel's blood pressure and trigger a second stroke. She had made Lexa promise not to ask anything *stressful*. Promise or no promise, Lexa had to know. Though there seemed to be no definitive answer. Today Gabriel remembered the island, but not the bungee jump. Alison Babbington was still her boss, but the FSA investigation meant nothing. 'Into the CDOs,' Lexa prompted. Gabriel became uncannily still, her eyes receding in their sockets. 'What?' she said at last. But Lexa had seen her register the importance of these initials she could no longer interpret and, for a moment – before this failure, too, was forgotten – the mask over her face had shown a terrible self-knowledge.

'Has anyone offered you a cup of tea?'

'In the loo?' Lexa queried.

Gabriel's voice throbbed graciously. 'I'll get the girl to make you one.'

Since the stroke, she had swapped her personality for an arbitrary sequence of role-playing. When her voice sounded childlike she became a child. When her eyes gleamed with that vulnerable light she was a cowering figure from Victorian melodrama. Smiling, she was a creature of pure joy. Currently she was the perfect hostess, although until July her idea of entertaining had been getting Amy to open a bottle of wine. It was as if she were an aerial picking up cultural static, the medium for a cast of thousands drawn from books, movies, soap operas, advertisements and her circle of friends.

'I got an email from Stuart Duffy this morning,' Lexa said.

'Me and several hundred others. A link to an online petition. You remember Stuart. My first big love affair—'

Gabriel's face was blank.

'—he got in touch three years ago. I told you. But you didn't tell me he'd been in touch with you.'

Gabriel started to sing.

'*Once a boy was no good*
took a girl into a wood—'

By now Lexa was used to these Dadaist stunts.

'*—bye bye blackbird.*
Laid her down upon the grass
squeezed her tits and skelped her arse
bye bye blackbird.'

'Are you trying to tell me something—?'

Gabriel looked up.

'—about Stuart?'

'*Took her where nobody else could find her*
to a place where he could really grind . . .'

Lexa cut across the song. 'Where did you learn that?'

'Don't you know it?'

'Not that version.'

Gabriel smiled like a child who'd deliberately used a naughty word, but might not know what it meant. 'Is the other one better?'

'Not really. It's about lynching blacks in the southern states of America.'

'No, you're thinking of 'Strange Fruit'.'

Lexa looked at her. 'You're right, I am.'

Gabriel's ping-pong ball stare was so wide that Lexa could see the bloody scribble around each eyeball.

This was how it went. For days on end she existed on a limited plane of bodily needs and childish humour, and then without warning there was a new awareness in those protuberant eyes. A conspiratorial glint, as if the inanity were a game they were both playing. But there was a catch. The game rested on implicit trust. Acknowledgement would kill it. And what if it was all in Lexa's imagination, what if Gabriel really was inane? Just bright enough to be crushed by the news of her lost intelligence.

Lifting her up again, Lexa caught a warm whiff of urine with a meaty trace of hospital food.

'I've got my knickers in a twist.'

Lexa rearranged them and pulled the joggers up.

Gabriel looked down at herself. 'Are you my friend?'

The moment when she changed personae was always disconcerting. Lexa caught the paralysed hand and, gently, shook her cold fingers. 'Of course. We've known each other a long time.'

That hovering gaze was suddenly sharply focused. 'What like am I?'

Lexa looked at the landslip that had been her jaw, her sunken cheeks, the half-a-head of lank blonde hair, the new growth over the shaven patch ash-white.

'You're just you,' she said.

The Royal Highland was an Edinburgh landmark: half-crag, half-fortress, a black stone railway hotel looming over the tracks like the bastard progeny of the castle and Arthur's Seat. As a child, Lexa had improvised a game of hopscotch on the tartan carpet and been told off by a waitress bringing her mother Nescafé and Peek Freans custard creams. Now the sooty stone had been cleaned to a dirtier-looking dun, and the travellers' lounge was called the Glamis Room and had hand-printed wall-paper and knole sofas upholstered in anchovy and taupe, and Lexa would never have crossed the threshold had she not been Alison Babbington's guest.

Three hundred bankers. A couple of hundred heads of division, perhaps thirty of them female; a few stellar names supporting the achievements of their staff; and seventy less-senior but better-looking women invited for what Alison presumed was the usual reason. Plus the odd wild card like Lexa with no reason to be there at all, except that Alison had paid for six tables and claimed she couldn't face it without a *neutral radical* muttering subversions at her side.

'An orgy of self-congratulation?'

'I would hope so.'

'For a sector that's taken eight-hundred-and-fifty billion from the taxpayer?'

'Just drink the champagne. You don't have to clap.'

So here they were, amid the young women in flimsy-floaty evening wear, and a few matrons in beaded cocktail frocks because, as Alison said, you might run a British bank, but you couldn't find a fucking floor-length dress that didn't show your bingo wings. Though, at the eleventh hour, a Japanese designer had proved her wrong with this cunning envelope of slate-grey silk-jersey that was more a sculpture than a dress. It was easier for the men, all of whom wore monkey suits or shortie jackets with tartan trews. (Because dress kilts were for back-office staff getting hitched in East Kilbride.)

At the aperitif stage of the evening the noise was ebullient but not yet deafening. It was still possible to pick out individual voices in the hubbub. A burst of ringing Anglo-Scots. That Edinburgh-boardroom baritone like gravel rolled in honey. Soon they would go through to the ballroom and, under a gold-and-white plasterwork ceiling lit by thousands of glass teardrops, unfold the sort of starched napkin that felt like an X-ray shield in the lap. Ahead of them lay five courses prepared by a television chef, with a different wine for every course, and Lexa found herself wondering – as she always wondered when she ducked under the red rope of privilege – *is this it?* A few out-of-season ingredients artfully arranged on a plate? A more subtly-nosed inebriation? No need to ask why money mattered in Cambusdyke, but the difference between what a lot of money bought and what an unimaginably excessive sum could acquire was less obvious. At least, to Lexa. It seemed to her that if there was a point to the pursuit of obscene wealth, that point was purely conceptual.

'I could say the same about driving a car with a hundred-and-fifty-thousand miles on the clock and wearing secondhand pants.' *Secondhaand paants.*

'Never pants. Or shoes.'

'You'd better hope those rampant consumers keep on shopping in Jigsaw and donating their cast-offs to charity.'

'So I'm a hypocrite?'

Alison took a sip of champagne. 'So I'm glad you don't wear someone else's pants.'

Women liked Lexa. Even the girls who talked nails and shoes, even the Cambusdykers saving for plastic boobs, even as they smirked at the jeans she wore with her wraparound dresses. But Alison Babbington's response to her was more than routinely affable. Seductive was the word, not necessarily in a sexual sense, not necessarily not. Lesbians, too, liked Lexa, perhaps mistaking her, or thinking she was near enough the border to come across. Alison wasn't a railway conductor with a number two buzzcut and a key chain dangling from her belt. She was straight enough to have a beef about her ex-husband. And yet . . . It felt like seduction. Maybe there was a Sapphic fling in the photo album, maybe it was late-flowering curiosity, or maybe she just flirted with everybody all the time. She was doing it now, working the room, giving them their fifteen seconds of intense unfiltered contact. They all felt special, then it was someone else's turn. Lexa could see it happening – the dopamine cut off, the system-shock of withdrawal – and knew just how they felt. For all her determination to keep her distance, the flattery was getting to her. There was every chance that Alison knew this.

She spoke to the woman because she had grey hair. Bright grey, beautifully-cut hair which emphasised her flawless skin, but still, in the context of this gathering, tantamount to a declaration of radical feminism. And she had to talk to someone.

The woman was standing with a man in Crawford tartan trews who was happy to be complimented on their punkish clash of green and magenta. He claimed to have been an actual punk in his teens but, when pressed, admitted this hadn't gone much further than owning the Sex Pistols album and a torn T-shirt that he used to smuggle past his mother under a Pringle sweater. His companion laughed but volunteered no evidence of her own youthful rebellion, so Lexa confessed to deceiving her parents to take the overnight coach to London and march in defence of abortion some years before her first kiss. At which point the schoolboy punk spotted an acquaintance on the far side of the room.

The grey-haired woman's name was Hermia and she worked in Exchange Traded Funds. She had an old-fashioned bluestocking's voice, with a testy note in its Oxbridge inflection. Her hazel eyes held no obvious wish to be liked. When asked what, exactly, her job involved, her glance slid over Lexa's shoulder into the room behind her.

Lexa played her trump card. 'I'm more at home with the benefits system. I work in Cambusdyke.'

The woman's mouth formed a shape that paid lip service to, and yet was not, a smile. She looked as if she were trying to listen to a very important programme on her own private radio.

'Do you not talk to ordinary people,' Lexa said, 'apart from your cleaner?'

A heavily-built man in a Chinese silk dinner jacket joined them.

'Excuse me,' Hermia said in her donnish contralto.

'What did you do to *her*?'

Lexa looked up into the fleshy face. For a moment all she knew was that she knew him. Then the memory slotted into place.

'Ned!'

The fringe was grey now, his Renaissance-portrait pallor a thing of the past, but the fat in his cheeks had kept the wrinkles at bay, and his eyelids were still fringed with those delicate lashes.

He closed the distance between them to graze his face against hers.

'So you double-kiss in banking now?' she said.

'Doesn't everyone?'

'Not on the sink estates, no.' Her heart was hammering. Her first contact with Goodisons in twenty-five years. 'What are you doing here?'

'Didn't Gabriel tell you? I work for Alison Babbington.'

Charlie Simmyn was renovating a cottage on Barra with environmentally-sustainable materials. Kit Meiklejohn ran marathons for cystic fibrosis. Hugo the quant's wife sold cupcakes to the yummy-mummies of Stockbridge. When the talk flagged, as it tended to, Lexa overheard references to Niall Ferguson and Dick Cheney from the diners behind her. On the far side of the circular table, Ned was talking opera. (Unless Wagner was an underling in Mergers and Acquisitions.) But of the four people she could feasibly converse with, three seemed determined to shift her view of bankers from sociopathic to blamelessly dull, and Alison was on duty and spreading herself very thin.

'You were warned,' she murmured while Charlie Simmyn was explaining his complex dietary requirements to the waitress.

'Does it show?'

Alison raised her dessert spoon and Lexa saw the strain of all those suppressed yawns reflected in its silvered back.

The noise from the other tables was raucous now, the faces

floridly animated. Some of the younger bankers had pocketed their bow ties. Obeying an old reflex, Lexa checked the expressions of the waiting staff topping up glasses at the rowdier tables. None looked overly stressed. At least two were laughing. It was strange, being among bankers again. Turning her head, spotting the types. The bloodless raptors made of cloth and claw and beak and glinting gold-rimmed specs. The rubber-cheeked golden boys they had once been. The inscrutable men with thinning white hair and stocky bodies toughened on Muirfield links. The pasty geeks with firsts in maths. The personable make-weights – one of them so much like Gavin he might have been a blood relative. And the category she found most troubling, the fiftyish alphas: burly, broad-shouldered survivors who wore their grey hair boastfully long and swept back from the forehead. A few weeks ago these men had been Gabriel's colleagues. She had left Goodison Farebrother, moved countries, put herself through all that upheaval, only to seek out the sort of predators she'd fled from. What was it she'd said on the island? *People want more. More art, more life, more money . . .* More pain? Did they want that too? And if not pain, then what?

The blaeberry cranachan had just been served. A skinny boy with narrow shoulders and dark springy curls took Charlie Simmyn's seat.

'Marcus Adobayo.'

She shook the caramel-and-pink hand, taking in his unbuttoned marcella collar, the lack of a jacket or tie, that flashy watch hanging loose on his slender wrist. He smelled faintly, disturbingly, like Alison.

'Most people call me Tropical.'

It was hard to believe a voice of such Shakespearian resonance could issue from that nine-stone frame. He could have played Mercutio. Or a latte Othello.

'Marcus is our regrettable contribution to global warming,' Alison said, knowing Lexa had already made the connection.

Tropical: the trader who didn't possess a coat, or an umbrella, or a car (which would have necessitated walking to a parking space), and no one was entirely sure he owned a jacket to match the pin-striped trousers he had made-to-measure by Yellowlees on George Street. There were reported sightings of a tie, but only once, and even then it had been draped, unknotted, around his neck. His life was lived in shirt sleeves at a constant twenty-six degrees, even in the icy bite of an Edinburgh winter, moving between home, bank, gym, bars, restaurants and nightclubs via a series of taxis which were warned to keep their heaters on 'high'.

'And you are?'

'A shareholder,' she said.

'Pension fund?'

'Taxpayer.'

Alison turned away to attend to something James Gordon Scott was saying on her other side.

'So not a shareholder in us,' he checked the back of Alison's head before lowering his voice to add, 'yet'.

'Should I move my account?'

'To China.' He read the question in her face and glanced towards Charlie, now back from the Gents and installed at another table. 'You can pay me later.'

He was a favourite of Ali's. *I know they're all doing it on hormones, but at least he's got a bit of style.* Style, and striking good looks. A chivalrous flirt, with a talent for buttering-up banking chiefs and maiden aunts. Bumptious, Lexa might have said in other circumstances, but the hours before what the menu quaintly termed 'carriages' seemed less of a prison sentence now.

'Do you mind them calling you Tropical?'

'You mean, because I'm a public-school nigger?' Leaning towards her, he applied his lips to her ear. 'Dey give me big respeck for da big cock.'

As it turned out, she was not to spend the rest of the evening *tête à tête* with him. Alison had barely started her pudding when she reached for her phone and breathed a soft *'Fuck'*, rising to take the call in the corridor.

Tropical murmured, 'The bell tolls for Structured Finance.'

Gabriel's department. Before Lexa could ask, Ned walked around the table to slip into Alison's seat.

'So have you missed me?'

She had forgotten the cherry-red shine of his lower lip when he smiled.

'Not much,' she said, 'have you missed me?'

'The first twenty years were the worst.'

He nodded at Tropical, who nodded back with the look of a man processing the past few minutes in the light of new information.

Ned was head of Mergers and Acquisitions, a post he had held for five years, since Alison lured him back from Hong Kong. There was more, but Lexa wasn't really listening. How many evenings had she spent with Gabriel in that time: three hundred? Plus phone calls and Sunday walks on the beach.

Ned asked where she was working these days.

'I'm on the peace-keeping force in Cambusdyke.'

There was a pause.

'You've never heard of it?'

'Is it very famous?'

'Notorious.' She wondered if he could be winding her up. 'It's a drug-ridden housing scheme on the west coast. A symbol of social anarchy. Most people worry about that sort of thing. Not bankers, obviously.'

'And you're saving them in spite of themselves?'

'You could say that.'

'Then what's there to worry about?'

It might have been the champagne, but he seemed more relaxed than he'd been in the eighties, less clumsy in his efforts to amuse as he talked her through the other banks' top tables, pointing out who was who. The CEO who'd redeployed his secretary to Aberdeen for serving him the wrong kind of coffee. The analyst who'd sabotaged a promising career by predicting the crash. The chief economist engaged to a Russian 'model' he'd met in an internet chatroom. The bond trader who was sleeping with directors at three rival banks. The heads of HR: 'All muff-divers.'

When she objected, he appealed to Tropical.

'The carpet-muncher mafia.'

Ned flicked the fringe out of his eyes. 'We're all pussy-whipped these days.'

'Under the fembot jackboot,' Tropical confirmed.

'So all these stories about bankers entertaining clients in lap dancing clubs: they're not true?'

Ned mugged disbelief. 'In Edinburgh? In the West Port pubic triangle?'

'Not unless they want to get beaten up by the hod-carriers,' Tropical said.

So then they were a double act, vying to make her laugh. With the understanding that the head of Mergers and Acquisitions would always come out on top.

She didn't make a habit of joking with men. A certain humourlessness was helpful in her job, and she'd never had Gabriel's playful touch with *maitres d'* and other women's husbands. But she could feel some long-atrophied muscle twitching back to life, helped by the Jigsaw dress, and the freshwater pearls Alison had lent her.

'See the stunner in green, by the pillar—?'

She followed Ned's gaze. A pretty face, though few observers would get that far. Even by the candid standards of the night, her décolletage left little to the imagination.

'—India Walsh. Lost us fifty million last year but Alison can't off her. The only woman in her division. They parachuted Samira Macleod in from Fixed Assets as cover, but Indy outflanked them.'

'Pregnant,' Tropical glossed.

Ned winked at the waitress who brought him a clean glass. 'And now she could take a position on a Tel Aviv bacon factory.'

'Just remind me,' Lexa said, 'on the trading floor, is it eight to one?'

'Which makes them eight times as powerful.'

'As good as unsackable.'

She had a vision of her twenty-three-year-old self listening to this conversation. The anger she would have felt, towards the middle-aged woman as much as the men. 'Am I going to have to bring up Goodison Farebrother?' she said.

To her surprise, Ned looked uncomfortable.

She was dying to ask *how did it end?* But she didn't want to learn that it had followed the usual pattern. New faces arriving, old faces departing, a talent drain as everyone sensed the way the wind was blowing. The rumour-mill churning. The clients removing their business. The takeover. It was oddly unbearable, the thought that something so malign could have just . . . fizzled out.

Ned shrugged. 'Everyone accepts the girlies deserve an even break, but the pendulum's swung too far the other way.'

'Too much mentoring,' Tropical said.

'Networking clubs.'

'Interview coaching.'

'Help with *goal-identification*.'

'Golf lessons—'

How long was it since she'd heard men laugh like this?

'—workshops on banishing negative body image.'

Ned shook his head as if beaten, then came back with '*Intelligent wardrobe* advice.'

'*No!*' A delighted yelp.

'It's on the intranet.'

Tropical turned to Lexa. 'All in the bank's time.'

'An accidental *double-entendre* and you're out,' Ned said, 'even at my level.'

He seemed to be waiting for her to agree that this was monstrously unfair.

'Would you like me to raise your concerns with the CEO?' she asked.

A warning flared in Tropical's eyes.

'What concerns?' Alison's voice said, behind her.

Ned retrieved her cranachan, pushed away when he'd sat down. 'Bloody Jocks and their porridge.' His glance slid towards the boss, inviting a response. 'It's bad enough for breakfast.'

The Ladies was deserted, all seven doors ajar. Alison walked up to the mirror, casting a critical glance at the crumpled translucence under her eyes, the smudge of Tea Rose on her philtrum but nowhere, now, on her lips.

'It wasn't funny,' Lexa said to her reflection.

'It was funny-*ish*.'

'"What's the difference between a banker in bonus week and a paedo in a nursery?"'

'No children were harmed in the making of this joke.'

'And no egos were dented, either.'

The kippered-looking editor of *Scottish Investor* magazine had handed out his scrap-metal trophies and ceded the microphone to a second-string television comic, a suet-faced culchie whose rapid-fire delivery turned the Irish joke on its head. An entire routine built around banker-bashing. Within seconds of his sprint to the mic, the ballroom was revved-up, the younger tables baying with mirth. He had a sheaf of newspaper cuttings. Speeches by leading industry figures, testimonies to Commons select committees, quotes from the Chancellor and the Governor of the Bank of England. Some he gave a surreal spin, others he merely read aloud. Slow-ly. The room roared. Lexa's had been the only unsmiling face.

'I hear you're closing Structured Finance—'

She paused, giving Alison a chance to say that Gabriel too would be made redundant, but she said nothing.

'—what's the point of a managing director with no department to direct?'

'And when she sues us for getting rid of her when she's sick?' Alison asked.

'You know she's not going to do that.'

'I don't. And nor do you.'

'If she keeps her pension, you'll never hear from her again—'

Alison's eyes lost the focus Lexa had come to expect.

'—will you think about it?'

'No,' she said.

Her toughness. Her ambiguous deadpan. The doll-size teeth and designer subfusc. The way she said '*haerdt*' for 'heard' and rhymed 'first' with 'borscht'. Lexa had to concede the charm in all this. It was a long time since she had met anyone so enjoyable to be around. And a long time since she had felt herself so enjoyed. As good as a facelift: she could see it in the mirror. It wasn't just the fancy frock and borrowed pearls.

The outer door opened and one of the housekeeping staff came in. A small dark woman. South Indian, perhaps. Seeing them, her face emptied of expression in a way that made Lexa think of Gabriel. She bundled the used hand towels into her laundry sack and withdrew.

Alison nodded her head at the door. 'Put your weight against that for a minute.' She took a clean towel and wiped the shelf in front of the mirror.

In films, when actors snorted baby powder or baking soda or whatever they substituted for cocaine, they sniffed noisily and swiped their nostrils, running the same fingertip around their gums. Alison was neater. When she raised her head there was nothing to betray her. She moved over to the door, gesturing for Lexa to take her place in front of the second line of coke.

Lexa shook her head.

Alison was close enough to smell the black coffee she'd drunk after the meal. 'There's a first time for everything—'

Her eyes were brightened by the drug, but she wasn't turbo-charged by it as the Irish comic had been. She retained that ironic detachment.

'—it'll get you through the next hour.' She held out the rolled twenty-pound note. 'And then we can go home.'

Lexa wasn't a drugs virgin. She had smoked dope and taken speed in her teens. It wouldn't change her life to try it. She wasn't going to turn into Bammer's best customer overnight. But it was one vulgar cliché too many. The chandeliers, the champagne, the pretentious food . . . Who needed them? Not Lexa. She rejected what the world prized. It was the last shred of her politics. She might never stand on another picket-line, but she wasn't going to roll over and become a marketing opportunity. Good cocaine, killer heels, thousand-pound handbags, recondite spa treatments, the pricey labels flaunted by anorexic models and metrosexual footballers: a bulldozer in her brain shunted them all into the same landfill site of indifference. And power, queried the Gabriel who lived intact in her head, was she indifferent to that, too? Would she have enjoyed herself quite so much with an Alison Babbington who was not CEO of Caledonian Bank?

Alison shifted her weight against the door. 'What did she do to deserve your loyalty?' She laughed her husky laugh. 'I can't even get you to trust me.'

'It's not about trust.'

'No,' another laugh, 'with Gabriel it couldn't be. Unless it was trusting her to make herself look good at every opportunity. I would have thought that relentless egotism could get quite annoying.'

Lexa walked across to the sinks to wash her hands. 'Aren't all bankers relentlessly egotistical?'

'Most of them. But we're going to change that.'

Lexa knew what was coming. 'The answer's still no.'

'I could use you—'

She ignored Lexa's satiric smile.

'—I'm not thrilled that we got our fingers burned in Structured Finance, but it's a chance to build a kind of banking that people can trust. We can't just leave it to the boys, let them turn the economy into a wanking competition.' *Whanking competition.* 'We have to learn from them without becoming them. That's what feminism should be addressing, not why eight-year-olds all want to be Jordan. If you really want to make a difference . . .' She raised her eyebrows, not needing to say it. They both knew Lexa was never going to ply her talking stick on the Gaza Strip. 'Idealists are valuable people. I hate to see one who's lost her way.'

'I don't belong—' Lexa glanced in the direction of the ballroom '—with them.'

'Who does?'

'You *are* them.'

A bruise of affront darkened the translucent skin under Alison's eyes. 'This country needs the banks,' she said, 'and bankers.'

'Cut out the cancer and you kill the patient?'

Alison left the door undefended and stood beside her. Their reflections like something in the hall of mirrors. 'If that's the metaphor you want to use.'

Lexa turned off the tap. 'I've no interest in getting the call centre turkeys to vote for Christmas.'

'*One day a week*. With a view to something permanent. To get a feel for the place, see if there's a fit.'

Lexa needed the work, God only knew. Local authorities were running scared, second-guessing the cuts they knew were coming, trying to stave off redundancies by freezing posts and doing nothing. Already two of her projects were under notice. And yes, the idealist, or the competitor, in her was hooked by the challenge. *To learn from them without becoming them.* To forge a new institutional culture where only the real misogynists would believe women were handed promotion on a plate. Everyone agreed things had to change. A shift from short-term profits to long-term results, to stop the goldfish chasing their bonuses round and round the bowl.

But to go back to banking after so long. Working alongside those people in the ballroom, the raptors and the silverback gorillas. It was unthinkable.

And yet she was thinking about it.

She had achieved the autonomy she'd always wanted. No one told her what to do. But there was an irony in her happy ending. She had enjoyed the years of women's defence classes and reclaim-the-night marches, the heightened sense of self that came from opposition to all around her. She missed living in a world in which everything was personal. So much justified anger. It was strange that, in all their hours of fiery talk, the women she knew had never got round to discussing what would happen after they achieved their goal. It had never occurred to Lexa that she was more alive in her oppression than she would be after taking control.

'This is exactly the sort of scenario I spent years fighting. No advertised post, no interview, the CEO making room for a friend. It stinks.'

'Of course it does,' Alison agreed, 'and if you come aboard you can rewrite our equalities policy to make sure it doesn't happen again.'

Lexa met her eye in the mirror.

There was just the right amount of reluctance in Alison's laugh. 'And you can go on and on and on about *fucking* Gabriel.'

'But will I wear you down?'

'We'll have to wait and see. Irresistible force versus immovable object. I'd say we're pretty evenly matched.'

Lexa thought how Rae would crow, after everything she'd said about her taking on the bank's PR. Then she thought about meeting Hermia from Exchange Traded Funds again. *Oh hello. Yes, I'm working here.* How many years was it she'd been making conversational capital out of Cambusdyke? She'd be fifty before she knew it. She didn't want to look back on this as the evening she'd stood on the quayside and watched the future sail away.

Alison took out a lipstick and, with two deft swipes, repaired her mouth. 'I'll get HR to draw up the contract on Monday.'

The white plastic box above the door released a hiss of floral scent as she bowed to the remaining line of cocaine.

OCTOBER

On Wednesday mornings now Lexa drove to Edinburgh, parked the Nissan in its designated bay, nodded at the receptionist in his marble bower, and swiped her pass over the pinprick of light that activated the lifts. She had been allocated a small office in the tower, on the floor now vacated by Structured Finance. The only available space, she'd been told, when she pointed out that working in a building which housed the CEO, the chairman's suite, the boardroom, HR and Mergers and Acquisitions would hardly help her impartial profile. The best she could do was boycott the tower's meeting rooms, holding her sessions in the windowless chamber off the trading floor.

She had been prepared for the technological changes in banking, and the ungraspably complex financial products, but not for the shift in style. Gone were the antique desks and hunting prints and wicker wastepaper baskets she'd known at Goodisons, and gone with them that pose of gracious living interrupted by the regrettable necessity of work. Caledonian's trading floor was an open-plan hangar, more call centre than stately home. The heads of the most profitable divisions had glass-walled cubicles along the sides of the building, with the privilege of invisibility at the drop of a Venetian blind. Everyone else – some two thousand staff – worked cheek-by-jowl in the middle.

The Monday after that dinner at the Royal Highland, Alison had taken her into the bank late at night and shown her around. Walking through the vast, almost-empty trading room, she had been struck by its ergonomic echo of the afterlife. Walls, carpet tiles, furniture, the blinds at the distant windows: all in shades of not-quite-white chosen to promote calm and concentration. The air seething with the not-quite-white noise of several thousand plasma screens. Alison needed her to see this, to know that every civilising influence had been brought to bear, because by day the place was hell on earth.

In Commodities, Bonds, Currencies, and the other 'client-facing' areas the heat was almost unbearable. So many screens. No trader could manage with fewer than four. So many shiny-faced men in their shirt-sleeves jabbering into telephone headsets. So much banter and bombast and naked aggression. Such a pungent stink of Armani Code mixed with machine-toasted dust and ionised air. Once she got used to the place, she saw that some of the turmoil was female. And there were pockets of stillness amid the mayhem, chilly zones where the air-conditioning could be heard over the funereal hush of loan officers communing with their single screens. She had lobbied Alison to relocate these beleaguered souls to the tower, signalling a shift in corporate culture, a prestige-transfer to the risk-averse retail side. Alison had laughed, pronouncing it *something to think about*, and Lexa had known it would never happen. However dangerous the adrenaline-crazed gamblers, no one wanted to go back to being known as the bank of choice for newsagents and florists and Morningside widows.

When friends asked her how it was going, she found herself saying 'better than I expected'. The odd thing was, they'd never ask for details. So then she'd say it was interesting, spending one day a week out of the public and voluntary sectors, dealing with people who didn't filibuster all day long. And her friends would make passive-aggressive noises about how *the money must be nice*. These same people who used to moan to her about the 'let's have another meeting' culture. So she'd tell them, yet again, that she wasn't defending the swinging dicks. The workers whose jobs were being outsourced earned twenty-five thousand a year and struggled to meet their childcare bills. Someone had to see that their pensions were protected and they were compensated fairly for the loss of their cheap overdrafts and company cars. It was the sort of negotiation she could have done in her sleep. Her only complaint was being stuck in the tower, with no chance to meet the women on the trading floor.

Wherever they went to smoke and gossip and drop their guard, it wasn't the plaza. Crossing the grey marble at one o'clock on a sunny day, she could feel like the last woman alive. Or dead: a ghost invisible to the throng that gathered to sip take-out espresso and swap expletive-laden boasts in throaty Edinburgh voices. These were the money-makers, the men who would never be outsourced. They were bigger than her old colleagues in Leeds, their torsos top-heavy from the gym, but to her they looked like children. That flawless skin: rosy-cheeked, blueish-white at the temple. A barely-contained energy, as if at any moment they might form a rugby scrum, or remove somebody's trousers, or bankrupt a small country, just for the fun of throwing their weight around. Blue was their colour these days. Midnight blue suits, and overcoats, and socks. Shirts in the spring-sky hue that suited their puppyish faces and their doomed but as yet slender waists. Custom-made by a man in Rose Street Lane who knew how to cut four-hundred-thread Egyptian cotton so it fitted more ostentatiously than Thomas Pink, but not so tightly that it looked like nightclub wear. Lexa had never heard of bespoke shirts, but their pointlessness made perfect sense to her. Caledonian was not an exorbitant payer as banks went, but even here there were twenty-four-year-old traders taking home six-figure bonuses. Some two hundred staff were in Gabriel's income bracket or above, including a dozen earning more than the CEO. Once the mortgage had been paid on their Trinity townhouse and the weekend place in Perthshire, and they'd acquired a set of wheels with *a bit of poke* and a premier-marque four by four, and the school fees had been debited, and the Tuscan villa and the fortnight in Courchevel were booked, and the wine merchant's bill settled, and the wife's credit card topped up, and the dinners signed for, and the tailor kept sweet, and the cobbler in Frederick Street had made a last of both feet . . . what else were they going to do with their money? A shirt – or ten – was as good a use as any.

And for all her neutrality, Lexa was now a cog in the machine. That was why her old friends looked at her askance. Thanks to her, the bank and its stars could carry on making money free of petty distractions. One day she was a subsidised Band Aid on the weeping sore of poverty; the next, a specialist recognised by the corporate world, a professional whose *skill-set added value across economic sectors*. She had assumed her contract would be handled by HR, but it was Alison who'd pushed the letter across the table. Lexa had had to suppress a flicker in her gaze as she read the figure involved. Six thoughts had followed in quick succession. The shocked sense that a mistake had been made; realisation that there was no mistake; acceptance of the sum as no more than she was worth; a new dissatisfaction with the rate she was paid elsewhere; the suspicion that a banker would have haggled over this offer; and self-contempt for selling her gifts so cheaply. All of this in the split-second before she looked up and asked, 'Why so much?'

Smiling her ironic seed-pearl smile, Alison had uncapped her pen.

Gabriel sat in a hospital chair making protesting noises while Rae toured her face with a wet flannel. Chin, mouth, nose, a twist inside each ear. Though even Gabriel couldn't get chocolate in her ears. There was a brief delay while the washcloth was rinsed under the warm tap. She opened her eyes and quickly shut them again, seeing Rae bearing down on her for a last all-over wipe.

As soon as the flannel was put away she reached for another choc-chunk cookie.

Rae mimed a throttler's grip.

As a rule they split the evening visit, but tonight neither could make the early shift. And Lexa was curious to see how Gabriel behaved with Rae. Lately, comparing notes on the phone, they seemed to be talking about two different women.

When asked about her day, Gabriel was silent so long it seemed she'd forgotten the question. At last she spoke, 'We picked up beads with tweezers.'

'That'll come in handy in the big wide world,' Rae said.

She giggled, showing teeth coated in brown paste. Lexa mimed chewing with her mouth closed. If she understood, she took no notice.

'Did they give you any physio?'

'I did the wobble board.'

'And how was that?'

After another agonising wait, she said, 'Wobbly.'

Rae laughed and took a bite of her cookie.

Lexa managed a thin smile.

Three months, and she was still waiting for Gabriel's face to tilt upwards with its old rapt shine. She had changed over the years, as everyone did. Faint parentheses either side of her mouth. Plump half-circles under each eye. Her beauty less ethereal. Her intelligence, too, more earthed. But underneath she'd remained herself.

How could a person just *disappear?*

Rae packed the biscuits away. 'OK, Gabe, into bed.'

'What about her teeth?'

Rae's glance took in the biscuits, the chair, its distance from the sink, and the minimal chance of Gabriel spitting with any degree of accuracy. 'Be my guest,' she said.

Lexa supposed that the nurses could do them in the morning. 'Up you get.'

Gabriel didn't move.

'*Come on.*'

'Too tired,' she drawled.

Was she getting better? Neither of them could say. You took her one day at a time. And even then she could be shrewd, asinine, infuriating and heartbreaking in the space of ten minutes. You couldn't sift it in your head and judge how a good day compared with her best day last month, or the month before. All Lexa knew for sure was that her bad days came round with depressing regularity.

Standing either side of her chair, each took an arm. As soon as they got her up, she flopped. Rae muttered something about Candid Camera and Lexa glanced at Gabriel to share the joke, but she was staring at nothing with her hovering gaze. They marched her to the edge of the bed and sat her down, Lexa hauling her legs up and across, Rae supporting her upper half, avoiding each other's eyes as they worked her down the mattress, trying not to laugh. Though anything was better than acknowledging the pathos. Gabriel pretended not to notice, aloof and self-conscious. Like a dog, Lexa thought. A family pet intelligent enough to know it is the object of mirth without understanding why.

Once she was settled, her eyes focused again. Her good hand explored the hole in her skull where the shunt went in. Rae caught her fingers and returned them under the covers.

It was Lexa's habit to read her a digest of the day's news.

Catching sight of the *Guardian*, Rae pulled a disbelieving face. 'She likes a story this time of night.' She made herself comfortable on the edge of the bed, leaning sideways to whisper something in Gabriel's ear. Sitting up again, she said 'D'you reckon she remembers?'

Gabriel smiled her slow-motion smile.

Lexa was forced to ask 'Remembers what?'

'If I said Bollinger . . .?'

'I'd have no idea what you were talking about.'

Rae and Gabriel shared a conspiratorial look.

Rae had never wanted children. Lexa was the one who had regrets. But there was no mistaking the dynamic at work. Twinkling indulgence. Saucer-eyed trust. The little mother and her big baby.

She took a storyteller's breath. 'We were staying in a flat in Tufnell Park . . .'

Owned by her cousin, gone to Italy for the week. Two poky bedrooms, a put-U-up in the sitting room, and a small paved garden. A bolt-hole after Leeds, while they worked out what to do with the rest of their lives. Breakfast at a pavement cafe amid cyclones of litter stirred up by the lorries on Holloway Road. Felafel and tahini for lunch. Browsing the street markets, bringing back octopus and okra and plantain for dinner in the garden. The smog-filtered sunlight ebbing across the flagstones, Rae and Gabriel smoking between courses to drive the wasps away. So many hours spent keeping their bodies alive for the next day's eating, talking about anything except the deed that had brought them there.

'I remember the holiday,' Lexa conceded.

Rae reached across to brush a strand of hair off Gabriel's forehead.

The tale began with the Friday that Lexa had dragged them around the galleries. After the National and the ICA, Rae rebelled, and they'd joined the stream of tourists and office workers and Surrey couples up for the theatre looking for somewhere to drink.

'. . . we end up in this wine bar behind Charing Cross Road. A bit *oo-la-la let's pretend it's Montmartre*, but there's an empty table. We've been there half an hour when this bloody great bottle of Bollinger turns up. The waiter pours it out and points to these three guys. You're going to take a sip, but she—' Rae tipped her head at Lexa '—says *don't touch it*. So we sit there drinking our house plonk. The guys are raising their glasses to us, waiting for us to call them over—'

Dimly it was coming back to Lexa. Not the faces of the men, or the décor of the bar, or the three undrunk glasses of champagne. Something else, maddeningly particular but just out of reach.

'—when we finish our wine, she wants to order another three glasses of Chateau Horse-Piss. With a bottle of Bolly sitting on the table. I tell her, it's not like we take one sip and we have to shag 'em. They're just three geeks in Next suits. Then you get up and walk over to their table—' Rae laughed her smoky cackle '—one of them kisses your hand. You tell them our names. They're corporate lawyers. They think we're actresses, the usual bollocks. She is *raging . . .*'

Lexa remembered the end of the story now. Though it was more of a fable. Even as it was happening it had seemed too easy to be true.

Gabriel looked up from the pillow, 'There was a snake. Called Septimus.' Her eyes were very bright. Mischievously bright, Lexa would have said once upon a time.

Rae's expression became a little less indulgent.

'What sort of snake?' Lexa asked.

'A feather boa.'

Her lips puckered in secretive pleasure at Lexa's laugh.

'You don't get snakes in wine bars.' Rae looked at Lexa as if it were her fault. 'You said, "Thanks for the champagne, boys, but it's gone a bit flat".'

Gabriel's voice became insistent. '*Eine Schlange*—'

With a sigh, Rae abandoned the Bollinger story.

'—if it goes pear-shaped, I don't want to know. . .'

Rae and Lexa exchanged glances.

Lexa leaned forward, 'If what goes pear-shaped?'

'*Wie bitte?*'

'*Who* doesn't want to know?'

Rae shot Lexa another barbed look. 'Time you got some sleep, Gabe.'

But Lexa was not about to let go of the possibility that Gabriel's wanderings might lead somewhere. 'Are you talking about the bank?'

Gabriel's eyes swivelled between them. She was sensitive to any sort of mixed message. Her face acquired an uncanny stillness. Her bloodless skin turned to parchment.

The public ward next door was silent, apart from the hospital tinnitus, so familiar by now that Lexa felt spooked at home. Until the fridge fan kicked in.

'Gabriel?'

Rae laid a restraining hand on her arm.

As the consultant approached them, the frizzy-haired staff nurse began to hum a tune in such an abruptly casual manner that Lexa knew it was a signal. The consultant smiled to himself. In his outdoor coat he was easier to place. A weekend sailor or pilot. Something clean and light and solitary.

Lexa jumped to her feet a moment ahead of Rae. 'Can we have a word?'

'I'm just on my way out.'

'We'll get you down to the lobby, then.'

Doctor Kerr. A murmur of silver in his hair, a tender crinkle at the corner of each eye half-hidden by his glasses, and an army of subservient women in terror of his mildness turning to displeasure. At twenty Lexa would have seen him as patriarchy in the flesh. Now she just hoped he was halfway competent.

'It's Rae and . . . *Alex*, isn't it?'

'Lexa Strachan.'

'Lexa, of course.'

They fell into step, Rae casting a last cool look at the staff nurse. Something about Robert de Niro. A hit in the eighties. The nurse wouldn't have been born then. Either she had the same retro tastes as Stuart's clerical staff, or the joke was Doctor Kerr's.

'What can I do for you?'

Before Rae had a chance to answer, Lexa said, 'How long do you think it'll take Gabriel to recover?'

His mouth made a fastidious shape. 'When you say "recover" . . .'

A pedant. That was all they needed.

'I mean, enough to go back to her old life. Or is that too

much to hope for?'

'Not at all. In fact, we've just been discussing it. As soon as the home assessment team can get out and make their recommendations . . . grab rails and suchlike . . . she's ready to go—'

It was the last thing either of them had expected.

'—she should be home within the next two weeks.'

Mentally, Lexa inventoried Mackenzie Square. The permanently-ruckled oriental rugs. The bags of clothes waiting to go the dry cleaner's. The black sack of shoes needing to be re-heeled or soled. One trip hazard after another.

Rae was walking on the outside, her view of the consultant blocked by Lexa. She overcame this by moving ahead and turning to face him, bringing everyone to a halt.

'She can't go home, but there's room at my place on Blackwater Road.'

The name of Gemmell's most expensive street seemed to sharpen the consultant's attention. 'As long as Gabriel agrees.'

As if Lexa had spoken her thoughts aloud, Rae said, 'She can't stay at yours, up three flights of stairs.'

Doctor Kerr's lips compressed in what looked suspiciously like amusement. All at once Lexa understood the nurse's joke. Bananarama. A dig at Gabriel's Agent Provocateur pyjamas and Rae's Louboutins and her own Converse high-tops. A girlish trio, when the rest of their generation had paired-off. But now Rae and Gabriel, too, would be a pair, in Rae's gutted-and-refurbished arts and crafts villa with its ensuite wet rooms and clutter-free hardwood floors.

'And you'll take time off work?' Lexa asked, knowing hell would freeze over first.

'I can hire a carer.'

'A stranger.'

'Better than getting the third degree from you all day.'

Doctor Kerr murmured something about running late, and they continued down the corridor.

'So you've done all you can for her,' Lexa said.

She saw a flicker of caution behind the consultant's glasses. 'Everything that needs to be done in hospital. She'll continue to have physiotherapy at home.'

'And what about her cognitive skills? Is she ever going to be *herself* again?'

They had reached the waiting area by the lifts. Rae sat on the vinyl bench, having won the right to supervise Gabriel's convalescence.

Doctor Kerr took off his glasses. 'It's an interesting question—'

Lexa knew he was patronising her. Hospitals infantilised patients and their relatives and encouraged consultants to behave like God Almighty, and that was fine with her, absolutely fine. As long as Gabriel got better.

'—I'd say most people recognise the person they knew. In time.'

'She thinks the ward's infested with *flying squirrels*.'

His lips were so thin they disappeared when he smiled. 'We call it confabulation. If the brain is damaged, causing memory disorder or disinhibition of associations, it carries on trying to make sense of experience.' He glanced at the lift button, checking that the red call light was still on. 'It makes things up to bridge the gaps.'

'For the rest of her life?'

'Every stroke is different.'

'You must have some idea.'

'It would only be a guess.'

'All right then, *guess*.'

Doctor Kerr shrugged. 'My guess is she'll be rational.'

'But will she be *herself*?'

Doctor Kerr put his glasses back on.

'We're a long way from being able to map the brain and say a bleed here or there will have this or that effect on personality. It may not even work like that. There's a well-documented tendency for very severely brain-damaged patients . . . I'm talking about people much more badly injured than Gabriel . . . they seem to behave less erratically, more *characteristically*, in the presence of a husband or wife—'

It was the stress, Lexa thought: she was nodding, but she had no idea where he was going with this.

'—which would suggest that the self is not located in the brain at all. Or the body, for that matter. The current thinking is that it's a process of interaction. If Gabriel's *self* is anywhere, she's in the space between you.'

Meeting his eye, Lexa saw pity there.

'Now,' Doctor Kerr glanced at the call light again, 'can I ask you something—?'

She shrugged.

'—do you think Gabriel *wants* to be the person she used to be?'

Rae looked up from the bench. 'What's that supposed to mean?'

The consultant's cheeks pinked. Lexa wondered how she hadn't noticed before. He was the type who liked small, sharp-toothed women.

'Some people don't have that will to pick up where they left off. A husband, children. Even . . .' The barest hesitation. Just enough to show he knew full well who his patient was. '. . . a job they love. These things seem to make a difference.'

'And that's scientifically proven, is it?'

Doctor Kerr did not know Rae well enough to recognise this quietness as lethal.

'I'm sure most of my colleagues would say the same.'

'So you all agree it's the patients' fault when you can't cure them. That must make life easier.'

With a musical *ping* the lift arrived.

The corridor outside Lexa's office was swarming with hipster girls in skinny jeans and puffa jackets scouting for the *iconic view* of Edinburgh Castle. Boy-men in layered T-shirts and beanies and hiking boots clumped past with film lights and tripods and aluminum camera cases. A woman in a New York Yankees cap loitered with an air of having nothing to do that could only mean she was the director. They all had maniacally friendly smiles, as if secretly filming a toothpaste ad, or under orders to feed the fantasies of their blatantly movie-struck clients. Rubbernecking quants from Risk and Valuations held their stomachs in as they sauntered to the water cooler. Mason, bodypopping to a groove inside his outsize cans, was taking orders for a Starbucks run as if auditioning for the *X-Factor*. Toby somebody from Public Affairs was filming the film crew with a point-and-shoot camera. Only the formidable Brenda held out, insisting there was *no way* the CEO was going to crouch-sprint across the roof and take off in a helicopter . . .

The buzzwords of the bank's new media strategy were *adventure* and *responsibility*. Let the breeders bitch all they liked about the country paying for the bankers' mistakes: every penny they earned went on keeping their boomerang kids in pizza and iPhone top-ups. The markets to target were the grey-pound empty-nesters and the lucky percentile of the eighteen-to-thirty demographic with a job. Focus group research showed they shared many characteristics. Technophilia, concern about environmental issues, personal optimism, interest in self-realisation . . . Which was where Alison had paused to glance at Lexa.

'You think it's bullshit?'

'Don't you?'

'It's a rebranding strategy, not psychoanalysis.'

A film had been commissioned. A ten-minute promo to be streamed on the net and salami-sliced into a series of television commercials. Various bank-sponsored charities and arts projects would be featured. A collaboration between opera singers and allotment gardeners in Falkirk, a sterilisation programme for Glasgow's feral cats, a school for dyspraxic children in Andhra Pradesh. Goodlooking Scottish mountaineers, fashion designers, paraplegic athletes and rap musicians would be asked about the importance of risk in creative endeavour, and invited to share their worries about air quality in China and broadband slow-spots north of Dundee. Though unscripted, these interviews would be edited to foreground the word 'trust'.

'I thought it was you.'

Lexa glanced over her shoulder, but there was no one else the woman could be addressing.

She came closer. One of the meeters and greeters condemned to wear a pink-and-purple tartan jacket but not, at this time of year, a company hat.

'You don't recognise me?'

For a moment Lexa wasn't sure. Blonde hair scraped into a bun. Neat features. The sort of white-mouse face that others' wizardry turned to beauty in the pages of *Vogue*. With a small shock, she placed her. Christie Dodds, the disaffected shareholders' poster girl.

'Good disguise,' she said.

'Ssshhh—'

Her eyes held a baffling expectation.

'—I'm Christine. You helped my maw, Sharon Reid.'

Sharon Reid. One of her early equality cases. A bank cleaner paid per shift what Lexa had occasionally spent on a cab when she missed her last train. No minimum wage in those days. Sharon and her four children had lived in a post-war four-in-a-block on one of Glasgow's dystopic housing schemes. Two glass eyes in a street of boarded windows. Lexa had heard the horror stories. Black mould speckling the walls, floorboards prised up and burned on the fire, babies' bottles filled with ginger fizz. None of it had been more disturbing than the sight of Sharon Reid being mothered by her own ten-year-old child.

'Christine! No wonder I didn't recognise you.'

In the 1990s, when Sharon first approached her, part-time

women workers had had to wait for their twenty-sixth birthday before joining Caledonian's pension scheme. (Male employees were admitted at twenty-one.) And if a woman were so foolish as to get married – as Sharon did, to the father of her youngest child – she was kicked off the scheme and given a token 'marriage gratuity' to muddy the discriminatory waters. Her union rep didn't see the point of challenging it: she'd only spend a pension on plastic tat for the grandkids while living on the same cheap processed grease. But Lexa had felt the old acid burn of visceral indignation, and Sharon had won her case.

A long time ago now.

Christie had put some thought into minimising her assets. No make-up, no curves. (A sports bra under that buttoned jacket?) Hard to reconcile this squeaky-clean facade with the greasy hair and mossy teeth Lexa remembered. That nervous habit of pulling her eyelashes out.

'You must have been at primary school the last time I saw you.'

'And you'd have been about ages with me now.'

They both smiled at this thought.

A gum-chewing film technician in a hoodie and neon Wayfarers turned the corner and asked the way to the Gents. The silence they observed until he was through the door had a conspiratorial flavour.

Christie's white-mouse eyebrows lifted, 'You working in movies the now?'

'Conciliation.' Lexa felt the need to add, 'It's a short-term contract.'

'Is that right?'

This phrase, delivered with this intonation, was a staple of Scottish discourtesy. No one knew it better than Lexa. But this was wee Christine, whose lashless eyes had followed her with such awe.

'I'm just a tourist here.'

'Aye? I'da said Cuba was more your kinda thing.'

Their eyes met. It didn't take a genius to work out who she was planning to ambush, and yet she didn't seem worried that Lexa would give her away.

'So you're a shareholder these days?'

Christie returned a moss-free smile. 'A wee anniversary present from my husband.'

The gum-chewer emerged from the Gents. Again they waited until he was out of earshot.

'Maw's dead.' Christie touched the corner of her left eye with the ghost of that childhood habit. 'Lung cancer.'

Lexa did a rapid sum. She hadn't lived long enough to collect her pension. 'I'm sorry to hear that.'

'We got her the best.' Christie named a private hospital on the outskirts of Glasgow.

A *bona fide* assistant in the bank's sugar-plum tartan walked past without giving them a second glance.

The expectant look was back in Christie's pale eyes. 'I used to think about this. Running into you again when I was grown up. I'd be rich and famous. You'd be dead impressed.' Her mouth twitched as if shrugging off her own childishness. 'I never thought you'd be on the other side.'

'I'm not on any side.'

'No?' she said. 'I never thought you'd be that either.'

While she waited inside the restaurant, Lexa passed the time by counting all the nights she had eaten at Alison's, or been her guest elsewhere. There was the charity concert in the Perthshire castle, and the reception for the Chinese diplomats, and the talk on Afghanistan by an aid worker Alison said was an MI6 asset, and the health club where they'd sat in the rooftop Jacuzzi laughing like hyenas in the pelting rain. She had been Alison's 'plus one' in two – no, *three* – Edinburgh New Town homes with finger-marks around the door handles and candle grease on the walls and great-grandmama's furniture still going strong. In her memory these evenings blurred into one long meal of over-roast lamb and under-poached pears, surrounded by people whose ancestors had known David Hume. Academics, judges, charity directors, psychoanalysts. The sort of people who could write a joint letter to *The Scotsman* and get a news story on the front page. Not so long ago Gabriel would have teased her for breaking bread with the Brahmins, for being so flattered by the attention of these softly-spoken men and their hawk-headed wives. These days, when she was teased, it was Alison who teased her.

There was no putting it off, a return for all this hospitality was long overdue. She had thought about it: her guest surveying the junk-shop fixtures and fittings, the chain-hung glass lampshade and red formica table, exclaiming *I used to have one of these!* Or else falling silent. But that wasn't fair. Alison might have been charmed to find her living in a time capsule of the bohemian 1980s. The point was, Lexa would have felt judged. Much easier to foot the bill at this tapas bar, an Edinburgh institution, so popular it had colonised the pavement, slinging a net of halogen stars over the street and keeping the chilly night at bay with a tin forest of patio-heaters. What did it matter if Alison – heading towards her through the candlelit tables – was thinking it was the sort of place that people chose for a date?

Lexa had friends who greeted her with a double cheek-swipe, and others who did the robotic clinch-and-release, and even one or two (oddly, women she knew only medium-well) whose hugs were like sinking into a feather duvet. Alison's style was the graceful swoop, giving Lexa the impression of wings closing around her. It was striking enough to come back to her at odd moments through the week. The brief, overlapping circle of their arms, and the riddle of what it sealed between them.

Alison slumped into her chair with a grateful sigh and Lexa knew that, underneath the table, she was using one foot to lever off the other's high-heeled shoe.

'I hope your day was better than mine.' She pushed her wine glass towards Lexa, who topped up the modest measure the waiter had poured and slid it back across the table.

'Is that an official enquiry?'

'*Oh no*, I have spies to tell me everything I need to know.' She took a long swallow.

'You get your money's worth.'

She looked up from her glass, 'Lexa Strachan, I can read you like a book.'

'Printed in Sanskrit.'

It was their standing joke. Lexa's professional independence and Alison's more or less harmless curiosity. The all-important distinction between contractor and employee.

Alison picked up the menu. She was ravenous. She'd wasted her lunch hour practising her *smile palette* with a stand-up comedienne. Charismatic leadership in six easy archetypes. Corporate Matriarch, Blue Chip Goddess, FTSE Princess . . . She waved a dismissive hand across the table. 'I forget the rest. If she weighed seven stone I'd be surprised. This little head the size of a grapefruit, a pink hoodie and a pixie cut.' She paused. 'Big ears.'

'*Big ears?*'

'If you'll let me finish . . .'

Lexa signalled her willingness to listen by turning her head and fingering her own more than medium-sized ear.

'. . . the ears and the nose are the parts' – *paerts* – 'of the body that carry on growing your whole life. You can't be a *little girl* with big ears. Forty if she was a day. She might like to get that sorted before she starts laying down the law to grown women. I felt like asking her, if you're such an expert on leadership, why are you the one telling jokes' – *chokes* – 'in cellar bars while I'm running a bank, hmm?'

'But you didn't.'

'I wouldn't want to upset the Chairman' – *dgaermenn* – 'who thinks I've so little to do I can spare an hour a week to learn how to *smile*.' She lifted her wine again. 'When what I really need to learn is how to stage a nuclear explosion every six months. To remind the boys they'd rather deal with the *charismatic* me . . .' She glanced at Lexa. 'Go on, say it.'

'That's why I got out in the eighties.'

'Like a book,' Alison said. She tipped back her glass. 'I think I might have to get pissed tonight.'

She'd had a filthy week. It was bad enough when it was just the chorus of outrage on the letters pages, and those superior bastards in the financial blogs. 'Now it's every teenager with internet access. That *fucking* YouTube clip is showing eight hundred thousand hits.'

Moments after speaking to Lexa last Wednesday, Christie Dodds had barged in on the promo shoot to announce that the UK shareholders were sueing and a class action was on its way in the US. The suit-and-tie filming the film crew had turned out not to be from Public Affairs. The footage had gone viral, boosted by Brenda's attempt to wrestle the camera out of the intruder's hands. The soundtrack was a collage of scuffling and panting and swearing and Rae barking at Brenda that she was making it worse, the picture yawing crazily but still managing to capture the CEO, motionless in the eye of the storm, wearing the ghastly smile of her own latex mask.

The bank's core investors – a trio of fund managers known as the Father, Son and Holy Ghost – were badly spooked. The board, too, was panicking. The non-executive directors, who'd signed up for four meetings a year and seventy-five thousand, had suddenly realised the buck stopped with them. The chairman had promised action. Alison pronounced the word in inverted commas, knocking back the rest of her wine.

'They could have hired a numbers man, but they wanted a human being, someone to manage the egos of the boys who make the money. *Now* I lack the requisite *technical understanding*—'

Looking up, she caught a waiter's eye and pointed to her empty glass.

'—she's working for the hedge funds. Oh I don't *know* it, but it's the only explanation. They select the stock they want to short, and hit the phones. *Hello old chap, any idea what's wrong at Cally?* Get the shareholders to run crying to the papers . . . Why would she do it? The stock just goes down faster, she's cutting her own throat. She could get out, she's only holding fifteen thousand. What's she doing buying shares in the first place: it helps her relax after a hard day's pole dancing? You know who she's married to? Tommy Dodds the Rangers striker. Do you think he reads the *FT*—'

Lexa thought about saying it. *I saw her just before she ambushed you and I didn't give her away.*

'—all right, she could be doing a doctorate in string theory for all I know. She's still a wee bitch.' Alison paused until the waiter had filled their glasses and moved out of earshot. 'Is that me with a black mark now, for unsisterly language?'

'It wasn't very Corporate Mummy.'

'I see myself more as a Blue Chip Goddess.' She glanced at her quivering phone and switched it off. 'I suppose she's been griping to you about how unfair I've been—'

Lexa became very interested in her wine glass.

'—you do know what I was paying her—?'

Rae, she meant. Lexa nodded.

'—with that sort of money, you don't get a second chance. It shouldn't have happened, and it was on her watch.'

'I hardly see her these days.'

'I suppose she's got her hands full looking after Gabriel.' With a throb of humour in her voice, she added '*Don't* do that thing with your glass again, *please*.'

Lexa put it back on the table. 'So that's the real reason you've got rid of her.'

Alison's little teeth showed. 'It might have had something to do with it.'

They spent the next hour picking at plates of bread and olives and grilled halloumi and chargrilled artichoke hearts, and a complimentary salad of peppers and some muscular fish that Alison found delicious until Lexa decided it was eel. For a moment she mistook Alison's grip on her wrist for a spoofing show of alarm about this.

A tall man was looking in through the restaurant window, breath pluming from his lips in the cold air. He pushed through the door and crossed to their table. Forks paused between plate and mouth as people turned to look. He had the manner of a C-list celebrity. Gleaming pewter hair, self-love singing from his pores, that coat cut to show his toney body when most men his age were hiding shrivel or bloat. Lexa couldn't understand how he made an ordinary pair of black leather gloves look so sexual.

'I don't think you've met Laurence,' Alison said.

According to Rae, he'd been so keen to cut loose he'd signed his rights away. A clean break just months before his wife had become a four-million-pound meal ticket, leaving him scraping by on a chief accountant's salary. He had a newsreader's symmetrical features, a face that said 'goodlooking' without sticking in the memory. What was it Rae had said? *You wouldn't kick him out of bed.* But you wouldn't marry him, either. Not if you had any sense of self-preservation. He gave Lexa the sort of glance she hadn't received in she didn't know how long. And yes, it churned the parts it was meant to churn.

He raised his eyebrows. 'Is this . . .?'

'No,' Alison said shortly.

His pout parodied disappointment. 'She looks like she might.'

Lexa glanced between them. 'Might what?'

She was fairly sure she knew, which was why she made a point of asking.

He gave Alison a *shall I?* look, before starting, 'My wife . . .'

'*Ex*-wife,' Alison said. 'You have another one now.'

Laurence glanced down at their plates. 'No chorizo?' He turned to Lexa, his lips a sly rosebud. 'I didn't catch your name.'

His vowels conjured the chintz-armchair-and-springer-spaniel gentility of the 1950s, a world that still held Lexa's mother in envious thrall. There would be citizens who could tell from his accent which of Edinburgh's public schools he had attended, maybe even in which street (India or Ann, or Heriot Row) he had spent his childhood.

'Lexa Strachan.'

He gave her a bright blank look he'd picked up from Alison. Unless she'd got hers from him.

'It's always a pleasure, Laurence.' Alison lifted her glass. 'But we won't keep you.'

'I just popped in to give you the good news.' He smiled toothily. 'Tashie's got a little brother.'

Alison's deadpan held for a second, then underwent spectacular collapse.

Having engineered her shock, Laurence seemed irritated.

'You knew she was pregnant,' he said, and Lexa recognised the authentic cutting voice of a bad marriage.

Alison set her glass down and it toppled, flooding the table with tempranillo. Lexa jerked backwards, but not quickly enough to avoid the splash. Neighbouring diners offered their napkins and she soaked up the spillage. A waitress hurried over with a damp cloth.

Laurence watched the fuss with his bright blank stare.

Eventually Alison recovered enough to say, 'You could have sent an email.'

'I wanted to tell you myself.'

For the first time she looked him full in the face. 'Why?'

Even he could not make light of the animosity packed into this syllable.

'Do you mind if I borrow my ex-wife for a minute?'

Alison stood up, 'If I'm not back in five, call my lawyers.'

Taking her elbow, he steered her out to the pavement where the late-night shoppers were staggering past with their laptop cases and bags of groceries from Marks and Spencer. Lexa watched them through the window. Alison's face was shockingly expressive, at once suffering and more alive.

Out of the corner of her eye, Lexa noticed a woman in a headscarf approaching the smokers' tables outside. Her nose was cartoonishly-red in her pinched white face. Her hands looked flayed by the cold, raw steaks protruding from the sleeves of her liver-coloured mac. Her expression was at once defiant and closed-off. The wrong face for the job, even without that off-putting card laminated with Sellotape.

Something attracted the woman's attention. Other heads, too, were turning. Even at this distance, without the benefit of sound, it was clear that Alison and her ex-husband were arguing. Or rather, Alison was arguing and Laurence was attempting to contain the situation. Her cheeks were mottled. Her brow strained like a joint of meat tied with string. Laurence was speaking now, eyebrows raised reasonably. Like a farmer handling a flighty animal, his gloved hands settled on her upper arms. She pulled away, the jacket twisting on her shoulders, and Lexa saw the shift in him, the moment he said the words he had been saving. The look on her face tore Lexa's heart. He gathered her into a clumsy hug that doubled as forcible restraint. The late-night shoppers were staring. Just inside the window, a party of glossy-haired girls and young men in professionally-laundered shirts tittered to see the oldies making idiots of themselves.

'He has this thing about ants. When I was pregnant we hired a gîte near Carcassonne. He went round the garden pouring boiling water on their nests. If he saw them in the house he'd squeal like a stuck pig—'

They were back in the warmth of the restaurant. Laurence had gone, taking his kinky gloves with him.

'—I had to stamp on them, and fetch the spiders out of the bath. I used to wonder what Lord Hulley would say if he could see his chief accountant shouting for his wife to deal with the beasties.' She poured a puddle of olive oil onto a plate, soaked a piece of bread and ate it. 'Stop me next time I do that.' She sucked her fingers clean of the oil. 'At home I'd pick up his socks, and put away the marmalade when he'd left it out with the lid off, and throw away the cardboard tube when he'd used the last of the loo paper. Change the roll so he had something to wipe his arse with next time. It's such a *fucking cliché*.' That *huf* of amused breath. 'But just as demeaning to keep on and on making a fuss about it. I'm a pushover for an alpha male. Always have been, always will be. And they're all arseholes, every man jack of them—'

She reached towards the bread basket again. Lexa moved it.

'—the time *after* this, I meant—'

Lexa squinted at her, but let her have the bread.

'—when he was sick I'd make raspberry jelly, let it half-set, and feed him with a spoon. Like a baby. He used to call it runny' – *rhunnie* – 'he said it in bed sometimes, as a joke. "Make me some runny, Ali".' She dipped the bread and swallowed. Lexa saw the effort it took to get it down half-chewed. 'Am I embarrassing you?'

'A wee bit.'

There was a darkening in the translucent skin under her eyes. 'I hope the little bastard ripped her in half, coming out.'

'It's meant to hurt,' Lexa said, 'that's how you know you're alive.'

Alison's startled look held a glisten of tears.

Laurence had demanded a change to the access arrangements. It would do Tashie good to spend more time with a proper family. She'd told him to come off it: even he wasn't insensitive enough to think this was the time and place to get what he wanted . . . Neither of them had noticed Lexa, until she was standing in front of them.

Across the table now, Alison smiled. 'Amazon Warrior' – *whorrier* – 'that was another of Big Ears's archetypes.'

Lexa's blood buzzed with adrenaline, as if she were still marching across the pavement, propelled by the sort of blind impulse she spent her working life getting others to curb.

'*Taxi for Bluebeard!*'

It was one of those catch-phrases that pass for wit in the west of Scotland and, by chance, there had been a party of Glaswegians sitting nearby. Their roar of drunken appreciation set off laughter at neighbouring tables. So far, Laurence had taken the role of calming influence. Now he found himself the butt of the joke. And at that moment the woman in the headscarf handed over her Sellotaped card. Distracted, he took it. He was on the point of telling her to get lost. Lexa saw the impulse in his face, and then the calculation. So many people were watching. As he pulled out his wallet, Lexa and Alison had made their escape.

'I thought he'd have some come-back,' Lexa said now.

'Against *you?*'

She twitched a shrug.

'It wasn't nothing,' Alison said softly.

'You'd do the same for me.'

'I doubt it.' She had regained her ironic poise. 'You wouldn't put yourself in that position.'

Lexa felt a draught and turned to see the *maitre d'* escorting the beggar off the premises.

'How do you do it?' Alison said. 'How do you live without intimacy—?'

Four months ago Lexa could have challenged this description of herself.

'—or is there something you're not telling me?'

'A man, you mean?'

Alison fingered her Boudicca necklace. 'Not necessarily.'

'Which was what your ex was getting at.'

Alison gave her a searching look. 'No,' she said at last, 'he was getting at me.'

Her skin was creamy again, that husky control back in her voice. Even with her shoes off under the table, she was every inch the CEO. No trace of the dumpy woman with raw-lidded eyes who'd made a show of herself on the street.

'He wasn't my first disaster by a long way. I had quite a track record. When he traded me in for a younger model, I thought, *here I go again*, I'm going to spend my life making the same mistake over and over, because that's the sort of bastard I'm attracted to. I know the world is full of good men. I just don't want to sleep with them.' She picked up a piece of bread, then put it back. 'When I did my MBA we had all sorts of speakers, not just business people. Artists. Philosophers. A man who'd run the New York Met, one time. He said something I've never forgotten. If you find yourself stuck in a pattern of unproductive behaviour, just do the opposite. So I tried it.' She looked up into Lexa's face, 'You don't seem very surprised.'

'Don't I?'

Lexa had known some sexual switchers at university, one of them a notorious man-eater before she decided it was women she loved. And 'women' had always been the sticking-point for Lexa: all those anonymous breasts and muffs. But Alison was in a category of one. A better listener than any man she knew, and amusing, and incisive and, yes, *charismatic*, and a relentless flirt. So really, any woman in Lexa's shoes, looking back on six years without a sexual touch, would have let the thought cross her mind.

'Did it work?' she asked.

'The sex? Oh yes. The best I've ever had. But she was just like Laurence. A user. We had completely different assumptions about what happens between two people. For me, a relationship is a set of scales in balance. She was beautiful, and smart in an unusual way. I was better with people, more professionally successful. I'm not saying I belittled her career. If anything, I gave her too much . . .' She stopped.

'Too much?' Lexa queried.

'For her, the world was a ladder. She'd look up to you, and want you, and after you'd given her a hand up, she'd stand on your back to reach the next rung—'

For the second time in half an hour her face showed that arresting blend of vitality and suffering.

'—she was shocked when I said it was over. I think she really did love me. But loving me was perfectly compatible with seeing me as less than her in every way. Less brilliant, less sophisticated in my understanding, less attractive. To Laurence, among others. Oh it was all right me being a better cook. Though if we'd been *out* as a couple, and had friends over to the house, who knows? And I was so blinded by my own idea of what loving someone means, she had to make her contempt obvious to a room full of people before I could see it.' She was silent for a moment before she shrugged. 'I must be pissed, boring you like this.'

'I'm not bored,' Lexa said.

'But do you know what I'm talking about?'

Did she? Lexa too was a little drunk, but she noticed that Alison's eyes had lost their ironic glint. Whatever she was being asked, it mattered.

'There've been times I've thought, if I give up on men, there's always women. But I've never taken that step.'

Alison released the breath she'd been holding. 'My advice is, don't die wondering.'

'That wasn't the greatest commercial for a lesbian affair.'

'*Ah no*,' Alison pointed an admonitory finger, 'that was *her*. And even with her, there's a closeness between women that a man and a woman can never match. All these feelings I'd never had before. Not even when Natasha was born. Touching her skin and feeling that touch in my own. Not really sure what was her and what was me. I never knew sex could feel so . . . real.' Another *huf*. 'I read somewhere – where was it? – that girls reach their peak around the age of ten. Imaginative. Confident. Curious. Intensely attached to their friends. Then their hormones kick in and all they want to know about is nail varnish and boys.' She chased a breadcrumb across her plate. 'It's funny. I see these actresses on TV, playing – what do they call them, BFFs? – but to me it's all . . .'

'Narcissistic commodification,' Lexa said.

She gave a pawky smile. 'Drag queens, I was going to say. It's like we can't imagine affection between women unless it's about showing off to somebody male. We can't just *be ourselves* . . .'

'Nobody else's business.'

'. . . two people who understand each other and enjoy each other and want the best for each other. Do you think that's possible?'

'Yes,' Lexa said.

'Yes,' Alison took up her glass again, 'I know you do.'

Siobhan and Eilidh were telling their celebrated anecdote, *Hogmanay in Dundee Bus Station with a bottle of crème de menthe*. Ruth was lecturing Stefan on the misogyny of the Taliban. Rowan was boring Karen about herbal HRT. Iseabail was teasing Judith about Roddy's lifelong crush on her. Mo was telling Gosha how the bastard let her down. And Gregor and Paul were trying to sell their cottage in Lochinver, in a pleasantly low-key manner, until Kay butted in with, 'You told me the neighbours were a nightmare.'

Rae raised her glass, 'To Gabriel.'

'And her friends,' Gabriel added, being arch or dissociated, it was hard to know which.

There was a ragged chorus of '*Gabriel and friends*' from the cluster of guests around the settee.

The mulled wine nipped Lexa behind the eyes the way mulled wine always did and for a moment this could have been any of Gabriel's parties: the yellow candlelight in the pumpkin lanterns, the smell of warmed spice and peat smoke and stargazer lilies, the houseful of middle-aged women hell-bent on a good time. After Martin walked out on his marriage, the Mackenzie Square Halloween party had become an annual fixture. And here they were again in their trick-or-treat gladrags, as if nothing had changed.

Rae leaned towards Lexa, 'Everything OK?'

'Fine.'

Four months ago one of them would have insisted that they talk this through, but really, what was there to say? That Rae blamed Lexa for the loss of the Cally PR contract. That she felt guilty to the depths of her Catholic soul, but could never atone for scapegoating Gabriel, and would soon get sick of her living in Blackwater Road. That Lexa was ready to take over as carer, and was putting down a marker for the future by holding the party in Gabriel's old home. None of this needed spelling out.

Rae turned away to move Gabriel's wine glass to a less precarious resting place.

There were around thirty interesting women in Gemmell and Gabriel knew them all. Without turning her head Lexa could see a belly-dancing instructor, a self-taught Gaelic speaker and published poet, a Croatian dentist currently working as a barista, one of Scotland's last Communists, a breeder of Kashmir goats, a silversmith who worked with sea glass, a shiatsu masseuse who dabbled in wicca, and the usual assortment of support workers, renewables specialists and creative-links officers. A heterogeneous crowd, though their homes were tellingly similar. Driftwood on the windowsills, pearly shells in the bathroom, appliquéd wall-hangings and home-made quilts. In the warmer months they filled their hearths with pastel-coloured stones smoothed by the ocean into womanly curves. Most were employed in the subsidised voluntary sector, or salaried by the state, or consultants like Lexa who took the bulk of their fees from the public purse. For all their indignation about the fiasco in Iraq and the failure to honour Kyoto, they had done well out of New Labour. Now they were nervous. Lexa could hear it in the heartfelt way they spoke of *looking forward to Christmas*. Two weeks of eating, and drinking, and carol concerts, and nativity plays, and not thinking about next year's election and the inevitable public spending cuts. Few of their jobs had existed fifteen years before, and Lexa had a hunch that few would remain fifteen months hence. And then what would happen to the homespun utopia they had created together in Gemmell? There were cliques and coolings as in any community, but by Hogmanay everyone had had everyone else to dinner, or rung them for a favour, or stopped for a chat when they met at the shops. It was decades since any of them had used the word *sisterhood,* but Lexa thought now (as she did every Halloween) that they were as close as anyone came to seeing a youthful ideal made flesh.

Her first glimpse of Gabriel unchaperoned was in the hall. She was coming out of the kitchen, only a couple of metres away, but she didn't notice Lexa. Rae had taken her to Glasgow for a cut and colour, and dressed her in a velvet hussar jacket. A good choice, hiding the worst of the weight loss and the hang of her dead arm. She'd made a nice job of the party paint, too: eyelids smeared in thundery blue, smudged charcoal under the lower lashes to draw attention away from her collapsing jaw. Gabriel had the face of a woman ten years older, but an attractive older woman. Down the corridor, someone put Joni Mitchell on the stereo. 'Song for Sharon', a track they both loved. Lexa looked for a smile, or just a glimmer of recognition.

So much of her life these days was spent waiting for Gabriel to snap out of this vagueness. She blamed Rae: still babying her, expecting nothing, clearing every obstacle from her path. Who'd have guessed she had the patience? Day after day of listening to that slurring drawl, watching her lips frame that faltering smile as if befuddlement was a charming joke. As if the old Gabriel was not still in there somewhere.

The kitchen door opened, pushing a wedge of platinum light into the dingy hall. Lexa saw Martin, in those red plastic devil horns he was born to wear, putting a tray of treacle tarts in the oven. Rae bustled out with a steaming pitcher of mulled wine. Like a freeze-frame jolting into life, Lexa moved forward. Gabriel saw her and smiled. There was a flashy burst of boogie-woogie from the piano, and then Eilidh started to play 'He Needs Me', heavy on the left hand like Nina Simone. The guests drifted through to the drawing room. Cigarettes were extinguished, glasses drained, conversations put on hold. Gabriel's parties were famous for their singalongs.

They sang 'Cry Me a River' and 'Ae Fond Kiss' and 'Natural Woman' and 'Bridge Over Troubled Water', which was cheesy, but at least they all knew the words. Gabriel too: moving her lips soundlessly, gazing around the shining faces. Lexa caught Amy's eye mid-note and the anxious push of the girl's lips curved into a smile. They had sung these songs at every party Gabriel had ever thrown.

Halfway through 'Summertime' Lexa heard knocking. Gabriel must have heard it too because she shuffled out of the room, but during 'A Case of You' Lexa heard it again, or thought she did, so she went into the hall to check and found the front door open and Gabriel, hunched against the cold in her huzzar jacket, standing on the path outside. With her was Ned, in a long black coat and, half in shadow, a tall, thickset figure in a chalkstripe suit.

She had time to wonder if Ned might be gay, if his interest in her all those years ago had been a cover. She didn't ask why he was here. It was Gabriel's party. She could invite whom she liked.

Gabriel turned towards her with a crooked smile and the man in the suit stepped into the light. She saw the fleshy pallor of a bald head.

'Hello Alexandra,' he said.

Inside, the guests were singing 'Every Time We Say Goodbye', their faces grave, seduced by the beauty of the song. Rae didn't hear the first time, so Lexa told her again.

'And you've left her with him?'

'She doesn't remember.'

Rae met her eye. Later Lexa would regret not challenging her to explain exactly what she meant by this look.

The three of them were still standing on the path. Lexa had a sense of earnest conversation abruptly broken off. Gabriel shuffled indoors and leaned against the radiator. Ned took off his coat and draped it over the banister, a faint smile on those cherry-red lips. Piers Kinsella walked in as if he owned the place, to stop opposite the open door of the drawing room. Curious faces turned from the piano. Unwillingly Lexa saw them through his eyes. Shapeless women who flaunted their grey hair, or dyed it paint-box red. Eilidh in ten-year-old Jaeger, Jacqui and Gill in matching fleeces, Lauren's latest eBay find, Rowan's black velvet and silver pentangle. The muddle of comfortable clothes and compensatory accessories. Hand-printed scarves and craft-shop earrings, pashmina shawls.

'I'll-*aah* have a beer, thanks.'

He had turned into a bruiser, broad-beamed, bull-necked. Even his head was bigger, and hairless as a hard-boiled egg. Only the voice was familiar.

'Must be twenty years.'

'Twenty-five.' She wondered if she had conceded something

by knowing exactly.

Rae, too, seemed stunned by the change in him. 'What do you want, Kinsella?'

'A Hoegaarden, if you've got one.'

'*Why are you here?*'

'Nothing to do with you.'

There was a sexual edge between them even now.

'You got married,' she said.

Lexa checked. Sure enough, he was wearing a ring.

'If I'd known you-*aah* cared I'd've waited. Too late now, I'm afraid. There are children involved.'

Lexa didn't need to look at Rae to know what she was thinking. They had sentenced him to a future of one-night stands and grappling in the dark, not school runs and bedtime stories and unselfconscious nakedness in the master bedroom. Despite their best efforts, they had not ruined his life. She didn't know whether she was disappointed or relieved.

He looked around. 'Does Scottish hospitality run to-*aah* sitting down?'

'There's beer in the kitchen.' She glanced at Rae who nodded and went to lean on the radiator beside Gabriel.

The kitchen door tended to swell in winter, she had to slam it shut. Kinsella raised an eyebrow at Ned. She knew she shouldn't let it pass, that it was in these first moments that the balance of power would be decided, but her mind was stuck at the open front door. *He's here, in Mackenzie Square,* when the whole point of the life they had made here was that it had nothing to do with him.

He accepted the bottle without thanks, as if she handed him beer all the time. 'Rae's wearing well. Still got that chavvy look, but the-*aah* tits are holding up.'

'Looks like you've grown your own since I last saw you,' she said.

Ned was careful to keep his eyes away from hers when she passed him the Grolsch.

Kinsella raised his bottle. 'To-*aah* old lang zine. Isn't that what you Jocks say?'

'Only if we like the person.'

And then she felt it, a tightening at the base of her throat, a physical memory of the way his mood could turn, and the last wisps of disbelief were burned away. It was him all right.

He surveyed the room. 'Very-*aah* boho.'

The Arne Jacobsen chairs around the old pine table, the pantry door warped permanently ajar.

'I hear you've-*aah* come back to banking.'

She had never thought of him as an intelligent man, or even emotionally intelligent, but he had always known where she was vulnerable.

'I'm a consultant. It's just a contract.'

'And what are they-*aah* consulting you about?'

Ned would have told him. He just wanted to make her say it.

'I do mediation. Conflict resolution.'

'Ah yes, you were always a dab hand at that—'

She steeled herself to look him in the eye.

'—does it pay well?'

'There's a lot of job satisfaction.'

He turned to Ned. 'Sounds like it doesn't.'

'Get to the point, Kinsella.'

She wasn't trying to imply she knew why he was here, but for a moment he lost the advantage. And then something unexpected happened. Ned, the eternal sidekick, took control.

'Shall we all sit down?'

Kinsella had left Goodisons fifteen years ago, after it was swallowed by the Krauts. He ran a hedge fund now. PKP Investments. A portfolio of four billion that had been averaging thirty per cent returns before the crunch. He didn't believe in silos, bought what he fancied. Equities, bonds, futures. Mostly UK, but he'd take a punt on a gold mine in bongo-bongo land if the right tip came along. When your track record was good, the investors didn't ask questions. Asset management was run by tossers. It wasn't hard to milk the opportunities they missed. The Gresham Club buffers kept their balls in the safe, the twenty-four-year-olds didn't have his contacts. Who did they know? Some fucking swami they met on their gap year. It took time to build the network he had. Decision-makers in the

FTSE 100, sources in the markets, chaps like Ned in the banks.

Without looking up, Ned took a slug of his beer.

There were too many amateurs in investment. They saw a hedge fund pulling in twenty times what they could hope to make and said 'must be dodgy'. Yeah, he operated close to the edge, his contacts told him a little bit more than they should now and again – it wasn't *insider trading*. Anyone could see the big funds had been stiffed by their own incompetence. But if they flung enough shit, reputational damage could be done. Sooner or later those toss-wipes in the FSA would come sniffing around, maybe a steward's enquiry. *That* his investors wouldn't like. Not that there was-*aah* anything to find, but by the time he was given the all-clear it'd be too late . . .

She stared at him in wonder. *He was still the same.* Did he never look at the world and think 'times have changed'? Did he never look in the mirror? Physically, he was someone else. Details she had never noticed back then were now distinguishing marks. The crowding of his lower teeth, the cleft in his chin. Surely the passing years had left some impression on the man within?

She felt a creeping self-consciousness and, turning her head, found Ned watching her.

'You have to hand it to her,' Kinsella was saying. 'Back in August I thought she was toast. But she's-*aah* never going to hold her own with Stephen Hawking, is she?' His eyes bugged in imitation of Gabriel's ping-pong ball stare.

Lexa wanted to hurt him. The thought came to her unbidden, as natural as breathing.

She got up, taking longer than strictly necessary to retrieve the wine from the fridge. Steadying her hands on the cold bottle. Filling a glass. Telling herself it was the shock. But the shock of what? The discovery that this man she had forgotten for a quarter of a century still existed? Or that this woman slept within her, waiting to be woken by his voice? Friends who did school reunions claimed the intervening years just melted away. Suddenly you were sixteen again, sucking a strand of hair, gnawing at a cuticle, giggly or sarcastic or drunk with sex. Or, in her case, twenty-three and angry. She could feel it now, like lava in her chest, smoking fissures in the crust of calm.

Sitting down again, she was aware of having missed some wordless communication between the two men.

Ned touched his beer bottle to her glass with a light *clink*. 'How much do you know about Gabriel's job?'

Of course. It had to be this.

'Not much. Why?'

Ned glanced at Kinsella briefly, then back to her. 'She never mentioned particular investors?'

She looked at Kinsella. 'A CDO?'

'A synthetic,' Ned said.

'And the mortgage-holders defaulted?'

'Yeah, but he owned the swap. Effectively he shorted it.'

Kinsella said quickly 'Let's not blind anyone with science.'

Ned raised his hands. 'Whiter than white. Completely legit. But in the current climate—'

She waited for his smirk, but it seemed this wasn't a laughing matter.

'—everything's coming out of the wash looking grey.'

'And will it come out of the wash?'

'Not if everybody keeps their mouth shut,' Kinsella said.

Ned picked up her wine glass, passed it under his nose. 'I wouldn't want it getting out, if I was Gabriel.'

'Why's that?'

Kinsella leaned across the table. 'She doesn't know what fucking planet she's on. She could say anything. *You*,' his jabbing finger stopped just short of her breasts, 'had better make sure she doesn't.'

She glanced down at his finger and up at his face before saying distinctly. 'I don't take orders from you any more.'

Ned's voice was bluff. 'There's no need for this to get adversarial . . .'

Kinsella slammed his beer bottle on the table. '*You owe me.*'

It seemed to Lexa that all three of them stopped breathing. She refused to think about what Ned might or might not know about that night in the tattoo parlour.

'Fuck off and talk to Rae,' Kinsella said.

Ned looked at Lexa. She nodded.

When the door closed, Kinsella got up and walked over

to the fridge to examine a postcard Rae had sent from Bali. His eyebrows flexed in that old derisive way at the message on the back.

'Have you heard from-*aah*, whatsisname, that short-arse Union rep you had a bit of unofficial action with?' He opened the fridge, took another beer, found the bottle-opener in the drawer. 'I take it he had a normal-size todger. Unless you could fit all of him up there.'

And here it came, the old helplessness. A passivity that could only be overcome with galvanic rage. Might he, too, be a different person out of her presence? Was it something in each of them, together, that created this?

'*Hello*,' he said in a new voice.

There was a brief delay before Amy slipped out from behind the pantry door.

Too sharply, Lexa said, 'What were you doing in there?' and saw the pale face flinch.

She had that white-around-the-gills look she got when she was found out. Reluctantly she walked over to the table and Lexa smelled the oily sweetness on her breath. Marzipan.

'It's a good hiding place,' Kinsella said in that new, creepy, Father-Christmas voice.

Amy, usually so sensitive to nuance, looked up at him trustingly, 'Joe always hides in there.'

'And where do you hide?'

She moved to the window, crooked a finger. It was always startling to Lexa how much Amy liked men, how flirtatiously sure of her powers she was, like all little girls. She had no idea what she was flirting with.

'Down there.' She pointed.

'I see,' he said, though she must have known he couldn't. 'I'd never think of looking there.'

Lexa crossed the kitchen to stand behind Amy, placing a hand on the countertop either side of her, forming a physical barrier. Kinsella was so close she could smell him, his beefy odour catching in the back of her throat.

The three of them stood gazing out into the night.

Suddenly he pointed. 'Look!—'

Lexa looked. Chains of red and white on the motorway, the orange scribble of residential streets, the chalk-dust cube of the floodlit all-weather pitch.

'—did you see it?'

She hated the intimate warmth in his voice when he spoke to the child.

Amy nodded. 'A shooting star?' But it was a question, not a statement. 'Can I make a wish?'

'As long as you don't tell us what it is,' Lexa said.

There was a constipated couple of seconds while Amy made her wish, before she breathed out again. She was so needy since her mother's stroke, desperate to please, wide open to any casual exploiter. Her eyes lifted, scanning the heavens, terrified of missing a second meteor. Unless it was their reflection she was watching: the ersatz family portrait superimposed on the lights across the valley. She gave a queer little sigh and tipped her head back against Lexa's chest.

'Go and find Joe, chickie. Make sure he's all right.'

It took her a second or two to rouse from her trance of safety.

Afterwards, there was a moment when they stood looking at the door she'd not quite closed behind her.

'How many do you have?' Lexa asked.

'Six.'

She had to glance at him to check this wasn't a joke. 'I thought that was just benefits scroungers in the *Daily Mail*.'

'I can afford them,' he said.

A hundred-and-fifty thousand in school fees every year, plus a couple of foreign holidays. And she couldn't see them flying economy. No matter how many nannies and boarding-school house-masters were involved, he was a father. His children would love him. Until they were old enough to know better.

'If I was at work,' she said, 'I'd be looking for a way out of this that everyone could be happy with.'

She could tell from the way his head turned that she'd surprised him. 'Are we *in conflict*?'

'Aren't we?'

This smile was a new addition to his repertoire of unpleasantness. 'You're-*aah* one of those, are you?'

'One of what?'

'What do they call them? *Reflective listeners.*'

She absorbed this. 'Have you had therapy?'

'Why would I need therapy?'

'I thought you might tell me.'

'Why would you think that?' He tired of the game. 'I make money, that's my therapy.'

'I don't know what that means.'

Another unpleasant smile. 'Just as well you got out of banking then.'

His back was against the countertop. The rubbery moon of his bald head floated on the darkened window behind him. His ears were flaccid, old-mannish. His neck, in that open shirt collar, an uncooked sausage roll. When he lifted the beer bottle to his lips she caught a glimpse of straining waistband. Greedily she noted each flaw. But so what? Money might or might not be therapy, but it was a talisman against common humanity. What could touch him? State spending cuts? He'd be treated in private hospitals, his children educated in those extortionate schools. Street crime? When was he ever on the street? He'd shop online, live in a gated community patrolled by uniformed thugs. He might get drowned by a tsunami on holiday or blown up by a terrorist bomb, but the odds were against it. He'd probably miss the rush hour, too: starting early, finishing late. The worst he risked was a waiter sneezing a new virus over his Michelin-starred plate. Maybe a lap dancer coughing as she jiggled her breasts in his face. He had no idea of daily life as lived by his fellow citizens, but he'd get to bend the ear of the Chancellor at the Mansion House dinner.

'How long have you and Gabriel been in touch?'

He made her wait, taking another swig of beer. She averted her eyes, not wanting to see his lips tighten around the neck of the bottle.

'A couple of years? No – three.' He saw her dismay and had to compound it. 'She made the approach, through Ned.'

Lexa believed him. Why would he bother to lie?

Out of nowhere she recalled that holiday in London, in Rae's cousin's flat. The week that had ended with Gabriel conning an unopened bottle of Bollinger out of three geeks in Next suits. They'd made a run for it, grabbing a black cab luck had placed outside the bar. Ten minutes later they were sitting in the garden, squealing at the *pop* as Rae forced the cork out of the bottle. All week Gabriel had been a little crazy. Shrieking on the street, flirting with barrow boys and waiters, trying to pass herself off as the sort of ditzy blonde who might tattoo a man's groin in a hilarious madcap jape. Lexa had felt it too, that same desperate gaiety, helpless with laughter as they squashed into the taxi. Yet even as they'd howled and whooped she had been praying that Piers Kinsella's desire for revenge was weaker than his fear of dismissal for insider trading, or the shame of exposing his disfigured flesh to the police.

'She needed a hedge fund. I was a contact,' he said.

'And you two had such happy memories of each other?'

Lager glinted wet on his upper lip, 'This was business.'

Who knew? Perhaps that was how bankers thought. And yet Gabriel hadn't lived like a banker. That had to count for something. Her friends were those women down the corridor. Joe went to the state primary and would, in time, join Amy at the local high. Say what you liked about the man she'd chosen to marry (and Lexa had said plenty over the years), he had no interest in money.

Kinsella fetched the wine bottle, setting it down beside her empty glass. '*Are* you still in touch with Stuart Duffy?'

'What's it got to do with you?'

For the first time, it seemed to her, his smile held genuine pleasure. 'Let's-*aah* see if you can work it out.'

NOVEMBER

They walked through the hotel garden, between beds of black earth, along a stone path slippery with rotting leaves. As they passed through the gate the ground began to rise. Not steeply, but the land stretched flat for miles, making the slightest incline into a hill. Then it was tarmac, not stone, under their feet, and she could smell the sea, and hear it slipping up a shingle beach, unless it was just the grind of traffic on its way to the trading estate. Lexa looked up. The sky was a swarming blue between dusk and darkness, not raining, but so saturated that she could feel its moisture beading on her face. They came to a lane lined by strange little one-room houses. Just huts, really, but built with chimneys and pitched roofs. A bay window here, mock-Tudor timbering there, or pebble-dash, or peach stucco, or scab-coloured brick. An odd time of year for them to be occupied, but more than a few had lighted windows, the curtains not drawn, so she could see the tiled fireplace and mantel, the pictures clustered on the shrunken back wall. A whole family – mother, father, teenage son and pigtailed daughter – crammed into a sofa, eating off plates on their laps. A man in a Motörhead vest scraping mud off a football boot. A dressing-gowned woman at the ironing board. All of them overweight, lard-white, the sofa family goggle-eyed behind their glasses. She knew she shouldn't look, but these yellow squares of light in the blue dark were tantalising as doors in an advent calendar. Had she seen them on the white walls of a gallery she would have taken them for faked tableaux, exaggerated stereotypes of the underclass. But they were just people living their lives.

Between the houses and the sea was a trailer park. Four rows of static caravans crowded together against the persecution of coastal weather. Most were shuttered for the winter but, as she threaded between them, she could hear the scratch of a televised voice through fibreglass walls and see the flaring blue cast by a moving picture. A man in jeans and a track-suit top sat smoking in a picnic chair, a gummy-eyed poodle wheezing at his feet. She was ready to be challenged, but he nodded as they passed. Then they were out the other side, on open ground. It was fully dark now. Looking down, she could just make out a row of untenanted concrete pitches. To their left, wet grass slid into the nothingness of air and sea.

'Watch yourself near the edge,' Stuart said.

It was a perverse choice for a union conference, he admitted, but cheap. An English seaside town that no one could call a resort. A place threatened by coastal erosion and shunned by half the High Street chains, with sandbags and vacant shops everywhere you looked. An Army recruitment office opposite the cash converters, a tattoo-and-piercing studio between a bakers full of curranty pastry and a store selling objects nobody needed for the bargain price of ninety-nine pence. The Union had its regional dues to pay. A disproportionate chunk of the member-ship lived around here: minimum-wage workers servicing the food grown in these flat fields. Flour millers, pea-processors, packers at a plant that turned out frozen potato croquettes. These were Stuart's people. But the conference wouldn't be coming back next year if he had anything to do with it. And he would have something to do with it, as long as he kept his nose clean between now and March.

She let him tell her all this, keeping her expression neutral, giving nothing away. It was a grossly unprofessional thing she had done, cancelling the feuding school governors and driving all day, but her anger had got her through the hold-up outside the Tyne Tunnel and every stretch of contra-flow, and even through the moment when he'd looked down from the platform and she'd read his mind as clearly as if the word 'stalked' had been written across his forehead. She'd thought, *he's here with a woman*. As if she cared about that.

'God sake, Lexa, you've got to stop ambushing me like this.'

But then he'd decided he was pleased to see her. His hand on her arm as he led her through the half-empty rows of stacking chairs, into the lobby with its assorted stalls. Greenpeace. Fair Trade. Compassion in World Farming. He had been heading for the palm court lounge with its yuccas and tub chairs and delegates sinking pints of lager at four in the afternoon, but she said no, she'd rather see him alone, hiding the anger so well she had to plead for air, in case he thought she wanted to go up to his room. She opened the French doors into the garden and he cursed the damp but followed her out. And now they had been walking for twenty minutes and she still hadn't broached the reason she was here because, despite everything, there was the pleasure of being with him in the mild, wet, salt-scented dark.

They came to a service road for the caravan site, sealed off with *Danger!* signs and concrete blocks. He moved beyond the barricade, his eyes trained on the ground, holding up a hand to stop her following him. Finally he beckoned. A couple of paces from where he stood the tarmac ended in a sheer drop. A blurry moon had risen, shedding just enough light for them to see the tide was in. The North Sea moved like cold, silent, bubbling soup. Grabbing her arm, he inched closer to the ragged edge. At the bottom of the cliff, but raised above the sea, was a stretch of perfectly-preserved road. Black tarmac. Double yellow lines. So preposterously normal that they laughed.

She looked back at the trailers behind the line of abandoned pitches. 'How long till the next row has to move?'

'A year?' He thought about it. 'Bit we're standing on could go any minute.'

And then it wasn't funny any more. She remembered his face on the platform, the way it had changed. He was the one who'd kept in touch these past weeks, emailing a joke that had tickled him, a link to a YouTube clip. It was strange being in regular contact after a quarter-century of silence. Not so strange for him, she supposed. All sorts of names from the past would be washed up on his cyber beach to resume the virtual friendship of Face-book-postings. But no one was meant to claim him in the flesh.

'So you're going to be General Secretary.'

He was staring out to where the horizon would have been,

had they been able to see it. 'Someone's got to fight for a better standard of living for 'em.'

'High-definition TV? Cheap flights to Disneyland?'

'If that's what they want to spend their money on.'

There was a light wind blowing off the sea. She could feel it stirring her hair, smell its faint whiff of bladderwrack and tanker fuel.

'What?' he said.

'You wouldn't have said that in 1984.'

'They didn't have high-definition TV in 1984.'

His gaze sharpened, as if he'd seen something out at sea.

She heard a wave slap against the shingle far below them. 'So it was always about money?'

'What else?'

'A culture, a way of life.'

'Christ,' he muttered, 'the last o't' great romantics.'

'I thought you were fighting for a class who believed there was more to life than money.'

It happened again, his eyes narrowing, that sudden shift in focus. Something in her blind spot.

'Times change,' he said.

'*You've* changed.'

'You can't fight for a class that dun't exist.'

'No,' she said, 'I guess that's right. All we can do is hold out, keep our own hands clean—'

Then she saw it too. A flash. There and gone. A lighthouse.

'—would you say?'

He let go of her arm. 'Is this where I frisk you to see if you're wearing a wire?'

She ignored this, refusing its train of distracting thoughts. 'I had a visit from Piers Kinsella. He's wondering why you've not been taking his calls.'

Another pinprick of light was swallowed by the darkness.

In a new, businesslike voice Stuart said, 'How much d'you know?'

Most of it, but not quite all, it turned out.

Gabriel had helped the miners, not with her own money, but by introducing Stuart to an investment opportunity. She constructed a synthetic CDO, one of those profitable parcels of thin air she had described so enthusiastically that night on the island. She didn't suggest he put his money into that. It was the *swap* she recommended, the financial product that paid out if the coleslaw of real-life debt shadowed by the synthetic went bad. And those debts had gone bad. And Gabriel and Stuart and Kinsella had known they would.

In the beginning, the sliced-and-diced debt had been mortgages in New York and Massachussetts. But the prospectus allowed the substitution of other loans, provided the ratings agencies viewed them as equivalent, as was the case with mortgages in Nevada and Florida, mortgages that anyone not employed by a ratings agency would have known were more liable to default. Gabriel was within her rights to switch the debt. The broker's discretionary powers were fully detailed in the small print. But who bothered to read it? Not the investors. All they wanted was their share of the easy money.

Lexa squinted. 'You're saying she deliberately sabotaged her own financial product?'

He shrugged. 'Cally owned a load of rubbish. Loans that were never going to be paid back. So she moved some of 'em off bank's books, into CDO. Alison Babbington should have given her a medal . . .'

'But she couldn't be told, because it was bent.'

'It's a financial product. Bent, straight: it's meaningless. Buyer beware.'

'Did she do it for you?'

She felt the violence in him before she heard it in his voice. 'I don't want to hear you saying that again. And you can tell Piers Kinsella an' all.'

'I'm not here to carry your messages.'

'What are you here for, then?'

Gabriel had put Stuart in touch with PKP Investments and he had bought a share of the hedge fund's swap, their *sure-thing* bet on a certain percentage of the mortgage-holders defaulting. Kinsella had told Lexa this. And she was here so Stuart could tell her Kinsella had twisted the facts. But the moment she'd seen his face on the conference platform, she had known that wasn't going to happen.

The economy was shot. Millions would lose their jobs, their homes, their promise of a secure old age, or, for the young, their hopes of independence, the adult rites of passage Lexa's generation had taken for granted. Unless their parents could afford to buy them a flat and fund them through an internship. London would continue to prosper as a holiday home for Russian mobsters. Edinburgh could always rely on the tourists. But communities like Gemmell and Dudderthorpe and this white-trash Riviera would grow ever more marginalised, small-time consumers in a country that had forgotten people could be defined any other way. And despite what she'd told Gabriel on the island, the severity of the crisis held a kernel of satisfaction. All the bitter medicine she'd had to swallow over the past twenty years: capital had to be given its head, wages driven down for those at the bottom, the wealth generators' incentives insanely inflated; the free market knew best . . . All this had failed. The unfettered pursuit of short-term profit had brought the global economy to its knees. The brightest and best and most testosterone-charged had squandered trillions on a market they didn't understand. How could there not be satisfaction in seeing them brought down, even if they barely acknowledged their humbling, even if they would be the last people to pay the price? Even if Gabriel had been one of them. Somehow Lexa had managed to live with this fact, until she learned that Stuart had joined the gold rush.

'Where did you get the stake?'

The lighthouse flared again.

'I were caretaking this pension fund I sit on.'

A billion pounds docked from county council salaries. The financial manager had been signed off sick for two weeks that became another two, and another. Always on the point of coming back. Stuart stood in one day a week, made sure the shares portfolio was ticking over. The only room for manoeuvre was forty million earmarked for alternative investment management. He'd taken twenty-five per cent and put it into PKP.

The amount, too, was news to her. 'You handed Kinsella ten million quid?'

'He doubled it in six month.'

'*What?*'

Stuart shrugged, 'He had this offshore fund in Cayman Islands. He put it through that. Turbo-charged bet.'

'Turbo-charged it how?'

'Borrowed another ten.'

Ten million, she reminded herself. 'How?'

Cornered, he snapped. 'If I told you, you wun't understand it. I put lot on black and that's where ball landed.'

'And if the ball had landed on red the pension fund would have been twenty million pounds short?'

'But that were never going to happen—'

The cloud had thickened, obscuring the moon, reflecting the barest glimmer of light pollution from the town. His face was no more than a pattern of shadows.

'—I split difference, half for Mick and rest of 'em, half back to pension fund.'

'It wasn't your money.'

'They got fifty per cent return. They'd never have got that without me.'

Theft, or maybe embezzlement. The courts came down hard on breaches of trust. Never mind insider trading.

'I can't believe you were so stupid,' she said.

'I din't know banking system were going to go belly-up, did I? One golden goose lays rotten egg: it's law of averages. Nobody's going to look twice. Mick gets to live another ten year. You telling me you'd have done any different?'

'But now Gabriel's been suspended they're going to scrutinise everything she touched.'

His silence said he'd already reached this conclusion.

'Buyer beware,' she murmured.

It was a throwaway line, an echo in her head that made it to her lips, but he heard it as a taunt.

'I'm not like you. Stopping chavs knocking lumps out of each other. It's not my idea o' making a difference. You have to get your hands dirty in this life.'

'And it doesn't come much dirtier than getting into bed with Piers Kinsella in the Cayman Islands.'

'He's no worse than rest. They've robbed us blind for years. I got a bit back, that's all.'

'Which makes you just like them.'

'We're all *like 'em*. Try finding NHS dentist these days. Or getting your kid through university. God help you if you've more than one. They'll all need bankers' salaries to pay off debt. Try being told you've got cancer, and there's drugs to keep you going, but you'll be dead in six month. You'll care about money then. What's *moral position*: feeling good about earning what scumbags in City spend on lunch, or getting those miners another few year? *Game's rigged*. If compensation case had come to court, you think it'd've been any different? You pay for justice like you pay for owt else. We'd have had some sad bastard off the rank, they'd've had top o' range QC. We all need money. It's what you do with it that matters.'

'Speculating on a fraud?'

Again she sensed that violence in him.

'You're the one dressing windows in fucking banking!'

Stepping back, she felt the ground creak under her weight. Adrenaline sharpened her senses. A pinching between the eyes, a sinus buzz. Stuart grabbed her arms, pulling her towards him. Behind her, the sound of loose earth and stones dropping down the cliff.

The room was much as she expected. Smaller than a Travelodge, but with a mini bar and an easy chair. Outside the window, a string of brake lights signalled the Monday evening rush hour.

He opened a miniature of Bells and sat on the bed, leaning forward to clink his teacup against her tooth glass. They drank. He put the cup down on the bedside shelf, licked the pad of his thumb and swiped at a mark on her chin.

'Muck,' he said, 'it's gone now.'

His touch set off a light ringing in her flesh.

'You saved my life.'

She meant it as a joke, or thought she had.

He drank some more whisky, his lips taut as if his gums were stinging. 'Don't be daft. It were thirty feet. You'd have survived.'

'With a couple of broken legs.'

A shudder passed through her.

'Drink up,' he said.

They sipped in silence for a while.

'I'm going to have a shower. I'll be two minutes, then I'll run you a bath.'

'I did wash this morning,' she said.

'You're *shaking*.'

She lifted her hand and discovered this was true.

He shut himself in the bathroom and she heard the droning of the extractor fan. There was no question of her staying. She had to train a roomful of relationship counsellors first thing tomorrow.

He came out of the bathroom bare-chested, water glistening on his shoulders, a towel wrapped round his belly. She looked, and he saw her looking.

'That's your bath running now.'

'Won't they be missing you,' she asked, 'downstairs?'

'They'll think I've got a click. It'll be all round conference by now.'

She had stopped counting the years since she had last made love. Rae was right, she couldn't blame her age. She had seen it happening to younger women too. The jamming of signals. Nothing going out, nothing coming in.

'I'd forgotten you had hairy toes,' she said.

He gave a soundless laugh.

'The rest of you is pretty much as I remember.'

'I'm a couple o' stone heavier.'

'It suits you.'

Another almost-laugh. 'You trying to make me blush or summat?'

'You're the one walking around in a towel.'

His gaze dropped to the carpet. 'I'm married, Lexa.'

'Oh,' she said lightly, 'you were separated the last I heard.'

'Three year ago.'

'So this is wife number what?'

He didn't rise to the bait, making allowances for her in her embarrassment. 'I'm still with Lesley.' He cleared his throat with his old scraping grunt. 'It's not perfect, but what is?'

'And you were apart how long?'

'Four month.'

She managed a smile. 'Four months is a sulk, not a separation.'

She knew she should be glad, for him, and for herself. There was nothing to regret. Nothing she could have said or done that night in Glasgow would have made any difference.

He reached for his teacup of whisky and sat back down on the bed, one hand tucking the towel more securely in place. She could hear the gushing of the taps through the bathroom door and, faintly, laughter echoing in the hotel corridor.

'Are you with . . .'

'No,' she said, before he could finish the question.

'How long's it been?'

She thought about the various answers she might give.

'Three-and-a-half months. But I still see her.'

His head lifted at that 'her'.

'Gabriel,' she said.

She tried to explain it in terms he would understand. Always in and out of each other's houses, never off the phone. But she could think of a dozen women, married and single, whose friendships worked like that. Full of shining moments, ordinary and perfect, like a song. So she described the sense she had of carrying Gabriel inside her, knowing what she would think and how they would differ and filtering everything through that dialectic even now.

'You were lovers?'

She shook her head. 'Just the love of my life.'

He moved his neck as if an invisible collar were chafing him. 'And she . . .?'

'Loved me? I think so.'

He frowned as if he were about to say something.

And of course it had crossed her mind: how he might have filled those four months he was parted from his wife.

They went for a curry, a radioactive dansak on a stained table-cloth under fluorescent lights. The hotel receptionist said it was a better bet than the place with smoked-glass mirrors and a guy with a scimitar on the door, and only ten minutes' walk. Which became twenty when they took the wrong turn and had to retrace their steps. Pilau rice, ladies fingers, a complimentary plate of poppadoms with raita, chopped onions and chutney. The sort of cheap meal they'd shared in their twenties.

The turbaned waiter was glad to see some customers at last. His cousin worked at Stuart's hotel. They weren't missing much by eating out, except maybe a dose of e-coli. He went to get Stuart's pint of lager, calling across to ask if they wanted the music on. Why not? Stuart liked a bit of bhangra. The tape started mid-song, Noddy Holder belting out *It's Chri-i-i-istma-a-a-s!* Their eyes met for a stunned beat. And then everything was funny. The green chilli he bit in his first mouthful of dansak. The look on his face when his cuff trailed in the chutney. All the ELO and Supertramp and Jennifer Rush he was missing by dogging the conference social. ('Wagging it, you mean. Dogging's summat else.') He had changed into moleskins and a zip-necked jumper, that nubuck jacket on top. Bone, oatmeal and rust. Underneath, his skin pink with steam. The fuzz on his chest thicker than before but grey now, not black. It was all there, preserved on her retina.

They talked about this part of the country. Everyone on minimum wage, and still the farmers used smuggled Latvians to harvest the brussels sprouts. His wife had grown up in the next town. Pubs full of bare-legged women in white slingbacks, the Corn Exchange booked out with heavy metal bands. Lesley had been the school snob because her house had a piano. She hated the place. Went back once a year to see her mother. Three hours and she'd be checking her phone, hoping they needed her at the hospital. She worked in paediatric cardiology, really cared about her patients, but sometimes he wished she pushed paper nine to five. When they went on holiday, it took her a week to come off the adrenaline. It was like finding the woman he'd fallen in love with, for three or four days, before she started stressing about going back to work.

Not that it was all one way. He wasn't the easiest to live with. After Irena, he'd felt this pressure to make it work, didn't want to be one of those guys with a string of broken marriages behind him. So it was flowers every Friday night and tables at classy restaurants. A weekend trip to Paris one time. *'Pack your bag, we're on the eight o'clock flight.'* She made him cancel it, said they'd switched the rotas and she was on call. Maybe she was, but it was the quietest weekend Leeds General had ever seen. A couple of days later, he phoned this woman he knew at Unison. He had the odd fling in the nineties, daft stuff, no one he really cared about. Then there was all this hassle with Anna, his step-daughter. For the first few years she lived with them they got on great. Till she turned fourteen and started fighting with Lesley. It got so bad she went to live with her dad. She was out the door five minutes and Lesley wanted to have another one. He thought she'd get over it, but she was like a dog with a bone. One day her pills weren't by the bed. So he asked her. She went mad. How dare he? It was none of his business what went into her body. He told her: he hadn't enjoyed nappies and sleepless nights at twenty-four, he wasn't going to go through all that again at fifty. That was when they'd split up. Water under the bridge now, he said, clearing his throat, aware how far he had strayed from jokes about dogging.

They ate the sugar-coated seeds that came with the bill and each left a ten pound note on the saucer. Five minutes after setting out for the hotel, they were lost again. Stuart had to admit it: they hadn't passed this bar on the way there. Yellow walls stencilled with black cacti and sombreros. A group of policewomen in short skirts and high heels had taken over the aluminium tables on the pavement. They were past the giggling novelty of fancy dress and the high of the first few tequilas. Some smoked, staring into space. Others checked their phones. One young woman, slumped forward over a table, needed a taxi home.

The pack leader was standing on the kerb, tiger-stripe highlights in her hair, cigarette clamped between her lips. Not so many years younger than Lexa. There was only just room on the pavement to get past. Their eyes locked.

'D'you want us to arrest him, darlin?'

She felt Stuart smiling at her side, 'I'll come quietly.'

The women shared a dirty laugh.

Safely out of sight, round the corner, Lexa echoed: '*I'll come quietly*?'

'It spiced up their night,' he said.

'Lucky them.'

In the end, he suggested following the railway line. He could see the trains from his hotel room.

It was a small enough transgression, a bylaw infringement at worst, but it brought back that distant summer when they'd dodged roadblocks and run from the police. A section of the chain-link fence had been peeled away from its concrete post, leaving a triangular gap. On the other side, walking the corridor of waste ground that bordered the track, they fell into their old rhythm, the old blend of intimacy and containment, talk and easy silence, a lone shoe remarked on, or not remarked on, the inevitable traffic cone, a switch box webbed with gang tags. It was a no man's land of fly-tipped rubbish and brittle winter scrub but, in his presence, it had a kind of poetry. Brick dust and clinker pierced by the feral weeds that flourished in such spaces. Brown sprays of buddleia, seed-headed Michaelmas daisies, docken spikes dark as old blood.

'What d'you reckon Kinsella's playing at?'

'Nothing nice.' She stepped over a broken skateboard. 'He made our lives a misery at Goodisons.'

'Aye, Gabriel said—'

The casual way he pronounced her name, the consonants rubbed smooth with use.

'—what's he think I'm going to do? Turn myself in to FSA? We're both int' same boat, we might as well trust each other.'

'Kinsella doesn't do trust. He has to feel he's got something on you.'

'What's he got on you?'

Two possible answers.

'You,' she said.

At first she'd thought he wanted her to put pressure on Stuart, but he wasn't the weak point in the triangle, the one with nothing to lose from cutting a deal with the FSA. It was Gabriel he was worried about. She couldn't be pressurised, only policed. And so the woman best placed to do that – or best placed as far as Kinsella knew – had been given an extra incentive.

'I don't get it,' he said.

'He knows we were lovers.'

He looked sceptical. 'Long time ago.'

'He must think I'm the sentimental type.'

They walked on through the weeds. To their left, a lumber yard. To their right, an industrial estate shamed with a rash of 'To Let' boards. Security lights flooded the railway land with the drab but detailed brilliance of a *Crimewatch* reconstruction. She thought about him phoning Gabriel in 2006. Their acquaintance, too, had been *a long time ago*.

'Why did she put you on to him?'

'She were trying to help.'

'If I wanted to help somebody, Kinsella's the last person I'd involve.'

'Aye, but you din't want to help, did you?'

She took this. What else could she do?

'It doesn't make any sense. Getting in touch with him after everything he put her through.' She trod down a bramble cane. 'For you.'

'She felt bad about cancers.'

He tilted his head to scratch under his jaw. Years of conflict work had left her with a highly-developed instinct for the evasive gesture.

'What are you not telling me?'

He sighed. 'A sum o' money were settled—'

Lawyer's language, she thought.

'—on some o' old-timers.'

In the middle of that long-distant summer. Early retirement for one miner and lump sums for two others already retired. All three had signed the papers accepting the cash *without prejudice* before Faxerley was sold. No loose ends when Beronex took possession, no reason to do a health and safety audit. Her mind's eye conjured that twenty-eight-year-old with his steel-bright hair. Not so different from the man walking beside her, after all. The decision taken then leading inexorably to where he was now.

'So Brian Netley took the money.'

'I thought it were one-off. Three sick men needing help. I had another two hundred with families who needed jobs. Harrison told me problem were brake linings on underground engines . . .'

She raised a hand to stem the tide of detail. 'And Gabriel handled the payments.'

He nodded.

The time when Lexa had felt most alive. First job, first love, the strike, her first chance to make a mark on the world. But she'd been wrong. She was just a bystander.

'And I thought I minded you buying in to casino capitalism.'

His head came up like a boxer's, 'If I'd kicked up stink about asbestos Beronex would never have touched that pit. All of 'em would've had P45 by end o't' week. Claims had been on books two, three year. Harrison were letting it drag on till they dropped dead. By rights Stan Richardson should've been long gone. It were only thing keeping him going, getting compensation. Then out o't' blue I get this call, are they ready to sign confidentiality agreement? It were good result. Hundred-and-fifty grand paid out. Families looked after. Pit got bought. Two hundred jobs safe . . .' His eyes dared her to state the obvious. 'For five year I thought we'd got away with it. Then Andy Lockwood died. Eighteen month later Roy Easton were diagnosed. Glen Ashton, Bob Leigh, Gary Scrivener. Mick . . .' His upper lip tightened. 'God knows who else. It can take forty year to show, like time bomb ticking inside 'em. I don't know what's worse, knowing you've got it, or waiting to find out . . .'

It was coming back to her now. That day they'd made love at the Norman chapel. She'd worn sunglasses, a minor perversion, more like what he called *mucking about*, but she'd felt the first stirrings of a new erotically-daring self. Then meeting Brian Netley. His cloak-and-dagger manner. Using her power to coax the facts out of Stuart later. Had he been working with Gabriel even then? No – wasn't it *she* who'd suggested involving Gabriel? And say she hadn't passed the buck, say she'd dealt with the situation herself, would Mick be dying now? Would she have called in the inspectors, with the risk that they'd shut the mine? She should be glad it hadn't been her responsibility, glad to have escaped that crushing weight of guilt. Instead, she felt she'd lost the only part of herself she cared about.

He put his hand on her forearm, turning to look back the way they had come. She looked too. A white light. A long way down the track.

'Why didn't you tell me all this in August?'

He shrugged, then half-laughed. And here it was again: the anger she had all but forgotten, the impetus that had made a three-hundred-mile drive seem like nothing.

'Go on,' she said.

'You weren't that helpful when I came to you three year ago.'

'I had my reasons.'

'Aye, and you might have had reasons in summer an' all.'

She could hear the train now, a low grinding in the distance.

'So why spend the morning with me?'

He expelled a deflating sort of breath. 'I din't know how much you knew.' Another glance back down the track. 'Turned out you knew nowt. It were a weight off my mind.'

She pushed the humiliation away, fed it to the fire.

'So why tell me the truth now? If it is the truth.'

He screwed up his face. 'What'm I going to lie about? You knew it all when you got here.'

'Not about you gambling with the pension fund. Or Gabriel rigging the CDO.'

He looked at her. 'I trust you.'

The words lodged themselves in the place she still kept for them.

He grimaced. 'And I need you to get rid o' Gabriel's yellow laptop—'

She could make out the headlamp now, and the twin blades of reflected light reaching along the parallel rails towards her. They stepped away from the track.

'—there's nowt they can't retrieve. Dun't matter if you delete it, it's all there—'

Some sort of goods train.

'—smash hard drive up, take it to dump. Somewhere they do metals reclamation – but not if they leave stuff lying for weeks.'

'Is there anything else—?'

He looked at her.

'—if I'm going to make myself an accessory to a financial crime, I think I have a right to know.'

The train was much closer now, moving as fast as an express. He raised his voice to be heard above the engine, 'Know what?'

'It must have taken a lot of negotiation, a lot of late nights.'

'*You think I shagged her*?' He grabbed her arm again, shouting now, 'Is that what this is about—?'

The driver had seen them. They heard the horn's two-tone blare.

'—I knew it were summat. You've had a face like a smacked arse all night . . .'

'I'm just asking if you used sex with her like you use it with me.' She too had to shout to make herself heard. 'Am I not supposed to have noticed?'

'I don't know what you're talking about.'

'One minute you're married, the next you're giving me the sob story on how incompatible you are.'

'I thought I were talking to a friend.'

'Aye, sure you did.'

'What do you want? A to Z, everyone I've ever slept with?'

'I don't give a *fuck* who you sleep with. Just drop the doggy eyes act when you're using me . . .'

It was a big, blocky diesel locomotive pulling an endless line of trucks. She had never stood so close to something so big moving so fast. The noise was pulverising. She felt it in her teeth, her bones. A cacophony of buffers and axles and coil-springs and dampers. They gave up trying to make themselves heard, but the train seemed to take over the quarrel, filling the air with hammers and knives. Truck after truck slicing past them with a black flash of night before the next, and the next.

The hallucination came out of nowhere. She *felt* them fucking, there, against the chain-link fence, his hands on her breasts, her thighs in the strangehold of pushed-down jeans and knickers. Her brain acknowledged his lustless grip on her sleeve, yet she could *feel* the heat of his body on hers, his breath hoarse on her neck, the ravening contact of their flesh. His eyes were stark in his face as if he felt it too. Stronger than hallucination. More like a glitch in time turning what had yet to occur into a *fait accompli*. Her ears were bursting with the slicing sibilance of metal crossing metal, the clangour of the freighted hoppers, the fusion of volume and speed and rhythm and sensation outside and inside, body, brain, sternum, bowels . . . And then the turbulence was past and they were looking at the flickering red lamp on the back of the last truck.

Stuart's face was like a plate that had been shattered and clumsily glued together.

'Coal,' she said.

'South African. They ship it into Immingham, take it down line to Ferrybridge.'

A wink of red, almost out of sight.

'*Jesus wept*,' he said.

They skirted the fence until they came to a supermarket trolley, turned wheels to the air, offering itself as a stile.

The hotel terrace was lit by the uncurtained windows of the function room. She recognised the saxophone break from an old Roxy Music hit. On the other side of the steamed-up glass, trades unionists were dancing.

He exhaled and the air tasted briefly of garam masala, 'Are you going to get a room?'

'They'll be fully booked.' She thought about the offer he would feel bound to make, 'The roads'll be quiet now.'

He raised no objection.

'So.' She knew she should just get in the Micra and go. 'Good luck with the general secretaryship—'

He scuffed his foot, scraping something off the sole of his boot.

'—I'll deal with the laptop.'

She turned away.

'*Lexa*—'

She looked into his face and the hope that had flared in

her died again.

'—yeah I'd like to make general secretary. I'm worried about FSA. I'm not sleeping. First time in my life I've got eczema. I'll live with it.' He met her eyes. 'I just don't want Mick thinking it's my fault he's dying.'

She had been dropping in on Mackenzie Square every other week, checking for leaks and mice and signs of forced entry. The first time, back in August, she had looked into Gabriel's room and seen the still-rumpled bed, the duvet kicked to one side as she'd left it the morning they set off for the island. The sheet was so cold it felt wet when Lexa lay down. She thought she heard the scuttling of insects, but it could have been her own blood in the ear that was pressed to the mattress. On the bedside table, under a blanket of dust, was a novel she had lent Gabriel two years before, the corner of page seven turned down.

Usually she walked, but today she couldn't muster the energy. She had managed four hours' sleep between the night-drive back from England and a demanding day at work. She saw the 'For Sale' sign from the car, and the mountain of black bags on the pavement, but still she parked and got out. Used her key in the door. What she found inside took her back to the day she and Gabriel and Rae first crossed the threshold. The brimming silence of those unfurnished rooms. A faintly fecal smell of damp.

Rae opened the door in tailored shorts and sleeveless cashmere. She had started showing off her arms, now that everyone made such a fuss of Michelle Obama's. Behind her blazed the Klieg-lit hall with its limited-edition prints framed in mounts that matched the carpet. Vivaldi was playing. Since moving to a big house she had discovered a taste for light classical music, though she still listened to Madonna in the car.

'I've come to see Gabriel.'

'She's having a shower,' Rae said in a voice Lexa hadn't heard in a long time, and hadn't missed.

'On her own?'

'Amy's with her. I don't leave her on her own.'

Behind Lexa the street lamps came on, though it was only

half past four. That brief barley-sugar glow before the filament warmed up.

They both knew why she was here

'I drove by Mackenzie Square just now.'

Rae toe-poked a dead leaf off the step. 'It's a dodgy time of year, but they reckon we might get a buy-to-let.' She raised her eyes. 'Barnardo's are taking the wardrobe on Monday.'

'You have been busy.'

'Somebody had to do it.'

And that somebody should have been me. Though they both knew Lexa would never have been a party to selling Mackenzie Square.

'Does Gabriel know?'

Rae looked at her for a good three seconds before replying 'You think I'd put it on the market without telling her?'

'She might not have taken it in.'

'*She knows.*'

It was cold out here, even with the heat escaping through the open front door. Rae tucked her hands into her armpits.

Lexa's fingers, too, were raw. 'Can I come in?'

Rae's gaze slid off to the side. 'She'll be awhile.'

'I can wait.'

'She's tired today.'

'It won't be the first time I've seen her tired.'

'She's not up to it.' Her Goodisons voice, sandpaper and razor wire.

'*It?*'

'*You,*' Rae said. 'You expect too much. She can tell she's disappointing you. It makes her feel bad, shuts her down.'

'She's shut down anyway.'

'Not like she is when she's seen you.'

A family entered the garden next door and made their way up the path. The parents pretended not to notice they were interrupting an altercation, but the children stared. The neighbour opened the door and ushered her visitors inside.

Lexa began with her competitiveness, her readiness to sacrifice anything and anyone to her need to be top dog. She couldn't bear it that her best friends' primary bond was with each other. And yes, Lexa knew that as one of seven, she'd had to fight for every last jammy dodger, but she wasn't five years old any more. She was a control freak. She'd never found a man she wanted to sleep with that she could stand having in the house, her sisters had driven her crazy, the only one of them she hadn't wanted to murder was poor Theresa. But it did Gabriel no favours, being turned into a substitute for a dead Bergin with learning difficulties, wrapping her in cotton wool when she needed to be challenged . . .

By now Lexa couldn't hear her own voice over Rae's sandpaper and razor wire.

It was rich, accusing *her* of making Gabriel into something she wasn't. She'd stayed out of it before. If Gabriel was happy with the situation, that was her business. But now she couldn't look out for herself, and it was stressing her. Why couldn't Lexa accept what was obvious to everyone else?

'. . . this is who she is now. What you see is what you get. It's sadistic to keep on rubbing her face in the things she's lost.'

The neighbour's front door cracked open and closed again with an emphatic *click*. It wasn't a street where women harangued each other in public.

'So it's not sadistic to take away her hope?'

'At least I'm not pushing her into another stroke.'

And as bad as anything either could say was the physical humiliation. Being made to stand on the path like a Kleeneze brush salesman while Rae looked down on her from the doorway. Rolling her eyes, a tic Lexa had seen too often not to know the weight of contempt it carried. She hadn't been alone with Gabriel since Rae brought her back from the hospital. Her best friend, and she couldn't even *speak* to her. Why would Rae not mention that she was selling Mackenzie Square? She had racked her brains, but could find no other explanation: Rae had *wanted* her to feel that heartsick wrench when she saw the 'For Sale' sign. She had stopped her seeing Gabriel out of jealousy, and to hide that – maybe even from herself – she'd re-cast her as some sort of Angel of Death, when in twenty-five years she'd only wanted the best for her. But anyone could see Rae was going to get tired of playing house with her big baby.

She'd meet a new man and want to stay out all night, or stay in and have screaming sex on the kitchen table, and what was going to happen to Gabriel then? Was that when she got dumped on Lexa?

Rae's lips drew back, exposing her narrow bite. No need to worry, she'd put her in a home before it came to that. 'She's spent twenty-odd years trying to make it up to you for shagging Kinsella. Now you've found another stick to beat her with. Well not while she's living in my house.'

The closing door took Lexa by surprise. She tried to get over the threshold but Rae blocked her. For a small woman, she was surprisingly strong. Lexa was stronger and heavier, but hampered by a higher centre of gravity and the responsibility of superior force. They shoved against each other in silence, as if what was happening would be deniable later so long as neither spoke. All Rae had to do was retreat, breaking the deadlock. Lexa would have staggered forward, looking foolish, and they could have laughed. But Rae wouldn't give ground. Electricity jumped in Lexa's muscles, a physical intelligence urging her to stamp on Rae's suede-shod foot, drive a knee into her weight-bearing thigh. She did neither. She had some self-control. Amy appeared at the other end of the hall, calling, 'Is everything all right?' Rae looked round. Lexa took advantage of the distraction to lunge for the newel post at the bottom of the stairs, intending to anchor herself in the house, but before her hand got there Rae had turned back and moved to intercept her. She made a sound which seemed out of all proportion to the blow but was impossible to doubt. Amy, too, cried out. Lexa felt appalled and unlucky and elated all at the same time.

'It's OK,' Rae said, though the intensity of the groan lingered in her voice. 'Go back to your mum.'

Amy dithered by the kitchen door.

Lexa stepped forward. 'She's fine, Amy. Go on, I'll see you in a wee while.'

Reluctantly Amy did as she was told.

Rae sat on the carpet, one hand cupped over her eye.

Lexa knelt beside her. 'Are you all right?'

'Fuck knows.'

'Let me have a look—'

Rae pressed her hand more tightly to her face.

'—I might have to take you to hospital.'

'I'm not seeing those butchers at the Infirmary.' She lowered her hand, but when Lexa tried to push her hair out of the way she shrank back.

'I'm not going to hurt you.'

'That's what *I* thought five minutes ago.'

She tucked the curtain of hair behind her ear.

'Nothing to see,' Lexa reported with relief.

'I've got that buzzing feeling that tells you something's damaged.'

'In your eye?'

'The bridge of my nose.'

'I didn't touch your nose.'

'Can we find out if I need to go to Casualty before you get started on the defence?'

In the handbag on the hall table Lexa found a mirror. Rae inspected herself, wincing as she palpated the skin under her eyebrow.

'Do you think I'll have a black eye?'

'Do you want one?'

'I want you to feel like shit every time you look at me for a week or so, yeah.'

'I didn't do it on purpose.' But she could still feel the thrill as her fist had made contact.

A car with a slipping fan belt drove past the end of the street. They listened until the sound was swallowed into the rumble of Hamilton Road. A blackbird was tossing leaves on the path, its beak a vivid yellow against the Caithness stone.

'It's not been easy for me either,' Rae said. 'Sorting through her stuff. I was trying to spare you that. There's clothes she wore at Goodisons. That green watered-silk suit.'

'It used to set my teeth on edge.'

'Tell me about it—'

Lexa was relieved to hear a throaty humour in her voice.

'—just putting it in the bin bag . . .'

Gabriel had worn it the evening Lexa took her to see *Silkwood*.

Afterwards they'd walked through the park. A late-summer night, warm and dark, with a scent of fermenting cut grass. They sat on the swings. Gabriel was soon so high that the iron frame creaked and a warning quiver slackened the tension in the chains. Lexa had pushed with her legs, steadily gaining height until by some fluke she and Gabriel were swinging in parallel, separate but together, feeling the same loss as gravity reclaimed them, the same exhilaration as they surged towards the sky.

'It's like you're throwing her away,' Lexa said.

'She's someone else now.'

'Do you never think, what if she's all there inside? When she says something so . . . typical?'

'She's putting it on? Give her an Oscar.'

'I'm not saying that—' Or was she? What was it Tropical had said? *I hear they've got her on the Ernest Saunders ward.*

'—did she tell you why Kinsella turned up here?'

'It was three years ago. It's who she is *now* that matters.'

Three years, not twenty-five.

Rae re-examined her tender eye. 'You need to get your boss to sort it.'

'Have we not had this conversation before?'

The blackbird hopped on to the step, close enough to see the yellow ring around its eye.

Rae's glance flickered in the mirror. 'I couldn't find her laptop when I cleared the house.'

'I've got it.'

She nodded, unsurprised, 'Find anything interesting?'

'I can't crack the password, and I'm not going to destroy it without knowing what's in there.'

That got her attention. 'You'd better fucking not—'

The blackbird flew off.

'—there's got to be something you can use as leverage. But be careful. If Alison Babbington thinks she's being backed into a corner, she'll cut her own arm off before she'll give you what you want.'

Amy was back, looking for clean towels. The ones in the wet room were soaked. She gave Lexa a mistrustful look on her way up the stairs.

Lexa lowered her voice. 'What you said just now. About Gabriel spending twenty-five years trying to make it up to me. What did you mean?'

'I was pissed off.'

'I did notice.'

They shared a wry grin. For all that divided them, they both had this streak of mordant humour.

Rae cast a precautionary glance back down the hall towards the wet room. 'The night it came out she'd slept with Kinsella, she was shitting herself—'

'I remember.'

'—yeah, but she wasn't frightened of him – well, OK, she was – but she was more frightened of you. What you'd think. When you gave her another chance, she was *so grateful*. The look on her face. It was like giving her a loan she could never make the payments on. And I know it didn't feel like that to you, you didn't think you were doing her a favour, but you were. I mean, I liked Gabriel – who she used to be – she was a good laugh, but she was never as fantastic as you thought she was. But the thing is, when she was with you *she* bought into it too. She loved it. Who wouldn't? But it was a hell of a strain, living up to your idea of her, keeping the rest of her under wraps.'

Lexa shook her head, 'She didn't care what anyone thought of her.'

'Ninety-nine times out of a hundred, no, she didn't. She didn't give a shit what I thought. That's why we got on. But the people who hooked her. Martin. Kinsella, till it got out of hand. You—' Lexa had the impression Rae was about to add another name to the list '—she'd've done anything to keep you in the fan club. You didn't want her to be somebody ordinary, fancying a bit more dosh, not too fussy how she made it. She had to be better than that. So that's what she gave you. Till Kinsella crawls out from under his stone . . .'

'When did she tell you?'

'I was in the Jag with her when he rang. It was on speakerphone. She cut him off quick, but it's not a voice you forget.'

Pure chance, then. Lexa felt like crying. 'And you didn't say anything?'

Rae raised her head. '*Yeah I fucking said something*. It was too late by then. I thought about telling you, but what was the point? There was fuck all we could do about it.'

Amy appeared at the top of the stairs, wanting to know which colour towel she should take. Rae called up that it didn't matter.

'And before you ask,' she said quietly, 'I don't know. She wasn't going to see forty again, things had fallen apart with Martin, but she was OK. Making all that money. A managing director. Maybe she wanted him to see her like that. Maybe she *wanted* to fuck it all up. When I asked her, she just said he was all right now.'

Beyond the open front door, Rae's garden was dead. The iron-hard earth, the laurels and rhododendrons with their waxy obdurate leaves. The street lights had settled down to a medicinal orange. The forecasters were predicting snow. Lexa longed for it, an innocent emergency of frozen pipes and abandoned cars.

'That password,' Rae said. 'Have you tried "Alison"?'

Lexa arrived at the bank next morning to find that Leveraged Finance had overridden her standing reservation of the room at the end of the trading floor. Most of the tower had been cordoned off by the FSA.

Installed in a room mysteriously excluded from the building's heating system, she opened the session, as always, by setting perameters. Two hundred bank staff would be transferred to Trubills with the outsourcing of the Accounts division. Over recent weeks she had met with the Union, the divisional staff, the bank's employee relations team, and its counterpart at Trubills, mapping potential areas of compromise and sticking points. The purpose of coming together today was to hammer out an agreement.

She paused, allowing her glance to circle the unhelpfully-rectangular table. To her left was Francesca, the rangy, perma-tanned director of HR. Then her deputy Sandy, the woman around the table most likely to be a lesbian. Then Jane, the bank's employee relations manager, flinching every time Francesca spoke in that *Mummy-left-me-half-of-Morayshire* accent. At the end of the table sat Malcolm, Jane's opposite number at Trubills. To his left, Gerry from the Union head office, with his wicked little goatee and that secretive-smiling thing he did that even Sandy seemed unsettled by. Beside him, Aonghas from Accounts, the only person in the room directly affected by the transfer. Then Carol and Dawn, the lay Union representatives. Carol in a High Street copy of Francesca's tailored business suit, too much viscose in the wool-mix giving it that tell-tale tendency to wrinkle at the seams. Dawn was smarter in every sense, with a 1960s air-hostessy glamour. Neither could hide their consternation at Lexa's jumper dress, boots and woolly tights.

'So.' She smiled, opening her hands in an *anything is possible* gesture . . .

All heads turned towards the door.

The man who walked in looked a baby-faced forty. Glossy brown hair, oily skin. Lexa expected him to apologise and withdraw when he saw the room was in use, but he addressed her by name, wondered if she had a few minutes. She was afraid not. Just a few minutes, he repeated. Jane suggested a comfort break, reaching for her cigarettes. Lexa gave her a look that translated as *I'm chairing this meeting*, then announced that they would reconvene in twenty minutes.

There were two of them. Lexa liked the boss on sight. The pink-shaven back of his neck. The buckled shoes that marked him as a fellow refuser of the sartorial code.

His name was Paton, his sidekick was MacNab. He gestured to a seat in front of a digital recorder. They would need her permission. To prevent the errors that tended to creep in with manual note-taking.

'There's nothing I can tell you.'

Paton had a mildly inexorable face. Like a postman.

She shrugged.

'Ten forty-two. Fifteen eleven o nine. Meeting room seven, Caledonian Bank. Present: Robert Paton, Andrew MacNab, Alexandra Strachan. Ms Strachan has consented to be interviewed without legal representation . . .'

Tropical knew by mid-afternoon.

Most Wednesdays he'd put his head round the door and she would filch him a cup of the superior espresso made by the assistant to the assistant of Ali's PA. She had no illusions: he was a trader, it was his job to cultivate every contact fate threw his way. But every now and then he was useful as a sounding board. As long as she didn't mind whatever she said being all round the bank by close of business.

'I hear the Stasi came a-calling?'

She looked at her watch. 'Three-and-a-half-hours: I'm impressed.'

'I heard before lunch.'

'But have you heard why?'

As usual when he didn't know, he told her something else.

There was a rumour going round the building that Paton and his goons were only days away from finding their crock of shit. Not the sharpest knives in the drawer, mostly HMGs and jumped-up accountants. If they were really good they'd still be bankers. But, like the Mounties, they always got their man.

'HMGs?'

'Home-Made Gents. Nice suits, but don't ask where they went to school.'

The concensus on the trading floor was that the CEO had jumped the gun, making Gabriel Findlay walk the plank before she'd been investigated. It might have upstaged the shareholders' protest, but now they were going to have to fish her out and throw her overboard all over again. With a bigger splash, this time. They had to get it over with by Christmas. New Year, new probity: that was the plan. A highly-public line drawn under the past, to make the hedge funds rethink and get the share price rising.

He frowned distractedly, as if the question were so trivial he'd almost forgotten to ask. 'What was it they wanted with you . . .?'

How would you describe your relationship with Ms Findlay?
  We're friends.
  Close friends?
  Yes.
  And you were colleagues . . .
  Ms Strachan, were you colleagues?
  Sorry, I didn't realise that was a question. Yes, we were colleagues in the mid-eighties.
  Did she discuss her work with you?
  In the eighties?
  Over the past four years.
  No. She compartmentalised life and work.
  Compartmentalised?
  Kept them separate.
  I understand the word. Did she give any reason for this compartmentalisation?
  Lexa had decided she didn't like Bob Paton after all. *I'm not a banker. I wouldn't have understood even if she'd told me.*

You're not a banker?

I left the sector in 1984.

Have you seen Ms Findlay since she was discharged from hospital?

The doctors saw no point in keeping her. That's not the same as making a full recovery.

Answer the question, please.

Yes I've seen her a couple of times.

You held a party for her?

You know I did. Why ask me if you already know the answer?

. . .

Yes we had a party.

Were any of the guests employed in banking or finance?

Nodding at Terrie (who was on the phone) and body-swerving Kath, Lexa barged her way through the sequence of exclusion zones into the CEO's office. Alison was eating cottage cheese and crispbread at the table.

She raised her fingers to her lips to check for crumbs. 'I'm retro-dieting. Trying to con my metabolism into thinking I'm still nineteen. I'd kill for the body I was trying to lose then.'

Brenda hurried in, mortified to have been caught away from her desk, leaving the boss unguarded. Alison waved her back to the outer office.

Lexa said, 'You put the FSA on to me.'

Alison hadn't turned cold on her like this since that first evening at her house, 'Brenda's right, you wouldn't have got past her. I have a lot to do this afternoon.'

'You mean, besides stuffing your face with crispbread.'

Had she said it after six o'clock, Alison would have laughed.

'I'm going to ignore that, because you've had a nasty surprise.'

Lexa put the envelope on the table.

'Oh for heaven's sake, Lexa. You can't *resign* from a six month contract.'

'I can if I give you four weeks' notice.'

'We can waive the notice period, if you really want to go.'

Their eyes met.

'You could have warned me.'

'No.' Her tone was firm. She pushed away the dirty plate. 'I can't afford anything that looks like collusion.'

Lexa stored this fact away. 'Is that why you put me on the payroll, so they could question me?'

'It was a factor.'

'In other words, all these weeks I've been knocking myself out I might as well have sat downstairs doing the crossword.'

'Don't be such a drama queen. I didn't say it was the only factor. I told you: I could use you in the corporate structure.'

'After I sell Gabriel down the river.'

She looked surprised. 'Is that an option?'

There was a beat of silence.

Alison's mouth twitched. 'Please sit down. I'm getting a pain in the neck from looking up at you.' That faint *huf* she used to signal the dropping of pretence. 'It's not Gabriel's scalp the FSA is wanting—'

She nudged a chair out from the table with her stockinged foot and Lexa sat down.

'—it's mine.'

Andy Hornby and Fred Goodwin had gone. The regulators were hoping for a Scottish hat trick. If it came down to an objective choice, chairman or CEO, there was no contest. She was the one the bank needed more. But because Sir Mungo was such a duffer, his resignation would make no difference. The hedge funds wouldn't care. If anyone was going to fall on their sword, it would have to be her. The thing was, she couldn't afford to quit. Every penny she had was tied up in property and stock options, and the only thing falling faster than the housing market was the price of Cally shares. It was *Natasha's future*. And why should she go?

'Show me a bank that didn't lose a fortune on derivatives. Oh I'm not saying mistakes weren't made. I didn't understand what we were doing. It was explained to me, and the explanation seemed logical, but . . .' She sighed. 'No one could understand everything that goes on in this place. *You* try getting your head around vega effects in long-term equity anticipation securities.

So I was guilty of ignorance. But the people who *designed them* couldn't predict what was going to happen. It's not like running an ordinary business. You can't do what we do and keep it all under control. I know: you think we shouldn't do it at all. But where else would the government have got the two hundred billion they've taken off us in taxes over the past six years?'

'Is that before or after the eight-hundred-and-fifty billion bail-out?'

'That's the business. You don't get the booms without the busts.'

Lexa recalled the graffiti on the wall of the old dole office in Gemmell. *Capitalism is the cause of your suffering.*

Alison laughed. 'You might as well say *being alive* is the cause of your suffering. They could do away with money tomorrow – well of course they couldn't, but let's say they did. Nothing would change. There'd still be winners and losers. You know why we give our people bonuses? *Because they're lucky.* Sometimes they're lucky two, three, four years in a row. But not forever. They've got number-crunchers at Princeton studying ten-year returns across the sector. You know what the graph looks like? The probability curve. Only not as good. We'd get a slightly better result in the long run buying random portfolios of stock and leaving them untouched. But banking isn't about the long run. And if we just programmed a computer, we wouldn't need traders and support staff, and the people employed by the independent analysts, and the ratings agents, and all the waiters and shop assistants and taxi drivers we keep in business. *And,*' she lifted her index finger, giving Lexa a shivery feeling of recognition, 'if we pay enough to attract the brightest people, once in a while they'll come up with something our competitors haven't thought of, and beat the odds short-term. Until everyone else starts doing it. And then we get a bubble, and then the long-term trend reasserts itself with a crash.' She shrugged. 'Which is where we are now, and where we've been before, and where we'll be again after the next boom.'

'You sound just like Gabriel.'

Something happened under that deadpan expression.

'I see her in you, too,' Alison said. 'No – I see *you* in *her*. She had a streak of integrity, underneath it all.'

'Maybe that's why you chose her.'

Whatever had happened in her face happened again.

'As a scapegoat,' Lexa clarified.

'She chose herself.'

'By being unlucky?'

'If that's all she was.' Alison leaned forward and Lexa knew that, under the table, she was working her feet into those punishing heels. 'It was her job to cover all the bases, and she didn't. If handing her over to the firing squad will satisfy the public thirst for blood, I don't see that's so very unfair.'

'And you can trust her to take the bullet.'

In the silence, Lexa could hear Brenda turning somebody away next door.

Alison's pupils contracted. 'I'm not sure I follow you.'

If she thinks she's being backed into a corner, she'll cut her own arm off before she'll give you what you want.

'The stroke,' Lexa said. 'She's hardly in a position to defend herself.'

If the CEO had her suspicions, she didn't say.

It happened every time Lexa passed the ironmonger's where the old man in the tobacco-coloured coat used to call Gabriel *ma'am*. In the post office, where the ancient postmistress remembered her as a wee girl with *these blue eyes that saw right through you*. In Morrisons, where the boy behind the cold cuts counter had been three-quarters in love with her. And every time Lexa saw a Land Rover, or a Gauloises packet, or a copy of the *Sun*. But lately, when she thought about Gabriel – about the Gabriel who still lived inside her head – that mobile face had a waxwork quality, the rapt look merely glassy. The detail of what had happened where and who said what was as vivid as ever, but the woman who starred in these memories was growing indistinct. And who was to remember her, if not Lexa? There were days when all she had were the mannerisms she had appropriated without noticing. A tone of voice, the way she said 'splendid' and 'horrid' and '*hoots!*' At these moments she was more Gabriel than Gabriel was herself.

"You didn't want her to be somebody ordinary . . . She had to be better than that". Better or worse: Lexa was no longer sure. But different. Extraordinary. Though Rae had half a point. The world had caught up. Three or four of their friends in Gemmell now had beautiful, heedless, shining daughters. The word 'patriarchy' meant nothing to them. They had no idea that the self could be obliterated by the body's surface. They were astonished to hear that this had been the fate of their mothers' generation, millions of young women, pretty and plain. But not Gabriel's fate. A beauty so expressive it defied objectification. A personality so strong. Lexa had never met a woman more shamelessly self-centred. A small miracle, almost a revolutionary act. And if Kinsella had briefly doused that flame, she had come back stronger than ever. Self-centred, but not self-sufficient. The day they met she'd claimed Lexa as a friend. To be chosen by one you yourself would choose, what else was love? Over the years a handful of people – women, mostly, and the odd jealous lover – had told Lexa that women's friendships *weren't like that*. To which she could only reply, *ours is*.

Why hadn't it been sexual? The question had never arisen until now.

There had always been an imbalance, all the way back to Goodisons. Gabriel so bright and beautiful. But so what? Not minding had been Lexa's gift to her. (*Like a loan she could never make the payments on.*) Even during the years with Niall, and later, in that brief, intense *folie à deux* with Duncan, what she felt for Gabriel had been the part of her that nothing could touch. The one true feeling that didn't change when Niall got the job in Sydney. She had come home after dropping him at the airport and looked in the mirror, and still liked herself, because she was the woman who loved Gabriel. And loved her consistently, year in, year out, knowing her – or thinking she knew her – as you could only know someone over twenty-five years. Fully conversant with her failings, able to predict what she would do in any situation, and still finding her, somehow, full of wonders.

Trust. When did it become stupidity?

For the first time Lexa was thinking about what it might mean to be more beloved than loving. The range of inadmissible feelings involved. Boredom. Contempt. Or something more ambivalent, something to do with needing but not wanting, or not wanting to need. Gabriel had known her feelings for Stuart. Whichever way you looked at it, regardless of whether they'd slept together, what she did was a betrayal. But what sort of betrayal? The thoughtless kind? Or an answer to the impossibility of rejecting someone who asked for nothing while giving everything, a way of squaring her limited room for manoeuvre with the overwhelming urge to refuse?

But this smelled of self-pity. Gabriel had loved her, in her own way. Just not as much as she'd loved Alison.

*

I wonder if you'll read this, or scan a
couple of lines and recycle with extreme
prejudice. As is absolutely your right. If
you want to flip to voice-mail when you see
my number, or get the saintly B to fib that
you're too busy to talk, that is your
prerogative. But it was too cruel of you not
to let me in last night. I could feel you
standing there on the other side of the door.
YOU HAVE TO TELL ME WHY. If you don't, I shall
go mad.

Rae had been right about the password. Lexa found the
message in the *sent items* box. February 16, 2006.
ArchGabriel@freeserve.co.uk to AlisonBabbington@callybank.com

I'm not going to wail and gnash and
beseech, or try to rouse the pity in your
lovely cruel breast. Were we too much, is
that why you killed it? And now you can't
bear to be reminded. But you can't kill it
in me. I will always remember. Don't be
cross. Be glad. You're loved. You see (if
you've stuck with me this far) I'm letting
you off. I hate what you've done to us, but
I don't hate you, and I never shall. I will
always want the best for you. And I will
always be here, if you need my help.

DECEMBER

When Lexa lifted her eyes to the great glass cupola, blocking out the cocktail-hour babble and replacing it with a churchy hush, she could just about match this place to her memories. The walls had been coffee-coloured, with pegboard boxing-in the volutes above the then gloss-painted pillars, which had made the breasts of those nymphs in the mosaic floor all the more scandalous. She used to come here with her father, the year they lived in Edinburgh. Always the queue leading to the smiling woman with the purple eyeshadow and the curly black hair. Though in the context of childhood, 'always' could have been twice. The woman used to smile at Lexa too, and once stamped the back of her hand with 'Caledonian Bank' in purple ink. One day Lexa's mother brought the cheque book and the woman didn't smile and when they got home her mother told her father that the curly black hair was a wig.

And now the building was a bar with booths and leather sofas and gaudy gold paint picking out the Hellenic mouldings. More exclusive (or more exclusively-priced) than most of the meat markets that had taken over the nation's banks, libraries and places of worship. A space where women in false eyelashes could gather to drink Manhattans and laugh about sex, safe in the knowledge that they wouldn't be disturbed. Unless they wanted to be. It wasn't hard to spot the customers hoping for company. That group in white, working the *après ski* look in the Edinburgh slush. The hen party in shorts and black tights and specially-printed T-shirts. The Christmas shoppers with a dozen classy carrier bags tucked under the table, eyeing up those lawyers or land agents or chartered surveyors bonding after a tough day.

Lexa had a sudden uneasy thought. Was Wednesday singles night? It would explain why there were no couples. Apart from the two of them.

'Do you-*aah* come here often?'

'Not since I was nine years old.'

'Was that legal?'

'It was a Cally then.' She met his eye, 'I thought it could be a talking point.'

'Who'd have guessed you were so manipulative?' He took his overcoat off, folding it and placing it over the end of the sofa before holding out his hand for her parka.

'I'm cold,' she said.

The revolving door spooled in a crowd of young men with the pink-cheeked, damp-haired, recklessly-unbuttoned look of freshly-showered sportsmen.

She tried to see him with the same unbiased eye. Pale-cinnamon tweed and brogues. Man-about-town gone up-country. With a full head of hair he'd have looked just right. Affluent, fashionably posh, the easy-going product of a privileged life. Bald, he looked like a gangster. His eyes too small amid all that unoccupied flesh. The fastidious way he'd folded his coat.

'The pink socks are a nice touch,' she said.

'I have done this before.'

She shot him an unguarded look.

'Champagne,' he said to the waiter.

A group in Santa hats and flashing reindeer horns walked in to take over the far side of the room. Of course. Not singles night, just not the week for couples. It was at least a decade since she had attended an office party, but she remembered this unstable mix of duty and transgressive excitement. The guffawing men and overdressed women drinking themselves into hysteria. Those girls in the corner singing along to 'I Saw Mommy Kissing Santa Claus'. The quiet ones, heads down, doggedly anaesthetising themselves against the night to come.

Kinsella checked his flashy gold watch. She realised they had absolutely nothing to say to each other.

Unnervingly, he smiled.

And now the boy was back with the bottle and a free-standing ice-bucket. The sportsmen cheered at the popping cork, universal code for a red-blooded male on his way to a result. Startled, Lexa saw the two of them from the outside. The intimate angle of armchair to sofa, the mirrored tilt of their heads and canting of their torsos, the simultaneous lifting of glass to lips.

When she walked in he'd kissed her.

'Fuck! Tastes like liebfraumilch jizzed with Alka Seltzer.' But already he was topping up his glass. 'Might as well make the most of it.'

He was virtually teetotal these days. The plods wouldn't check for finger-prints if some scroat helped himself to your silver, but they were shit-hot on drinking and driving. He was out half the night getting the kids back from somewhere or other. Guitar, rugby practice, conversational Japanese. Freezing his bollocks off every Saturday, watching them lose on the other side of London.

Feeling the alcohol start to warm her, Lexa unbuttoned her coat. 'Aren't you a bit old for all that?'

'Second hatch. Two with Mia, four with Trudi. Got off lightly first time round. Trudi doesn't approve of boarding schools. Doesn't want to miss those-*aah* precious minutes when we see them in the rear-view mirror.'

She wondered if he'd always had his personable side, but just never felt the need to charm her before. And she did need to be charmed, to give the impression of liking him, just for this evening. If she couldn't manage that, they were both wasting their time.

'I haven't been up to the dacha for months. Seven hundred acres. Not far from Kirriemuir. I-*aah* don't suppose you shoot?'

'Not till the revolution.'

'Pity. Not much else to do up there. Since the kids got old enough to have a social life I've been paying the keeper and his wife to watch daytime TV.'

'I expect you can afford it.'

It was the hour when bars signalled the transition from conviviality to lust by dimming the lights. The Beverley Sisters faded out.

'Still, if you ever fancy a weekend in the wilds . . .'

She took a gulp of champagne. It wasn't that she found herself *liking* him exactly, but she didn't feel the old loathing. A blessing, really. And yet she so wanted to feel it, to flush out his true hateful self.

The DJ put Beyoncé on, cranking up the volume. That song about single ladies, taunting their men for not putting a ring on it. Over Kinsella's shoulder, she saw the Santa hats getting up to dance.

'How much does the boss of a hedge fund make?'

'The year before last, between eight and nine.'

'Eight *million*?'

'No, eight hundred.' He snorted as if he found her naivete amusing. 'Yes. Eight million.'

'And how much tax did you pay on that?'

'About two hundred grand.'

'Two-and-a-half per cent?'

He shrugged. 'It-*aah* hurt, but it had to be done.'

The women in white stood up and joined the dancers.

She asked, 'What about last year?'

He moved his arm, breaking the symmetry between them. 'There was a bit of a downturn. Maybe you heard about it?'

'You're a hedge fund. Did you not hedge?'

'Not against fucking nuclear meltdown.'

His old speaking shout. Just hearing it through a closed door used to make the secretaries jumpy.

'But you're still a player?'

'It was a *global financial crisis*. Everyone got their bollocks singed. We did better than some. Shorted the right banks. Got into maize before the pack.'

'And what do you tell your kids,' she said, 'when they see the food riots on the news?'

He was on his feet, reaching for his coat.

'Where are you going?'

'Back to the hotel, see if I can get a flight home tonight.'

She was pretty sure he was bluffing.

'Kinsella . . .'

'The name's *Piers*.'

All she had ever wanted was the admission that it was a fight.

I am not a woman who can't take a joke. This isn't a laugh. To say what she meant and be understood: was there a better definition of equality? Well, she'd achieved that.

She knew what she had to do.

'I'm sorry.'

His scalp looked moist, like a peeled potato. He was sweating.

'Get up.'

His headmaster's voice. After all these years, she still felt that reflexive dread.

'*Fucking stand up.*'

A couple of the sportsmen looked round.

She stood and he turned her, pulling off her parka, dropping it inside-out on the sofa. A flesh memory shuddered through her. A room in the middle of the night, his hands on her back. And then, with no less revulsion, the memory of her hands on him.

'That's better,' he said.

They sat down again. He placed her coat on top of his, leaving the seat beside him clear.

For the first time in twenty-five years she allowed herself to remember what had happened that night, after they'd tied him up. She was the only one who'd seen it done, who knew about the Vaseline and dipping the needles in the ink and how much pressure to apply. It was her hand on the buzzing machine, and still it felt like his choice. His refusal to say the words that would get all four of them out of this. But she must have wanted to hurt him. How else could she have done it?

When Gabriel held his boxer shorts out of the way, he hardened. Lexa could see it through the fabric. She thought: when will he be frightened, *what does it take?* And then the needles bit and he screamed in pain and fury, and she had her answer. Tattooing was more difficult than it looked but, with Rae and Gabriel pinning him down, she managed to write the word in blood and ink on his skin. 'Sexual harasser' wouldn't have had the same impact. But now she had to concede that those six letters had been a lie. Whatever he was, he wasn't a rapist.

Afterwards he had withdrawn into himself, still tethered but no longer struggling. They had not known what to do with him.

They couldn't leave him to be found by the tattooist in the morning, but nor could they run the risk of freeing him. Rae was all for fetching her car and dumping him outside the city, still tied-up. Gabriel was worried he'd be found by the police. But that was going to be a problem no matter where they left him. The discussion had gone round in circles. Dawn was breaking, if they waited much longer there would be people on the streets. Finally, Lexa had proposed a deal. They would let him walk away if he promised to go without attacking them. Rae said they'd be mad, but he looked at Lexa and nodded his agreement. Of all the details she had tried to forget, none was more harrowing than that moment of mutual trust.

'Did you have it removed?' she asked.

He met and held her look. '*It's none of your fucking business.*'

A woman had come in and was scanning the drinkers on the far side of the room. Catching sight of them, she waved and picked a path between the tables, over the bare-breasted nymphs. Lexa glanced down at Kinsella's left hand.

'I've taken it off,' he said.

'Hoo!' Pulling off her gloves, unwinding her scarf, she presented her frozen-flushed cheek to Lexa to be kissed. She was breathless with rushing, or with the cold, and becomingly self-conscious under the scrutiny of a stranger. 'Sorry I'm so late,' Her glance brushed across Kinsella, 'but at least you had company.'

The waiter appeared with a third glass.

Lexa said, 'Alison, this is my friend Piers.'

2010

JANUARY

The sign at the cemetery gate directed Lexa to a squat building dating from the 1940s, with a gritstone Gothic chapel next door for those who preferred to bury their dead. A drab day. Black branches, wet road, grey sky heavy with vapour, a minimum of colour in the lifeless turf between the clumps of dissolving snow and the higgledy-piggledy gravestones. The rain stopped, releasing her from the monotonous scrape of the windscreen wipers. The car park was full, the mourners inside their cars waiting for the preceding service to finish. She parked between an ageing, boxy Volvo and a brand-new retro-styled Fiat. A black limousine blocked the exit, too big to fit in a parking space. A female driver subverting her professional weeds with plum-coloured hair and a salon tan. The crematorium doors opened and a dozen people came out. Hands were shaken, cheeks kissed. The Daimler drove away.

Car doors began to open, discharging the next batch of mourners. There was an improvised look to their outfits, any garment passing muster, no matter how informal, so long as it was black. Lexa regretted her bottle-green parka, but there was nothing to be done about it now. Several of the men had teamed leather jackets with white shirts and thin black ties, giving them the appearance of off-duty waiters. Caroline was shivering in a cheap-looking black two-piece, her hair scraped into a bun that showed how her monkey-face had shrivelled further since the summer. Beside her stood a heavily-made woman as saturnine as her father had been twenty-five years before. A blonde in a black sheepskin coat approached and, reaching out to mother and daughter, took their hands. With a start, Lexa recognised Irena, Stuart's first wife, a little less succulent these days but still a beauty. Stuart saw her too yet made no move to greet her. He looked terrible, his face ashen above his expensive suit.

The mourners filed inside, squashing into the long pews to make sure everyone found a seat. Caroline sat at the front, with her daughter, and two men in their early thirties who had inherited their father's build but not his colouring, and their wives, one of them heavily pregnant, and a tiny woman who looked like Caroline with white hair. Lexa spotted Frank in the row behind, next to George, his tattooed hands hidden in the sleeves of his suit jacket. Stuart stared at the coffin on the curtained dais, lost to himself, blocking the aisle until Lexa touched his arm. He nodded at the nearest pew and they sat down.

The vicar was young, with an unfortunate lift to his upper lip when he spoke, so that he seemed to be smiling in embarrassment. Lexa tuned out of the religious mumbo-jumbo but listened to the address, learning that Mick had married Caroline on his seventeenth birthday, the summer she had been crowned Coal Queen. He'd entered Faxerley Colliery in the footsteps of his father and grandfather (a striker in 1926), and had been a Labour Party member for thirty-nine years. It occurred to Lexa that this was the sort of pedigree that got read out in a funny voice on Radio 4 sketch shows. Though the joke was nearing its sell-by. In ten years' time, would anyone understand?

A taped organ played the introductory chords of 'The Lord is my Shepherd' and the congregation shuffled to its feet. She was surprised by the volume of sound produced, the men's meaty baritones and the thin sweet notes rising from the women. When the hymn ended, Stuart stepped into the aisle. In the first few seconds, as his voice resonated against the ceiling, she assumed he was reading a passage of scripture.

'If men live together, forming tribes, nations, communities, societies, like stones accumulated in heaps, Society is only a collection of separate men, laws are only rules preventing their hard corners from knocking against the sides of their neighbours, the State exists only to maintain the heap (and not that necessarily). In such a unity the individual man alone counts. Individualism must be the predominating idea. Liberty is the freedom of action of the individual, and is a thing of quantity, every limit imposed on its extent – as for instance the legal command "thou shalt not kill" – being a curtailment of it . . .'

In the front pew, the small white-haired woman shifted impatiently.

'. . . if, however, Society is a unity of the organic kind, totally different conclusions follow. The individuals composing it are still separate and conscious, but they depend very largely upon the Society in which they live for their thoughts, their tastes, their liberties, their opportunities of action, their character, in brief, for everything summed up in the word civilisation . . .'

He looked up, distracted by something in the pews behind Lexa. Gradually she became aware of sounds within the silence. Rasping and wheezing, the whistling scrape of laboured breathing. Not one or two people: half the congregation. A spasm passed across Stuart's face.

'Caroline's here to say goodbye to her husband. Donna, Kevin, Roderick, are seeing off their dad. But I'm here for man I worked with, and drank with, and argued toss with for thirty-odd year. What he saw in Doncaster Rovers I'll never know—'

There was a collective grunt of humorous appreciation from the pews.

'—they say we'll be online twenty-four seven int' future. I'm halfway there already. It's handy for work, but it's not what I call *connection*. Not like we were connected at Faxerley. One thing about miners, they talk. We heard about pits where they took you off face to see manager, offered you fifty quid in hand if you broke overtime ban. Never tried that with us. They knew better. I'm not saying we were all saints, but there were a standard, and we lived up to it. Mick Sharp never walked past lad who needed help. In thirty-three year he had one day off sick. Craic were that good we missed it when we went on holiday. Sounds like sentimental crap now.'

In the front pew somebody tutted.

'Day strike ended we marched back behind banner. Mick, Frank Cuckney, George Spender, Tony Glossop . . . you know who you are. Fifty walked up there with us. Women, kids, old-timers, dogs . . .'

He closed the book.

'That were last good day we had. Beronex put new management in. Big stick brigade. Anyone going back had to sign up to new working practices. No negotiation. What did we have to negotiate with? We'd shot our bolt. They had strikers and scabs working side by side. Head down, get on with it. Nobody talked to each other. It weren't just about maximising profits. We had to work for them, not for us-selves. Then they pulled plug, walked away.'

His mouth worked soundlessly for a moment.

'Day they shut Faxerley there were men crying. I were one of 'em. I din't even cry when Irena left me . . .'

Lexa's glance strayed to that black sheepskin coat.

'. . . What I'm saying is, we're here to say goodbye to Mick, but he weren't just one lad. He were part o' summat. They killed it off, Thatcher and Blair and rest of 'em, but it were summat bigger than all of us while it lasted. And that made Mick Sharp bigger than all o' them.'

When the vicar asked the mourners to pray Lexa sat with her eyes open and her head unbowed. The red velvet curtains closed around the dais in an undignified sequence of jerks. An electric hum as the coffin descended. The jaunty notes of a clarinet sounded through the loudspeakers. The vicar shut his prayer book and simpered. Most people identified the tune before Paul McCartney began to sing. A hit from the year Mick had married Caroline, the time they'd been happiest, before the hunting through his pockets for phone numbers and condoms, the knowing and pitying glances on the street. 'When I'm Sixty-Four'. He had only made it to fifty-eight.

Out in the car park the faces relaxed, glad to have the ceremony over. No one had cried. Stuart was surrounded. Lexa couldn't say what she had to say in front of an audience, but nor could she go home without telling him. She felt a tap on her elbow and turned to find Pecker at her side. The blueish gum around his front crown was still there, but less noticeable now than the mushroom-coloured bags under his eyes.

'You remember me?' she said in wonder.

'Course. You're the lady merchant banker, Stuart's posh tottie.'

It struck her that this was a label she would have found objectionable back then. Now it seemed harmless, even funny. 'I was never posh.'

'You were like queen to us.'

Her smile faded. She glanced around her, 'It's a good turn-out.'

'There's a lot more cun't get. What with pneumoconiosis and COPD and cancer, we'll keep this place going for next twenty year. They've had scientists out this week, taking DNA samples.' His eyes creased sceptically. 'They reckon we've got higher than average statistical incidence. Could be summat int' gene pool. They wanted Caroline to donate body. She wun't entertain it, knowing he's in jam jars in laboratory in Sheffield. Anyroad, they won't have to wait too long for another one . . .'

Lexa's eyes flicked across to where Stuart stood, still deep in conversation.

Pecker turned his head to let her know he'd noticed. 'You're coming to funeral tea?'

'Am I?'

'Course you are. We've had whip round, put hundred quid behind bar. We're counting on your boyfriend to match it.'

'He's not my boyfriend.'

Pecker grinned with that blue-edged tooth, 'How d'you know who I'm on about, then?'

The upstairs room at the miners' welfare no longer conjured the spartan aesthetic of the Soviet Bloc. Racks of spotlights had replaced the fluorescent tubes. There was carpet on the floor and a row of optics and beer taps had been installed in one corner, the surrounding space set out with tables. Three trestles laid end-to-end, covered with paper cloths, displayed the purvey. Someone had forgotten to take down the banner that proclaimed, in glittery capitals, *HAPPY NEW YEAR!*

Lexa picked up a plate and helped herself to a ham sandwich and a soggy samosa. There was tea in gallon teapots for the old ladies but most people were nursing drinks from the bar. She was tempted to do the same, but deterred by the thought of the long drive home. Instead she drifted around the edges of conversations about football and boxing and betting, and how the new KostLess on the bypass would drive Abdul's mini-mart out of business, and why the police had not arrested the dealers when everyone knew who they were. Though nobody mentioned Mick's name, it seemed to her that all this talk was a sort of grieving.

'Lesley, isn't it?'

'Lexa.'

She had shed the flamboyant sheepskin to reveal a black close-fitting dress and high boots. Though Lexa remembered her as a natural blonde, there was a metallic brilliance to her shoulder-length hair, a cosmetic bloom on her skin darkening to brick-dust under her cheekbones.

'I'm Irena.'

'I know.'

'I reckon it's a toss-up between you and me.'

The soft voice suggested girlish confidences, but Lexa detected razor blades under the candyfloss.

'I'm sorry?'

'The least welcome guest.' In a stage whisper she added, 'They don't like outsiders.'

Stuart looked up, caught sight of them together and set off across the floor.

'I thought you grew up here,' Lexa said.

'Aye, but I moved away. They hate that.'

'They've always been fine with me.'

'Oh they will be, to your face.'

'All right?' Stuart said.

Irena smiled as if she had just won a bet with herself. 'What were that load of rubbish you read in chapel o' rest?'

'Ramsay MacDonald.' From the way he said this Lexa guessed that political goading had been one of their games.

She caught Lexa's eye. 'He's been dead a long time.'

But Lexa didn't want a front-row seat at the Stuart-and-Irena show. 'He was right about Dudderthorpe.'

Irena batted her mascara-heavy lashes. 'Come again?'

'A community trying not to be a pile of stones.'

'You reckon?'

Stuart was watching them, a glint in his eye which took Lexa back to the summer they had spent as lovers. He was making her self-conscious. Her voice sounded egregiously Scottish in her own ears.

'I thought what Stuart said was very moving. The right balance of personal and political.'

Irena lost her mocking detachment. The plucked flesh between her eyebrows pinched into an angry pleat. 'You should have tried being Polish and growing up here. Yeah, pits are shut. Big deal. They've got jobs, most of 'em. Two weeks in Lanzarote: they're happy. And there's fight for compensation, they still get to point finger at somebody else . . .'

'Pack it in, Irena.'

Surprisingly she complied, and Lexa caught a glimpse of how they must have been as husband and wife.

'Just making conversation.' She was nettled about losing face, but the look she gave Lexa indicated that, overall, she'd got what she wanted. 'I thought Lesley'd be a bit different.'

'I'm sure she is,' Lexa murmured.

Stuart's lower teeth showed in a fleeting grin.

'Well I can't stand here chatting to you two all day.' She leaned towards her ex-husband. Automatically his glance dropped to her breasts. She smiled and allowed her cheek to be kissed. 'See you at next funeral.'

Lexa watched her cross the room, noting the rhythm of her buttocks under the black dress. Mick had been right, all those years ago. It was hard to believe they had been chosen by the same man.

While Stuart queued for the drinks, she laid claim to an empty table. Dudderthorpe still divided along gender lines to socialise: women sitting, men on their feet around the bar, with a unisex area under the windows where Caroline was receiving expressions of condolence. She remembered the last time she'd stood in this room, the pent-up anger of the strikers. Meeting Irena had stirred up old sediment. Had Mick alerted Stuart to her presence in the bar that day, they might have continued as lovers. She might have dragged the asbestos into the light, closing the pit, saving a few from fatal exposure. Maybe more than a few. One thing was certain: they would not have thanked her.

Stuart returned with a pint of beer and a glass of white wine, though she had asked for water.

'What happened to the teetotal regime?'

He sat down. 'That's for days I don't bump into ex-wife.'

'Was she always such a nippie sweetie?'

'She's just jealous.'

'A bit late for that.'

'Aye.' He had lost the watchful energy he had shown in Irena's presence.

'You look tired.'

With an edge to his voice, he said, 'They've just incinerated my best mate.'

'You don't have to take it out on me.'

She recalled them snapping at each other as lovers, but could not remember why. She had been too inexperienced to chart the currents flowing under their words, too young and green for a love affair. And now she was too old.

Stuart's gaze was trained on the far side of the room, 'You see tall lad at bar? Ronnie Townsend. He's not known long. Reckons he can fight it. Slaphead talking to Donna, Mick's lass, over there?' She nodded. 'Eric Paulden. He's known about twelve month. Des Lynam-lookalike's Carl. They reckon he's paid thousands to some private clinic in Canada. Old lad with tinted glasses is Gerry, chair of action campaign. He's not well. I din't think he'd make it.'

She stared at these men with their yellowing teeth and greasy hair and unfashionable spectacles. Every morning they awoke and counted off their remaining days. A year, two, five if they were lucky. She didn't know how they could bear to be here, how they did not swallow a bottle of paracetamol, or take a razor blade into the bath, or get hold of a shotgun and run amok until they were picked off by a police marksman. How they had not vanished inside their broken bodies like Gabriel.

'Do you ever think, what if it hadn't been us?'

'You what?'

His eyes held a warning but it was too late, the words were out. 'You, me, Gabriel. If if it'd been somebody else?'

He stared at her. 'You think I need reminding whose fault it is?'

'I'm not trying to . . .'

He tapped the side of his head. 'You think there's owt you can say that's not going round and round in here?'

Her chest cleaved with pity, as it had when he'd spoken at the crematorium. But he didn't want comfort. Or perhaps he did, but not from her. He was married, they lived three hundred miles apart, they would not meet again. And yet *something* persisted between them. Not desire as she remembered it, that thread pulled taut. More of an ache, a shared sadness that touched everything: the smell of coal smoke in the streets outside, the leaden sky, the blackly-gleaming branches in the cemetery, the faces he had pointed out.

'What were she calling you Lesley for, anyroad?'

Lexa shrugged. 'All cats are grey in the dark.'

'You what?'

'It doesn't matter.' But she watched to see if he remembered.

His voice rose a semitone. 'What're you on about?'

'Something you said once, when you didn't know I was there. You and Mick were discussing Irena and me. Comparing us.'

'When?' His tone was incredulous but she could see he believed her.

'That day we picketed the coking plant. Afterwards, I saw you in the bar.'

'And you never said owt?'

She flipped her hands. 'What was there to say?'

It took him a couple of seconds to work it out.

'And that's why you packed me?'

'More or less.'

He exhaled noisily. 'Owt else I should know about? Any more little secrets you've been sitting on?'

First the guilt, then the displacement into anger. She had known he would react like this. But there was another response she hadn't expected. A look on his face like a bereft child. He blinked and the moment was gone, but for the first time it occurred to her that it was not Mick's fault at all. She need not have walked away from him that day. She could have shouted over the bar and made a scene, or written him a letter, or taken one of his calls, and after he had grovelled sufficiently she might have accepted that she had caught him at the sort of empty swaggering men went in for among themselves. The relationship might not have lasted, of course. She would never know now.

'I was in love with you,' she said.

His astonishment was almost comical. 'You never said.'

'You weren't in love with me.'

'I din't know it were on table.' Cocky now that the news was sinking in, he said 'We could have had a kid. You never know, we might have produced normal-sized human being between us.'

'Is that how you see us, a pair of freaks?'

He heard the hurt in her voice. 'Lexa . . .'

Too late. He was a stranger to her now. The executive tailoring. His strong square head. And yet that *something* remained. Or the lack of something: the barrier between her and every other man. She felt the permission of a last meeting, the freedom to say anything.

'When I saw you again at that hotel in Glasgow, I hadn't thought of you for twenty years, but I still *knew* you. Your mouth, your lips, how they felt when we kissed. The way your tongue moves against your teeth . . .'

'Do you want to go?' he said hoarsely.

She shook her head, fighting the spell she was casting over them both, 'I need to talk to you about Kinsella.'

A shrill sound cut through the hubbub in the room, a rising scale which halted abruptly and resumed as a guttural wailing. Under the windows Caroline was weeping, her reddened monkey-face turned to the ceiling, her shrivelled features distorted as she flailed against the arms attempting to enfold her. The mourners fell silent, their expressions an uneasy blend of compassion and embarrassment. *Mick is dead.* Only now did it become real to Lexa. The small white-haired woman threaded between the tables and for a moment it seemed she was going to use her maternal prerogative to slap the widow out of her grief, but she merely caught her daughter's hands and held on to them, her thin arms jerking as Caroline, roaring now, tried to pull free.

Stuart looked away. 'If it comes out, it comes out. It dun't make any difference now.'

Lexa licked her dry lips. 'That's not going to happen.'

He led her down the stairs and out through the parked cars to the low brick wall which marked the edge of the recreation ground. The rain was in remission where they stood but persisted half a mile away, a sackcloth veil across the view. She remembered telling him this place had lost its romance, but in the ebbing light its ugliness had the stark, silvery glamour of a Magnum print. Turning her head, she could see the back of the mini-mart with its piles of flattened cardboard cartons, the shiny stove-pipe of the Chinese takeaway, an old helmet hairdryer rusting in the yard behind Curl Up and Dye. Beyond, the red-brick semis were still lit for Christmas. Santas parked sleighs on rooftops. Icicles flashed on guttering. Reindeer grazed on handkerchief lawns. One crazy house blazed from garden gate to chimney-pot like a cut-price Vegas.

'Come on then,' he said, 'suspense is killing me.'

She told him about Kinsella and Alison, and Rae phoning with the news that Gabriel had been retired on a full pension, and the rumour all round the bank that the FSA was hot on somebody else's trail.

'They're shagging?'

'It looks like it.'

'I thought she were your friend.'

'I didn't force them into bed at gunpoint.'

The night she introduced them, while Kinsella dealt with the bill, Alison had murmured in her ear *an alpha male with a hedge fund. You've been keeping that quiet.* And Lexa had not known how to deny any sexual interest in him without making it clear that Alison was being set up. Since then they had managed one quick drink in a bar round the corner from the bank. Neither had made any reference to Kinsella, though Tropical said they'd been seen together all over Edinburgh.

'What if he pisses her off?' Stuart said.

'He's bound to, sooner or later.' For Alison's sake, she hoped sooner. But not too soon. 'She might cut the crotch out of his suits, but she'll keep him out of the hands of the FSA. Too many people know they're a couple. If he goes down, he takes her with him.'

'And she can't protect him without protecting Gabriel?'

'Which protects you.'

Over his shoulder she could see the Rover she'd noticed last time, still on the soccer pitch, amid the scabs of frozen snow. Some joker had placed a lavatory bowl on its roof.

'And this bloke they're after now, what's he done?'

'No idea. Something he shouldn't't've.'

A carousel of gulls circled above the Chinese takeaway, bone-white wings against the grey sky, as if waiting for the giant bins in the back yard to offer up their treasures. The curtain of rain was getting closer. Any minute now the tarmac would show the first spots of wet and Stuart would start to worry about his suit. And then they would part.

He sighed. 'Two thousand and ten. Tories'll be back in by summer.'

'It might trigger a socialist revival.'

'Nah. They'll be smart this time. They'll talk about hugging hoodies and mending broken Britain while they take food out of us mouths.'

A barman came out of the back door and emptied a crate full of bottles into the recycling bin.

'I went to Gemmell,' he said.

Of course. He would have to see for himself.

Rae had asked him to stay to lunch. Even after everything Lexa had told him, he hadn't expected to find Gabriel like that.

'Gemmell were an eye-opener an all. Your pal's all right, up on Millionaire's Row, but rest of it . . .' He blew out his cheeks. 'We all have to come from somewhere, but you don't have to serve life sentence there.'

She thought of him on Gauze Street, browsing through the paperbacks she had donated to Barnardo's, then getting in his car and driving home. She would have cancelled anything to see him.

'I'd better go,' she said.

'Not yet.'

'It's a long drive.'

'*God's sake*, Lexa.' He caught her hand. 'It's bad enough saying goodbye to Mick without you walking off into sunset. I could do with your company for a couple of hours, is that all right?'

She remembered standing here a quarter-century ago, when

the brick wall had been a fence, and there'd been no closed-circuit television camera to hold them in its sights, and Stuart had been a man she hardly knew who had stepped forward on a whim and changed her life. And it had been dark, which had helped. Even now they were shy of each other, their heads bowed, watching her hand in his grasp as if it were an event independent of either of them.

They heard knocking and looked round to see Pecker at one of the upstairs windows, working his eyebrows like Groucho Marx. Stuart gave him the finger with his free hand.

'Life's too short to waste it in Gemmell. You can't push her round in bath chair for next thirty year.' He adjusted his grip, kneading her palm. 'If your pal's happy to do it that's her look-out—'

She tried to ignore his words, to concentrate on the seal between their hands and the heat it was transmitting up her arm.

'—I know what it's like, holding on. You've got to cut your losses. Get out. Try summat new.'

'In a recession?'

'You could do owt you put your mind to—'

Through his hand she felt some resistance overridden, like a car changing gear.

'—I've got spare room if you want to give Leeds a try.'

She smiled at this fantasy. A little harmless nonsense to keep grief at bay.

'I bet your wife'd love that.'

'She's gone—'

They both felt the weight of the following seconds.

'—got someone else. Seemingly it's been going on for a couple o' year.'

'And you found out when?'

He shrugged. 'Day I emailed you about funeral.'

A gull cackled from its perch on the shiny stove-pipe above the Chinese takeaway.

'So you're on the rebound?'

A long moment passed before she saw the glint of his bottom teeth.

'Summat like that,' he said.

Gabriel stood on the flat roof looking out over the city, irradiated by the setting sun. Not quite on the edge, but with no railing or parapet or even a raised lip between her and the drop. She did not turn, though she must have heard Lexa's footsteps on the wooden decking, above the rush hour traffic and the chink of scaffolding being dismantled somewhere and the whispered white noise of the bank's heating and ventilation systems. Was it a game they were playing, bluffing it out to see who spoke first?

Lexa looked around at the wrought-iron furniture and the gas barbecue and the lemon trees in terracotta planters. A lawn, bordered by low box hedging, occupied the remaining two-thirds of the roof.

'They should get a flock of sheep up here.'

Or maybe she really couldn't hear.

The wind pushed at Gabriel's skirt, worried strands of her hair that the sun turned to gold. It was more than two months since they'd last spoken.

Louder this time, Lexa said 'I've missed you—'

The sinking sun was level with the roof, a presence that expressed itself through absence, the lack of colour in the surrounding sky, the impulse to look away. Lexa's hand shielded her eyes and still her vision was strung with lilac spots, yet Gabriel stared steadily westwards.

'—are you not blinded—?'

Two paces would have taken her over the edge.

'—Gabriel.'

Finally she turned. The sun traced her profile in gold filigree, leaving the rest of her face in shadow. 'Where's Rae?'

The words were quite distinct, with no drag in her diction.

Lexa came alongside her. 'Searching the building for you. Along with half of Security.'

Though Alison had known exactly where she would be.

A hip-hop bass line pounded from a car down on Morrison Street. Far below them, the plaza was washed the colour of clear honey. Little people with long shadows crossed the grey marble, carrying their possessions in identical reinforced cardboard boxes. They moved in clusters of two and three, talking, and even laughing, alight with the vitality of bad news. They were young and resourceful and, sharing their fate with so many others, saw no reason to feel ashamed. Some held their boxes under one arm, using their free hand to capture the scene on their phones. It took awhile to pick out the sleepwalkers in this swarm, the solitary and stunned. Here and there, an upturned face gazing towards the windows of Alison Babbington's office.

'*Nos morituri te salutamus,*' Gabriel said in a voice uncannily like her old clear chime.

We who are about to die salute you.

Lexa thought about the hope that never quite died, no matter how many times it proved false.

An Audi estate had pulled up on the bank's private road. A cameraman got out. They could see Rohese Quenn, the new PR woman, homing in on him from the far side of the plaza. It had been her idea to get Gabriel in to clear her desk and shuffle across the trading floor. What better way to draw a line under any suspicions of a carve-up? Rohese had guessed the cameraman's game but, in that skirt and those boots, hadn't a hope of heading him off. Lexa watched him set up the perfect shot of the box-carriers battling their way through the wind tunnel between the bank and the building society headquarters next door. Unbuttoned jackets lifted like capes. A skirt flew up, hiding the wearer's face but exposing the scarlet thong beneath her tights. Tonight's news bulletin would show this footage under a Scott Joplin rag, and the smirking viewers would think *serves them right*, and maybe it did, but many who deserved worse had kept their jobs. When the bonus pot was made public in ten days' time, Alison would explain that the bank was steering a responsible course between restructuring to ensure the mistakes of the past would never be repeated and retaining the talent pool that could so easily be lured elsewhere. A few liberals would write sarcastic letters to the *Guardian*, the Bank of England would print some more magic money, the supermarkets would put up their prices, thousands of guiltless workers would lose their jobs. And Lexa would feel as indignant and powerless as any other taxpayer. She too was here to clear her desk. When three divisions were made redundant without her being told, it was time to take the hint.

A faint blaring of sirens rose from the rush hour traffic. Down in the north-east corner of the plaza a leather glove scurried along the ground. The carelessly-placed lid of a box whirled away, releasing a cyclone of A4. The sirens were louder now, trapped in the gridlocked streets below. In the plaza the exodus had halted. People who'd got half way to the car park were turning back. The crowd thickened outside the bank's main doors. Moved on by Rohese, the cameraman was filming the press posse, and so missed the drama of two detectives and a uniformed escort abandoning their cars and, with the wind behind them, all but flying into the plaza. As they arrived at the bank, two colleagues emerged. Their chain-store suits gaped at the shoulder, unlike the tailored second skin of the man sandwiched between them, his shirt the prescribed shade of blue, his hair cut in the recognised style, his pleasantly-nondescript features suddenly remarkable in the battery of photographers' flashes.

'That should have been you,' Lexa said.

Squinting against the sun, she studied Gabriel's face.

One of the police cars had found a way into the plaza. They watched the tallest detective place a hand on the banker's head and fold him into the back seat. Any minute now Rae would appear on the roof. No knowing when they would be alone like this again.

'Did Alison make the running? Is that how it worked? In the beginning, I mean. Once you were together, I can see that—'

The two of them up here on summer evenings, a bottle of Prosecco wedged in the shade of the box hedge, Alison kicking off her shoes, a bright bubble of laughter rising in Gabriel's throat.

'—but you'd never slept with a woman. Or not that you told me. Was it her idea?'

Gabriel's head shifted. Their eyes might have locked, had Lexa not been blinded by the sun.

Here was Gabriel's chance to say that she had been seduced with the same deadpan provocation Alison had used on Lexa, that keeping it secret had half-killed her, that doing business with Kinsella had been a last resort. Lexa would understand, but she had to *say* it.

She felt the seconds ticking by. Twenty. Thirty. Above them, a passenger jet drew a vapour trail across the sky. She watched until it disappeared.

'Last summer,' she said, 'when you were in the Infirmary, she came and sat by your bed, watching you sleep. I can't think why she would do that, if she didn't love you.'

Gabriel took a clumsy step towards her. Lexa opened her arms.

What was it Doctor Kerr had said? *If her self is anywhere she's in the space between you.* Nothing stood between them now. Lexa could feel their lungs filling and emptying together, their blood pumping to the rhythm of a single heart, peace spreading through her as if she were held with Gabriel in the healing circle of her own embrace. But even as she surrendered to this feeling, she understood.

Some nights, coming back from the hospital, she had sat in the dark for hours, lacking the power to move. Yet hope had always returned, until the next ping-pong ball stare, the next faltering smile. As no doubt it would return again, if Lexa stayed in Gemmell. But right now she knew that Gabriel was never going to do a hundred on the ring road again, or deface another sexist tabloid, or lie her way into another job, or look back and laugh at the surreal remarks the stroke had put in her mouth. They would never have the conversation where Gabriel took her hands and said *thank you* and Lexa asked *for what?* and Gabriel said *believing I'd come back*. She wasn't coming back. And the Lexa who would have held that conversation with her: she, too, was gone.

Slowly, making sure Gabriel kept her balance, she pulled away.

The sun's platinum blaze had contracted to a fierce copper disc. It was a relief to turn their backs on it and cross the decking to the door that led down into the bank. The Medieval castle walls were stained rosy pink. A faint hallucinatory platform announcement reached them, carried on the wind from the railway station.

ACKNOWLEDGEMENTS

Almost everyone I know has contributed to this novel in some way. I would like to thank Mary Alexander, Roben Antoniewicz, George Bell, Bernard Chandler, Jeremy Close, Medani Close, Geraldine Doherty, Rob Hands, Karen McKellar, Mark O'Neill, Siobhan O'Tierney, Paul Philippou, Heather Reid, Mary Reilly, Ivan Sedgwick, Christopher Swaine, Fiona Thackeray, Catherine Walker, Alice Walsh and Peter Zombory-Moldovan. Dave Douglass and Steven Wrigley also provided invaluable help.

I owe a huge debt to Ursula Doyle for selecting me as one of Blackfriars' authors; to Judy Moir for her tirelessness and faith in me; to the Scottish Arts Council for supporting me through two residencies; and to Jim Melvin for living in a *menage à trois* for so long (him, me and this book).